Little
Wing

Also by Freya North

Little
Wing

FREYA
NORTH

WELBECK

First published in 2022 by Welbeck Fiction Limited,
part of Welbeck Publishing Group
based in London and Sydney
This paperback edition first published in 2022
by Welbeck Publishing Group
www.welbeckpublishing.com

A CIP catalogue record for this book is available from the British Library

Paperback ISBN: 978-1-78739-763-7
E-book: 978-1-78739-762-0

Printed and bound by CPI Group (UK) Ltd., Croydon, CR0 4YY

10 9 8 7 6 5 4 3 2 1

For Jonathan Lloyd, my agent and friend, who has had my back for 25 years – thank you.

Tell me, what is it you plan to do
with your one wild and precious life?

Mary Oliver, 'The Summer Day', 1990

We have time, there's no big rush.

Jimi Hendrix, 1970

Prologue

Colchester, February 1969

Nothing will ever be the same again.

This I've known these past long weeks as the waves sweep through me in rushes and ripples, pulling me under, lifting me up.

Wave after wave after wave on a tide that only ever comes in; ribboning through me with pitching fear but wonder too; excitement cresting on the surges of dread. Elation roiling with loneliness and curiosity undulating with panic.

But there is the swell of love. There is the flow of contentment.

How is that? That I love you?
You. Little tiny nonsensical you.
The flutter of you. The beat and the rhythm of you and me.
We're inextricable now – the making of each other.

A wave of nausea.
I've heard that this should stop after twelve weeks.
I count almost eleven.
The trouble and the joy that you will bring.

Colchester, February 2005

With a heave and a hoick while berating himself for being a stiff old bastard, Frank struggled from his chair and Zimmer-framed his way over to the window. He tapped on it. And again. If they couldn't hear him, surely they could see him – he was a colour-blind eighty-year-old man with untameable hair; he was quite dazzling to all. He waved in their direction, grinned and gave a big thumbs-up. Not long, fellas – she's on her way.

Three times a week, Nell climbed the stairs to Frank's flat on the third floor. She'd done so for more years than either of them could remember. She never took the lift, reasoning that by not using it she was extending its life for those who needed it most. She was tired today; the café had been manic and she'd only heard the strange noise coming from the fridge as she'd been closing up.

'It's me, Frank – just Nell,' she called through the door as she unlocked it and prepared for the wall of heat to hit her. She liked his home, though – the rooms weren't big but they felt spacious on account of him having few belongings. What he had plenty of, however, were paintings of seafaring adventure, which transformed the walls into oceans. Some he had painted himself. *Not from memory*, he once qualified in case she thought he was as old as Captain Cook. But despite the drama on the high seas, there was a calm that permeated Frank's flat and it always smelt of toast. He was all about toast and Walnut Whips – and Nell did worry that, on the days she didn't visit, that was all he ate. Not the walnuts, though. These he'd prise off and leave on a plate, waiting for her.

'I'm in here!'

She smiled to herself – when was Frank ever anywhere other than in here?

'I'll just pop into the kitchen and prepare the banquet,' she called back. She opened the fridge, checked the milk and placed the cheesecake inside, then she set the oven to preheat, put a plate and cutlery on a tray, took a square of kitchen roll and plumed it into the glass. She noted a little washing-up that she'd do before she left; she'd put a clean tea towel out too. Frank had a small mirror just next to the door and she glanced at her reflection, thinking she looked a bloody mess, retying her ponytail before going through to the sitting room.

'Hello, love.'

'Good evening, mister – wow!' Nell took in his bright red shirt and equally vivid clashing cardigan, his hair appearing to have had the shock of its life. He looked like someone who worked at Woolworths with a sideline in clowning and his dentures appeared to be dancing.

'Wow yourself,' Frank said.

'I'm wearing supermarket jeans and a crap sweatshirt.'

'They won't mind,' said Frank, still by the window, supported by his Zimmer. 'I've told them you're coming.'

'I think I heard them when I arrived.' She hadn't but she believed white lies to be an essential kindness for people like Frank who could go from visit to visit without human interaction.

'Would you be so kind—'

'—of course!'

And Nell fetched the saucer of walnuts, making a note to change the antimacassar on her way out. Empty the bin and put the newspapers in the recycling.

'You know it's not a Walnut Whip if you don't eat the walnuts, Frank.'

Today, the window latch was stiff even for Nell and it took a shove to swing it open.

'Break them in two, even three, Nell. They're big'uns. Put them right there – and there – and there. Perfect.'

The nuts were lined up on the outside sill. Nell and Frank watched as the birds, at first warily, descended to feast. Frank always looked triumphant. Job done, he'd say, job done.

'Here.' Nell handed him today's newspapers that had been left at the café.

'The *Telegraph* and the *Mirror*,' Frank mused. 'Right and Left, you see. This way and that. Back and Front. Both ends of the spectrum, Nell – and that's what one must always set out to consider.'

'You never know, next time it might be *The Sun* and *The Star*,' said Nell.

Frank's teeth clackered at the thought of it.

'Did you bring me my scraps and leftovers?'

Nell laughed. 'Cheeky! You know I always dish out your portions before we even write them up on the blackboard.'

'One day,' said Frank, 'I'll come to your café and eat my tea there.'

4

'You'd be very welcome. I could pick you up, if you like.'

'One day.'

They'd had the same conversation for years.

Home. No mail. Nell walked up the communal stairs, subliminally noticing new scuffs on the paintwork, new stains on the carpet tiles. The corridor on the fourth floor had that vague silence she'd grown accustomed to. Only as she passed other doors could she detect the faint sounds of other people's lives: a TV tuned to a kids' channel, a vacuum cleaner, random banging, an argument. It was just gone half five when she shut her front door behind her and felt she could quite easily don her pyjamas, watch crap telly, maybe drink crap wine and fall asleep without actually going to bed.

Nell slumped down on her sofa. Or her settee. She wasn't sure of the difference. Actually it was an oversized armchair erroneously called a love seat because only Nell had ever sat on it. She looked at her walls and imagined how just one of Frank's paintings would affect the emptiness and numb white. She'd feel seasick, she decided. She didn't like clutter and she never bought anything that had no use; however, she didn't think of her flat as bare; she thought of it as a clean, contemplative space which in itself had supreme purpose in her life. But she saw herself just then, sitting in silence with her new phone, flipping the lid and snapping it shut over and again. And she realized she could quite easily sit there, doing just that, for hours on end.

There was a time when she'd have phoned Philippa while *Corrie* was on, or *Silent Witness* or *Friends* or *Cold Feet*, and it was as if they were together, magically inside the stories, known to all the characters, part of the action playing out. But these days

Philippa had two small children and lived in New York and she and Nell were on different episodes of *Desperate Housewives* and it never felt like they were watching it together at all. There was also a time when she'd have called her mum so she could listen to her theatrical discourse of the day. She could prepare an entire meal and eat while her mother veered off on her fanciful tangents. But there was no point Nell phoning her any more because it was just a grim episode on repeat.

Hello, Mum?

Hello?

Hello – Mum.

Who is this?

It's Nell, Mum.

Who?

Mum – it's *Nell.* How are you?

Who is this?

It's Nell – Mum. It's just Nell. I was just calling to see how you are.

Nell?

Yes! Yes, it's Nell! Mum!

Nell—

Your daughter? Nell.

Who are you? I don't know you! I don't have children. Leave me alone.

So Nell wouldn't be phoning the mum who'd forgotten all about being a mum. And she wouldn't call Philippa in another time zone. And she'd break her phone if she fiddled with its flip-top much longer and there was sod all on the telly anyway and bugger all to eat in the fridge.

Debbie, Nell's friend and co-manager at the café, had said why don't you sign up for a ceramics evening class or something? Zumba? Or something. Or go for a run.

Run?

Where to?

Away?

Nell only had Converse trainers – you couldn't do running of any merit in those anyway.

* * *

The Chaffinch Café was known by everyone as the Chiffchaff Caff, which was erroneous because chiffchaff is not a diminutive for chaffinch. They are an entirely separate species. Though rarer than the chaffinch, the chiffchaff is just a small warbler, unspectacular in its olive-brown plumage and its repetitive song. And that's what always bugged Nell – who only ever referred to her place of work as the Chaffinch. To her, there was nothing dull, *ordinaire* or monotonous about the café or the people who made it what it was. It was a place as colourful, spritely and joyous as the bird after which it took its name. She'd worked for the Chaffinch Foundation for six years, initially in the residential home, now as manager at the café in Colchester, open to all, run by Chaffinch staff and residents and featuring produce from their thriving allotment and the local farm shop.

Nell never thought of her crew as remotely challenged. In fact, she often felt it was the customers who had special needs which her staff fulfilled and surpassed all the time. Tea and sympathy. Coffee and a breather. Cake and a chat. The Chaffinch operated at a different pace to other establishments – and that pace changed from day to day. Some days the staff brought a rambunctious energy, with loud singing, random interpretation of customer orders and a certain amount of spillage; other days the pace was meditatively slow, albeit with the same liberal attitude to what had been asked for. Serendipitously, customers seemed to time their visits for when the café provided the ambiance they most needed. Only very occasionally were visitors to the town unable to hide impatience or irritation with the pace and the gentle cack-handedness for which the café was held in such affection by the locals.

At 8.30 in the morning, behind the vibrant blue shopfront, in a denim skirt, trainers and a robust top the colour of oatmeal which could obscure a multitude of splatters, Nell gathered her workforce around her. She'd known this gang since their teens. Daniel who proudly introduced himself to everyone as Danny Downsie, Rachel who found speech onerous but was fastidious about how food looked on the plate, Alex and Sanjay who were slow on the uptake but an entertaining double act when it came to making sandwiches, Libby whose jolly disposition cancelled out her clumsiness, and AJ whose barista skills were worth the lengthy wait. Today, Nell also had Siobhán volunteering although, with her boyfriend troubles and money worries, she gave the lot of them a headache.

'Listen up, team. Soup today is sweet potato, leek and watercress.'

'Sweetato and waterleaks,' Danny repeated.

'There is quiche,' said Nell, 'which is veggie, obviously. And there's a mixed Mediterranean salad with freekeh.'

Everyone looked appalled.

'Just say superfood salad,' said Nell. 'Also, chocolate mousse cake, Rice Krispie chews and banana bread.'

'It's not bread.'

'I know, Sanjay – but it looks like a loaf, so.'

'It's not bread. It's cake.'

'It's sweet,' said Alex.

'It's cake,' said Sanjay.

Nell thought about it. 'You're quite right. Let's call it banana cake.'

'Queue,' said Rachel in her rasping voice.

Nell looked out the window. Toddlers straining to get out of their buggies and strained mothers in need of caffeine. Two builders who were long-term members of the Danny Downsie fan club. The clerks from the bank which opened in half an hour.

'Are we ready?' Nell looked at them all. Siobhán was sending texts. AJ was polishing the coffee machine. Libby was in her own world. Sanjay and Alex were still talking about bananas. Danny was by the door with his arms crossed like a bouncer.

'Are we ready?' Danny sang out as he opened the door. 'Welcome to the Chiffchaff Caff!'

Nell experienced that peculiar energy surge. Apprehension and joy. It was always the same. Even when things went wrong on the surface which was, inevitably, a daily occurrence, beneath it all Nell knew this was the best job in the world.

The builders said *awright mate* to Danny and ruffled his hair while calling out their order to Libby who told AJ a latte with two sugars and tea with three, while Rachel very carefully put brownies in two separate paper bags. The mums were order-ing cappuccinos and babyccinos, which AJ loved making most of all. Sanjay sneezed into the chopped iceberg but told Nell immediately which was a great improvement on last week with the hummus. Danny told Rachel she was an old slowcoach but a raised eyebrow from Nell saw him apologize straight away. Siobhán said her life was a fucking nightmare and everyone behind the counter told her off for swearing. Two tables were undercharged but then overpaid. All the red crayons had gone so a toddler had an enormous tantrum. Danny dispensed cuddles. Rachel cried a little. Sanjay needed a sit-down. Libby was singing Madonna's back catalogue. Nell's jumper gamely hid splashes of food and drink and Alex announced to everyone who came in that there was banana and it was a cake and by lunchtime, it had all gone.

Debbie took over from Siobhán for the afternoon shift so Nell and Alex prepared chocolate cornflake cakes and dolloped the mixture into paper cases in time for after-school mayhem. Alex was obsessed with telling her it's organic, don't panic and she hadn't the heart to tell him that, actually, it wasn't. Nobody wanted Alex to panic. It was supremely upsetting.

It had been a good day. The takings were good and the fridge sounded fine. Debbie organized the crew into a crocodile of sorts and Nell waved them off, watching them dawdle and dance their way down the high street. She turned the sign from Open to Closed and went through to the kitchen to sit down for the first time that day. Need to put the glasses into the dishwasher. Change the tea towels for tomorrow. Check milk. Butter. Loo roll. Buy red crayons.

She ladled herself the last of the soup. Sweetato. Brilliant, Danny – brilliant. Libby's left her bobble hat – drop it in later. She thought, I'll bring Frank here one day. I'll just put him at the corner table and he can stay my entire shift. And then she thought how these days, she could never do that with her mum.

*   *   *

White gloss paint. Awful. In this room, it was everywhere. The door, the skirting boards, the radiator. None of the surfaces had been rubbed down first, giving the impression the paint had been daubed over everything in a rush. It all looked a little pockmarked. And why pale blue for the walls? Just so cold. And that insipid framed print of an unconvincing bowl of fruit.

Today, though, none of that mattered because Nell's mother was chirpy, patting the space on the bed for Nell to sit.

'It's *Eggheads*!' she cried. 'I love *Eggheads*! Oh Florence, I *love* that man!' Her mother waved the remote control about. 'Oh, whatshisname.'

'It's *Nell*, Mum,' said Nell. 'Dermot Someone.'

'Oh, what's his *name*, Florence?'

'Dermot Someone – shall I make you another cup of tea? Nell, Mum, *Nell.*'

Nell's mother cradled the cup as if it was her last. It was indeed her last – a 1953 souvenir cup and saucer produced by Clarice Cliff for the Coronation. When Nell had moved her here two years ago, she'd condensed her mother's life into two suitcases and a box and the cup had come too.

Today, however, it wasn't her daughter sitting by her side, watching TV, but someone called Florence. Some days she knew, some days she didn't.

Out of the corner of her eye, Nell kept watch. She observed how frequently her mother's inner gaze wandered although her eyes remained fixed ahead, how her mouth would twitch in silent conversation, how she'd suddenly scratch viciously at her arm or tug at her hair. Sometimes, Nell's task was to calm her mother from childlike distress, other times it was to ignore the insults hurled at her. Often it was simply to remind her that she did definitely have a daughter because here she was and her name was Nell. Mostly, though, Nell just needed to let her know she was safe, that life was good, that everyone around her cared and was kind. Sometimes Nell tried to distract her, to guide her backwards to times she might remember and access the comfort that could bring. Nell, Mum – it's Nell.

'Hey, Mum – do you remember? Remember when we went *up west* – as you used to say – to John Lewis Oxford Street? A long time ago – I think I was about eight. Have a think. Do you remember John Lewis, Mum?' Nell persevered, with a little nudge. Her mum was still looking at the television. 'And we'd been shopping for hours on end. The haberdashery department. Spools and reels of ribbons and silky cord in every colour? Do you remember? Every colour of the rainbow?'

And Nell remembers so vividly being eight years old, in John Lewis with her mother spending a fortune in the haberdashery department. Metres of ribbon of different widths: velvet, satin, grosgrain, plain. Every colour imaginable.

This one! her mother laughs out loud. And this and this and this! Nell so loves her mother at these moments of extreme effervescence, feels swept along on waves of joy. Swathes of chiffon being bought too, genuine silk chiffon because Nell's mum says can you imagine anything softer and lighter than air? It's true and Nell has never felt anything as exquisite. Buttons – they buy so many buttons too. What'll we do with all of these things, Nell asks, what'll we make? And her mum takes her chin between finger and thumb and says, let's just have them because they are things of beauty.

And then they are trying on all the perfumes and Nell's mum has little red marks all over the backs of her hands and the insides of her wrists. It could look disturbing but it's only tiny strikes of all the lipsticks while she hunts for the perfect shade. And then she finds it and she buys five. They run – run! – to the toy department and Nell quite likes the fluffy bunny, which looks so real, looks at her so longingly, but her mother says look at this chap! Look at him! It's a great big cuddly toy dog, like a German Shepherd, and her mum has a paw on each shoulder and she's dancing around the shop floor, light as you like on her tiptoes. For a moment, Nell thinks wow – she's going to do it! She's going to buy me the hugest and most expensive toy in the whole shop! But then the dog is dumped and her mum's saying she's tired, oh my God so tired and then she says, I know! I know where we'll go next! Come, Nell – come!

The top floor, where the bedroom furniture is.

Over twenty-five years later, it was all so suddenly vivid. The buttons and ribbons and the toy department and the lipstick. It was Revlon and it was called Transparent Burgundy. But she'd forgotten about the bedroom furniture department until now.

'Do you remember?'

Her mother, though, was still staring at the TV, not watching.

'It was the top floor,' Nell said quietly. 'It was very quiet – not many customers. We had all those bags, all those lovely things that we'd bought. You tested the beds like everyone tests the beds – with a good old push on the mattress. But then you chose one. It had a lilac headboard. And you lay down on it and I was laughing. But then you turned the other way and you curled up onto your side and you told me to go away because you were going to have a sleep.'

Nell paused but there was no way of knowing whether her mother was listening.

'Then the sales assistant came along and said, madam, may I help you? And you said nothing. I knew you were awake, but you said nothing. I was standing there with all our bags. *Madam – I really must ask you—*'

Nell paused. She thought back to that day. The rising panic she'd felt. She could taste it again now, the anxiety shooting through her blood. She knew her mum wasn't asleep on the bed on the top floor in John Lewis, she *knew* she wasn't asleep. She was just lying there, lying about sleeping, leaving it all to Nell.

Madam – really!

'My mum is just really tired,' Nell had told the man. 'Please could you leave her alone just for maybe like five minutes? Please, mister?'

And he'd gone but not before Nell had seen the look on his face that said he thought her mum was repellent. So Nell had counted to sixty, five times, marking each off on the fingers of her left hand. You really have to get up now, Mum. That man's going to come back soon.

Nell looked at her mum, touched her hand but, just like that day, there was no response. That day back then, over twenty-five years ago, Nell had stood at the foot of the bed looking at her mother, not quite able to see her face, wondering how deeply she was fake-sleeping, watching as the salesman and another man approached. Oh, how she had silently, desperately, prayed her mum would just stop it.

She remembered that now.

She nudged her mum again, fought away a tear.

Sylvie came in with her mother's dinner all expertly cut up.

'Hello, love.'

Nell liked Sylvie the best. All the staff here were kind but some could be a little brusque. Sylvie was always cheery, always patient.

'How are we today?' Her big sing-song voice.

Nell answered for her mother. 'Calm – but I'm Florence again.'

'Calm is good,' said Sylvie. 'We like calm, don't we, Mrs H?' Sylvie looked at Nell. 'You don't look like a Florence.' And then she looked at Nell the way Debbie from Chaffinch would look at Nell. And, occasionally, the way that Frank did too: with concern. 'And how are you today, Nell?'

It compelled Nell to feign immediate lightness.

'Me? Oh fine! Fine. I'd best be off.'

She kissed her mother's cheek. 'Bye, Mum – I'll see you soon.'

Her mother spun her head sharply and regarded Sylvie pleadingly. 'Who is she? And why does she think I'm her mother?'

A silent drive home, Nell's mind both heavy and blank.

Every time her mum denied she had a daughter, Nell felt less and less that she had a mother.

Home.

Along the corridor and past the sounds of the lives of others.

Into her flat and down into the love seat.

Maybe she'd fall asleep in her clothes.

Colchester, December 1968

Love.

It's all any of us need. Love is everything and I can't understand why some people don't realize this – why the politicians and that lot stop seeing this. It's the truth, love is. I try not to hate – I try not to use the word. Instead, I'll say I despise *politicians* and I detest *the H bomb* and I abhor *all wars.* I really loathe *boiled fish in milk* – which we have every single Thursday at home. I can't stand *school.* But I just try not to use the word HATE. Love is what rules. It's all you need. Just listen to the Fab Four.

It's very strange how my passion for Love and Peace puts my mother in such a bad mood. She huffs at me and turns her back at so much of what I say. And yet – she lived through the war! She actually knows what hate feels like! My stepfather, though, he laughs; not in a cruel way and I don't mind it because I love George. He isn't a man of many words – apart from saying 'aye, dear' to my mother a lot – and his soft Scottish accent seems to soothe her, thank goodness. What I like about George is that he gets me. That's quite far out for a grown-up. And he does listen – and then he chuckles or he'll murmur in response – he's quite expressive, really, in his mostly wordless way. I did hear him once defend me to my mum: 'She's a pacifist, my dear, not a commie.'

What my dad didn't know about love isn't worth knowing. I miss my dad. I haven't seen him half my life. Eight years on and I talk to him still, *to keep him here, to make sure none of the little details fade. But I do so in my mind only, as Mum doesn't like to hear reminiscences. Almost as soon as he died she said God had plans for him and who are we to argue or lament. I was eight and I wanted to do a lot of crying. Now I'm sixteen and I want to ask her what kind of a god is this god of yours, taking my dad and giving him a disease with no cure that killed him within weeks?*

I used to shake my fist at the sky – in case there was a god listening. Now, mostly, when I think of him I have a little smile and I say, oh, I wish you were still here, Pops! I say, Pops – you'd love this band. Listen to this song! Jimi Hendrix!

I imagine how my father and I could be talking about politics and peace and everything. I think he'd be proud that I sneaked to London twice to stop the Vietnam War, and once to ban the bomb with CND. He went on the Aldermaston march when I was seven. Not with Mum. He died three months later.

If he were here today I'd say, look at my dress, Pops, I made it from Annie's mum's tablecloth that she was going to throw out. And I'd say, Pops – won't you please speak to Mum about Joan's party at the weekend? I really so want to go. I'm sixteen and it's nearly Christmas!

So I like having these little chats with my dead dad. But, on Saturday, I'm going to sneak out of the house with Annie's mum's tablecloth dress in a bag and change at the hut in the park before I go to Joan's party. I know my dad wouldn't have minded.

Dad and George were very good chums. They're quite alike and that's why I'm so fond of George. George knew that I went to the Vietnam rally, he told me he was proud of me, he told me he wouldn't tell Mum. I do love George too.

I know my dad wouldn't have minded. He'd be happy for me.

Camden, February 2005

Dougie hurried down Hartland Road to Camden Town under-ground station laden; his kit weighed a ton. He slalomed between a pile of puke, a bundle of sodden clothes, a wet stodge of discarded takeaways, a homeless man sitting in a doorway begging for small change. Dougie chastised himself for feigning blindness to the beggar because usually he would give a quid or two but today he was in a rush. He'd make it up to him – he was there regularly. But just now, Dougie was late and his bags were cumbersome; something was digging into his shoulder blade like the sharpest of accusing fingers reprimanding him for some crime or other.

He thought about that analogy as he queued for his Travelcard.

The most recent crime, he supposed, was not wanting to move in with Suze after a year together. You're thirty-bloody-six, she'd said, get a life. And she'd thrown his stuff around and hit him across the face and told him she was done, she was fucking done. That was almost two years ago and still, on occasion, he breathed a sigh of relief. He reckoned his greater crime was that, more often than not, he let his father's phone calls go through to the answering machine. But certainly, to have to listen to his dad flummoxing down the line was punishment enough for that. His father hated answering machines and the messages he left were always faltering; he'd say very little but awkwardly and loud. Just thought I'd telephone, lad, see how you are. It's your dad, son, just – you know – calling.

Dougie regretted the impatience he felt at his father; in future he would answer the phone. In fact, he would call his dad before he had recourse to phone him again. He'd do so tonight. He bought his ticket and walked down the escalator saying sorry, sorry, sorry to everyone his bags knocked against on the way.

The studio today wasn't a studio but a warehouse. It was bland yet airy and therefore perfect for the assignment. Dougie had shot there a few times and when he arrived he noted all the models for the job crammed together and realized the days ahead would be long. There were three staff – but he hadn't worked with any of them before. Two blokes who looked bored already and a young woman who seemed bewildered as to why she was even there.

'Hey, I'm Dougie.' He shook hands with everyone. 'I'll just get set up, then.' He was relieved they made no motion to help. From experience, he knew it would be easier if he just cracked on. He hung and unrolled the swathe of white paper, rigged up the lights and softbox, positioned the reflector and tripod, set out his lenses and checked his battery packs. The silence was awkward so he whistled slightly tunelessly through his teeth. God, Suze had hated him doing that.

'Let's start with Belinda, Babs, Bernadette, Bella, Briony, Beth and—' He regarded the three assistants and couldn't tell whether they were nonplussed or just naturally gormless.

'I'm referring to the brooms, guys. Let's have the brooms, please.'

And it did cross Dougie's mind that this was where his photography degree had taken him, this was where his career was at; the arse-end of Colliers Wood, photographing tools and gubbins for an agricultural trade catalogue. When he had graduated all those years ago, he'd envisaged a life behind a Leica taking portraits, documenting faces the world over. Now, however, he was photographing powder-coated steel sheep hurdles and water bowsers. This commission meant a week here and then two weeks on the road: Derbyshire, Carlisle and Peterborough, photographing goods produced by smaller companies for inclusion in the catalogue. This week, though, was to be all about brooms, wheelbarrows, pitchforks and shovels and what looked like a multitude of aluminium hooks, bolts and prongs.

'Mate, meet Bella and Babs.' One of the staff had brought the brooms to him, holding them upside down so the heads were close to his own. 'Stunners – bit bristly, but stunners.'

And Dougie laughed.

'I'm Stevo,' said the man. He was overweight, bald, and there were intriguing gaps between all of his teeth.

The man's face intrigued him. In a glance, Dougie thought, I wish I could take your portrait. He thought, I love your broken nose – it's like it's being slowly sucked into your face. He thought, there's a story behind it and I'm pretty sure it's not rugby. But then he thought, I cannot photograph you.

Inanimate objects for work. Sometimes derelict buildings and lonely landscapes for pleasure. But not people, really, and never portraits these days. These days, Dougie denied himself from looking in too much detail at faces. It used to be that, when he looked at a face through the lens, he felt he could see beyond the surface details and straight into the human condition. But with Daisy, he hadn't seen it. He hadn't seen the pain. And then it was too late and she was gone. He couldn't risk it ever again – the seeing but not seeing.

Dougie left most of the equipment at the warehouse, taking only his cameras with him, but still he ached as though he'd done a day on a building site. He did wonder whether he should have driven. He hated the Tube but he hated sitting in heavy traffic even more and his car was prone to overheating. He ought to go to the gym – stretch it out, run it off – but it would be late by the time he was home and he was tired. He ought to cook something wholesome – lunch had been sandwiches, crisps and chocolate from a garage – but he was seduced by the vinegary wafts from Oh My Cod so he bought fish and chips and mushy peas and ate them off his lap as soon as he got in. He showered, inspected the silent march of grey in his hair. Suze had often said he should cut his hair short, but he'd always liked his waves and kinks – currently, though, it was way too long. Look – enough for a ponytail. He laughed at himself and called himself a twat, but he kept the elastic band in place and mooched about his flat in boxers and a T-shirt and put off calling his dad.

Phoning his dad always felt loaded. He left it another hour. As he listened to the phone ring 700 miles away, his eyes were drawn to the old framed map his parents had given him when he'd left to do his degree. The map that his great-grandfather had drawn by hand; black India ink now faded to brown, meticulous detail on thick cartridge paper now yellowed. Don't forget – they'd said without saying it – don't forget where we are, don't forget where you are from. Dougie looked at the place names, the coastline, the mountains, the land torn and strewn. His great-grandfather's handwriting. Their island, their home. It was almost a year since he had last been there. Homesickness for his childhood as much as the place itself gripped him.

'Gordon Munro. Hello?'

And hearing his father's voice tightened a knot so acutely that Dougie couldn't answer.

'Hello!' His father was shouting – like he was calling out to someone on the other side of the dunes.

'Da.'

'Douglas?'

Delight and surprise.

'Yeah, Dad – it's me. I'm sorry I've been – you know—'

'Aye, son – aye. You're busy. I know. I know.'

'How are you?' Dougie concentrated on lightening his voice.

'Oh now, can't complain – been a bit bitter, but nothing that we wouldn't know about.'

Dougie knew what bitter could be. The gale-great wind that screamed at you and sliced at your skin like a blade. The rain that lashed you like a beating. Days and days of it.

'Snow?'

'Just a flindrikin. How's that big life down there, then, Douglas? How's all that London?'

Dougie laughed but gently. 'It's fine, aye. Really great. It's busy – I'm working a lot.' He paused, waited to see if his father wanted to respond. Dougie pushed on. 'How's Ben, he's well, is he?'

'Oh aye – curled up at my feet right here – not getting any younger, but life in him yet.'

They'd always had dogs. They were always called Ben. This Ben Dougie did not know so well.

'I will come back – maybe in a month or so. You know – it's just with work and—' And Dougie's empty promises and lame excuses rang out around his flat like a kicked can.

Gordon waited a beat. 'These days you say "back" – do you hear it? You say "back" not "home".'

Dougie was aware of it. When he first moved to London, he would say so quite pedantically because London was home and he had to believe it. Nowadays, he did so automatically. He looked at the framed photograph hanging next to the map, of Luskentyre at the setting down of the sun, which he'd taken all those years ago with his first proper camera that God knows his parents must have saved and saved for.

'I'm glad you're well, Dad,' Dougie said quietly. 'I will look into dates. I'll keep you posted.'

'Aye – you do that.'

Dougie paused. 'It has been too long.' He paused again. 'And I'm sorry for that.'

He looked once more at the map drawn so fastidiously by his great-grandfather; for posterity, for future generations of the family – for someone just like Dougie who'd left the island without much of a backward glance. The map that said this is where we are. This is who we've always been. This place of yours that will always be here. This place you can always call home.

'Bye, Da. Bye for now.'

'God bless you, Douglas. *Oidhche mhath leibh*. Goodnight to you.'

Colchester, December 1968

Not a baby.

Mum and George were going out for cheese and wine at their friends on Saturday and they – or rather Mum – had asked Wendy to babysit. Those actual words. Wendy was as mad about this as I was. I am not a baby and my sister does not want to sit her way through a Saturday evening. It occurred to me that I probably wouldn't have to sneak out now – that I could just tell her. But part of me was quite looking forward to furtively stealing into the night. Wendy's only ten years older than me – she can't have forgotten what it's like to be my age.

Almost as soon as Mum and George left, Wendy's boy Jimmy arrived and suddenly it struck me that there might very well be a God so I laid the dress out on my bed, put the lipstick and false eyelashes next to it and then went downstairs.

'Wendy,' I said, 'you're cool if I go to Joan's, aren't you?' Everyone knows she's my best friend.

Just then Jimmy came in with two Martinis and he said, 'Let her go, Wendy.' And I'm assuming he didn't mean for me to see the wink he gave her.

Wendy looked at me and I knew exactly what she was going to say. 'It's your life; it's your funeral.' She said exactly the same thing when she caught me on the high street, when I played hooky from school. 'Your life, your funeral,' she said.

Well, skipping school didn't kill me – but being there threatens to do precisely that. I know what I want to be and I don't need school for it. I am going to be an artist – and to be an artist you need to be a free thinker, and that's something that boring old school does not encourage. My teachers say I'm bright – exceptional, even – but I say school dulls me right down.

So Wendy caught Jimmy's wink and probably couldn't wait for me to get out of the house anyway.

I went up to my room, changed into my handmade dress, and I glued on the falsies and added my cat's eyes perfectly in one swoop of black liner. And then I very casually walked down the stairs, checked myself in the mirror in the hallway and applied more lipstick. I didn't need rouge – my cheeks were pink and glowing with excitement. The sitting-room door was shut and I called out goodbye.

I said, 'Goodbye, kids!' I said, 'Don't wait up!'

It was only Jimmy's voice that replied. 'Be good!'

Of course our mother doesn't approve of Jimmy. She always looks pained when he calls on Wendy. Mind you, there's little in life that doesn't pain our mother. Wendy would have to marry a vicar for Mother to be halfway happy. Anyway, Jimmy was on side and I pretty much skipped all the way to the party, singing to myself thank you God thank you God thank you.

There were so many people! Everyone was like me – like we were a tribe; it was such a groovy vibe. 'Hello, I Love You' by the Doors was playing just as I arrived. It was perfect. Everyone was talking, singing, dancing. Friends from school and new people hanging out. But – best of all I met this boy, this dearest boy, an absolute knockout. None of us knew him – he turned up with Gerald and Martin and that lot. But as soon as I saw him oh! the flutter and the swell and if that's love at first sight then let my eyes see nothing else!

Even when I was really having a good talk with Joan about Sid, my eyes were pulled to him. But it was too much when he caught my gaze! I felt this incredible heat come over my cheeks and my chest, my skin prickled and my breath caught. I didn't know what to do about it – I asked Joan and she said, look! he's over there by the punchbowl. She said, just go over as if your main interest is a glass of punch and see, she said, just see.

So I did.

I went over to the punchbowl and drat! his back was turned but as I took a glass I could sense him, like he was as drawn to me as I was to him. As if our souls were sending out electric charges that were reacting mid-air, propelling us together. My hand was shaking as I spooned punch into a glass. It's excellent stuff to calm the nerves, is punch! And then I hear this lovely voice and I know it's him and he's saying, wow – I dig your dress! Far out!

And that's when I felt I could turn and look at him and I told him I made it and he said that it was the coolest thing. Somebody had put Jimi Hendrix on and everything just seemed magical, so clear and real, so right and so – in the Now.

We chinked glasses and our eyes were absolutely locked as we sipped at the punch. Which was very strong.

'I'm Peter,' he said.

We tapped our feet and nodded our heads in time with the song – and soon enough we were dancing. And when we weren't dancing we were talking. It was as if we'd known each other our whole lives. He's from South Africa but his family don't live there any more, now they're renting on the other side of the park – the well-to-do side. We talked for ages, we drank the rum punch, which was like the best pop in the world but with this hot and sharp delicious aftertaste that made you squint your eyes shut.

'Rum,' Peter said. 'Rrrrrum!' And he said it like a lion starting to roar.

We only had eyes for each other, we didn't care to talk to anyone else from that moment on. We're so similar. We danced and danced and it was as if everyone else at the party just melted into a silent background. Like they were black-and-white cutouts, like scenery. Really, there was just Peter and I. Someone had put on 'All Along the Watchtower' and he kissed me. And then oh how we smooched and I couldn't have told you what was playing then and I couldn't have cared who was looking. Jimi himself could have been right there, wanting to make my acquaintance, and I wouldn't have stopped. And I'll say this: I know that no other kiss will ever feel quite like it.

We smoked some pot and I felt so floaty with it and so springy from the punch. I've never felt so − here! − so alive! So my own person, so in love with being me at this time in the world's history! I felt so high! And 'Everlasting Love' by Love Affair just made me feel this overwhelming sense of YES!!! Me in my dress being the most Me I've ever been − and being kissed all the more for it. Could anything ever match this night, could feelings ever have this strength again? Once you've felt something once, is it diluted by repetition?

And then Peter took my hand and led me away. I know Joan's house as well as my own. I told him, I know where we can go − and we ran up the stairs and then tiptoed up the next flight too. I took him up to the attic, to Joan's brother's room − because he's away at university. We could hear people in Joan's room and even in her parents' room − but I knew Dicky's room would be empty. It was also dark. Warm. Lovely and warm. And so were Peter's lips which were all over me; my face, my mouth, my neck. Oh my, I was soaring and sinking all at once but I was safe in his arms and I was kissing him back. His hands. His hands were moving and finding and squeezing and I thought oh my goodness I'm going to pass out with *the pleasure. I mean, I've kissed boys before and they've had a feel over my clothes. But Peter – well, he discovered the flaw in my homemade dress, which is that the armholes are a bit gapey so he found a way in. And I'm so glad he did. Felt like my breasts were made especially for his hands. He was pressing against me and moving back and forth and I could feel It. It. His desperate hardness. His hardness. His desire. For me.*

He took my hand and led me over to Dicky's bed and we just lay on it, gazing at each other touched by moonlight, or maybe it was streetlight not moonlight. But anyway, he looked so deliciously handsome!

We were kissing so passionately and it was like he was dying of hunger, of longing. I gave his hands freedom because it felt good and nothing felt wrong. He ran them up my thighs and then between my legs and his voice was so soothing, saying, relax baby relax. When your parents call you a baby it's like an insult – but when the man you love calls you baby it's like honey. So I relaxed. It felt – I never knew! His hands, his fingertips – I never knew it could feel so – I never knew that about my body.

And he unbuckled his belt and unbuttoned his jeans and he took my hand down there and I never imagined it would feel so – warm.

And Peter said shall we?

He said I think we should.

He said that feelings like this are so rare and that not many people experience a connection like ours. He said that we have to live in the moment. I believe that too.

And I said I know, but –

And he said don't worry – I'll pull it out in time.

And I said I know, but –

And downstairs the Beatles were singing 'Hey Jude'.

And Peter said relax, baby, relax.

I'm so in love.

Nell

Sometimes Saturdays felt like Tuesdays and Wednesdays could feel like Sundays and Nell didn't mind that. She liked shift work, she didn't mind that her weekends were a movable feast. Invariably, whether she was working or not, she'd pop in to the Chaffinch anyway, to double-check she really wasn't needed. Saturdays, after all, were filled by a different crowd. Dads came in, bewildered by what their kids were allowed to eat, while their offspring said Mummy definitely lets me have the triple chocolate brownie with ice cream and double sprinkle. And Danny, bless him, always colluding. He'd figured out early on how dads tended to tip very well, especially if he called them mate and clapped his hand on their shoulders. Also at weekends, teenagers lingered in small throngs, commandeering the tables at the back, dawdling over cappuccinos and eking out one toastie between the lot of them. That she was treated like a minor celebrity on her impromptu visits was a crucial antidote to how monotonous and quiet she found her time off could be. Just occasionally, though, when she wasn't needed and her flat was too still, too empty, she yearned to be far away from everything and everyone. But she didn't really know how to get there, nor where on earth that could be anyway.

On this particular Saturday, after she'd popped in to the café and paid for a latte to go, Nell mooched up Trinity Street. She stopped by the archway as she always did to admire the Tudor splendor of Tymperleys and recalled how her mother would always tell her how it was built from an old ship's timbers before going off on elaborate tangents about life on the high seas, telling the stories in a rustic pirate's voice which she'd then forget to switch off. The window display of a candy-coloured lopsided old building caught her eye, antiques and bric-a-brac enticing her to enter. It was cold. As if she needed an excuse to go inside. She loved this shop. She examined a Toby jug, wondering on whose shelf it had spent its lifetime with its benign stare. Nell wondered if anyone was missing him.

'Do you a good price.'

'Oh – sorry – I was just looking.' Nell had long known that she was every shopkeeper's nightmare.

'Remind you of someone?'

She regarded the china face again. 'I don't think so.'

'I mean – someone who might have similar? Granny? Mad uncle? Bloke called Toby?'

'No,' Nell said, 'not in our family.' She put a vague smile on her face and turned her attention to a shoebox crammed with a jangle of old keys.

'Bet some of those could unlock a story of two,' the shop-keeper said. Nell nodded in an anodyne way, focusing on a basket brimming with balls of wool, so comfortingly soft despite lurid colours. She felt conflicted. It was the same every time; she felt she ought to buy something, not for herself but for the shopkeeper.

She never did. Her flat, though small, had space enough – but she let her enduring aversion to clutter govern her purse strings.

And then, on a small table which itself was for sale, Nell chanced upon the cups. They were laid out as if waiting to be filled. Some had cracks, some were tea stained, and some had price stickers that were jaw dropping. But Nell had spotted the one identical to her mother's: the commemorative Coronation cup with its bright blue crenellated edging and gold detail.

'No saucer – so you can have it for eight quid.'

'My mum has one,' Nell told him. 'With a saucer!'

'And the plate?'

'A plate?'

'If she has the plate too – well, you're looking at forty, fifty quid. *Trio*, they called them. Clarice Cliff.'

'Turquoise and gold,' Nell said quietly. 'So beautiful.'

'You can have it for a fiver.'

'I only need the plate – do you have one?'

'Not at the moment. You could try eBay. But I can't go lower than a fiver for the cup, love.'

Nell smiled politely and shook her head. She hadn't seen her mother for almost a fortnight. She ought to visit, it wasn't as if she had any other plans for the day. She could tell her about the cup. When Nell left the shop, she was struck by how warm it was, positively spring-like. As Dickens said, one of those March days when the sun shines hot but the wind blows cold; summer in the light, winter in the shade. Maybe she could take her mother into the gardens at the home. There was something about fresh air that made any conversation, no matter how confused, lighter.

Sylvie wasn't on duty today. At weekends, it was mainly agency staff and Nell did worry about this. With her mother's mind eddying, Nell sought consistency in everything around her.

'Knock knock!' Nell called through the door and went in. Telly on. Bed sheets crumpled. Chair empty and window ominously open, the curtains fanning a hostile chill. 'Mum?'

Nell was about to the press the panic button when she heard the toilet flushing and her mother appeared.

'Hello,' she said.

'Hello!' Nell kissed her cheek and whispered, *it's Nell, Mum.* 'I thought I'd call in – see if you'd like some company. A walk. Do you want to go for a little wander?'

'No.'

'Oh.' Pause. 'It's lovely out there.'

'Out where?'

'Out – *side*,' Nell said. 'Come on – a little stroll.'

And so, on a bench dedicated to someone called Hilda, they sat in companionable silence. Stealing glances at her mother, Nell saw that her eyes were soft and her hands were still and her mouth was not twitching. Birds were busy and the March sun, though now watery and low, threw glints of promise on the buds and on the grass. With their arms loosely linked, they sat awhile. The birds' chatter seemed far more random than her mother's today, and that was of strange comfort to Nell.

'When I'm gone, I don't want a bench. I don't want people's wrinkled arses on my memory. I'm getting cold.'

'You're not going anywhere for a long time, Mum.'

Her mother looked horrified.

'I meant – stop thinking of benches. You're in fine form. You are.'

But her mother remained turned from her. 'I'm cold, that's what I am.'

'Cuppa?'

'Oh, I'd love a cuppa, dear!'

'Shall we have it in the day room?'

Nell led her back inside, disturbed by how cold her mother's hands were. Nice and toasty, her mum used to say to her when Nell was a little girl, when she would feed mittens on elastic through the sleeves of her coat and help her wriggle her hands into them. *Like a bunny in a burrow.*

The day room was fairly quiet for a Saturday so Nell made tea while her mother crossed the room towards a table by the French windows. Nell noticed how she walked without stoop or scuff. You could call her many things but doddery was not one of them. Her mind, though, was cursed by a frailty beyond her years and that, Nell felt, was the greatest injustice. Her mother was the youngest here, by a decade surely, but she was far more scrambled than most of them.

They had their tea and they looked out over the garden where they'd just sat together. But there was no valid conversation, no point in suggesting the crossword and just then Nell felt a pang for teatimes with Frank.

'You'll never believe what I found today. A cup just like yours – the special one with the Queen on it.'

Her mother swivelled to regard her full on; there was an engaged intensity to her stare.

'And did you know, it's worth money! Well,' said Nell, 'if you had the plate.'

'But we *did* have the plate.'

'You did?'

'But mine broke – almost as soon as I got it.'

'The plate, the cup, the saucer,' said Nell, 'it was called a trio, apparently.'

'A trio.' Her mother looked suddenly bereft and a tear traced a jagged path halfway down her face.

Nell put her hand gently on her arm. 'I'll try to find a matching plate for you. I'll ask the shopkeeper to keep an eye. I'll look on eBay. Don't upset yourself, Mum.'

'Mum?'

But Nell didn't have the energy to say, it's Nell, Mum, it's Nell. She'd done so a number of times already.

'A trio,' her mother said again, mournfully. 'Could someone please take me home now?'

'Come on,' said Nell. 'I'll take you up. Perhaps we can see what's on the box.'

'Not you!' her mother cried out. 'That one! I know her!'

One of the care managers, Marcia, had appeared. 'Everything all right?'

'Almost,' Nell said. 'For a while there, everything was almost all right.'

'I want to go *now*.' Her mother was fractious, her voice brittle, edged with frustration or sadness or rage. Or maybe all three. She regarded Nell. And Nell watched as something akin to recognition, and something else that screamed fear, briefly surfaced in mother's eyes.

'Florence – go away! Go back to Harry's.'

Her mother started to weep.

'I know you're not really here!'

As Marcia guided her mother away, Nell sat for a while in the numb stillness of the room. Slumping into the chair, she took a sip from the green-glazed cup synonymous with institutions everywhere. What was it with the milk here? Why was there always a tinge of sourness? It tasted horrible. She'd bring her own milk next time. That's what she could do. She turned the saucer over. Beryl. The crockery was called Beryl and it made her laugh uncontrollably.

'Oh, Nell.' Marcia had returned. From the heave of Nell's shoulders, she thought she was crying.

'Your teacups!' Nell hooted. 'They're called Beryl!'

Marcia smiled kindly. Often enough she dealt with all levels of incongruous emotions among the visitors. Best just to keep on as if nothing was amiss.

'Her sister came by last weekend, you know,' she told Nell. 'Brought chocolates.'

'Really?' Nell's laughter slipped away into a sigh. 'Did my mum know who she was?' A little reluctantly, Marcia had to nod. Just then, Nell wanted to be as far away from this place as possible. If she wasn't known, what was the point of being here?

Driving along the lane towards the dual carriageway, she thought of her aunt. How long had it been since she'd seen her? She felt strangely irked at not knowing she had visited so recently. Their family was tiny – just the sisters left now, really. You couldn't count her father because they had never been able to count on him at all. She should go and visit her. Her aunt was only an hour or so further on. It was irrelevant that Nell had always found her somewhat frightening. She was family none the less and she ought to visit her, or at least phone. Nell, though, went home.

Nell in her flat, eating a second Pot Noodle straight after the first, squeezing the sauce out and then sucking the packet empty. It struck her that this was arguably the most pathetic way to spend her Saturday night. Debbie had sent a message to say a couple of them were going out for a curry but Nell had said, truthfully, that she had other plans. She didn't qualify what they were and she certainly wasn't going to say I'm going to eat Pot Noodles and hunt for a plate on eBay.

Her laptop was already very hot on her legs. Recently, it had been doing this more and more. She'd fully expected it to explode when the fabled Millennium Bug was meant to hit but miraculously, five years later, it was still functioning. She logged on to eBay and started to browse.

Discovering that there were quite a few examples of Clarice Cliff Coronation tableware was strangely deflating and that many were located in the United States just seemed wrong. She was relieved to see that the shopkeeper's prices had been fair. There were complete sets as well as various components being sold separately. Some were the same form, the same design just without the turquoise, some had flaws, some had damage but there were no single plates for sale. Cups and saucers. Complete trios. And just the one listing with a saucer and the plate and that's what Nell bid for. In fact, she didn't have to bid at all. It was Buy It Now for £10, with £3 postage on top. It was all a little unsatisfying; she'd been relishing the hunt, the anticipation of the shrewd last-minute bid. But with a single click, it was hers. The trio would be reunited. And Saturday evening stretched ahead.

Dougie

'Did you always want to do this?'

Michelle's question took Dougie aback. It was his last day at the shoot in Colliers Wood. Wheelbarrows, brooms and shovels, hurdles and gate mechanisms, bolts, ground spikes and galvanized storage bins had all been photographed and logged. Today was going to be a colourful finale. The remaining stock was comprised of aerosol cans of sheep marker in blue, green, red, yellow, purple, black as well as tubs of something called raddle powder, Stockholm tar in a can, vivid blue obstetrical lubricant gel and ketosis drench in bright pink, all in various sizes. There were shepherds' whistles in plastic or metal, ten different colours, and bottles of something called Insta-life with a retro-style label Dougie was particularly taken with.

'Did you?'

He looked from her to the array of products and picked up a can with a picture of a winsome calf and lamb on the label. 'To photograph umbilical spray? A career high, for sure.'

Michelle appeared to believe him and at once, he felt bad.

'I'm teasing you,' he said, 'it's those bolus applicator guns from yesterday that inspire me most. The shape of them, the glint of steel – how to capture in one shot all that they do and the lives that they save.'

She observed him for a moment. 'Are you taking the piss?'

'Yes.'

'Funny.' If she actually found it funny, her tone and her expression belied it.

Dougie grinned. Something had to lighten the monotony of the day ahead. 'Let's start with those calf sucking preventors – let's have them over there, no filter, natural light to present them in all their spiked glory.' He larked around, making a square frame shape with his fingers.

'Fuck off!' Michelle joshed. She picked one up. 'Looks medieval. Pretty kinky, even.'

'Poor cow,' said Dougie and Michelle looked at him askance. 'I'm sorry, I didn't mean you – obviously.'

'Take me out for a drink later?'

Dougie caught Stevo's eye who gave him a comedic lewd wink. Michelle was currently all hands-on-hips and a jaunty raise of her eyebrow, waiting for an answer. She'd moved from coyly flirty by Wednesday, to lingering eye contact yesterday and now this talk of kinky shit with a pout. So, go for a drink when the job was done, maybe get a little drunk, maybe have a fumble, maybe have more than that? Dougie thought how his cock could do with it, God knows.

'Sure,' Dougie told her. But it did cross his mind: the enormous hassle of lugging his entire kit back at some ungodly hour tonight possibly pissed; or tomorrow, no doubt hungover and reeling with regret. And he said to himself, why don't you simply say no?

'Let's do that,' he said. And then, in a moment of clarity he called out, 'Stevo! Radhu! You coming for a drink when we're done?'

They did.

But Stevo and Radhu had families waiting and they didn't stay long. It wasn't the sort of pub conducive to hunkering down for the evening anyway. It felt cold. The air was tainted with the sticky-sour smell of stale beer and seating was on hard wooden chairs at sharp square tables. On a main road, with its unattractive exterior, it was the sort of place to stop by for just the one drink after work or a quick one en route to somewhere else. The regulars were sitting at the bar, tapping the beer mats perfunctorily on the counter, hunched and drinking alone, silent.

'Well, it's been nice meeting you, mate,' Stevo said, making light work of two pints on the trot. 'Good luck with everything.' And it struck Dougie how plain it was to both of them that they'd likely never see each other again. It was what it had been – five days in a warehouse with agricultural randomness and meal deals from the local garage.

Dougie looked at the time. If he left now, the journey home would be stifling with rush hour and feel twice as long. If he left it, say, the time it took to drink one more pint, it would be more civilized out there; there'd be a seat for him and even a seat for his gear and he'd be back at his flat with much of the evening still left. It was as if Michelle could hear him thinking this through but she stared resolutely ahead, turning a deaf ear to it all. In her determination to get more drinks in, adding bags of crisps to her round, Dougie sensed she'd timetabled her entire evening.

She handed him another pint. This one with an even feebler head than the first. 'What part of Ireland are you from?'

Dougie choked on his beer. 'I'm—'

'I've been to Dublin loads of times – my cousin lives there and you sound just like him.'

He didn't want to embarrass her but he was biting down hard on the urge to say for fuck's sake I'm Scottish. His island accent was soft, melodious, almost Scandic in comparison with, say, a Glaswegian's – but it was unmistakably Scots.

'I'm from Harris,' said Dougie, 'the Outer Hebrides?' He watched her face carefully.

'Is that not near Dublin, then?'

He didn't know how to react now, really. His accent he would never disown and his homeland he would never deny.

'No – nowhere near,' he said. 'Excuse me,' he said, 'little boys' room.'

The toilets were dank: cold black institutional loo seats, two chipped urinals, a frosted window that didn't close, a cracked mirror mottled at the edges and a broken hand dryer. Dougie regarded his reflection. Maybe this was what anonymity could be. Not being Scottish. Not knowing Michelle's surname. Not needing to know much else about her cousin in Dublin or her weekend plans or her phone number or anything, really. After being so exhaustively involved with both the drama and minutiae that Suze had brought with her, perhaps the simplicity of just liking Michelle's face and of not really having to be the whole him could be refreshing.

God, you look tired, man.

Give it half an hour and the Tube'll have a seat for you and another for your gear.

Fuck's sake you're thirty-eight, not seventy-eight.

Just one more pint, then.

So there sat Dougie and Michelle, not chatting, not in awkward silence, just in a downbeat acceptance of why they were there and where they'd be going.

'Another?' Dougie went to the bar.

He also bought crisps.

She could fold the empty packets into small triangular purses. Dougie told her that it was cool. She just shrugged.

'It's not like there's any purpose,' she said, 'still gets chucked in a bin. It's just something to do with an empty crisp packet.'

Just something to do.

And Dougie told himself to get that bloody Tube and still have a good portion of evening at home to wind down. Takeaway curry, perhaps.

'Shall we go back to mine, then?' Michelle said.

Dougie had not expected the bluntness, certainly not so soon. There had been no preamble, no dancing towards and away from the topic. Is this how it's done now, then? He'd only been out of the loop for two years – was this progress?

'OK,' he said.

'You can't stay—'

He nodded before she had time to qualify it.

She went to the loo. He went to the loo. They put on their coats and left, leaving the empty glasses and the crisp packets in the little triangles and the crumbs and the four men still silent at the bar, pleading with their pints to dilute their woes. Out in the bite of cold air, it felt as if the rush of the traffic shoved him in the chest and Dougie wanted to be anywhere but here. But then he wondered if it would be too complicated, too insensitive now, to change his mind and get that train. It occurred to him that he was going to do the wrong thing, whichever direction he took. So he decided fuck it – I'll just go along for the ride, all the while thinking Jesus this is a bit grim.

Michelle shared a flat with two others who were nowhere to be seen. Her bedroom was cramped, mostly bed; a clothes rail, ill-fitting curtains, a fractured mirror similar to the one in the pub toilets. Brad Pitt in *Thelma and Louise* pulled from a magazine and put in a clip frame. And three stunning watercolour paintings, pastoral and halcyon, delicate and intricately observed, unceremoniously Blu-Tacked to the wall.

'I *love* these,' said Dougie.

'Oh.' She was nonplussed. 'I did them.'

It took a moment for Dougie to compute. 'They're amazing,' he said. 'Where are they of?'

She shrugged. 'I made them up.' She regarded Dougie's fuddled expression and presumed he didn't understand. 'You know, like you see on TV – lovely countryside places with stone bridges and streams and hills with those walls made out of rocks. Archways into secret gardens. That kind of thing.'

Dougie was transfixed. 'But Michelle – they're *really* good.'

'You think? Thanks!'

She was running her hand up his back now, across his shoulders.

He didn't want to have sex with her at the moment. If at all. But as he gazed at her paintings, it struck him that if he didn't have sex with her she'd feel shit and he'd feel crap about that. She'd refreshed her lipstick already. When they'd arrived back at her flat, she'd gone to the bathroom and reappeared slicked with fresh make-up.

'I really like your hair,' she said, tugging gently. 'You're really cute.'

And then Dougie thought to himself just close your eyes. Just close your eyes and feel lips against lips. Tongues. Find breasts to squeeze, feel hands around your cock, perhaps a mouth too, if you're lucky. Go for the warm and the wet. What she wants and what you can have. The escapism and release of coming – knowing you won't be coming back. Coming and going. And after this you can just keep on going with your life. Just sex, that's all it is. People do it all the time with no need for it to be meaningful. Just a mutual chase-down of physical pleasure. Consensual and inconsequential. It's fine.

But.
Fuck.
How can it feel so isolating, so lonely?

Dougie was back at his flat at just gone midnight. Dumped his kit on the sofa and lay on his back on the floor of his sitting room, hands behind his head, feeling his body lengthen and unwind. His place; its unique scent, its warmth, the sound of the boiler. In the next room his bed, his sheets, his laundry hanging to dry. In his peripheral vision, the flashing of the answering machine.

It was his dad; loudly and with those annoying pauses.

'Son. It's your dad. I'm just phoning. You're not in. Just phoning to say hello. And it was nice, aye, to chat the other day. So. Your da. Yes? OK! OK! Bye now.'

And as Dougie hovered his finger over the erase button, his eyes rested upon his great grandfather's map. And just then, he felt desperately homesick again. He'd lived in London with relative swagger all these years, defiantly called it home within months of arriving – but not tonight. Right now he knew he was but one of the millions of disparate fragments making up this frantic city; an unspectacular dull little detail in the vast mosaic of dirt and noise, of dreamt-up watercolours and Friday-night regrets.

Dougie replayed his father's message and didn't delete it. He just stood in silence and Colliers Wood had nothing to do with anything. He longed for Scotland, for Harris, for the place of his birth, to be back home.

February 1969

I don't know how it happened.
But I do know how it happened.
It's the swinging sixties after all and sex is neither a mystery nor a sin.

I don't know why I went that far.
I do know why I went that far.
Because oh! I felt so free, so alive, so happy – so real.

We're living in the moment, my tribe, and we're to love life and ban the bomb and make love not war. That's what we're about! We're teenagers. They call us a new breed as if they're frightened of us, as if we should be tamed. Being a teenager in 1969 – nothing comes close! I feel sorry for other teens past and future.
It's the best.

Or – it was the best.
But now – just now it's not so good.
I went to find Peter. He has gone.

The whole world shuts down over Christmas – and I've always loved that. But when it opened up again, and cars were on the roads and shops were open and decorations were being taken down and new bicycles had scuffs and puppies were becoming tiresome, that's when I crossed the park to the beautiful houses, to where Peter and his family were staying. I knocked at a couple of doors. Well, four actually. Not here, everyone said. And 'not here' is not the same as 'not in'. There were more houses than I thought.

I gave up and walked back across the park to Joan's and asked her.

She told me, oh – they've gone. They were just staying in a house over the park during the Christmas break.

I asked Joan, where can I find him?

And Joan said New Zealand or Australia – one of the two – and she thought this was hysterically funny. When I didn't laugh so much she gave me a hug and said yes yes, he was cute – but.

And I thought if she says plenty more fish in the sea I'll scream.

She didn't.

She said oh dear – you have a big old pash on him, don't you?

And at the time I just said yes I do and I rolled my eyes at myself and we laughed about it. I put on a stupid jolly tone to Joan when really it hurt my heart and messed with my head knowing that he had gone before I could see him. That, actually, he'd gone without trying to see me again.

And I didn't even know then what I know now.

But soon it was back to school. Back to stupid irrelevant school where they force you to feel incapably young and they treat you like you can't possibly have any views that are worthwhile or any feelings that are true. I daydreamed about Peter all the time and I was told off for not concentrating. I tried to drop his name into conversation with anyone who'd been at Joan's that night but I started to realize that no one really knew him at all. In a roundabout way, I chatted to Martin and Gerald, trying to find out what I could, about how they knew him, if they knew where he was.

Martin said they'd met him in the park the day of the party and he'd offered them a cigarette and they'd invited him along. Gerald said they knew Joan wouldn't mind – she'd told everyone to bring their friends, to make it a night to remember.

And over and over again I've replayed that night I'll never forget.

I realized how that night was last year already – though it was only a month or so ago. It's odd – the fact that so short a time has passed but last year is now a long time ago. It's passed. It's past tense.

I think of how, when I was fourteen turning fifteen, if I was asked my age I'd say well! I'd say, I'll be sixteen next year!

I wanted to skip ahead – I wanted to leap into the future. I wished time away.

Now I want to claw it back.

And so I thought I had a bug.
My mum thought I had a bug.
Wendy said it was probably the bug that she and Jimmy had had.

But after three days, I came to see how the bug started to pass by mid-morning and by the end of the week, I knew. I just knew. I would have known even if I wasn't being sick. I counted the weeks off on my fingers. The cold scorch when the reality dawned on me – I've never felt so alone, so terrified, so amazed, so confused. The week my period should have come, I wore a pad every day believing that if I kept to my routine, if I just carried on with normal, maybe this extraordinary thing couldn't possibly be happening. But at night, lying for hours while everyone slept – my brain whirred so violently I'd put my pillow against my head and hold it tight, just to get it to stop, to slow down at least. I can hear my heartbeat loud in my ears, I can feel it in my mouth, sometimes I have to tell myself to breathe. Just breathe, I say. Just keep breathing. But in the mornings, oh the sickness.

I started to hide it from everyone in the house.
That's what I'm doing now.
It's so hard, so ghastly, trying to be sick as quietly as you can.

Only—

That night. That night. I'll never forget that night. I'll never regret that night. I want to find Peter. Really, I need to find him even though my mother will kill him. And God only knows what'll become of me.

And I think back to that night, that night of You. At the time though, You – as a notion – were so far from my mind. Truth be told, if You – as a Consequence of It – had crossed my mind, then I probably would never have done what I did. And that, my little one, would mean that you and I would not be here, growing together as we are. So.

What will they do to me? But you – I won't let anyone do anything to you.

Nell

'Going to pop out – anyone want anything?'

Debbie was off on her break. Mostly, the staff didn't have time to take breaks, nor did their work strike any of them as the sort of job where breaks were welcome or even necessary. There was rarely a dull moment at the Chaffinch – but today had been slow.

'I would like—' But AJ couldn't actually think of anything he'd like.

'Anything we need?' asked Debbie.

'I need a hole in the head,' Danny declared. He was famous for upcycling expressions.

'OK,' said Debbie, diligently writing this down. 'Anything else? Nell?'

'Paper napkins – go to Pounds Right. Here.' She gave Debbie a couple of pound coins. 'Oh and could you pop in to the post office – there's a package waiting for me.'

'At Pounds Right everything is one pound or less.'

'Can I open the package, Nell?'

'Don't forget Danny's hole.'

'Danny, you mustn't put a hole in your head.'

'It's a saying, stupid.'

'I'm not stupid.'

'You are.'

'Oi!'

'AJ used the "S" word.'

'The "S" word is for SHIT, stupid.'

'He did it again! He swore *and* used the "S" word.'

'*Oi!*'

There were days like these when everything seemed to teeter precariously on a brittle edge. Most customers patiently turned a blind eye and a deaf ear but today, there was less tolerance and two in the queue left. Nell saw it as part of the job, to manage this. Usually, she let it all wash over her; she'd trained herself over the years, to employ a type of personal Teflon against which discord and altercations had no purchase. But today she found it all a bit tedious. So when Debbie returned with Nell's package and Nell was mobbed by the group begging to help open it, she said no way guys – package-opening privileges are suspended until normal behaviour resumes. Danny tried to reason that none of them were normal – he said he was Danny *Downsie*, remember. He said they were all *specials* – and, though this worked on Nell at other times, today she stuck to her resolve. They asked her if she even knew what it was inside and when she said yes, it's a plate and a saucer, they all lost interest anyway.

'Open it, then,' said Frank. The birds had been fed their walnuts and his meal was warming in the oven. He was wearing an orange cardigan with oversize brown buttons over a yellow shirt and his golfing trousers though he hadn't played for at least a decade. 'If it arrives in one piece, I'll eat my hat,' Frank said, helping Nell unwrap the items. 'And if they've sent you what you thought you were buying – I'll eat a walnut.' He was enjoying this. 'Buying off The eBay? Madness. It's all a scam.'

'Well – they've packed them well,' said Nell, giving the bubble wrap a pop.

'We don't know *what* they've packed, as yet,' said Frank. 'Could be anything or nothing.'

'Look!' Nell was delighted as the bright blue edge of the plate appeared with a glint of gold detailing. They examined the china with quiet fascination. Fancy that, Frank kept marvelling, fancy that.

'They produced them with green detailing too, you know,' Nell told him. 'You see, eBay isn't all bad – you learn a thing or two as you browse.'

'I prefer the blue.'

'Me too. Did you have anything like this, Frank? For the Coronation?'

Frank thought about it. 'I didn't even get a day off work – that I do remember. The second of June 1953. I was working at the printers; we had the special to rush out. Your mum'll be made up, Nell, made up.'

'I hope so.' She paused. 'Sometimes – well, mostly – it's difficult to tell, really.'

Frank handed her the saucer and patted her arm. They sat in companionable silence for a few moments. Over the years, Frank never knew if the subject was a no-go area, always taking his lead from Nell. 'Terrible thing. Terrible. I've told you I was orphaned at four years old?'

Nell observed a glaze come over his eyes and Frank slumped a little. Like a child, Nell thought, and it made her sad. He was all papery skin and gammy hips now and his life was a long arduous shuffle from one side of an overheated room to the other, but Frank *had* been a boy once upon a very, very long time ago. He had been someone's little boy, even if for just four short years.

He tapped her arm again. 'You'll shoot me, won't you dear, if my marbles go? Or poison.'

'Stop it, Frank,' Nell said. 'Anyway, it's not the same with my mum – she's always been a bit – different. Always. She's always inhabited two different worlds, if you like. It's just, it's getting progressively worse. It's getting very bad.'

'Can't be easy for you, love,' said Frank.

'I just wish I believed that she still knows it's me.'

'Must've been hard when you were a nipper, just you and your mum?'

'It was fine,' Nell muttered. 'My father left when I was three. I didn't know any different.' She paused. 'Anyway, having a nutty mum makes for great popularity at school. She was so entertaining – almost exotic – to my pals. Children see bonkers as a quality.'

'Well, that's a shame in itself, isn't it,' said Frank. Nell shrugged. There was such kindness to his voice, and yet she felt irritated by his judgement. So she dished up his meal, checked the window latch, bagged up the rubbish, assessed the toilet roll situation, made her excuses and left.

Nell returned to the shop on Trinity Street. The cup was still there and Nell picked it up, triumphant.

'I came by a couple of weeks ago? And you told me about the trio – that originally it would have been a set of three?'

'Ah yes – I remember. Well, you can still have the cup for eight quid.'

'You said a fiver!' Nell laughed.

'Inflation.'

Nell wasn't sure if he was joking.

'Go on then, I'll take five.'

Nell took a breath and beamed. She'd been looking forward to this part. 'Well – look what I found!' From her bag she produced the saucer. She held it out to the shopkeeper who took it to scrutinize.

'What do you want for it?'

'I don't – you can have it. I did what you said and looked on eBay and found a plate and saucer going for a tenner. But I only needed the plate. So – you can have this. The saucer. You can just – have it.'

'But—'

'You can just have it,' said Nell, slightly taken aback that there was no smile coming her way, just suspicion. 'Seriously. My mum has the cup and saucer – she broke the plate, she said, when she first got it. So I found a plate – and, look, the saucer's for you.'

The shopkeeper examined the saucer again.

'You never know,' Nell said, 'maybe someone'll come by and they've got the plate and they're looking for these.'

'I can give you, say, a fiver off anything in the shop.'

'It's just for you,' Nell said. 'Honestly. I don't want anything for it. Just – have it.'

And then she thought oh shit, his eyes are welling up.

'It's the smallest things,' the shopkeeper said, putting the teacup onto the saucer. He took Nell's hand and held it. 'Thanks, love.'

Spring's imminence was a comfort akin to a favourite piece of music playing quietly in the background, all of the time. Mid-March wasn't spring proper, but there were bulbs in bloom, something about the sunlight being less watery and the air carrying a scent that was positively unwintry. Spring was defiantly on its way, winter was almost done. Nell felt light and happy leaving the shop, popping into the café to be hugged but not needed, and heading off to visit her mother; a sense of triumph wrapped up with the plate.

The tearoom downstairs was quite lively with families visiting and the scamper of grandchildren weaving a joyous energy through the legs of the tables and chairs, laughter bouncing up from the sofas. Nell wondered if her mother ever ventured down here at such times, to the welcome contagion of affection. She doubted it. Her mother would tell them to turn the volume down, more like. Nell smiled in the vague direction of everybody, waved to Sylvie and then climbed the stairs to her mother's room.

Telly on. Mum in a chair. Not much response.

'Hello, Mum. It's Nell.'

'It's Julie Andrews!'

Her mother was watching *The Princess Diaries*.

'I've never actually seen this film,' Nell said. 'Can I make you a cup of tea?'

'Shh, Nell, shh!'

If Nell's day had been a good one thus far, it had just got exponentially better. When *had* her mother last called her Nell? She sat on the edge of the bed, close to the chair, and didn't really mind whether they got round to the plate or not. Her mother had told her to be quiet. Shh, Nell, shh.

'Oh, I could watch that all over again!'

'They'll probably repeat it sometime soon,' said Nell. 'How are you, Mum?'

Her mother was zapping through channels, increasingly annoyed at there being nothing on that she wanted to watch.

'Cuppa, Mum?'

I'll keep saying it. I'll keep reminding you that you're Nell's mother.

And Nell made her mother a cup of tea in the Coronation cup. She'd brought KitKats too. She took the plate out from her bag and placed the cup and saucer on it.

'Here you go,' she said. And she waited.

'Thank you, dear. I love a KitKat.' She pulled off the paper and scored down the foil between the chocolate fingers with the edge of her thumb.

'Mum?' Stop looking at shit on the bloody telly! 'The plate? *The* plate?'

Very carefully, her mother put the KitKat onto the arm of the chair. She placed the cup and saucer, the tea untouched, on the windowsill. The plate was in her lap and they were both focusing on it. She lifted it up, tipped this way and that so that the light danced off the gold lines and spun depth into the turquoise glaze. A very young Queen Elizabeth looked out and over their shoulders while the lion and unicorn, dressed up to the nines, kept guard.

'But—' Her mother looked perplexed and her voice, when it came, was small. 'But this isn't mine. I broke mine.'

'I know,' said Nell.

'Is this yours?'

'No – it's for you. I found one – I found it for you.'

Her mother laid the plate gently on her lap, traced her fingertip satisfyingly over the undulating frilled edging. Round and round, anticlockwise as if rewinding memories, as if trying her hardest to wade backwards through the current fug to a time when things were clear.

'Do you remember how Mother always told us never to cry over spilt milk – but how she would roast us over anything else?'

'She died, Mum, when I was very young,' Nell said quietly. 'I don't really remember her.'

'But whose plate is this?'

'It's yours now – I found it for you.'

Her mother looked amazed. 'We were given them, by Grandpa. We were so excited – never mind the street parties and the flags, we were just so excited for the new Queen. And even more so to be given such a, well, *grown-up* set of china.'

'A trio.'

'We were. We were.'

'It was called the Clarice Cliff *trio*.'

'We were all given a set but I broke my plate. The very day I was given it. Gosh, was I told off.'

'But see – here's another. So it's complete again.'

'Is it yours, Florence?'

Nell took a breath against her mother's insistence on Florence. As she exhaled, she remembered how Debbie sometimes called her Maude. Sometimes Catherine. Sometimes, Debbie would run through various names including her dog and her daughter before she alighted on Nell. It was Debbie's *thing*. Maude Catherine Rosie *Nell*. Catherine Nell Maude *Rachel*. And Debbie would just blame last night's wine, or the menopause, or the need for caffeine but she'd always laugh it off.

'It's yours now,' said Nell. 'The trio is complete.'

Nell's mother looked at her sharply. 'No, it's not.'

'They belong together, don't they,' Nell pushed on, marvelling, thinking it was the best £10 she'd ever spent. She put the KitKat back on the plate.

'Grandpa gave these to us. The new Queen was just so very pretty. Mother kept saying she was far too young for such a role. Dad said, I blame that bloody Simpson woman. He said, poor man, that poor bugger – and we knew he was referring to the late King. He was genuinely upset about all of that but we were thrilled because Dad *swore*. Bloody *and* bugger! So unlike our father. But we didn't think of the poor King or of his bugger brother and bloody Wallace. All us girls wanted, really, was for our hair to behave so we could style it just like our new Queen's. Oh, we *loved* her!'

Nell sat very still, just drinking it all in, willing there to be more. It had been a long time since her mother had spoken so lucidly and at such length. She loved hearing of her swearing grandfather and stern grandmother. She loved to think of her mother as a young girl, willing her hair to stick to a style. She imagined the sisters with their commemorative plates and cups and saucers, gazing at Elizabeth. There was even some enjoyment in thinking of the plate breaking; real times, these true events, something undeniable and not invented.

Her mother was staring at the middle distance, tugging absent-mindedly at her hair. Bring her back.

'Do you remember if ever I broke something?' Nell said. 'Or dropped something? Or spilt something? You were never like that to me, like your mum was to you, when you broke the plate and got a roasting.'

Her mother's fingers were going round and around the plate again, faster, each direction, agitated.

'You never told me off for such things,' Nell continued softly. 'You'd say oh dear, just an accident. You'd call me—'

'Butterfingers.'

'Yes! That's right! You'd call me butterfingers. Or—'

'Clumsy clot.'

'Yes,' Nell laughed, 'clumsy clot! Do you remember when we had tea at that extremely posh hotel in London? I can't remember which. You always said the Ritz was the Pitz – so it can't have been there. But it was somewhere luxurious. My thirteenth birthday – a few months late, but who's counting?'

Finally her mother was eating the KitKat and she was savouring every nibble.

'I sent that dainty tower thing flying,' said Nell. 'The tiered plates with the finger sandwiches and the cakes-in-miniature and the scones. All over me, all over the floor. Everything – everywhere.'

KitKat finger number two. Did she remember? Oh, Nell hoped she did!

Nell kept going. 'And the waiter in the prim uniform with his nose in the air, he looked – appalled, disgusted. And before I could even think of crying, let alone apologizing – to him to you – you said, *It was an accident, Mr Snooty – bring us fresh cakes and shove your attitude in the bin with all of this.*'

And Nell remembered it all. She remembered being only momentarily mortified by her mother's reaction and by the posh people staring. The far stronger emotions of feeling protected and feeling proud, they were what had lasted.

'What day is it?' The KitKat was finished.

'It's Saturday.'

'Is it.'

'It is – all day!'

Nell watched her mother take the teacup to her lips, listened to her sip and sip and sip as if her mother's thoughts were keeping time with each. It was a peaceful day today. She hated it when her mother was agitated.

'Do you want me to take you out? For a drive? It's a lovely day – you can *feel* the spring.'

Her mother sip, sip, sipped. Then she got up from her chair and took the cup and the saucer and the plate to the little bathroom. Nell could see her washing everything.

'Here, I can do that. Let me—'

There was a pause, just a short one but long enough for the change to be manifest.

'You'll do no such thing. I'm not a cripple. I'm not an invalid.'

Nell physically slumped. She thought, come back, Mum – come back. And she thought, please, please don't go just yet.

Think of something!

'I heard Aunt Em came to visit!' Nell rushed. 'We could go and visit her one day – tomorrow, if you like. You like my little car! And it's an easy drive.'

But her mother didn't respond. She was holding the plate, the cup and the saucer. She carried it, as if in procession, slowly and reverentially, and she held the china out to Nell. 'Here.'

'But – they're yours.'

'Take them.'

'I don't want them, Mum. You love that cup!'

'Take.'

'And now you have the plate and you can look at Elizabeth and remember about her hair—'

'Take them.'

'They're special to you. Your dad swearing and your mum telling you off for breaking the plate.'

'I broke the plate the day we were given them.'

'I know – but I fixed it. It's a trio once more.'

'It cannot be fixed.' Her mother looked at her very levelly. 'It is not my plate. It doesn't belong here. It belongs to a long, long time ago. There was a trio – but then there wasn't.'

'But Mum—'

'Stop calling me that – what's wrong with you?' She was pulling at her hair again.

Nell's thoughts were in a rapid scurry. If I leave it she'll break it. Stupid bloody plate. Thirteen quid. I'll put it back on eBay. I'll do it Buy It Now for £15. Plus £3.50 p&p.

'You shouldn't be here, Florence. She'll kill you if she sees you. You have to get back to Harry's.'

Dougie

'Long way to come for a bit of rope.'

As greetings went, this wasn't the warmest that Dougie had encountered on his recent travels, but he was being paid to do a job, not make friends, so he followed Mrs Selwyn to the new barn behind the old stone farmhouse.

'That there's for cattle, that there's for sheep.'

In the barn, there were two trestle tables on which cream and white rope in fractionally different diameters and various lengths were laid out.

'And that there – that's horse whispering.' Mrs Selwyn motioned to an industrial-looking coat stand on which hung ropes in different lengths and colours.

Dougie went to inspect. 'Different colours for – different levels of whispering? Like karate? Or for different decibel levels?'

Mrs Selwyn broke into a deep and dirty chuckle. 'Summat like that. We just knot them and fix on the snappers and clasps. Sell like hot cakes. Different colour for every day of the week plus Sunday best, I reckon. You know what they're like with their horses.'

Dougie didn't. He thought it all looked like giant fresh pasta left out to dry.

'You'll want a cup of tea?'

'Please,' said Dougie, starting to unpack his equipment. He'd had nothing since setting off first thing. It was windy outside; the steel sides of the barn juddered with the gusts and the cold slithered under the doors and snaked its way up his back.

'Kettle's over there,' she said, still laughing as she left.

The previous two days had been three different locations in and around Peterborough. Today Dougie was at a farm in the Hope Valley in Derbyshire. Tomorrow he would be in an industrial area of Carlisle where the joys of photographing drum pumps, hygiene and bio security awaited. Today, though, it seemed Dougie was being given enough rope to hang himself. And yet, before long, he warmed up and found there was something oddly gentle about the ropes and halters; everything today tactile and uncomplicated after all the galvanized items of the last few days, those containers and grilles and steel contraptions that looked like things of torture. It was soothing working methodically and completely on his own, and there was something strangely con-templative about deciphering the Selwyns' spidery handwriting on the scraps of paper under all this rope.

He worked swiftly and efficiently and was finished by early afternoon but decided not to head straight for Carlisle and the Travelodge. Instead, he took to the hills beyond the village and walked. God it felt good to be buffeted by squally weather, to have rain and wind lash his face and to have so much space and solitude. He'd brought his camera; a sudden longing to capture ephemera and land and sky, to photograph outwards and expansively for the first time in God knows. He walked hard and fast up to beyond the tree-line, to where the landscape was no longer plotted and pieced, where the earth was wet and uneven beneath his feet, where he felt just that little bit closer to the sky. There, with the wind wild enough to catch his breath and the rain soaking his lops of hair into steely fingers which harsh-flicked against his face and into his eyes, Dougie felt he could exhale. Anchoring himself, facing north, finding stability amidst all of this. He'd leave Hope behind having rediscovered something else. All points north. Soon he would be closer to Harris than to Camden.

Joan wept.

But I had to tell someone about you. I was starting to feel frightened. What my body was doing, what my head was telling me. Oh, hells bells – what was I to do? It was getting a bit too much.

I count fourteen weeks. It's March now.
Little you.
Still making me sick as a dog.

Sometimes, just sometimes – in the moments before I fall asleep, in the dark of my room and the silence of the house and the blanketing aloneness of my bed – just sometimes I'd think it would be better if you didn't make it.

I have prayed for blood.
I have prayed for pain to say you've gone, to say you've said goodbye.
I have pushed my hands against my belly and pushed hard – down and away.
Tears streaming as I have prayed go away go away go away.

So I told Joan.
She cried and cried.
This isn't helping, I told her, crying too.
That bloody bloody bastard! she said.
That didn't help.
Why were you so stupid she said over and over again and, for the first time, I felt really ashamed. I realized that's how the outside world will see it, will see me.

Your mum will kill you, you stupid stupid thing, Joan sobbed.

I know, I said. I know that.

But.

Joan said, but what? And she stared at me good and proper. Oh God, she said – you're not thinking of keeping it! You can't! You have to get rid of it!

She called you It and I loathed her for that. And I detested her for making perfect sense about everything else.

She would not stop crying.

That bloody bastard! she said.

I just didn't have the energy to argue. In truth, it's become a daily battle to continue to love Peter.

Joan turned up at my house a couple of days later and I was terrified she was going to say something. Luckily Marjorie was visiting and the focus was on her and everyone was downstairs so Joan and I went up to my room.

She had a bag.

In the bag was a bottle half full of gin. She told me I had to take a Gin Bath – we were neither of us sure what that was, whether I was to drink it or bathe in it. She told me the water had to be very very hot. She said I was to have the bath and she would wait. She was whispering the whole time – like none of it could be spoken of out loud – though no one could have heard us anyway.

Listen, Joan, I said, listen. I'm not sure, I said. I'm not sure this is a good idea. I'm not sure what I want.

You do not want to have a baby, idiot, said Joan. She hissed it out, as if each word was a sentence. I cannot hate her – she is so very worried for me. She is my oldest and closest friend.

Run the bath! Run the bloody bath! Run it bloody hot! Drink the bloody gin.

Stop swearing, I said.

You've had intercourse — and you're chippy with me for swearing?!
OK, OK, OK! I'll run the bath!

And I called downstairs, 'I'm just having a bath!' We do this in our household.

I heard George call up, 'Right you are!'

I'm going to stay, Joan said. She said she didn't know how long the bath would take to work. She had her school clothes with her — she told her mum we were studying.

I left her chewing her nails, sitting on my bed, calling me a stupid, stupid girl.

I ran the hottest bath and poured half the gin in. It smelt queer and it made me queasy. I didn't want to drink any of it. I had a sip and it was so sharp in my mouth, like fumes. Just one sip and I could feel it burn right down my throat, I could feel it hot in my stomach. I thought of the sweet punch at her party. I thought of Peter. Joan was at the door whispering you must drink it all down.

Get in the bath and drink it all down!

I got in the bath and I drank it all down. There was probably about half a glass left in the bottle.

And I cried silently as I watched my legs turn very pink. The water was scalding. My stomach looking like it was blushing. My arms looked broiled. And I said, I'm sorry, little baby I'm sorry I'm sorry I'm sorry.

Joan at the door. Has anything happened? Are you crying? Is it hurting? Has it come out?

Me in the bath. Sobbing as secretly as I could.

So hot. Feeling sick. Stroking my tummy and saying sorry to you.

It was Wendy who told me Mum had found the gin bottle which I'd forgotten I'd hidden at the back of the bathroom cupboard under the basin, ready to throw away. I begged her to say it was hers, or even say it was Jimmy's. But she just said your life, your funeral and my goodness did my mother give me a roasting the next morning.

At least I didn't have to hide throwing up – they'd just think it was the gin. But she roasted Joan too. She told Joan she'd be telling her mother. And I loved Joan for sharing the blame and the punishment with me. But before we went to school George passed us in the hallway as we were putting our shoes on and he smiled at us and said gin?! On a school night?! and I really loved my stepfather just then. Because if it had been just about gin on a school night, he had our backs. But none of them knew it was all about You.

The gin bath didn't work.
Joan was so upset.
I, though, was relieved.
She could tell.
You have to stop this, she told me. You have to think of your future! Or think of the poor little baby – it's no life.

She is wrong. You are my future. I had felt you flutter by then.

I stay late for art club on Thursdays. Obviously, it's the only thing I like at school. I'm doing something really groovy – a psychedelic painting, huge, based on music. I love Jimi Hendrix most of all and, as I thought of his music and his passion and his brilliance, I chose the colours. I let his music define the shapes and create the energy and the result was swirls and pulsing blobs. Sounds disgusting but it's really worked.

That Thursday night it was very strange because nothing had changed on the outside of our house – but as soon as I opened the door, something was very different inside. Everything looked the same. But something had happened and it wasn't the same. Nothing was how I knew it.

Joan.
My mother.
George.
All in our sitting room.

My mother. White as a sheet with disbelief and disgust.
Joan. Red with shame and fear.
George. Softly grey with concern and kindness.

I didn't hate Joan. Or even my mother. Certainly not George. Because I try not to hate – and anyway, I'm so full of love.

But when my mother told Joan to leave, I felt a terror I could never have imagined.

Not what they have in store for me – but what they might have planned for You.

Nell

Nell didn't really know where to put the china. She didn't have shelves. She didn't need them. When she rented the flat, the landlord told her it was a blank canvas and said she was welcome to put up whatever she wanted and if she needed shelves, he'd supply them. She told him she wouldn't need them. She didn't need shelves because Nell didn't tend to buy things that had no practical use, nor did she keep things that might impinge on space, not even books. She liked things to be clear. She liked to be able to see. Books she read and enjoyed she passed on to Debbie, the rest she'd take to Oxfam. She liked candles because they had a purpose and also a lifespan and took up little room but their presence was felt; she also had two houseplants years old that were still going strong. When her mother had left the house for the care home, all Nell took was the old pine trunk that had been at the foot of her childhood bed. Photo albums, her rag doll Holly, a bunch of mix tapes and, strangely, her English exercise books which had been stored in there for years. They were out of sight and therefore there they could remain. Now, in her flat, the trunk was an excellent base for the television, the phone and answering machine. Often, Nell found herself just sitting in a daze, not watching the TV, tracing instead the shape of the trunk's iron hinges with her eyes, remembering her childhood home, the crowded chaos of it all.

In her bedroom, she had four framed Ansel Adams prints of Yosemite, which were from a calendar. In the sitting room, a poster of Picasso's dove and another of Matisse's snail, both in clip frames. In the kitchen, she had a corkboard bursting with photos from over the years, which she never changed, only added to. She often lost herself in these when she made herself a coffee or ate beans straight from the tin.

Frank wanted to know all about the cup, but Nell didn't want to relate what had happened. She walked around his sitting room, picking things up and asking him to tell her about them.

'My mum loved all her bits and bobs,' she said. 'Some were quite lovely. Mostly, though, they were fairly hideous. She'd spend money we didn't really have. Said she was *helpless in the face of gorgeousness*. Really, she just loved buying stuff.'

'And do you think she misses her things?' Frank asked. 'Or just misses shopping?'

Nell thought about it. 'I don't honestly know. It's hard to tell what's forgotten. I don't know what she misses.'

Frank put his hand through Nell's arm.

'I think you miss the mum who loved the bits and the bobs,' he said. And he noticed Nell's almost imperceptible flinch from kindness.

It was early evening after a long shift at the café when Nell went to see her mother. She found her downstairs with a group of other residents, playing card games and drinking coffee out of the dull green cups called Beryl. Effervescent and present, her mother was trouncing everyone, her eyes sparkling and her smile lively. For a while, Nell just watched unseen. Rummy and whist. They were playing for matchsticks. Her mother's pile was impressive. Nell watched her shuffling the cards exuberantly, fanning them and tapping them and throwing them from hand to hand. It struck Nell that her mother was happy, happy in the here and right now. And Nell thought she's probably far happier than me – and the notion made her laugh. The party looked up and saw her and no one seemed to know who she was.

'Hello.' Nell gave a little wave.

'Are you joining us?' asked one of the group, an elderly gentleman whose moustache was so white it looked violet.

'I'm useless at cards,' Nell laughed.

'Nonsense,' said her mother. 'You used to beat us all hands down – from when you were knee high! Watch it – she's bluffing! She has the best poker face in the world. Watch her like a hawk, I tell you – don't be fooled.'

Nell couldn't remember ever winning a card game against her mother, not even snap.

'Are you joining us?' the man asked again.

'It looks like quite a tournament and the stakes are high – I don't want to interrupt,' Nell said, but she hovered and everyone looked at her as if to say *you're hovering*. 'I'll leave you to it.'

'Goodnight!' the man said cheerily.

'Aces high!' her mother was calling out.

'Mum – I won't see you till next weekend, so I brought these back.' Nell produced the Coronation trio to oohs and aahs. 'I'll pop up to your room and leave them there.'

Everyone looked at the space Nell left.

'Daughter?' someone said.

'I thought you didn't have any children?' said another.

'It's not mine,' she said.

And no one was sure if she was talking about the china or Nell.

Dougie

At the services north of Lockerbie, Dougie sat and contemplated the plate in front of him, now denuded of the enormous cooked breakfast save for a smear of brown sauce and two baked beans suffocating under the skin that was all he had left of the grilled tomato. He'd been there over an hour and he hadn't yet phoned his father. He told himself this was so that he could make the visit a surprise but he also knew that this enabled him to change his mind and his father would be none the wiser. He needed to work it all out.

There was one ferry crossing and it was at 3 p.m. but he was almost 300 miles from Uig in Skye. He knew, realistically, he wouldn't make it. It would take six and a half hours on a good run but the weather was squalling already; the rain flinging hostility at the window by which he sat. It was a day for the indoors, not a day for a ferry crossing or hurrying in bad weather through the Highlands. Nor should he be spending hours southbound on motorways.

It was a day to stay put.

'Get you anything else?' The waiter seemed to hope not.

How could he still be hungry?

'Um.' He scoured the menu. 'I'll take a couple of rounds of toast, please.'

'White or brown?'

'Brown, please.'

'We're out of brown.'

'White, then.'

'Drink?'

'Bit early, isn't it?'

His joke was lost on the waiter.

'Tea. No – make it coffee,' he said. 'I've a hellish long drive ahead.'

The waiter wasn't remotely interested.

Dougie had been driving for two and a half hours and was only now at Tyndrum. He had no chance of making the ferry and yet he was still heading north. No doubt his father, in his inimitably laconic way, would just call this *a bit of weather* but actually the conditions were appalling. The rain and the wind had become a monumental entity, bigger than anything, devouring the landscape only to expel it now and again in gauzy and ghostlike apparitions. Occasionally, through the wafting and glower, a glimpse of a hillside scarred by silver streaks of wet; a valley suffocating in a shroud of dark mist. The mountain edges could occasionally be seen, trying valiantly to cut into the sky only to be swallowed up by it. Everything was purple and black, like new bruising from the assault the weather was wreaking.

Glencoe. Dougie always stopped at Glencoe, but not today. He was still three hours from Uig. He asked himself over and again, why am I doing this? why am I still driving? I'm not going to make it. He doubted the ferry would sail in this anyway and even if it did, it would leave in two hours. If by some miraculous time travel he made it, he'd puke his way over the waters of the Minch, that was for sure. But still he drove on. Jesus, would they not close the Skye Bridge in this?

Nearing Fort William, Dougie called it a day. Called himself a stupid bastard. He was tired now, too tired to drive on or drive back. After booking into a B&B on the edge of the loch he could not see, Dougie sat on the side of a single bed and put his head in his hands. Despite the gloaming, the lashing rain and the hurl of the wind, the proximity of home confronted him. His fingers ran absent-mindedly over the candlewick bedspread. He'd had one like this on his own bed, growing up. He remembered his mother teaching him to make a bed, snapping the sheets tight, smoothing the blankets and hospital-cornering the lot before tucking the bedspread under and over the pillow so that it looked just right, she said. A couple of years after she'd died, Dougie bought his father a duvet for Christmas. Gordon said she'd turn in her grave seeing how quickly he could make his bed now.

Dougie went out for a walk along Loch Linnhe, the water whipping and lacerated like a small sea. He wanted to feel it all, to be drenched right through, to shiver and not feel his fingers and have earache from the wind. It was getting dark but whether this was true dusk or the untiring weather was unclear. Sodden, he found a pub where a pint of heavy was pulled for him before he even asked. There was a peat fire lit and he went and stood by it until steam came off him, his body shaking, his cheeks starting to burn, his hands thawing, finally, though his fingers remained wind-swollen and stiff.

The beer helped and a whisky was settling and a stool was pushed towards him by a local called Ken whose face was as etched and as craggy as the landscape. Dougie sat awhile, mesmerized by the glowing peats. Eventually, he came to. He checked his phone for a signal and dialled.

'Gordon Munro, hello.'

'Da?'

'Son?'

'Aye.'

They both took a beat.

'Aye,' said Dougie again. 'It's me.'

'You all right? Dougie?'

It was only just gone five in the afternoon, a very odd time to be taking a phone call from his son.

'I'm outside Fort William.'

'*Fort William?*'

'Aye,' Dougie sighed, pushed his pint away, took a moment and gave his father the same. 'I was on my way, Dad – but the weather! I was coming to see you.'

There was silence. Gordon prayed for his mind not to be playing tricks, for his memory not to have failed.

'Did I know this, Dougie?'

'No,' his son said quietly. 'I was going to surprise you.'

It was all a bit baffling. 'Well,' Gordon said, 'that's – well, that's—'

'I should have called, given you the heads-up. I'm sorry,' said Dougie. 'I've been working away this week. Peterborough, Derbyshire, then Carlisle last night and I thought I'd come – back.' Why could he never say 'home' to his dad? Why always 'back' or 'for a visit' or 'to see you'?

'You'll have missed the boat.'

'Did it even sail today? In this?'

'I believe it did. Will you come tomorrow, then?'

Dougie considered his answer even though he knew what it was. 'I'm not sure I can. I need to head back, you see.'

His father paused, continued slightly stunned. 'You were coming home – for just for one night?'

Dougie realized then how stupid the concept had been and how lame it all sounded.

'I just thought – it occurred to me I was closer than I was to London. I just drove.'

'You'll stay in Fort William.' Dougie hadn't heard his father strict for some time. 'I'll not have you driving to England in this bit of weather.'

'I'll stay here tonight, Da. And next time I'll plan it properly.'

'That'll be grand, Douglas.' Gordon floundered to make sense of a visit that wasn't known about and hadn't happened.

'OK – well, bye now then.' Dougie listened to the solid pause. 'Dad?'

'Aye.' Gordon sent another pause down the line to his son. 'You be safe on your way, laddie.'

'I will.'

'Almost home,' said his father.

The worse the weather, the more crowded the pub became. Beer and whisky and bravura and camaraderie. Hikers from Sweden and Canada had the piss gently taken, regulars swore gamely at each other and matched the landlady at her chirpy insults, and Dougie was treated as one of their own. His jeans were drying against his skin, a sensation odd but not unpleasant. He got drunk. They all got drunk. He wasn't sure how many drinks he paid for nor how many were bought for him. He thought he'd ordered food. He spoke to a girl called Inge from Sweden with mesmerizing blue eyes and hair so white and silken that he was compelled to stroke it. He told the Scots he was from Harris, he told the foreigners he lived in London. He told Inge that she was beautiful and he wanted to photograph her. He told the craggy man he'd first met that he wanted to take his portrait. He told them he photographed wheelbarrows for a living.

That he later found his way back to the guesthouse was nothing short of miraculous. He had no idea what the time was or how much he'd drunk but his hangover was so bad the following day that he spent another night in Fort William. But the pub today was almost empty. The storm had passed and folk had hiked on or gone back to work. He went to sleep at 7.30 and left Scotland at first light the next morning.

When Dougie finally arrived back at his flat in Camden, it was as if he hadn't been there for months. Stuffing clothes in for a wash and bread into the toaster, he sat on the sofa, looked around him and it felt now like he'd never left. All those drum pumps in Carlisle and the ropes in Derbyshire and whatever it was he had photographed in Peterborough. And the joyless waiter outside Lockerbie and the beautiful hiker in the pub, the tiny bed in Fort William and the howl of the wind and the lash of the rain and his new best friends slapping his back as drinks were downed – it was all so implausible it became dreamlike and forgotten.

Nell

Nell had sat in her car, stationary, for a good ten minutes before reluctantly turning on the ignition. Now she was halfway there and reminding herself, out loud, that she was doing this to shut Debbie up. To shut everyone up. Nell really couldn't think of anything worse than a blind date – nor anything she'd less like to do on her day off – but Debbie had announced it with aplomb in the café as if it was her greatest achievement to date. Guess what everyone, she'd said. I've got Nell a date, he's called Tobes and apparently he's gorgeous and he's seen Nell's picture and he's dying to meet her.

Rachel grinned from ear to ear and said *bridesmaid* to Nell in her wavery whisper.

One of the mums called over that she met her husband that way.

AJ asked if Nell would be having sex.

Danny told AJ to shut up because she was going to marry *him*, aren't you, Nell.

Alex asked if it meant Nell had to pretend that she was blind.

Libby needed to know what Nell would wear.

Danny said not your grey sweatshirt, it's too grey.

Sanjay said not the trousers with the big pockets on the side, they're horrible.

Libby said wear a red skirt, it's important.

One of the builders in the queue said you want to be careful, love. Make sure someone knows exactly where you'll be.

Debbie said Jesus – it's a date with a nice guy called Tobes, not some random axe murderer.

Nell said what sort of a name is Tobes anyway?

And everyone looked at Nell. Everyone. Staff and customers alike. Everyone threw their exasperation at her.

All right all right! Bloody hell! I'll go!

Nell didn't have a red skirt, nor did she have any inclination to buy one. She stuck her head out of the kitchen window and detected only a slight breeze; put on jeans and long brown boots and two gauzy tops which she hoped was what layering was meant to look like. She added a necklace then took it off. Slung a wide belt around her hips and thought not bad. A little make-up and a lot of nerves.

Why am I doing this?

Because everyone's in the background rooting for you.

And as Debbie said, it's only for lunch – not for ever.

Bury St Edmunds – an excellent pub and a perfectly nice-looking Tobes. Within minutes though, Nell was quietly wondering how she could best describe him to everyone desperate for details on Monday.

Really sweet guy – just not my type.

Nice bloke – but not for me.

Lovely man – I'm not sure I'd want to take it further.

Why not! they'd demand.

Because he was so dull I wanted to stick my fork into his hand just to see if he had any other expressions.

Because he only asked me one direct question: which route I'd taken, before telling me which route I should have taken, turn by turn.

Because I don't want the mess of anything with anyone.

And actually, fundamentally, because I just couldn't imagine kissing him.

Heading for home at half past two under the hastily contrived excuse of needing to feed her neighbour's cat, Nell pulled into a lay-by, rested her head on the steering wheel and groaned. She sat where she was, looking out at what had been fly-tipped: bathroom tiles in bright blue that someone must have chosen originally and now someone else had rejected, a builders' bag with polystyrene spilling out, a bin bag tied up concealing an indefinable mass, a doll's pushchair, a scatter of beer bottles depressingly close to the bottle bank. She glanced away from it all, looked at the road sign instead. She had a missed call from Debbie who was probably phoning to chastise her for not giving it a proper try, for leaving so soon it was rude, for lying about a cat. Or maybe Debbie simply wanted to see how she was. But Nell didn't want to speak to her. And she didn't want to go home just yet. She flipped open her phone and made the call. If she'd messed up Tobes's date and Debbie's best efforts, she might as well perform a good deed with what was left of the afternoon.

When Nell was young her Aunt Em had intrigued and terrified her in equal measure. She was her mother's older sister but she seemed to inhabit a different time altogether. Tall and formidably straight, even now in her late sixties, always in a well-cut and sober skirt or trousers, blouse ironed starchily, a V-necked cardigan, buttoned, and not a hair awry in her immaculate bob. It was one of the consistencies of Nell's life, that Aunt Em never changed and nor did the sensation for Nell of being peered at judgementally. From under that severe fringe and over those rectangular tortoiseshell specs, Nell had been assessed and categorized over the years by those steely eyes. Her aunt was always sharp, pointedly so. She was all about order and control; she had a fiercely active brain and no time for nonsense. She could not be more different from her sister.

Her aunt's spotless Nissan Micra was precision-parked outside, with straight wheels three inches from the kerb. Nell rapped the door, brushed herself down, retied her ponytail and it felt like waiting to see the headmistress.

'Well!' said her aunt, answering the door. 'Now this is a surprise.' Navy-blue skirt, tan tights, navy shoes with a modest heel, pale blue shirt with white dots, a blue cardigan around her shoulders. Nell felt herself being scanned from head to toe.

The house was straightforward and neutrally decorated, the green twist carpet showing the satisfying swathes from daily vacuuming. Somewhere, a clock tocked, even and low. There was the pervasive scent of cleaning products and coffee. Nell took off her jacket and put it over the newel post where it was swiftly removed and hung on a hanger, placed in the coat cupboard.

'Tea?'

'Yes, please.'

'Go through to the sitting room.'

'Can I help?'

'Go through – dear – to the sitting room.'

Nell did as she was told, and sat carefully on the edge of a velvet-upholstered chair, her hands politely in her lap. She looked around; she hadn't visited for a long time. There was an oil painting above the fireplace she didn't remember, a traditional village scene where raucous peasants were being ignored astutely by a fancy couple taking a stroll. There were five paperweights on the windowsill, each placed an even distance from the next. And had the curtains always been that colour? Her aunt had lived here for decades, new curtains were not unreasonable.

When was Nell last here? Christmas had been in a hotel restaurant the last few years and though Nell phoned every once in a while, she appeased her conscience because her aunt was staunchly independent and always so busy; still teaching occasionally at Cambridge, still writing papers on whatever sciencey thing it was that was her calling.

Tea was brought in on a tray, cups and saucers and a plate of digestives. Paper napkins. Milk in a jug, sugar in a lidded pot, two teaspoons. 'Well, this I was not expecting.'

Unsure whether this was a reproach, a slight on poor manners, Nell changed tack. 'Thank you so much for visiting Mum the other week.'

'She told you?'

'No, Sylvie – the bubbly one.'

'It was a good visit – one of the better days, I should imagine.'

'Lucky you,' Nell said into her tea. They busied themselves with biscuits.

'And what are you doing these days, Nell?'

'I'm still at the café, I'm manager now,' Nell said cheerily. 'I love my work.'

'It's hardly *work* – it's a *job*. And yet you had such a good brain on you.' Her aunt sighed. 'Who knows where you'd be now, had more care been taken with your education.' The tea was replenished. 'You know I did suggest boarding school to your mum – you'd have sailed a scholarship.'

'I couldn't have left Mum!' Nell said. 'Anyway, I like my work – it's challenging and stimulating, and I make a difference and an OK wage.' Nell couldn't read her aunt's expression. 'How's – your world?'

'Oh, they won't let me truly retire!' her aunt exclaimed. 'But I only lecture twice a week now – which means my research has so much more of my attention these days.'

Nell nodded enthusiastically. She feared that if she asked for details her dumbness would be amplified. 'Good for you,' she said instead. 'Good for you.'

And it seemed neither of them was quite sure what to talk about next. Her aunt broke the silence. 'And your flat?'

'Love it.'

'I've been in this house thirty-odd years.'

'And have they been odd?'

She gave Nell a pitiful smile as if to say that if that was wit then it was lacking.

Nell felt more awkward now than ever she had as a child. Back in those days, her aunt laid a towel out on any surface Nell might sit on and her mother brought snacks and a bag of toys with her. Only they weren't her usual toys – they were the boring things like jigsaws and illustrated reference books and a Rubik's Cube. It was as if her mother, too, avoided being judged or frowned upon. Nell remembered being set up in the hallway while the sisters' muffled voices and shadowy figures could be detected behind the mottled glass of the door into the lounge.

'I did ask Mum if she'd like me to bring her here one day,' Nell said.

'And she said?'

'Well – she didn't, really.' Nell paused. 'I don't know where she goes, in that head of hers. I don't know how much she hears.' She shrugged at her aunt. 'And I don't understand so much of what she says.'

And, perhaps for the first time, Nell noticed a wisp of sadness momentarily soften her aunt's rigid features.

'But mostly I *think* she's happy,' Nell said. 'I think she is. She lives within the TV programmes she mainlines and I think that makes her happy. If escapism is her drug, let her take it.'

'The staff are wonderful,' said her aunt. 'Wonderful.' She was going to take another biscuit but thought better of it. 'When I'm incapacitated, mind or body, I wouldn't mind whiling away my latter days somewhere like that.' She paused. 'But perhaps in Cambridge. Better standard of inmates, one would imagine.'

'Inmates? It's not a prison!'

'I was joking, Nell.' Her aunt placed her cup and saucer back on the tray, folded her hands in her lap and observed Nell. 'It can't be easy for you, to see her, at her age, surrounded by ancient people – and yet she's more off her rocker than the lot of them.'

For some reason, despite Aunt Em's steady and emotionless tone, Nell found this funny and she laughed. Her aunt regarded her quizzically.

'Sometimes I see glimpses of recognition,' Nell said. 'If I keep talking, keep recalling. I try to find things to show her that might take her back and spark something. But I don't have much luck.'

'I know.'

'Sometimes it's horrible. Sometimes, when she doesn't know it's me – it's awful. And when she denies she's ever been anyone's mother.'

'I know.'

'Teflon,' said Nell.

'Pardon?'

'I try to coat myself in imaginary Teflon.'

Her aunt looked puzzled.

'When she's mean or angry – I don't let it stick. When she keeps calling me Florence – I just let it slip off.'

'She keeps calling you Florence?' Her aunt's voice was brittle and a mottled red now crept up her neck.

'I don't even know a Florence,' said Nell. 'I don't remember her ever mentioning a Florence. Does she call you Florence too, then?'

'No!' her aunt barked and then softened. 'Marjorie.'

'I always forget,' Nell laughed. 'Aunt Em-for-Marjorie.'

'You really should call me Marjorie now. Aunt Em is so – babyish.'

But Nell thought how the name Aunt Em carried with it a hopeful softening of her aunt's spikiness. They sat in silence and looked out at the garden, the derelict bird table, a squirrel leaping like Tarzan onto the nut feeder hanging from the apple tree, the lawn so neat its edges were surely snipped by nail scissors. Teatime dilute sunshine, inky shadows starting to seep across the scene. Sitting there quietly, the awkwardness became companionable enough.

'I ought to go,' Nell said. 'I said I was going to feed a made-up neighbour's imaginary cat.'

'Very good, dear,' Marjorie said.

Nell was puzzled; wasn't that precisely the sort of nonsense her aunt would leap on to dissect? She thought of Frank, how sometimes he would suddenly come over so weary, how after a hearty chinwag he was content just to sit in his chair while Nell went about the chores quietly before leaving. Maybe Marjorie was the same, just a little tired these days.

'Here,' said Nell, loading the tray, 'let me take it in for you.'

Nell went through to the kitchen, which was so spotless it was as if nothing had ever been cooked there. On the windowsill an incongruously vulgar ornament of a bright green frog holding a lily-pad umbrella emblazoned with *I'LL NEVER FROGET YOU*. Next to it, a white dish with a nailbrush. Next to that, an old-fashioned kitchen timer. To her side, a tea towel ironed crisply. The water was satisfyingly hot as Nell washed up and looked out at the garden, the squirrel still pilfering nuts. She dried the plates and the cups and the saucers and opened cupboard doors to find where they lived.

And there on the shelf, the exact same Clarice Cliff trio that her mother had. She took it out. Pristine – plate and all. Marjorie wasn't the type to drop or break anything.

But.

Wait.

Look.

Behind it – another set, identical and complete.

'Each of us had a set. We were all given them, in 1953.'

It made Nell jump; her aunt was standing right behind her.

Marjorie spoke thoughtfully. 'We each had a set – but Wendy broke her plate the day she got it.'

I heard the door shut.

It was Wendy, back from work. I heard my mother call her into the sitting room and the door was shut. I was in my bedroom wishing I could be absorbed into the walls, the floor, the furniture. I'd been sent to my room like a child. A child with child. My mother had called me some terrible things, really. Language I had no idea she knew, let alone would dare to say aloud. She called me a slut and said she couldn't even look at me. How could you? she said. How could you do that? How could you be so bloody bloody stupid. You're no daughter of mine, Florence. You bloody little whore slut.

So up to my room I went, listening to her on the phone to Marjorie.

You need to come home, Marjorie – yes, dear, I know you've only just gone back. But something has happened. That slut little sister of yours. No – not Wendy! Florence! Oh, I can't say it – truly I can't say it! But you need to come home. Family crisis, Marjorie. Well, tell your professor. Tell him what? Oh, but I can't say it! Oh, Marjorie – she's gone and got herself. Gone and. Speak to George! I can't – Speak to George! George – George – speak to Marjorie. Tell her she needs to come home. Tell her what her youngest sister is.

And up in my room I heard Wendy come up the stairs. She always skips up the stairs; she has this funny way of walking practically on tiptoes.

Jesus, Florence, she said. Jesus Christ – what did you do? It was that night, wasn't it – before Christmas. Joan's party – when I said you could go. Jesus, you stupid little fucking idiot.

How mad is Mum? I asked.

Wendy shook her head, ran her finger grimly across her neck, looked genuinely scared.

What should I do? Should I run away?

It was the first time I cried. Not because of my situation, not because of the trouble I was in, but because I was terrified of what I didn't yet know.

Wendy cuddled me. What were you thinking, you idiot idiot girl? She started shaking me, silently. She slapped my face hard and then she kissed me over and over. She said I love you I hate you I love you I hate you – over and over again. Then she pulled at her hair and rocked back and forth. She does this when she's stressed. She pulled small chunks of hair right out. She's always done that too – when I was little, I used to tickle her arms to make her stop.

What'll happen? I wanted to know. What should I do?

I haven't a clue, she said, distraught.

Then she gave a huge grin and cupped my face in her hands. Anyway! she breezed. Look! And she held out her hand and the sparkle of the ring filled the room. I'm engaged! Jimmy and I are getting married. Oh, isn't it the best!

Wendy can do that – she can be one way and then immediately the other. She can be down in the depths one minute, then soaring at a dizzying height in a split second without you seeing how she got there. She can be with you – and then away from you. She's always been that way.

All she did after that was talk at me about wedding dresses and cakes and who would be at the reception. And it was just such a relief, if momentary, to escape into the fairy tale of my sister's making.

Wendy, I pleaded when finally she broke for breath, Wendy – won't you please help me?

Help you?

She'd completely forgotten.

With – don't let our mother. Please – I don't know what she's going to do.

To do?

About me – and my baby.

I watched Wendy deflate and wither away from her joy and the dream of her wedding into the dreadful situation of her little sister being knocked up. Out of wedlock. Aged sixteen. To a boy who is nowhere to be found.

That night, in the furthest corner of my bed, so close to the wall I could smell both the wallpaper and the cold brick behind it, I slept in a curl. I imagined myself like a frond of bracken, tiny but tight against the elements, protectively furled around what lay within. I woke like that. And when I woke I realized that, beneath the gut-wrench of terror, I didn't feel sick. And I said to you, you've done it! I said to you, we're on our way. I felt proud.

I dressed for school and went downstairs. George was there behind the newspaper, the smoke from his pipe rising like comments. He crackled the paper shut and looked at me.

And how are we this morning? he said.

And it struck me he was talking about you and me.

OK, I said. I said, we're OK.

I looked at the floor and asked where my mother was.

George said he wasn't altogether sure.

Joan looked so ill the teachers kept asking if she was feeling all right – all I could do was tell her it's OK when she kept saying sorry sorry sorry.

What'll she do? she kept asking. Your mother?

I'm not sure, I said.

We sat in a huddle whenever we could: at the back of the class, in the quiet corner of the lunch hall, in the furthest part of the playground, on *the back of the bus home – and we wondered, silently, what was going to happen.*

Can I come to your house after school?

Yes, said Joan.

Can I come and live with you?

Joan started to cry.

If I were to run away, I said, do you promise PROMISE that you won't say a word?

She wiped her nose and we had a long tight hug.

If I do run away—

Don't run away – I couldn't bear it.

But if I do – I'll let you know, secretly, somehow.

At Joan's I ate a hearty plate of toast and I did all my homework – it was like I was trying to strike a deal with God or something, that if I behaved, everything would be OK. I stayed at Joan's house until the two of us just sat there, opposite each other at the table, silently knowing that actually I had to go home.

Wendy was the only one there. She said Mum had gone to collect Marjorie from the station. We gave each other a look; we're both faintly terrified of Marjorie; she's too severe to be a sister, let alone an ally. She's only five years older than Wendy and almost twice my age but I just hope that when I'm thirty I'm nothing like her. Wendy and I knew she'd be mad at being summoned home, away from her studies and professors and papers and importance. Neither of us could figure out why she was being brought into the mix. George was next home and he seemed relieved that it was just Wendy and me. I don't think he much likes Marjorie either – she's often so curt with him, talking down at him, talking across him. He may be uneducated in her eyes – but he's wiser than us all.

Well – I'll be off then, George said, all red around the face. *Dominoes and darts.*

It's his thing, once a week.

Oh please, George, I said and oh how tiny my voice was. *Please stay.*

But it's ladies' matters, you see, he muffled.

But George—

I'll be home later – that I promise you. You'll be OK, a leanabh, *you'll be OK.*

I love it when George says things in Garlic – which is how he pronounces Gaelic – or Gàidhlig as it is spelt. I don't know what they mean but his tone of voice is everything.

So my mother and Marjorie arrived while I loitered at the bottom of the stairs. Wendy, the darling, rushed up to our sister and said *look! look! I'm engaged to Jimmy!* She said, *love is in the air!* She said, *it's good news it's great news it's the best news ever!* She said, *it's to be celebrated, isn't it!* She said, *come on, Marjorie! let's have tea! let's sit down! let's go for a walk! let me tell you all about everything.*

Marjorie, though, barely looked at her. She glanced at me and then away. My mother still couldn't look at me.

'In,' Marjorie said to me, motioning at the sitting room. She and my mother sat and for some reason I believed I should stand. Wendy was by the window, in a daydream. I don't really know Jimmy that well but how I wished that he'd walk up the path right then. And I wished for George's darts and dominoes to be cancelled.

'Florence,' Marjorie said and when Marjorie says anything, you are compelled to stand to attention. 'Sit down, for God's sake.'

She turned to my mother. 'Options,' she said.

I thought to myself if we had a blackboard, she'd write them up like one of her academic sequences.

And then I felt you flutter. And I wanted to laugh. I wanted to rejoice.

'The Act came into effect last April,' Marjorie was saying.

My mother and I looked at her not knowing what she was going on about.

'The grounds will be wide. Mother's health – physical and mental. To prevent grave injury. If the child is at risk of severe abnormalities. And so on. And so on.'

Now I knew.

My mother knew too.

My mother went white.

'Twenty-eight weeks,' Marjorie said. 'Up to twenty-eight weeks, it will be permissible and legal. How far gone are you, Florence?'

And I couldn't think and I couldn't count and I couldn't remember and I didn't know – and when I said I don't know, my mother and my eldest sister looked at me with such disgust I felt their eyes rip into the flesh of my belly.

'There are, of course, alternatives,' Marjorie told my mother, though her steady steel gaze did not leave me. 'How would you like a crochet needle fishing around inside you, Florence? That'll set you back ten pounds. But for fifty pounds they can puncture the fetal membranes and squirt bleach into you through a rubber tube – that should do it. At best you'll get an infection, most likely permanent infertility – at worst, you'll die.'

My mother cried out – stop it stop it stop it!

'Or there's off Harley Street,' said Marjorie, 'legal – if you have the money.'

My mother roared. My mother stood and charged into the centre of the room. 'I will not go against the Word of the Lord!'

And I thought to myself, what's the Word of my mother's Lord got to do with my body and my baby? But my mother appeared to be against Marjorie so I decided it best to say nothing.

And then George suddenly appeared. Darling George had forsaken dominoes and darts and the pub and the blokes for this maelstrom of female bile and fury and he very calmly said, thank you very much, Marjorie, but Thou Shalt Not Kill.

He had his back to me. My mother and my sister had been glowering and glaring at me with disgust and revulsion. George, though, had his back to me as if he didn't know I was even there. I couldn't see my sister or my mother because he was blocking them out.

He spoke to my mother and my sister, he spoke softly, his accent having its familiar calming effect. 'We can send Florence away. She can have the bairn in secrecy and peace – and then. Well. And then.'

And I realized then that George did know I was there. His back was a mighty wall of protection and trust. And I thought to myself my dad would have stood like this too.

I glanced over to Wendy. She was fiddling with her engagement ring and giving tiny bounces from foot to foot. She caught my eye and showed me her ring with a grin.

'Jimmy and I won't have babies for at least five years,' she announced, and she's so absolutely beautiful when she smiles like that.

'I'll speak to the church. Oh dear,' my mother was weeping. 'Oh, but I can't. The shame! The shame!'

'We will not need to speak to the church,' said George. 'My brother – in Harris. She can go there. There she can stay.'

Everyone was quiet.

'No one need know,' he told my mother.

'Where is Harris?' I asked.

'It's far away,' George's back said. 'It's a long long way away from here. From all of this.'

And again I felt you flutter. Like you couldn't wait to get there.

Nell

'What are you chuckling about?'

Debbie and Nell were at the Chaffinch early to bake the overnight bread they'd prepared yesterday.

'I was just remembering something,' Nell said. 'About my mum.'

Debbie waited. It was rare for Nell's mum to be the cause of much mirth.

'When I was in Costa this morning,' Nell said. 'It popped into my head. Is the oven hot enough?'

'Yes. Slash the tops.'

Nell used scissors to cut into the tops of the rounds of dough so that they would rise perfectly. 'It's odd, isn't it, how at the time we cringe then later, we laugh.'

'Ah,' said Debbie, 'the kindness of years.'

'She'd often do it. Very politely – she'd say *excuse me, can you help me?* If we were out – in a shop, a library, the supermarket, a café – wherever. And it didn't matter to her who they were – old, young, male, female, whether they could even speak English – but invariably they were never staff.'

They placed the loaves into lidded pots and Debbie opened the oven door. 'Half an hour,' Debbie said, 'then we'll give them fifteen minutes uncovered.' She was silently willing Nell to keep talking.

'*Excuse me, can you help me*, she'd say. And more often than not they'd say oh sorry, I don't work here. And that didn't bother my mother one bit. She'd just carry on. *Yes*, she'd say, *but I need – I'm looking for – I want—*' Nell paused and giggled. 'She didn't care if they worked there or not – she needed assistance and she chose people whose faces she liked. Sometimes she'd even take their arm.'

Debbie laughed. 'Did they offer help?'

'Always!'

'Wow. I think I'll try it.'

Nell's eyes were lingering in the middle distance.

'I remember being in a café – and she asked someone on their way out to order her another cup of tea and a Fanta for me. They said sorry, love, don't work here. She said oh I know, I know – but could you order me another tea – and a Fanta for Nell here.' Nell shook her head. 'And they did. Bonkers,' she said. She was running the water hot to put the bowls in to soak. They still had half an hour before the troops arrived with Siobhán and another hour before they opened. She and Debbie sat with coffee. 'We were in Safeway's once and Mum was on the hunt for pillow rice – we'd only just arrived at the shop and she made a bee-line for this elderly chap who so obviously didn't work there. I can see him now. *Excuse me, can you help me, I want pillow rice.* Anyway, he hardly spoke English – but that didn't bother her at all. The two of them – speaking louder and louder at each other. Babel right there in Essex. Then Mum starts acting it out, like charades, pretending to go to sleep, puffing up the imaginary pillow, doing tiny things between her fingers to signify rice. That poor man.

He had such a lovely grandfatherly face. I mean – what the fuck is pillow rice? She had an audience by the end.'

Nell's laugh was contagious and soon enough she and Debbie were bent double for the ache. They snorted and sighed and then started laughing all over again.

'But Nell – did you even get it?'

'Get what?'

'The pilau rice?'

'The—' Nell stopped, her eyes widened, darting over Debbie's face, visibly stupefied. 'Oh my God.' It was the most extraordinary revelation. 'Debbie!' Nell clapped her hands over her mouth and just stood there. 'Twenty-five years, must be,' she said eventually. 'I didn't even think. *Pilau*. That's the thing with my mum – she's always been so – well, you know. And I just thought – probably everyone in the shop just thought – there's that batty Mrs Hartley, off on one about pillow rice.'

'So you didn't get the rice? That day?'

Nell was lost in thought. 'No,' she said after a while. 'Daft thing is, if she'd asked a sales assistant – instead of a little old man – we probably would have.'

'Well, think of it this way – what your curry lacked that night your mum made up for with the merriment she gave her audience.'

The coffee suddenly bittered and Nell's face dropped. She shook her head vehemently. The milk tasted sour. 'No. They were *gawking* at her, Debbie. She was a spectacle. It was always the same. Wherever we were, they'd always look at her like that. With a sort of intrigued revulsion. I felt it. I hated it.' And Nell's eyes were on her shoes, her cheeks red and her fingers fidgeting. And Debbie thought, this is muscle memory. Debbie thought, this is exactly the way Nell would had stood on that day in Safeway and on numerous other occasions – a small girl desperately trying to juggle embarrassment and love and shame and protection behind her mother's back.

'I hated it,' Nell said quietly. 'I hated them. And actually, I hated her for all of it. I longed for a normal, boring mum. I prayed for one. I felt very bad about that.'

She looked at Debbie. 'But I gave up the praying a long time ago. Now she calls me Florence and either ignores me or shouts at me and says she has no daughter.'

When Siobhán led the crocodile of helpers in, Danny instinctively knew Nell needed a cuddle.

'He's not worth it,' he said to her because her eyes were red and she looked so sad and he'd seen women with this look on the telly. On the telly it was always the same. The ladies just needed to hear one thing. 'He's not worth it,' Danny quoted. 'Silly arse.'

And Sanjay told Nell she looked awful but he said it with such affection that she thanked him.

So Nell was blissfully unaware just then that this would be the day when everything that was known would be obliterated, when she would discover that everything she thought had happened had not, when she was to find out that she wasn't who she thought she was. But at 9.30 in the morning, with the espresso machine malfunctioning, she hadn't the time to consider how football stickers six hours later might be the catalyst for irrevocable change. She didn't compute just then that the seeds had been sown already when she visited Frank yesterday and they'd watched the blackbirds pecking up the walnuts. First there were two. Then there were three. For the time being, however, it was just Tuesday at the Chaffinch. Bread to be taken from the oven. Heads to be scratched over the coffee machine. Switch it off again. Clean it down. Switch it on again. Bingo! Thank you for waiting – your latte is on the house.

It was busy, really busy already and Libby had just dropped an entire bowl of couscous. A toddler was having a meltdown. The main door was jamming but it was still too chilly outside to keep it open. Nell did what she needed to do, what she had done countless times before, and she popped the memory of her mother and the pillow rice into a compartment at the furthest reaches of her mind.

After school, a mother came in with her two young boys. She looked frazzled, as if the day had already been far too long but a significant and irksome portion still stretched ahead. Thomas and Freddie, take your blazers off, boys, and go and sit at that table over there, please. Watching her, Nell wondered for a moment if the woman might just walk right out of the Chaffinch and hop in a cab to start a new life.

'Do you know what I'd really love,' she told Nell at the counter, scouring the menu. 'Toast and Marmite. Would you have Marmite?'

'We do indeed. And for you?'

'That is for me!' She was rooting around in her handbag saying shit shit shit under her breath. 'Also, cheese-and-tomato sandwiches for the boys – and two of those Rice Krispie cakes. Shit where the shitting heck is it?'

'Anything to drink?'

'My bloody purse. Oh, there it is. Oh, just water for the –
Freddie! No! Sorry – I'm so sorry.'

They looked over to see that the boys had already helped
themselves to water from the jug and much was spilling over
the table and onto the floor.

'Don't worry about it at all – soon have that cleaned up,'
said Nell. 'So, water for the boys and a huge gin and tonic
for you?'

The mother looked at Nell with such hope that Nell felt
terrible. Luckily the woman was happy enough to have a
cappuccino with two extra shots.

'Coming right up,' said Nell. 'Danny – can you take kitchen
roll to Table 4?'

Though it was their busiest time, she loved this part of the
day. After the customary mid-afternoon lull, a surge of infec-
tious energy accompanied the after-school crowd. Nell and her
staff girded themselves, primed and ready for the onslaught, the
fractiousness and hyperactivity, the tangle of schoolbags, the
tears and the giggling, the noise, the high demand for sweetness
and carbs.

Nell tackled the obstacle course of bags, books and pencil
cases between her and Table 4.

'I thought I'd bring the *You Know Whats* in a bit,' she
winked conspiratorially at the mother. 'Ensure that Thomas
and Freddie eat their sandwiches first.'

'Genius,' she said. 'And thank you. Yummy – look, boys!'
There was a lot of wriggling on chairs. One of the boys said
not boring old cheese. The other one complained about crusts.
They both clamoured for football stickers.

'You promised us!'

'You did, Mum – when you dropped us at school. You said we'd each get a packet after school.'

Nell stepped in. 'Chiffchaff rule,' she said. 'Stickers after sandwiches.'

The boys stared at her while their mother spooned cappuccino foam into her mouth as if it was ambrosia.

The older boy, who Nell thought was about seven or eight, looked at her as if she was the wicked witch of the café.

'It's the rules,' Nell shrugged. 'The rules of the café.'

The younger boy tipped back on his chair, glowering at his sandwich.

Nell saw it in slow motion and somehow made it to the chair before it fell right back.

'Boys! Both of you! Settle down, for goodness' sake!' Mum's little moment of cappuccino heaven had passed. 'I'm so sorry – they're revolting.'

'Oh please,' said Nell. 'I've seen far worse.'

'I've told you! You can both have a pack once you've eaten your sandwiches. Football stickers,' the mother explained to Nell. 'I use them for leverage. Tactical bribery for making them eat, wash and shut up.' She turned to her sons. 'Both of you will get your football stickers one you've eaten your food.'

And then one of their school chums came in and the boys called over, hey, Joe! we're getting football stickers when we've finished our food! Joe's face lit up and he rushed over to the table.

'Mum – if Joe eats his food up – can he have a pack?'

'I think I only have enough for both of you.' She rummaged around in her bag. Ordered another cappuccino from Nell. Then she turned to the three boys triumphant, and fanned out three packets of stickers. 'Look! One for each of you! When you three have eaten every last crumb, you will *all* have one.'

We were all given a set but I broke my plate. The very day I was given it. Gosh, was I told off.

We each had a set – but Wendy broke her plate the day she got it.

The floor was moving under Nell's feet and the ceiling was pressing on her head and all the tables and chairs were whirling. The usual cacophony had suddenly dissipated, replaced instead by a searing tone, as if her eardrum had just burst. It felt as if the entire café was in a manic swirl, Nell at the centre, going down a plughole.

'Are you all right?'

Are they talking to me?

'Do you need to sit down?'

Who? Me?

She swayed as a hit of adrenaline shot its freezing path around her body before sending the most terrible heat through her.

Florence.

I need to sit down.

Yesterday I was watching walnuts with Frank. Two blackbirds and plenty of walnuts for both. Three blackbirds and enough walnuts for all of them.

Two birds then three.

Two kids then three.

Both of you.

All of you.

Two sisters. No – three.

Nell limped to a chair and sat heavily, unaware of the nonplussed
family whose table she was invading.

We were all given them. But Wendy broke hers the day she got it.

'Are you all right?'

'Mum, what's wrong with that lady?'

'Hello?'

'Why's she at our table? Why's she looking like that?'

'Nell? Nellybelly?'

Somehow Danny's voice managed to find a way through the
din that was ricocheting around Nell's head.

'I told you – he's not worth it. Got to listen to your Danny.
You know so.'

Nell looked at Danny. He didn't like her eyes like that. She
looked like she was a crazy lady. He'd go and get Debbie.

'I think there was a third sister. I think her name was Florence.
All this time my mum's been insisting that she has no child and
I thought it was just her being – *her*. But now I think – I think I
might be Florence's daughter.'

For a few precious minutes afterwards, Debbie and Nell
just sat in silence in the storeroom, Nell's hands in Debbie's,
Debbie's eyes on Nell, Nell's eyes trying to scan through a
million incidents and memories.

'Everything makes sense and none of it makes sense.'

'What'll you do?'

'I don't know.'

'Speak to your mum, maybe?'

'I've been speaking at my mum for the last five years not knowing what she hears, what she understands. Not knowing what she's talking about when she does respond, not knowing what's true or what's imagined, what might have happened or what's been reinvented.'

'Your – dad?'

'Come on! He left when I was three! I haven't seen him for over thirty years!'

'Your aunt, then?'

Nell thought about Marjorie. 'You see, she went really quiet when I said about Mum calling me Florence,' she said. 'I just thought she was tired, that I'd outstayed my welcome.'

'There's probably a really simple answer to everything,' said Debbie. 'And honestly – it might not be what you think it is.'

Nell nodded. She could hear Debbie. It all sounded logical. But there was a small and terrible inkling growing with every thought she had.

'But what if I'm not who I think I am?' said Nell.

'You are Nell.'

'But whose Nell am I?'

With a stagger and a lurch, Nell spun from one notion or theory to another. Her head hurt. Debbie had told her to go early. She couldn't remember driving home and, as she climbed the stairs, Nell stamped down on thoughts, turning them into little more than the stains already there. Down the corridor, past the cheery doormats of others, the sounds of their lives muffled but there.

Her doormat was plain, no words, no images; she'd bought it because it was called a DirtEater which seemed better value for money than one saying Welcome. She closed the door and slid down it, sitting there looking in on her life. There wasn't much to see, an empty love seat and the mug from this morning's tea. She closed her eyes and tried to trace her steps around her childhood home instead. So different from her flat. She could remember her dad's coat, so long and dark on the hook against her small red one with the furry hood and her mother's flamboyant jackets. She could see her dad's shoes, slip-ons, by the front door and if she walked her mind along the hallway and turned left into the sitting room – might she see him there?

No.

When she thought of her dad it was just the man in the photograph. Summer and an ice cream and a lopsided hat; her father with shirtsleeves rolled up, wearing staggeringly wide flares, a cigarette in his hand, two-year-old Nell on his hip, a smile for the camera. But she couldn't see him in her memory walk, just her mother in a rainbow dress dazzling and happy in a kitchen that was in utter chaos. She could see her childhood bedroom, all organized and neat with toys in a line and books undulating like the pipes of an organ. She could see her mother's bedroom, strewn with clothes and cluttered with stuff. A bottle by the bed and one in the wastepaper basket. One shoe here and another over there. A Babycham glass on the windowsill and a forgotten cigarette in an ashtray, just one long perfect snake of ash.

Nell rested her head on her knees and wrapped her arms around her legs. Why hadn't she asked more questions? Why had she always just accepted any information given? What was her mother capable of answering? What was her aunt willing to reveal?

Three stupid lovely Coronation china sets. One each.

There were three of them, who was the third?

And when *had* her mother started calling her Florence? About four years ago – when she let her hair go back to its natural colour and she grew out her crop? She couldn't really remember.

Nell went to the bathroom and turned the dimmer switch to full. She stared at herself in the uncompromising brightness. Who did she look like? Did she not look like her mum? Whose nose is this? And these lips? And this eye colour? Her mother's eyes were brown; Nell's a greenish grey, edged darkly.

She phoned Philippa in America, saying no – you can't phone me back in half an hour something has happened and I need you to listen. Her oldest friend with such a different life now, thousands of miles away in another time zone. Kids and a husband and a high-powered job. Their friendship had spanned the years, but how much longer could it maintain its closeness over the distance, across the gulf between their lifestyles? She'd never doubted it but, just then, Nell doubted everything. Philippa said fuck! fuck! She said Jesus Nell, as mad as it sounds, maybe there's something?

'My life feels cluttered with lies and secrets,' Nell said quietly, 'And I'm choking.'

'But do you want to find out, Nell? Because once you do – nothing can go back to how it was.'

Nell sat in her car outside the care home. Questions to ask and imagined answers fought around her head. The notion that she'd been lied to – what possible reasons could there be? And Nell thought, but Mum – it was always you and me – you'd knit your fingers through mine and admire the lattice. Look, Nell, you and me, woven together.

And Nell thought, I would cook dinner for us when you were in a slump on the stairs.

I would put you to bed and finish my homework.

I'd be as full of hope as you were, when a new boyfriend came into your life. And I'd try to cuddle your pain away when they left.

And you defended me at all those parents' evenings.

And you told Rosie Philip's mother that her daughter was a conniving little liar.

And when Lee dumped me when I was fifteen you took me to a drag club on a school night and had all the queens fuss over me and then you slept on my floor so you'd be there when I woke sobbing in the small hours.

And in and out of the years you'd cup my face in your hands and ask what you'd done to deserve a gem like me.

In her car, looking at the building keeping her mother out of harm's way, Nell sat for almost two hours until it was too late to visit. She made her way home and drifted around a muddled sleep and then, for the first time in all her years with the Chaffinch, she phoned in sick.

Marjorie. It would be more productive to go and see her aunt in the first instance. She couldn't risk nonsensical ramblings from her mother nor could she cope with possible silence and that infernal television. She phoned to no answer so she drove to her aunt's but Marjorie was not at home; it must be a Cambridge day.

A half-hour drive later, Nell left her car at the park-and-ride. She knew Marjorie was something in Natural Sciences, a Professor Emeritus these days, but that's all she knew. Now, she was heading for the unfathomably beautiful old colleges without really noticing anything, busy rehearsing what to say when she found her aunt. It hadn't crossed her mind to check the internet before she left. At any moment, Nell expected Marjorie to appear across some quad or cloister, her academic gowns billowing around her like dark secrets. Eventually, Nell gave up and approached a student, saying Natural Sciences as if she was part of it all.

Which?

Pardon?

Natural Sciences – which? There's about sixteen different departments.

So Nell had to walk for twenty-five minutes to the West Cambridge site, leaving the dreamy creamy spires and hallowed arches and flying buttresses and stained glass for expansive modern buildings and space. Finally, after trying one office and then walking to another, she discovered that Marjorie was indeed lecturing today. Biotechnology – and her lecture was in full swing.

She crept into the back of the lecture hall and sank down into a seat right at the top, up high. The air felt dense with the brainwaves of the gifted and the screen down there at the front had words and symbols that were a foreign language. There was Marjorie, upright and formidable, barking out her supreme knowledge for all to admire and clone. And all Nell could do was try to formulate a coherent sentence from the scrum of muddled questions.

A small line of students stayed after the lecture to honour Marjorie with their convoluted questions and queries. And then they were gone and it was just Marjorie and there, way up high, Nell. Nell who had forgotten the sentence she'd been honing over the last half-hour. But from up there, Marjorie didn't look quite so tall and imposing.

'Marjorie.'

Speak louder.

'Marjorie!'

Louder still.

'Dr Lawson.'

Louder.

'*Aunt Em.*'

'Nell? Good God! What are you—?'

'Who is Florence?' Nell bellowed.

Marjorie paused only momentarily before continuing to gather her papers, switching things off, putting things away. She buffed her glasses and put them in their case. The snap of the closure carrying all the way up to the back. Shielding her eyes, she looked hard to the back of the hall.

'I will not speak to you if I cannot see you,' said Marjorie.

'But you can hear me,' Nell called down. 'Who is Florence?'

She's walking out! Marjorie was ignoring her and walking to the exit! Nell started to make her way down the steps but at the same time Marjorie stopped, figuring out that a scene in an empty, soundproofed lecture hall was probably preferable to one playing out in the foyer in front of an audience.

'Who', said Nell, 'is Florence?'

She was a tier up, but close now to her aunt who kept her hand raised like a peaked cap across her forehead. Nell didn't think the lighting warranted it and it made it hard to decipher Marjorie's expression. Was that regret or annoyance? Were her lips pursed in anger or disquiet or simply to keep secrets contained? And her eyes – indignation or remorse? What was going on in that soul of hers and was her heart beating hard behind that crisp cotton shirt the colour of summer skies?

'Florence,' said Nell again, not caring that her voice cracked. 'Who is Florence?' She searched her aunt's face but her expression remained unnervingly illegible. 'You were *all* given those cups and saucers and plates with the Queen and her nice hair. My mum broke her plate the day she got it. Is that Florence's set in your cupboard?'

'Yes,' said Marjorie. 'It's hers.'

Nell's head pounded. What was she to say next? Why was this lecture theatre so cold? What was written on her aunt's face?

'Who – is Florence?' Simple question and one yet to be answered.

'Florence was the youngest,' Marjorie said simply.

'Youngest sister?'

'Yes. I was fifteen when she was born. Your mother was ten.'

Nell sat down. It was true, then. 'Why did I not know this?'

Marjorie wasn't going to answer that.

'Where is she now?'

Nor that.

What next. Keep going. 'Why—?'

'She was born in 1952,' Marjorie nodded, her voice steady and unemotional.

'Aunt Em—' Nell rubbed at her face. 'Is there something I don't know?'

Marjorie looked straight at her, steel eyes and emotionless. 'On a need-to-know basis, no – I'd say no.'

'If I asked my Mum, if I ask Wendy, what will she tell me?'

Marjorie shrugged, an eyebrow raised, nothing soft. 'I have to go, Nell. This is all quite unexpected. A colleague wants to see me. And I have a meeting. And my research.'

'Oh, fuck your bloody research!'

Two students had entered but quickly exited.

'I beg your—!'

What was her aunt going to do – tell her off? Give her an F?

'Why does Mum call *me* Florence?' Nell paused but her heartbeat was so fast, so audible, it was as if her body was trying to block out the sound of the possible answer. 'Why does my mum say she has no daughter?'

Why won't Marjorie answer?

'Do I look like her? Do I look like Florence?'

The redness creeping up Marjorie's neck, a different tone of voice when it came, one Nell had never heard. It carried with it defeat. 'Yes, Nell. You do.'

'I do?'

Her aunt nodded. 'You look like Florence. You always have.'

There was only one word. 'Why?'

Marjorie's gaze tried to slice straight through Nell as a warning but Nell barricaded herself with all the imaginary Teflon she could envisage.

'Florence – was your mother.'

Nell sat down heavily as if weighed down by all this nonsense.

'Why? Why has no one – ever – told me this?'

Marjorie hugged her lecture notes against her. The question had finally come and it sounded undeniably reasonable. She knew that any answer she gave would sound flimsy. 'We thought it was best,' she said. 'That was what was decided. That's what we all agreed. We thought it best – for everyone.'

She watched Marjorie walk away, bone-brittle and stooped. Nell couldn't move and, for another hour, she sat where she was. She sat through an hour of chemical engineering and was asked by the neighbouring students if she was going to the departmental social later.

And Nell thought to herself, I'm not who they think I am.

Somehow, she managed to find her way back to the park-and-ride and drive herself home from Cambridge. She kept the windows rolled right down, needing cold air to prevent her brain overheating, needing it to signal the here and now, needing the buffeting to help her concentrate on the road. She said names out loud. Florence. Wendy. Marjorie. Her mum was ten when her mother was born. What kind of a fucked-up sentence was that? Calculated her mother must have been sixteen or seventeen when she gave birth to her. Wendy would have been twenty-six. And Marjorie thirty-one. But who had called her Nell? Was that Florence or Wendy? And why had Florence given her up? And where was she now? Why – and when – had Wendy become her mother?

Her dad.

Jimmy.

Thoughts of her dad were rarely accompanied by emotion of any magnitude but, just then, Nell felt waves of confusion and dread. Did this mean that Jimmy had been Florence's—?

Florence's what? Did Florence have an affair with her mum's husband?

Why hadn't she asked Marjorie about Jimmy?

Why hadn't she asked where Florence was?

But most of all why – please – please – why had no one told her anything about any of this?

In the care home car park, Nell took her mobile phone and very nearly called Debbie and very nearly dialled America and was about to phone Marjorie at home. She flipped the phone's lid back and forth, snapping it shut, pinging it open and then, crying out in despair, she threw it into the footwell and stamped on it.

Sylvie on the desk.

'Oh, hello, Nell love!'

But Nell could offer only a fake smile as she climbed to the first floor, the threat of vomit in her throat.

'Knock knock who's there it's Nell, Mum,' she called out as she entered the room.

There she was, watching the telly gormlessly, trying to inhabit the world inside that bloody box.

Nell went to the cupboard and took out the Coronation crockery.

'Hello, Wendy!' she said, all light and jolly. 'Tell me – whose is this, Wendy? Is it yours – or does this one belong to Florence?'

Her mother inspected it, glanced at Nell and rolled her eyes. 'It's yours, silly – I broke my plate the day we got them.'

'Wendy!' Nell said. 'Wendy!' She shouted. '*Wendy!*'

Her mother frowned, stared hard at her, as if willing Nell to come more clearly into focus. She looked confused, perhaps frightened, and her vulnerability confronted Nell on a cellular level. She went and stood behind her mother's chair, zapped the remote control to turn off the television. 'Wendy,' she said over her head, giving the chair a forceful nudge. She fought to control her voice, crushing the scream she wanted to emit, for a lightweight and conversational tone instead. 'Wendy – what happened to Florence?'

The stillness, the weight of hidden words.

'What happened? To Florence?' Nell stayed where she was.

'Well—' And her mother sounded so fragile, so fearful. 'Well—'

'What did Florence do?'

Her mother's voice came hoarse and fragmented. 'Bloody well went and got herself knocked up.'

'What happened?'

'I had to have the baby. I never had a baby. But I had to have Florence's. After she'd gone.'

Nell thought *listen*. She told herself to listen, to vanquish the adrenaline and just to focus. You've just heard it. There. You are not Wendy's daughter but Florence's. This is not your mother. This is your aunt.

'Why?'

'I had to have the baby – Mother said so. After.'

'After *what*? After she'd gone where? Why couldn't Florence keep her baby?'

Wendy didn't answer or wouldn't answer or couldn't answer because now she was crying. Not crying – weeping. Not the usual histrionic overexcited sobbing that Nell had grown inured to, but with the hoarse depth of one who was broken. Nell went round from behind the chair and put her hands on her mother's shoulders. They felt alarmingly bony, hollow somehow.

'Is Florence's baby Nell?'

Nell shook her.

'Where is Florence? Is she alive? Dead?'

She shook Wendy hard, felt flesh slip off a rattle of bones.

'Why couldn't Florence keep her baby?'

She was shouting, she couldn't help it. She shook her mother as if she was a rag full of dust and dead things. 'Where is Florence? What's happened to her? Why did you take her baby?'

And Sylvie came in. 'Nell! Good Lord – what on earth is going on?' Sylvie pushed Nell aside and wrapped Wendy in soothing tones and gentle hands. 'There there, Mrs H. – what's going on, eh? No need to upset yourself.' She turned to Nell, appalled, disappointed, and she hissed. 'What on earth, Nell – what do you think you are doing?'

'I don't know,' said Nell and she didn't recognize her own voice. 'I don't know. She won't say. She won't say anything that makes any sense. Nothing makes any sense any more. Nothing.'

Gordon

Gordon Munro knew something was amiss – not wrong, not dangerously so, just not quite what it should be. Something was not right. His son, he sensed, was at odds in his world and that was not good, not good at all. Gordon lit his pipe, put a hand on Ben's head and stared at the fire. Ever since he'd been a small boy, he'd always felt that the fire gave him what he needed. Warmth. Perfectly cooked toast. Herring cured to perfection. Hot water. Familiar peat reek. Comfort. Answers. Aye – Dougie wasn't right. That business the other week – Dougie driving in a storm when he knew he hadn't a chance in hell of making it. Telling Gordon he would only have had the one night anyway. And, since then, nothing. Two messages he'd left on the boy's machine, the last five days ago. Now, that's not like Dougie. They might neither of them be overly conversational on the phone – it's an awkward thing, a voice coming disembodied down a wire with no face to read – but his boy always called him back before long.

In the fire, the flames licked and furled their way around the blocks of peat. It had been cold for late March these last days – bright but cold with it. He remembered Dougie as a wee one on days like these, how he'd say to Gordon that the sky

118

said it was summer and please could he go swimming. How his wife, God bless her memory, would tell him no, you'll catch your death and how Dougie would persist, saying he'd catch the *sgadan*, that's what he'd catch – herring. Gordon looked at the hook at the top of the fireplace. How long had it been since the *sgadan* had hung from there while the heat and the peat smoke worked on it until it was the most beautiful taste in the world? And how long had it been since his boy had been home, sitting on that chair there, enjoying the fire with his father?

Around the room Gordon's eyes travelled. Everything in its place. Above, the sound old roof keeping out the elements, beneath his feet those flagstones rising and falling with the earth beneath and now worn smooth. When did his lad last skate over them in his socks? And here, his own father's chair with the leather burnished now to a deep red – Gordon remembered it from his childhood being the colour of tablet. Near the fire, Ben's basket and above it, Dougie's photography books. On the wall, Dougie's degree. My son the college graduate. My son the photographer. And Dougie's mother had lived to know about both and though Gordon missed her, Lord how he missed her, he thought to himself how glad he was that she wasn't sitting here worrying too. That she hadn't lived through all that terrible business of what was it now, almost fifteen years ago. He'd never wanted her to worry about a thing, that's why he'd married her, to protect her like the roof protected the house, to provide a foundation most solid, his arms around her like these very walls, strong and sheltering and standing the test of time.

This house of the Munros, for three generations, a breathing living member of the family. Old MacCuish had asked him the other day how long Gordon had lived there and Gordon had told him since the day he was born. Seventy-two years, coming. They were taking Old MacCuish to a flat, so they were, up in Stornoway. His children had paid a price for it – apparently it came with independence but also a buzzer he could ring if he needed assistance. Shopping delivered, if he so wished. Dominoes or cards, tea and company, downstairs every afternoon. So the MacCuish house was for sale – a sight none of them thought they'd ever see.

'Not for us, Ben, hey laddie?'

The dog looked up at Gordon. Licked his lips and stared at his master beguilingly. Gordon chuckled. He would feed the dog, put the stew on and phone Dougie while it was heating. He levered himself out of the chair telling the dog, as he always did, that it was the old wood creaking, not his bones.

In London, the phone rang in Dougie's flat. He knew it was going to be his dad and called himself a shit for not having returned those two other calls. He shouldn't let it go through to the answering machine. But.

It was his dad. Of course it was.

'Hello? Yes – hello? It's your father, Dougie. Twenty-fourth of March. Hello? I'm telephoning you today – it's Thursday – to say hello. To see how—'

The machine cut him off.

In the kitchen in Harris Gordon cursed under his breath, dialled again.

'Yes, Dougie – it's your father here. So! Well aye – you're not in so I'll just leave a message to say I was phoning to say hello. See if you're there.'

Gordon tapped the handset against his forehead. What a bloody stupid thing to say.

Dougie listened to the pause, his father's jumbled awkwardness, willing his father to continue. The answerphone clicked off once again.

Gordon looked at Ben. 'I'm not a man of many words, am I, boy? But I cannot finish a sentence when I'm speaking to a damned machine.'

Phone again, Da.

Come on, Ben, let's take a walk around the garden while the stew warms. Come on, boy.

Gordon thought he'd try Douglas one more time, just before bed. He dialled half the numbers and then paused. Was Dougie in – and would he pick up? Gordon asked himself if he wanted to be answered by a machine. No, he did not. But nor did he want to hear the brevity in his son's voice masking something else. He clicked the call dead.

Nell

She kicked the wall. As she was climbing the stairs to her flat it felt like she was invigilating a discordant conversation in her head between her mother and her aunt and she just wanted them both to shut up so she could hear herself think. So Nell kicked the wall. She'd grown to know the individual scuffs on the paintwork of the communal areas; they were a nice consistency, like familiar bystanders to her comings and goings. For the first time, she left her own mark and it was a big one, an impression of almost the entire underside of her rubber-soled boot. There was a limping anger to it.

In her apartment she stood, cursing herself for her minimalism because there was nothing for her to throw around or break. All those films where distress is appeased by swiping everything off tables and shelves and surfaces. If her life could be judged on her flat, then there was very little in it. Even her answering machine was empty of messages. It struck her that, in her flat, silence came not just from soundlessness but from the blank absence of things, from the quietude and order she so meticulously engineered. And, just then, it was deafening.

Nell would drive to Debbie's. That was a good plan. Debbie was gifted with two great qualities: she was kind and sensible, she'd know what to say and advise what to do. Only Debbie wasn't in. How could she not be in? Nell placed her forehead against Debbie's front door, too tired to swear. She sat on the doorstep until a numbing chill told her to stand up, get a grip and either go home or wait somewhere warm for Debbie to return. With one last futile knock on the door, Nell left. She hovered by her car then walked away from it, heading from the river up East Hill towards the castle. As she walked, she recalled how frightened she'd been of the castle when she was young; it was nothing like a fairy-tale castle. It was imposingly squat and masculine and its narrow arrow-slit windows made her feel she was being spied on. The mortar around the bricks and stones looked like it was dissolving, like some vicious acid was at play. They learned about the castle at school and when she used to glimpse it at night, the ghosts of all those who'd been locked up there over the centuries called out to her. Especially the witches of the sixteenth century, tortured in the castle then cast into the river to see if their guilt floated.

Now, as the castle came into view, Nell thought back to being eight or nine years old, how one night her imagination ran away with her and she scurried into her mother's bed shaking and sobbing about the poor souls locked away. Hadn't her mother sat bolt upright, taken her hands and said well, we must go and release them!

How reasonable her mother had made it seem that they should put socks and shoes on, and coats over their night-clothes and march on a mission along the silent sleeping streets to the castle. How safe Nell had felt grasping her mother's hand so tightly, being pulled along until they were there, in the dead of night, gazing up at the vast keep. In a whisper Wendy asked

Nell whether she had heard Roman prisoners or those from the time of William the Conqueror? Or the medieval ones, when the castle became Colchester's jail? But Nell told her no. She told her mother about horrible Matthew Hopkins the self-proclaimed Witchfinder General. It was the poor witches I heard, Nell said. So they walked as close to the walls as they could, her mother brave and no-nonsense, ears peeled.

'I don't think there are any prisoners at the moment, Nell. Definitely no witches.'

'But how can we be sure?'

'Prisoners!' her mother suddenly cried out, theatrically but deadly serious. 'Be ye here? Be ye guilty of yon sins or be ye miscarried of justice?'

She cocked her ear with her hand and told Nell to do likewise. There they stood together, listening hard until her mother, triumphant, concluded that all was well behind those immense walls and Nell believed her.

And now Nell was standing as close as she could to the floodlit castle, swallowing down on tears, imprisoned by sudden grief and total confusion mingling with all that fury.

She meandered along the high street and headed to the George, ordering a double vodka for the scorch and the fume to cauterize the rawness and still her mind. And another. And soon enough this became her favourite place in the world. It was lively and warm and everything was bathed in a cheery orange light. The friendly and simple scent of chips and scampi and garlic bread and crisp crumbs and spilt beer; the melodic sound of chattering and joshing and laughing by everyone around her. Everyone! Nell drank her vodka, the power and the punch of it newly delicious; she made friends, best friends, and her glass was being chinked by all. Here – let me buy you a drink, love. I'm Tony, this here's my wife Sue. Graham. Cindy – pleased to meet you, Nell. Pat – and I'm a postman, that's why they all call me Postie.

I'm Jake and you're gorgeous.

Hello Jake, buy me a drink?

Handsome Jake with his broad shoulders and smattering of stubble and his dazzling smile and Nell thought, I'm old enough to be his mother, almost. And Nell thought how fit and charming he was, and so generous with the drinks and the compliments and the intent focus. And Nell thought – so what. She thought, I don't care. And Nell thought, I just want to *feel*.

I just need to feel. I just need not to think. I just need to feel not so hollow.

'Where do you live, JakeyJake?'

'I live on the way . . .'

' . . . buy me another.'

'Same again?'

'In fact, sod the drink – let's go back to yours.'

She watched him react, was that bafflement? Or could he not believe his luck? She decided she'd go with the second. She decided she'd go with JakeyJake, back to his place *on the way*. On the way to where? Nell didn't really need to know that. If someone could just fuck her brains out for a bit, she'd forget about absolutely everything else.

In the early hours of the morning, Nell woke with a start and lay in a clammy sweat in a cold room wondering where she was.

Christ, her head. Suddenly, she was aware of a massive looming face gazing down at her, eerily hypnotic and intense. She felt pinned to the bed, unsure if she was dreaming, telling herself to wake up. Then her focus adjusted. It was Jimi Hendrix. Just a huge poster of Jimi Hendrix.

Gingerly, she sat up. Jesus Christ, her head was banging and her throat was so parched her tongue was stuck to the roof of her mouth. Her hair stank of cigarette smoke and she felt sick. She looked away from Jimi and across the bed to where a man slept, snoring. His name was Jake, she knew that. She remembered them crashing into the flat and ricocheting off the walls. She vaguely recollected a nonplussed flatmate. And taking a can of Stella into Jake's room, sitting on his bed, sipping beer and smoking fags. The floor strewn with clothes and crap and therefore easy enough to add hers to the melee. A floordrobe. And she recalled how she told him to stop talking, to stop it with the compliments and the come-ons. And she knew that she grabbed for him first. But sitting up now next to his snoring silhouette at God knows what o'clock, desperate for water, for paracetamol, for her own bed, what Nell couldn't remember was how any of it had felt. To be kissed again, fondled, desired, penetrated, held. Nothing.

Out on the street, Nell walked along the terrace trying to locate herself, cursing herself all the while for breaking her phone, for drinking too much, for going home with a bloke she didn't know who lived on a road she didn't recognize. She'd just walk. She'd just have to put one foot in front of the other and maybe soon there'd be a garage and she could find out where she was and also buy a bottle of water. And so Nell walked, cold and unsteady but her head clearing with every step. Then, like a friend not seen for years, her old primary school greeted her. She was on the other side of town from where she lived but just streets away from Debbie and her car. Ten minutes, perhaps fifteen on account of her throbbing skull.

On her car a piece of paper on the windscreen.

Just knock. Whatever the time. Don't go home. Just knock. Dxx

I can't knock at almost four in the morning.

Nell opened her car and crawled into the back, curled into a ball and hid her face from the coming dawn. It was freezing cold. She clambered into the front and turned on the engine, chanting at the heating to hurry up and there she sat until, at last, everything slipped and blurred and she wasn't here and she wasn't there as she slid into sleep.

It wasn't Debbie who woke her, it was an elderly neighbour walking an ancient dog who tapped on the window and lessened the shock of it with a kind if gnarly smile.

'All right in there? Lose your key? Want a cuppa?'

A cup of tea. A cup of strong builder's, two sugars and a slice of hot buttered toast. Hands around the mug, blowing soft concentric circles on the surface. Guaranteed to make everything better. Nell gazed at the stranger who repeated himself but she was acutely aware that her car was fumed with boozy breath and regrets and she couldn't bring herself to roll down the window, much less open the door. She thumbs-upped, instead. Both thumbs and forced a grin and nodded her aching head and the pensioner went away happy. Moments later she left the car and headed for Debbie's front door.

Debbie opened it in a blear of sleep and bewilderment and an oversized T-shirt of two cuddling teddy bears that needed to be kept private from the world. But she took in the sight of Nell and, in one glance, instinctively knew not to register shock or judgement.

'Oh dear,' said Debbie. 'Hello, you.' And she ushered Nell into the warmth of her sweet-smelling house.

'I'm fine.'

'You don't look fine.'

'Well – I am.'

'Well, you don't smell fine – it's seeping out of your pores. You shouldn't come in to work today.'

'I'm your boss. I'm coming in to work.'

'You're not my boss – we're a cooperative.'

Nell looked at Debbie and Debbie looked at Nell.

'Shit,' said Nell. 'I forgot that bit. You're right.'

'Anyway, you look like crap and you'll scare small children,' Debbie said and just then Nell really loved her.

Debbie provided steaming mugs of tea and pints of water and the time and the space for Nell to warm up and speak.

'Any paracetamol?'

Taking birdlike sips at the hot sweet tea, Nell watched Debbie rummaging in a drawer for painkillers and listened to her sing-song muttering. Just then, she felt she was in the safest and most comforting place in the world. That's why, when Debbie popped out two tablets into Nell's hand and whispered, drink, Nell, there's a good girl, Nell finally cried. In a tumble of emotion and with words in a tangle, somehow it all came out.

'And last night I had sex with someone called Jake who keeps his clothes on the floor. And Jimi Hendrix watched us smoke fags in bed.'

Debbie nodded. What else could she do?

'And I can't actually even remember the sex bit.'

'Perhaps you didn't do it?'

'There was a used condom in my shoe,' Nell said.

'Ah well then,' said Debbie, taking a measured sip of tea. 'Perhaps you did.'

They sat and drank and looked at each other.

'In your shoe?'

'Yes.'

And then they were laughing, snorting into their tea, laughing until they wheezed and Nell begged to stop because her head was splitting.

'*Misery acquaints a man with strange bedfellows*,' Debbie murmured.

'The last time I had sex was with Billy,' said Nell. 'God – that's almost two years ago.' She looked at Debbie searchingly. 'And my mother's called Florence and my aunt's a cold old bitch and my other mum isn't even my mum.' Nell paused. 'And no one told me. And no one will tell me anything. And I don't understand. And I got completely pissed and shagged a stranger. Which isn't me. But the thing is – none of it is me. Nothing. It's all been a lie.'

She rested her head on her arms on the table, Debbie's hand between Nell's shoulders.

'Just go with it, Nell,' Debbie told her.

'I don't want to. I want everything to go back to how it was.' Nell paused. 'And what's so alarming is that all the while I've been assuming it's just my mum's batty ramblings. But now I find there's truth in it.'

'You're raw and tired and on your way to the hangover from hell. I'm going to run you a bath and then you stay here for a few hours – come in to work if you really feel like it, but first just rest up here awhile. OK?'

Nell looked up. She wanted to say to Debbie won't you stay with me? Wanted to confide that she dreaded going to sleep because when she woke up she'd have to deal with the huge wave of facts flooding back and engulfing her.

'Have a duvet day,' Debbie said.

'Sometimes my mum couldn't go to work,' Nell said. 'She'd be—She'd just lie there with her eyes glassed over. She couldn't talk on those days. Sometimes two, three days at a time.' Nell paused. 'I'd stay home from school. I couldn't leave her.'

'That's really hard, Nell. For a little one.'

Nell shrugged. 'But when she came to, she'd compose these extraordinary letters to the school to explain my absence. Beautifully written crackpot fiction. So I'd copy her handwriting and write my own and say I'd had a slight temperature for a couple of days, that's all.'

It was novel waking up at midday within the fresh sheets of someone else's bed. Being woken up in the small hours by Jimi Hendrix now seemed a hazy dream belonging to someone else entirely. Nell scissored her legs; the sheets were cool and she was warm and Debbie's sofa bed cocooned her in comfort and safety. She felt peaceful at last, lying in the slatted light from the venetian blinds and gazing at all the interesting belongings and books, art and photographs and odd little ornaments and knick-knacks, that told the story of Debbie's life. The room was replete with possessions and everything had its place. The purpose of everything was memories and proof, little mementos of a life lived, small objects that gladdened the heart. Nell's head started to swirl again with disjointed thoughts about Wendy and Florence and Florence and Marjorie and Marjorie and Wendy and where, in their fucked-up triumvirate, Nell fitted in. Just briefly she was accosted by memories of the Jake bloke from last night, of reeling around the bar and his skanky room, and the booze and the fags and the shit sex and she was appalled. But most of all she hated herself for having shaken her mum, for shouting at her, frightening her in a fit of frustration and hurt.

She needed more painkillers, more water and she either needed to be on her own or in company, but she couldn't figure out which. After the bath she pottered around Debbie's flat wishing she lived there, in the company of things, with the souvenirs of good times and memories to be proud of.

Enormously tired but wired with adrenaline. Back to her building and up the stairs and there was her boot stamp on the wall. Along the corridor blocking out the sounds of lives going on beyond the doormats and behind the walls of her neighbours. She headed for the calm in Flat 428. Today, the white walls and minimalism seemed staringly cold. Nell sat on the love seat surrounded by a dull and sterile silence and she longed to be back at Debbie's. She was so tired and her head was still half full of fuzz, her eyes stung and her stomach ached. This time yesterday – no! But yes – this time yesterday she was just back from Cambridge and about to visit her mum. Stop.

She turned away from her thoughts and went over to the kitchen, opening and then shutting the fridge and the cupboard before eating baked beans cold, straight from the tin. Her eyes slid around the photos of her montage and all that smiling. Little had she known. There, near the top corner, a bleached-out photo of Nell on her sixth birthday with Wendy grinning wildly amongst a scatter of children in fancy dress around her. Marjorie in the background, po-faced, as straight and as cold as a steel rod. Nell pointed her fork at the picture, nodding slowly. She had answers, that woman, and Nell deserved to hear them.

The previous evening Marjorie had sat quite still in her chair, hands loosely on her lap, television off, anticipating that Nell would be hammering on her door with a battering ram of questions. She'd stayed like that until almost eleven o'clock, unaware that, at the time, her niece was roaring drunk in a pub. Now, after the briefest of phone calls, Nell was on her way and Marjorie told herself to concentrate, to be prepared and, when her doorbell rang less than an hour later, her wits were already neatly gathered about her.

Marjorie did not offer tea, or coffee, or water or anything, she simply led the way to the sitting room and motioned for Nell to sit. The curtains now concealed the paperweights on the sill. The curtains, Nell thought with some satisfaction, were actually horrible. And there they sat in silence. Nell not knowing what she wanted to ask, or what answers she was most dreading. Marjorie just wishing she'd get on with it.

'Mum was useless,' Nell said.

Marjorie was not having that. 'Don't you dare – don't you ever!'

'Yesterday,' Nell qualified evenly. 'She was no help yesterday – she was in gaga land.'

Marjorie bristled. She did not like being wrong-footed. She looked at Nell levelly. 'Nell – what *is* it that you wish to know?'

So much, Nell thought. I want to know so much I don't know where to start. Her mind was so full that, momentarily, she had nothing to ask. But then Nell thought about her absent father remembered only from the details of a few photographs. 'Did my mum – Wendy – did she know about Jimmy and Florence?'

'Jimmy?'

'My dad – Jimmy?' Nell read the confusion on Marjorie's face and she felt herself grow a little thinner. 'Is Jimmy my dad at all?'

'No.'

Nell's blood was churning. 'Then – but who *is* my father?'

'I don't know.'

Nell sat back, deflated. 'You don't know?'

'None of us knew. And believe me, we hunted. It's not as if we had Google back then.'

'Is it Harry?' said Nell.

'Harry?'

'Mum bangs on about Harry sometimes.'

'As I said – I don't know who your father is.'

'Just say!'

'I do not know and that is the truth!'

Marjorie took a big breath in and then exhaled, emitting a faint whistle from her nostril. She wanted Nell to go, she wanted her head clear. Memories served her no purpose, they were indulgent and interruptive. They were interfering with her head and her home.

'Why didn't Florence bring me up? Why did Wendy get me? Why not you? Did you toss a coin for me? Toss a coin *not* to have me? Did you win?'

Marjorie shuddered. It wasn't so far off the truth but the girl did not need to know that. She left her chair and sat down on the sofa next to Nell. It all felt awkward and contrived. She just wanted the whole thing to be done with.

'I will tell you, Nell, all that I know. Florence was sixteen and got herself knocked up at a Christmas party. The boy was not local. He could not be found. Wendy was engaged to Jimmy. Florence was sent to distant family in Scotland and Wendy brought you up after she died.'

Wait wait wait.

Florence *died*?

I can't go and meet her? My actual mother died?

'Florence is dead, then?'

She's definitely dead – just look at Marjorie's face.

'Nell,' said Marjorie, 'I really do feel that none of this can be helpful to you. You've got this far in life without having recourse to any of it. All families are complicated and rife with secrets! There was so much shame. We did what we thought was best in a dire situation – for *you*.'

She made it all sound so annoyingly trivial. She wanted to make it sound like they had put Nell first.

'I have a right to know,' said Nell. 'About what happened. And it's not as if I can ask my mum. Either of them.'

'Don't you cast me as the villain, Nell!' Spittle underscored Marjorie's words. 'Don't you suddenly overlook how I have protected you all these years.'

Protected me? Nell could only sit and stare, feeling her brow contort with confusion and despair. She rubbed at her forehead. Protect me? She glanced over at Marjorie. She wanted to yell, to throw a paperweight through the window or at the mirror or at the stupid clock with its super-calm low tock. She could so easily tear into Marjorie. But she told herself to think.

What was it she did when AJ became fractious? Or Libby or Alex or Sanjay? She softened her voice and lowered her energy and quashed the need to emote.

No eye contact, lighter tone, don't mention first names. 'What family in Scotland?'

'Our stepfather.'

'Granddad George?'

'Yes – George.'

'I do vaguely remember Granddad George – he was lovely.'

'George's family in Scotland.'

'In Scotland. Where in Scotland?' Nell made it sound like advice for a holiday destination. 'And she died, Florence died? In Scotland?'

'Yes.'

'Of?'

'She was ill.'

'And I was—'

'Very young. A year or so. Two. I don't know. I can't remember.'

How Nell wanted to smack her aunt, who sat there alarmingly emotionless, as if having to remember any of it was tedious and unreasonable.

'Would you happen to know where Jimmy is these days?' Nell asked.

'Good God, no.'

'Would my mum? Perhaps? On a good day?'

'No.'

'Then what about Harry?'

'Harry?'

'Mum – she often tells me to go to Harry's.' Nell felt tears welling, her throat tight and constricted. She swallowed hard. 'I just want to know. What happened. The truth. Who I am.'

And it was then that Marjorie had had enough.

'For goodness' sake, Nell – digging all this up! Upsetting everyone all over again. My youngest sister gave birth in her teens and tore her family apart! She was the death of my mother! She was the ruin of my sister! Just leave the ghosts – just leave them. I have work to do. Please – I think you should go now.'

To her staff at the Chaffinch, it was as if Nell had disappeared off the face of the earth, so rare was it for her to take time off for illness or holiday. They found her absence unnerving. Especially Danny, whose levels of joy and stability were dependent on everything being just so, and he'd been begging Debbie to phone Nell every ten minutes for what seemed like *years*. When Nell arrived just in time for the teatime rush, everyone was too busy to react so she slipped back into her duties. Danny could only wag his finger at her before jigging his way over to Table 7.

Debbie mouthed, OK? and though Nell nodded, she wondered when anything would ever seem OK again.

Nell and Frank watched the walnuts being snaffled up. Frank thought it best to focus on the birds than to pass comment on Nell's unkempt appearance, the uncharacteristic downturn of her mouth, the dullness which had swallowed her usual spark. Dark around the eyes. Shadowed.

'Look at this little greedy bugger.'

'I've found out I have a dead mother I never knew about,' she told him. 'And a living mother who hasn't a clue who I am.'

'Well,' said Frank gently, 'I didn't have a mother at all.'

They stood where they were and he sensed Nell slump a little, as if she was a rag doll and her stuffing was being tugged out with each of her thoughts.

'I just want to know,' said Nell. 'That's all. I just want to know – *something*.'

They went and sat on Frank's sofa and she lost herself in the picture he'd painted of a wooden boat hugging the waves in a sunset and oh, what she'd give to be there.

'Have I ever told you how I came to be an orphan?'

He had. But just then, Nell wanted to hear it again because growing up without a mother seemed preferable to having two. Frank's lovely voice, gravelly soft, flowing back over the decades to what he knew of his early years. Nell was so tired. Frank's flat so warm. And, in the painting, the lulling waves of a temperate sea. Perhaps she'd just close her eyes while he spoke, Frank's voice like a lullaby, over eighty years to recount, so soothing.

Frank let her doze for a while. You only had to look to know that the kid was knackered, spent, hollow. The granddaughter he'd never had, that's how he thought of Nell. And her sadness and exhaustion were a terrible thing to see. It wasn't right, any of this.

'Why don't you go?' he said, shaking her shoulder gently. 'Why don't you go?'

The sailing boat was sinking into Frank's sagging sofa and Nell woke with a start.

'Why don't you go?'

'Of course – of course.' Nell scrambled up, slightly mortified. What time was it? 'God – I'm so sorry, Frank – I can't believe I drifted off. Of course I'll go – let me just pop the meal in the oven for you. Do your recycling. Then I'll be off.'

Frank touched her head gently.

'To Scotland, I mean,' he said. 'Why don't you go to Scotland? Find your facts, Nell. They're more likely to be there than in your mother's head or between the lines of what your aunt isn't telling you.'

'I can't just go to Scotland.'

'Why not? You do know I can heat my own food up. It's not all about Walnut Whips. I can cook tinned spaghetti.'

My mother can barely look at me.

Sometimes, though, I catch her – and her expression is hard to fathom. I've heard her say, 'She's finished me off.' And I want to say, 'But Mum . . .' but I don't.

I haven't seen Marjorie – she's gone back to her university.

Wendy comes into my room often – and she'll hold both my hands and scan my face and then she'll either talk about me or about Jimmy but I never know which it'll be. She said to me, 'You're too little to have a baby.' I told her I disagree. Sometimes, though, when I wake up in the night, I lie there and I think to myself that I am too little to have a baby. I'm still going to school while everything else is organized. I don't look at all pregnant. I'm forbidden from talking about this but I do with Joan. She's been trying to find out about Peter. It's brick walls at every turn. She feels she is being helpful – but actually, I don't think of him now and if I do I feel plain angry.

Joan managed to take a leaflet from the doctor's surgery about babies and we went to the library together and hid books on pregnancy and childbirth inside the atlas. So I know how big you are now, I know about your fingernails.

And we looked at the map of Scotland and tried to work out exactly how far away the Outer Hebrides are. They are the furthest thing west on the map of the United Kingdom. It doesn't look like there's much else after that, just St Kilda then the tips of Greenland and North America. I've never been west. We go to Great Yarmouth for our holidays, Scarborough once. I have no idea when I'm going or who's coming with me or how long it's going to take or how long I'll be gone for. What do I pack?

What happens when I get there? When will I be coming back again? With my baby?

I don't want to ask questions – I want to be in control of the answers. Joan and I have started to plan how we stay in touch. She says she'll come and visit. I've decided when I first see her hold you, then I'll ask her to be your godmother. When we were young we always promised we'd be each other's bridesmaids. But marriage isn't important to us any more. Society has moved on. But society has not moved on about being a young and unmarried mother. It seems there's no place for me, seems I'm a disgrace, seems most people think you and I should not be together. But I am your mother and no one is taking you away from me.

George has come knocking at my door. Asks if he may come in. There's just him and me in the house at the moment. I'm drawing – another of my psychedelic dream sequences of shapes and swirls and spaces and forms advancing and retreating. Pinks and greens and oranges and blues, with black outlines just now and then. All inspired by Jimi Hendrix of course. I think I'll do you a huge one and stick it on the ceiling above your crib.

George says, 'Wow.' He says, 'Never stop drawing and painting and writing, Florence.' He says, 'I used to paint and I stopped and now I can't start again.' He says it's a time thing, he says it's a confidence thing. And then he says, 'You're an artist, Florence – and that's a responsibility, that's what you must be.'

'It's all I've ever wanted to be,' I say.

'Your dad,' he says, 'my very best friend. I promised him I'd look out for you.'

We have a moment, privately and together, with my dad.

'I wasn't – entirely – truthful,' George says. 'But I had reasons enough for painting the outline of a picture and not filling in all the details.'

I don't know what he's on about.

'My brother and I left Skye to follow our hearts. Mine led me to England and my first wife, God rest her. For my brother Iain, it was a lassie from Harris and it's there that they made their life.'

This much I know.

'But she died a while ago,' George said.

You flutter but I slump. Now what? Now where?

'But Iain is a good man,' he's telling me. 'And he will look after you and the wee one. And in your own way, you'll be a good thing for him. You'll be cared for and safe, Florence – I swear to you.'

'Is this a secret?' I ask. 'Between you and me? About your brother's wife?'

George thinks about this. 'Let's just say it's information which we can choose not to share.'

I think about this.

'There may be a reluctance to send you there, otherwise.' George rubs his eyes and I notice the bags and the wrinkles that stay for a moment where he's dragged his skin. He looks tired. 'And then I can't guarantee where you might go.' He looks very uncomfortable. 'Your mother – I know she's – but she's a good woman. And I told your father – I'd look after all of you. All of you – and this is what I'm trying to do.'

I understand, I think.

But I need to know something else.

'But George, when the baby comes – then what?'

He nods thoughtfully, but then he is forthright.

'You stay there, Florence,' he says. 'The both of you. You turn your back on here, on everything here, everything you have known – greet your new land with an open heart and you will be welcomed, you will be safe.'

'I don't come back?'

'No.'

'I stay there? I live there? With Baby? On an island?'

'Yes.'

'But what about everything here?' And I start to cry. 'When can I come back?'

His hand gently on my shoulder. 'For now, everything for you is out there. In Harris. Bide your time.'

'But when am I going?'

'Soon.'

'How soon? Will you take me?' My voice sounds so young it shocks me. 'Please, George?'

His look is reluctant and sad – and it says no. And this I do understand. I understand. He is already taking me, in a way. But he can only take me so far before he has to turn back because his place is here.

I'm looking at the map of the UK. I am looking at the Outer Hebrides; they look like a tattered feather on the edge, on the very edge. They are a scatter of islands in snips and bits, strewn like snags of seaweed. And so much water. It looks like the land hasn't finished rising out of the sea.

Gordon

Gordon knew his wife would have called him *amadan*, a numpty. She'd have said it affectionately but she would have meant it. His wife would have made him sit down, have a wee dram and a proper think about it all. His wife would have changed his mind for him. She'd have put her arms around him and everything would have made sense, everything would have seemed all right. And he'd have laid his head against her and said, what'd I do without you?

His son, though, might well be appalled.

But too late for that now. His wife was no longer here and sometimes there's so little comfort from the dead that poor decisions are made almost in protest.

No time for the boat and the train and he'd worry about the cost another day. Loganair would fly him to Edinburgh and British Airways onwards to Heathrow. And then he'd just have to find his way into the city.

Dougie hadn't been paid from the last job yet, and that's why he'd taken this one. There was a time when he would have seen it as demeaning, being assistant to someone else, but these days he simply totted up that it was money in the bank and therefore worth it. It was a fashion shoot, all week in an echoey studio near Earls Court. 'Fashion' was stretching it, but there were models and there were rails of clothes for a lowbrow but perennially popular catalogue. Last week it was womenswear, this week men's. Dougie had worked with Len before and that's why Len wanted to work with him again – because Dougie was efficient and capable and quiet. He wouldn't lark around with the models, he wouldn't make suggestions or raise an eyebrow or get precious or moody, he'd just get on with it and do what was asked of him. He was paying him to have no opinion.

Sometimes, when Dougie's mind was so wired and active through the night, it was good to have the daytime to rest his brain. And it was very good not to have to lug all his own gear across London.

It was still cold at night – the warm drifts of spring that beguiled during the day were crushed by an invasive chill once the daylight had faded. There was something insidious about this when Dougie emerged from the fug of the underground – yet welcome if he was coming out of the gym. He liked the gym; he saw it as a place of amusing contradiction – the pursuit of health in a place where the air was cloyed with the taste of sweat, also the anonymity but amicability of everyone calling each other mate. Dougie liked to move, to really move, to move fast. It was just something he'd always done. When he was little he'd called it the jiggies – he'd call to his parents that he was going to get the jiggies away and he'd just go out the back door and run. Over the bibbled grass of the garden to the machair hinterland between land and beach and then on to the sand where time behaved in a strange way and his legs carried him indefatigably. Running had always been Dougie's physical and mental release; barefoot on sand or a pair of trainers for the hills and off he'd go for mile after mile. He was a familiar sight. There goes the Munro boy. There he goes.

His favourite pair of trainers was one of the few things that came with him to London. But though he lived not far from Regent's Park, from Primrose Hill or even the Heath, there was something about running in London that he just did not take to. He felt contained, enclosed and restricted in the vast city. For Dougie, when uneven paths and green collided with stretched tarmac and grey it was akin to running on glue. A rhythm eluded him in the parks but he felt nervous and irritated on the roads. He tried running the Outer Circle of Regent's Park, just off the kerb, but the clashing cadence of other runners was so distracting it made him quite misanthropic. However, the gym around the corner had a treadmill and though this should have been an anathema to him, Dougie discovered how running evenly for an hour without getting anywhere could be strangely transcendental. With headphones on and gazing through his reflection without focus, a different zone altogether opened to him, one in which he didn't have to think or notice or feel anything.

He wasn't getting to move much, assisting on the Earls Court shoot, so he ran for a good hour or so at the gym every evening after work.

Fuckin' hell, mate – you training for the Marathon or what?

Gordon was an excellent walker. His pace was a jog for most and even now in his seventies his familiar routes took him no longer than they always had. There was a local walking group, a couple of his friends were in it and though they asked him to join he explained that walking slowly made him trip and swear which wouldn't be good for any of them. But London did something strange to his legs; how does anyone walk in London? Not in a straight line, that was for sure. Gordon felt as though he was doing a jig, an arrhythmic and disjointed course to where he was headed. In London, it seemed to him, people were walking to a soundtrack of some very experimental jazz – avoiding each other with a quick-quick-slow, or dancing around one another, or getting right up against each other with too much apology or without any at all. On the train from Heathrow to Paddington, he'd looked at a map and thought he might walk to Camden along the canal but almost immediately there was vomit and rubbish and something dead in the water and skanky kids doing drugs so he took a taxi. His legs were twitching.

So here he was, standing in front of the street sign and reading it out loud. When he arrived at Dougie's door, he said the number out loud too. He looked at the three doorbells for a long time, thinking to himself he never knew that Dougie's neighbours were called Dr Ismail and J & U Loughrey, and that his son's handwriting seemed to have changed. Douglas Munro. Small and contained. His son was anything but. He rang the bell to no answer. Waited. Rang it again. Backed up a little and looked up while the emanating dark from the first floor descended all over him. And just then Gordon thought perhaps this wasn't such a good idea. What, exactly, was he here to achieve? How did he expect his son to react? He wondered how could it be that he had been at home this very morning and now look where he was. Did Dougie not feel the distance every day of his life?

Gordon rang the bell again. Told himself to go for a walk, so he walked. Around and around the block, stopping outside the building each time, looking up at the unchanged windows.

And off he walked again. He had to keep walking, he was cold. He ventured further afield, along Camden High Street, but the olfactory clash of all those cuisines was maddening. He was very very hungry – when had he last eaten? But he didn't want to stop anywhere because what if he missed his son? And anyway, what would he order and how much would they charge down here? He looked at his watch. It was half past six. Gordon kept walking.

At nine o'clock, emerging into the night's aircon glowing hot from the gym, Dougie headed home for a shower, stopping off on the way for a takeaway curry. He was gratifyingly knackered now. He calculated that he could be asleep in an hour and a half. Ahead of him, a tramp in a dark grey slump on his doorstep; not an uncommon sight with the hostel just around the corner. Usually, if he had a bag of shopping Dougie would give a packet of biscuits, a carton of juice, but he was going to be selfish with tonight's curry. The man appeared to be either blind drunk or fast asleep. Dougie thought, he looks a bit like my dad. The same soft beard of a lifetime, the hair once thick now tufty, spectacles so well known to the nose that the two appeared to meld. And when Dougie realized it *was* his father, his heart jumped and his brain ceased working and all he could do was stand stock-still. The pain he felt at knowing that he was more horrified than delighted. The momentary instinct he had to turn and walk away. The collision of questions like a high-speed chase in his head. Dad? What's happened? What's he doing? Why are you here? Dad?

Gordon must have sensed all the thoughts directed at him. He looked up and saw his son and he scrambled to his feet and raised his hand and couldn't find his voice.

'Dad?'

As the blood flowed back into Gordon's left leg, pain replaced the numbing. He raised his hand again and hoped desperately to be normal-looking. What was it the kids say? No biggie!

'No biggie.'

'What?'

'Hello, son.'

Dougie was next to him now. 'Dad?'

And there they stood, eyes pin-balling around each other's faces while their brains rebounded in cul-de-sacs.

'Hello, son,' said his dad. His voice. His face. Him being here. Dougie's curry and gym kit slid to the ground and he put his arms around the man who used to be so much taller than him.

'Jesus, man,' Dougie said. 'You're freezing.'

While Dougie was in the shower, Gordon stood in the flat feeling as though he was inside his son's body. This is how he lives. This is what he smells. This is what he sees around him. Gordon absorbed it all, cataloguing every book, taking in that the TV was Sony, his grandfather's map of Harris, a box set of something called *The Sopranos* that didn't look like opera, a roller blind – not curtains – walls a bit thin really, compared to home. Sounds from the shower telling him the water pressure must be quite good in these parts. Gordon walked softly down the short hallway to the galley kitchen. Does his washing-up, my boy. Not much in the fridge. The calendar he'd sent him, *Hebridean Light*, but nothing written on it. Back in the front room, Gordon ran his hand along of the edge of the semicircular table that flapped open from the wall. On it, the curry sweating inside the polystyrene, inside the plastic bag. He was warm now, but so hungry. He was fantastically tired and had trouble remembering why it was he left home this morning to come here.

Having settled his father in the front room with a steaming cup of tea and a blanket which Gordon said he didn't need, Dougie stood in the shower feeling that his brain was detaching. On the other side of this very wall, his dad. His dad had, on a whim, taken two planes, a train and a cab and come to see him. He could make no sense of the situation at all and he felt alternately so happy and yet utterly appalled.

My dad!

Christ – what the heck is he doing here?

Reappearing, Dougie regarded Gordon sitting on his sofa, noticing that he'd rolled the blind down. He'd refreshed his tea. He'd warmed up, there was good colour to his cheeks and the stiffness had gone. He remembered that shirt and that jumper – he'd asked his mum to buy his dad a nice jumper one Christmas when he'd been too busy to shop before the long trek home from college. It had cost £19.99 and she wouldn't hear of Dougie giving her the money for it.

'You hungry, Da?'

Gordon didn't want to say I'm starving, didn't want the boy to worry. He paused as if having to think about it. 'Aye,' he shrugged.

'Well, there's curry – and I've bread in the freezer. Beans and cheese too. Or eggs.'

'Oh,' Gordon shrugged again, as if anything would do – because actually, it would.

'Tell you what, we'll share the curry and top it up with bread and butter – how does that sound?' And it amused Dougie to hear how his accent was now just a little more Scottish than usual.

And so they ate together, quiet and appreciative. Dougie insisted on washing up so Gordon made tea. He'd brought some Tunnock's teacakes with him – he knew they were sold everywhere, but it wasn't the same. Yes, Dougie agreed, not the same. And thank you. No – thank *you*.

'I have to leave quite early in the morning,' Dougie said, too tired to tackle the elephant in the room. 'Got a big job on – in Earls Court.'

Gordon nodded, rolled the foil from the cake into a ball, focused on his tea, sipping down on his struggle for words.

His father's discomfort was awful; Dougie couldn't head for bed. 'Dad?'

'All good, laddie, all good.'

'But,' said Dougie, 'you are here?'

Gordon took some time to think about this. 'Aye. So I am. But.'

His dad sounded as though he was leaving one of his answering-machine messages. He didn't need to travel hundreds of miles to do that.

'Are you OK, Da?'

'Me?' Gordon laughed. 'Oh aye, oh aye.'

'But – you are *here*.'

Gordon fixed Dougie a look that his son had not seen in many many years, then he got up and straightened himself tall.

'I'm come to take you back home. For a wee while.'

Dougie stared at him. 'You've what?'

'Just for a time.'

'What?'

'Something wrong with your ears, Douglas?'

'You've come here – to take me back with you?'

'Aye.'

Dougie laughed. His father didn't. 'Why?!'

'Father's instinct.' Gordon levelled his gaze at Dougie. 'Because it seems to me it'd do you good, son.'

'Dad – I can't just up and leave and come back with you for a mini-break!' Dougie rushed a gulp of tea. 'I'm busy at work – and I have commitments. And anyway, I'm fine. Honestly – you worry too much. I'm touched – but I'm good, I swear to you, I'm good.'

'Well,' Gordon said, 'you're coming back with me. Just for a wee while.'

Dougie stood, now irritated, too tired. He'd planned to be asleep at least half an hour ago. He'd planned to have a curry to himself, on his lap, watching an episode or two of *The Sopranos*. But his dad was here. Here with a purpose and Dougie's conscience was rattled. 'Da – that's not possible. I can't afford to.'

'I'll buy your ticket for you.'

'I didn't mean that kind of afford.'

'What can't you afford, son? The time?'

Dougie was now moving around his flat while his father continued to speak. He stripped his bed and brought the linen through to the front room, dumping it on the arm of the sofa while he disappeared to lay fresh sheets on his bed for his father. He came back in with a bath towel.

Gordon watched him. 'Or would it be the possibility that once you're back home, *air ais dhachaigh* – back on the island – you might find it's precisely where you need to be? Is that what you are afraid of?'

If Dougie's frustration showed, Gordon ignored it, turned a blind eye to the muscles twitching in his son's cheek.

'I feel really bad that you had to come all this way.' Dougie tried a different tack. 'I wish you'd phoned, I could've saved you the journey.' He regretted that last sentence as soon as it was out.

'I did phone,' said Gordon levelly. 'Two – three times.'

'Look,' said Dougie, 'look.' He blinked his gaze away from the map of the island. 'I'm working tomorrow but why don't you stay for a couple of days. Give *yourself* a mini-break. Maybe you need it more than me. I'll take some time off – we can hang out. Do stuff. See places.'

Gordon, carefully planning his response, stared at the sofa.

'I'll kip on the sofa,' said Dougie. 'I've made my bed up for you.'

'Oh, here will do for me very well,' said Gordon. Where he was to sleep was irrelevant, really. 'There's something amiss, Dougie, in your life. And the answers aren't here – *a' fuireach air tìr mòr* – living in this big city and you just a tiny speck on your own.'

'Well – I've changed all the sheets now. And here's a towel. Plenty of hot water but I'd better think about my getting some shut-eye now. Like I said, in a month or two I'll take time off and visit.'

Gordon stood very straight, very still. 'You were almost home the other week – and your voice, Douglas. I heard it in your voice. You forget – I'm your father.'

Dougie rubbed at his forehead. 'And you forget – I'm thirty-eight years old.'

Gordon was resolute. 'All the more reason, therefore.'

He watched his son snatching and pulling the sheets into a semblance of a bed on the sofa, noted the redness to his face, the inwardness of his eyes, lips tight against further words.

OK. OK.

'OK,' said Gordon. 'We'll sleep on it and talk tomorrow.'

'I leave for work with the lark, Da,' said Dougie. 'It's always a mad rush.'

Could his son really not see that it was precisely this mad rush that Gordon had come down to London to do something about?

Dougie left for Earls Court far earlier than he needed to. His sleep had been erratic and uneasy and he awoke tired and fractious, blaming his father for it and not the narrow sofa. He dithered about writing a note – but that would suggest he'd given it all some thought and he needed to continue to demonstrate that there was nothing to think about. As quietly as he could, he left the flat for the station, the neighbourhood softly awash with a workforce he didn't usually meet.

But he couldn't do it. He just couldn't. He stood by the ticket barriers, immobilized and infuriated with himself, with his dad, baffled by it all. But however irritated he was, he couldn't leave the flat devoid of contact, he couldn't have his father wake to find no word from him. So Dougie turned and jogged home, composing a note to Gordon which, ultimately, bore no resemblance to the one he actually wrote.

'Douglas, darling darling boy, hold the bloody thing steady.' Len's effete side truly flourished when he had an audience and currently he had the attention of four male models in loungewear and a handshake of honchos from head office. He'd been tutting and eye-rolling theatrically for the last hour, and making unnecessary tweaks to the clothing, to the jut of a model's jaw, to the precise positioning of a hand on a hip. Today, for some reason, he was pronouncing Dougie's name Douglarse. 'Be a doll and make me a coffee, would you? Douglarse darling – would you? Gentlemen – coffee?' And Len snapped his fingers and Dougie, very slowly, picked up his coat and gym kit and then he walked away. And he walked away knowing he'd never be asked to work for Len again on a mail order catalogue of horrible clothes.

'I'm away home,' he said over his shoulder.

Gordon wasn't sure how late people in London worked until so he spent the day hunting out the green amongst the grey, searching for quiet in all the klaxonning of the city's soundtrack. A rose garden in Regent's Park. A boating lake. The other side of Primrose Hill where there were no views. He carried Dougie's short note in his head.

Don't go, Dad – wait till I'm home??

Although Gordon would always find it odd, almost hurtful, that Dougie called this place home, he found encouragement in Dougie's double question marks – it made it seem like a plea.

Dougie felt almost euphoric leaving the shoot; rebellious, principled. It felt strange but significant to tell them he was off home and to realize he was talking about Scotland and not Camden.

Just for a couple of days, Dougie told himself as he came up the escalators at Camden Town and into the afternoon.

And, as he strolled back to the flat, he told himself he was doing it for his dad. It was the right thing to do. It would be good for his dad to have some company, a helping hand perhaps. Just a few days, Dougie thought. He'd make himself useful. A week, max.

Nell

Sylvie eyed Nell suspiciously when she arrived but on seeing her wax-pale complexion and dried-out eyes, she softened.

'Not easy,' Sylvie said. 'We know that. We understand.' She gave Nell's arm a brisk rub. 'It's not easy for family, for friends. For us, sometimes. But she's having a good day today.'

'Can you come with me?' Nell asked. For the first time, she didn't want to be on her own with her mother. Today, she was not fearing what she might hear so much as what she might feel.

'I can.'

'Might you stay, please, for the entire time?' Nell thought she sounded like a child about to have an injection. Sylvie thought she sounded like any one of the residents fearful of sleep.

'I shall.'

Outside Wendy's door, Nell lingered. Thoughts of the last time ran through her mind and she turned to Sylvie, reluctant to go in. 'It's just she's not who I thought she was.'

Sylvie touched Nell's arm. 'I don't think she has been for quite some time.'

'No,' Nell said. 'I mean – I've found out I'm not who I think I am.'

Wendy was curled up embryonically the wrong way on the bed but she scrambled herself straight when Nell and Sylvie entered.

'Forty winks,' she declared. 'Well, probably a hundred and forty slow blinks but who's counting!'

'Hello—' Suddenly Nell didn't know what to call her.

Sylvie took over in her jolly and warm, bustling way. 'Look who's come to see you, Mrs H. Look who it is.'

And Wendy looked at Nell quizzically for an extended moment.

'Nell,' said Nell. And Sylvie repeated it.

Nell touched her mother's arm, noting the tissue just poking out from the end of her sleeve. Strange how she always had the presence of mind to make sure she had one of these. Nell's eyes criss-crossed her mother's face but today there was scant recognition from Wendy for either Nell or Florence or Sylvie, or even herself come to that. It seemed that just then, for Wendy, there were simply two soft-spoken, smiley women in her company and that was enough. Nothing on the telly this afternoon. Not hungry.

Smiles and kindly nods travelled a triangle between them, suspended momentarily for an occasional sigh about nothing or a gaze out of the window.

'Wendy,' Nell said eventually, as conversationally as she could. 'What do you remember of Harry?'

'Harry?'

'Florence's Harry.'

'I don't know of a Harry.'

'Oh – you know – Nell's father? *That* Harry.'

Wendy looked shocked. Like a secret had seeped out. 'But she never told anyone his name!'

Sylvie saw the frustration cloud down over Nell.

'Scotland.' Nell persevered. 'Florence went to Scotland.'

Wendy turned to Sylvie, as if it had been she who had spoken. 'She was the little one, Florence was. She was sent far away.'

'Scotland,' Nell said again.

'Sent to Scotland.' Wendy paused. She brought her finger against her lip. 'Shh! Not to be spoken of.' She glanced from the window back to Sylvie. 'She wrote to me a couple of times. I suspect there were more letters, but I expect our mother intercepted them.'

Sylvie could sense Nell standing stock-still, desperate not to distract, desperate for more. 'Letters, were they?' Sylvie said. 'Postcards?'

'Letters.'

'Lovely.'

'And once, a photograph. With the baby. Just one. I kept the photograph in the flap of the pillowslip inside my pillowcase.' Wendy smiled and cooed. 'Scrumptious. Little cherub. Little beautiful blonde doll.'

'Say Jimmy,' Nell whispered to Sylvie.

Sylvie looked confused, then shrugged. 'And Jimmy?'

But there was nothing from Wendy.

'Say Harry,' Nell said.

Sylvie nodded. She sat close to Wendy. 'And Harry? How about Harry?'

But though Sylvie and Nell scrutinized Wendy's expression from two different angles, there was nothing to see.

'Scotland? Say Scotland. Nell? Say Nell. Florence? Say Florence.'

Nell's whispers floating right over Wendy's head while the three of them stayed as they were, quietly apart.

But then Wendy shifted. She shifted her shoulders a quarter-turn, away from Nell and straight on at Sylvie.

'Sometimes I see her – Florence – sometimes she visits,' Wendy told Sylvie conspiratorially. 'And she asks all these questions and it's like she's forgotten that she has the answers.'

Nell sucked the sentences into her mind for later.

Wendy slumped a little, forlorn. 'She died, my little sister. Up there. Where they sent her. She sent me a photograph of the little dolly baby, though. Ever so ever so pretty. Little plump pudding.'

'Just ask who was the father, where is the father?' Nell hushed over to Sylvie.

But Wendy gave her shoulders a little shake as if she'd intercepted the question and it wasn't permitted to land.

'Your little sister,' Sylvie prompted.

'Yes – Florence. Sometimes she's here. Sometimes it's confusing because Nell looks like her, looks so much like Florence. But you see, sometimes it really is Florence who is here. I know it is. Not Nell.'

Sylvie and Nell quietly imbibed it all, Sylvie waiting for Nell's next question to whisper its way to her.

'I'm very tired with all this remembering,' Wendy interrupted. 'I should like to watch my programmes now.'

Sylvie plumped the pillow on the armchair and helped Wendy off the bed. 'Nice cup of tea?'

'But of course Marjorie had her studies, her research, her university life. All of it *very* important and none of us were to forget it. I think what Marjorie found far more difficult than any of her science and studying was that she came from a family of thickies.' Wendy started to giggle.

Sylvie looked over to Nell who was standing as still as she could against the wall behind her mother.

Wendy sighed away the last of the laughter. 'So the baby came to me.' She shrugged. 'Who else was going to have her? Certainly not my mother, certainly not Marjorie. And I was married, you see.' She paused. 'In a manner of speaking.' She fidgeted with an edge of the tissue poking out from her sleeve and then regarded Sylvie, wagging her finger. 'Don't marry a man just because he makes a delicious Martini and offers you a ticket out of home.' She paused. And repeated it. And then she took the remote control and started zapping.

Out in the corridor, Sylvie and Nell stood in steady silence a while.

'Thank you.'

To Sylvie, Nell looked more depleted than when she'd arrived.

'Not entirely sure what help I was – seems to me you didn't get your answers.'

Nell thought about this. 'I don't think I ever will. There's no one to ask. There is nobody who'd know that I'm looking.'

'Well, I'll keep listening,' said Sylvie. She linked her arm through Nell's and walked her along the corridor and back down the stairs. 'Really – that's what they want, people like your ma, at this stage. For people to just keep listening without prejudice.'

In her flat, a bowl of Heinz tomato soup on her lap untouched, Nell sat looking at the white walls quite peaceably. Shadows whispered in with the encroaching dusk like an audience to her thoughts, a soft and quiet company that stayed awhile and then moved on. A tear or two: from pure tiredness and because she was that plump blonde cheruby pudding baby, a secret in a pillowslip between sisters. Nell scratched and scratched for memories. Nothing. Only Frank, hazy on the horizon of her mind's eye. The Chaffinch crew, coming into focus in the foreground. Tomorrow, she'd be back in the land of the living with Danny and Debbie and the blackbirds and the walnuts. For now, though, she'd stay just here and wonder about the little dolly baby who came from Scotland, a hand-me-down from one sister to the other.

Nell wasn't going to eat the soup, it had gone cold and there was a skin on the surface now. She'd have an early night. She'd have a bath, light a scented candle then go to bed with the radio on. She hadn't slept well for days. She took the bowl through to the kitchen and tipped the contents down the sink, running the hot tap on full. She glanced at her montage by the fridge and alighted on a photograph of herself at sixteen, holidaying with her school chums in Greece after their GCSEs. She touched the photograph and smiled. All that retsina and miscalculating the drachma their entire trip. And they sunbathed slathered in baby oil and snogged unsuitable boys and they came home in love or heartbroken, all with peeling shoulders. And Nell thought, I liked the summer when I was sixteen. She remembered how her mum had laughed and cried and couldn't hug her for long enough when she returned. And then Nell realized that Florence would have been pregnant with her at that age and she couldn't even get close to imagining what that must have been like. Too tired to think more on any of it. Nell turned off the lights and went to run a bath. On her way through, in the corner of the room, the red blink of the answering machine. She detoured across the navy darkness and pressed play. Thinking, Philippa.

You have two new messages.

The first was the loaded crackle of active silence and then the bluntness of someone hanging up.

But then they tried again.

It was Marjorie. Marjorie clearing her voice. Marjorie about to hang up. But then she spoke.

'Harris,' she said. 'Florence,' she said. 'Florence was sent to the Isle of Harris.'

To Harry's.

Nell had one answer now and it pointed north.

I need to look ahead.

I have to focus on the horizon. Someone – a woman briskly patting my back – has been telling me to do so. The sea swell is awful and I feel so sick, the lurch and the pitch is worsening. The cold metal railing is sticky with saltwater and my fingers are reddened and wet, clinging on. A bad smell of boat. The sea is called the Minch and it is churning, sucked black and splattered with spume. I've already thrown up. My guts feel shredded. I've been travelling since yesterday. Trains and buses and boats, journeying away from the only home I've known, towards a strange island I'm being told is the only door now open to me.

This place is still over an hour away, somewhere over there on those lumbering mauve humps of land that seem to float and wail into view every now and then before disappearing behind the chucking rain.

What kind of a place is this?

Which idiot thought to colonize land surrounded by such wild water?

I can't believe I have to live there now. I'm livid about that. It's 1969 – what's the problem? So I'm young and unmarried and pregnant – it's just different, it's not uncool, it isn't a sin and I'm not wicked. Why didn't I just ditch the train and stay in London where everything would have been fine?

Instead –

the middle of bloody nowhere
in the middle of a hostile sea.

My people, my tribe – I would have found them in London. They're hardly likely to be waiting for me on a piece of forgotten land hurled into the sea.

My mother couldn't look at me before I went, but I saw how white and tight I've made her. She said May God go with you, *which is an improvement on* May God forgive you *which I've had hissed at me for weeks. She wasn't there when I left yesterday. I know it was the worst day of her life. For her, it was even worse than the day that Joan told her about me and about You. She'll never forgive me so I doubt very much whether her God will either. I wonder if I'll ever see her again — will she forget all about me? Will she even want to know?*

I've lost count of what day was when because it feels like I've been travelling for ever. There aren't just miles between me and home but mountain ranges and so much water. Wendy slept in my room on my last night at home. She came in, crying and cuddling me and calling me Oh Little One, then spent hours and hours talking about her wedding though she never actually mentioned Jimmy and never finished a single sentence. I envy my sister — she can change the subjects in her mind at breakneck speed, she can zoom her focus on one thing and forget everything else that might be connected. I wish I could do that, it would be so useful. Marjorie I haven't seen or heard from, not since that day in the sitting room when the wall of George protected me and my fate was fixed.

Joan and I never had an official goodbye because I didn't know I was leaving until the night before, nobody told me. So I wrote her a letter on the long train journey, at about two in the morning. I couldn't sleep. I couldn't get comfortable. My heart was thundering for hours on end as the train rumbled through the night, through England and into Scotland. I haven't an envelope but I want to post Joan's letter as soon as possible. I mean — they do have post offices over there, don't they? On those chunks of land in the distance that are looming from the ocean like a sea monster?

It was George who took me to London and saw me onto the train. He gave me a hug, a kiss on the top of my head. Soraidh slàn mo ghràidh *he said in Gaelic. I think it means farewell. He told me everything will be OK, he said just you wait and see. He knew I was shaking uncontrollably but he didn't even mention it – we both knew that there was nothing more he could do.*

Oh, I am going to be sick again.
This horrible wretched bloody bloody boat – when will it get there?
I am headed for Tarbert on the Isle of Harris. George's brother is to meet me. His name is Iain Buchanan. More than that I do not know.

And You.
Can you feel my stomach curdling? Does it affect you? Can you feel seasick too? Am I hurting you? If I'm being hurled around the boat, throwing up over the side, are you still safe inside me?

This will be where you are born.
This is where we will live together.
If we ever get there.

The further away we are from where we're from, the closer and closer we get.

Mr Buchanan found me.

Not that I'd have been easy to mistake. I was the only teenage girl on the boat. I actually wanted to kick the boat when I got off. I sensed a few people nearby on the harbour cast a glance but Mr Buchanan just nodded at them, took my suitcase and put his hand on my shoulder to guide me up the steep streets and along. He looks so much like George I wanted to hug him but, like George, he isn't the type. However, like George, in not many words and quiet gestures, you can sense kindness. He just appears to be more traditional, more formal.

I forgot to see if there was a post office. Tarbert thinks it's a town – but it is tiny.

I know why I'm here – but I haven't a clue where I am.

This much I know.

*1: The Isle of Harris actually occupies the same land mass as the Isle
of Lewis but they are completely different and there are mountains that
keep them separate. Harris is Norse for 'High Land' and this makes
sense. It's rugged and majestic and, in glowering weather, quite terrifying.
Mr Buchanan says the island is formed from some of the oldest rocks on the
planet. Lewisian gneiss. It's grey, with bands of white and black contorted
by pressure and shaped by the Ice Age.*

*2: There is a North Harris and a South Harris and they are connected by
just a skinny pinch of land at Tarbert. I am living ten miles away from the
town. I'm living in the middle of nowhere on the edge of what appears to be
nothing. There is water everywhere, water and a vast sky and so much quiet
and so few houses and so few people and somewhere in all of this is tiny little
me. I don't really know where I am – and in a strange way this often makes
me feel freer than it makes me feel lonely.*

3: There are hardly any trees.

*4: My address is: Buchanan, Seilebost, Harris. That's it. Seilebost has a
bank of sand dunes at right angles to a massive beach – so it's like a beach
within a beach. A vast horseshoe bay filled with white sand. I see a few
houses all the way over on the other side. I see the island of Taransay. But
mainly, I see the sea.*

*5: The Buchanan house is a plain building. It is situated on the west coast
of South Harris and Mr Buchanan's late wife's father built it on land that*

the family had previously occupied before the Highland Clearances shoved them off. It's painted white and positioned away from the prevailing wind. Otherwise, Mr Buchanan said, there'd be days when we wouldn't be able to open the door. The window glass looks black from the outside but inside the view from each is like a framed painting. Soft land or the sugar-white sand or the ever-stretching sea, skies brilliant blue or choked with swirling clouds, rain coming across the sea in solid pillars or sunshine so brilliant everything looks tropical.

Outside, there is a short run of ancient tumbledown low stone wall which Mr Buchanan has kept as a memorial, though his land stretches to either side. Nowadays it divides nothing from nothing, and from my bedroom the wall looks like a short and lumpy scar. The sheep like it though – they lie in a line right next to it. They're not even his sheep. After a day of sunshine, the stones feel warm but I'll bet my hand would freeze against it in midwinter. And oh! the wild weather here, the slating rain, the whipping wind and those waves that have been running for 3,000 miles across the Atlantic. Mr Buchanan told me that they have around 375 hours of gale force winds a year. There probably isn't much else to do here than count them.

6: It is a very quiet household. I think Mr Buchanan has forgotten about talking or humming or whistling as he's been here all on his own since his wife died, also they had no children. The floors have threadbare rugs on top of stone slabs and you can sense the earth underneath it all. The kitchen is neat and small and runs into the sitting room which has a worn leather sofa and two wooden armchairs gathered around the fireplace where peat provides the warmth. There's a stack of books on the shelf and a stack of peat outside, piled up like a huge brown honeypot. Cut peat looks like a slab of the richest chocolate. Mr Buchanan has only had electricity for four years and he doesn't seem to like using it. He hasn't heard of Jimi Hendrix and almost didn't believe me when I quoted some lyrics and tried to describe what his music sounds like. I showed him my swirly pictures inspired by this amazing musician and he seemed to like them. He has a wireless that takes a long while to wheeze into life.

There are a few photos of the late Mrs Buchanan – and she looked so warm and smiley. And that's when I catch myself about to cry because every so often I would like very much to cuddle up to someone like her, for them to shush me gently and tell me I'm all right, that everything will be OK.

7: The view from my room is nothing much to see – just endless stretches of waving marram grass that grows in sand, that looks so soft but is sharp like a whip. Just that and the dunes and the sea.

My room has curtains that let in the light and for the first few days I hardly slept because it's so quiet and empty and yet my heart raced through the night whilst my thoughts collided head on. My room has faded wallpaper decorated with flower sprigs, a bed and a cupboard and an old school lift-up desk. There are no marks on it, no one has carved their name or scratched a doodle and there are no inkblots. I'm glad I left my marks everywhere in my old school. I'll bet the kids see them and say 'Remember her?' but in just a few years I suppose I'll be forgotten.

Inside the desk I have put the few belongings I managed to squeeze into my suitcase. I brought with me notebooks, pens and pencils so I can write and draw. I brought Woofy, the toy dog I loved so much when I was little – I should like to give him to Baby. The framed photograph of my dad and me on my third birthday. Also, my school photo, rolled up in a tube – just so I can remember who I liked and what I hated. Joan and I are side by side, looking goofy. I brought my tablecloth dress. Also the mascara and the very pale lipstick Joan and I bought to share. And my favourite LPs. There's no record player here but I sit on my bed with them in a fan around me. If I take out the vinyl and tip it against the light so that my eyes can run along the tiny grooves, I can hear the music. I gaze at the album covers and sing along quietly.

Also in the desk is an envelope containing £20 that George gave me to give to Mr Buchanan who has refused to take it.

8: Mr Buchanan likes church – but not in the way my mother likes church. For my mum, it was the answer to her anxious everythings and something to brandish over us girls and what she saw to be our failings. For Mr Buchanan, it's far more straightforward – it's structure and community and a rhythm to his life.

9: Until last year there was no public transport, now there are three buses a day all the way to Stornoway and one bus connecting the east and the west. Luckily, there's a bicycle for me to use – I think it must have belonged to Mrs Buchanan. I posted Joan's letter and it took me over an hour and a half to cycle to the post office in Tarbert and almost two hours to cycle back because of the awful hill. But I met a very old lady on the way who was pushing a bicycle with two flat tyres. In the basket was all sorts, including two cats. Mr Buchanan says she's known as Mrs Mole and her sheep live in her house. He says she feeds them brown bread because she says white bread is not good for them. I hope I see her again.

10: I've been here over two weeks and in that time I have spoken to just a handful of people as I've only been back to Tarbert twice. They all have soft, sing-song voices. Some have regarded me most suspiciously – but whether that's because I'm from Colchester or because I'm pregnant I don't know.

11: It seems that I'm to be known as Flora. That's what Mr Buchanan calls me, that's how he introduces me.

I like it.

It feels as if being Florence was a million miles away in a totally different time.

12: And you're growing and I'm looking bonny, *so I've been told.*

Glasgow

Nell hated flying and had boarded the plane to Glasgow with a stomach knotted with nerves, which tightened during the short flight. Though she knew she was heading to the same destination as Florence, so too did she know that she was hardly tracing her birth mother's footsteps. She doubted very much that Florence had gone by plane. She imagined that the journey, all those years ago, would have been a protracted, hard slog via various trains and boats and buses. And Nell thought of Florence. How had it felt setting out on her own, banished, pregnant and so young? She must have been terrified. Florence: utterly alone and forsaken. How long had her journey taken, and were the family even aware when she arrived safely? And what of Wendy back then? With her little sister exiled – how had it been for her? Wendy, engaged to Jimmy but still living at home, emotionally all over the place, no doubt. And Nell wondered if all of this was the catalyst, whether this was what had triggered her mother's mental health issues? Did the family see it as Florence's fault? And just then, Nell wondered if perhaps it was. And then she considered whether Marjorie believed blame to be transferable. First Florence, now Nell, through mother to daughter, like a kind of genetic blight. She'd always felt her aunt had disliked her. Marjorie was very good at finger-pointing, Nell reasoned. She blamed me. She blames me still.

Within an hour, England melded with Scotland and the plane made its descent. Nell felt strangely emotional disembarking, knowing she was stepping onto new yet native soil. Did Florence never return to England? Was she ever spoken of again, in either country? Memories could be hidden but could they be forgotten?

And also—

—am I Scottish, then?

Nell sat in the airport waiting for Loganair to fly her onwards to Stornoway. The flight would take pretty much the same time as the one up to Glasgow had. The departure board listed destinations she'd never heard of and the names were compelling. They sounded dramatic, romantic, far-flung. Benbecula. Islay. Barra. Tiree. Stornoway. Outside, a tiny propeller plane that looked like a toy. Please not that one.

'Where you headed?'

She didn't really feel like talking but the whiskery man sitting three seats away had kind eyes and a slightly sad smile and there was no one the other side of her so she couldn't pretend he was talking to someone else.

'Stornoway,' she said.

'On your holidays?'

Nell wondered how to answer that one. Officially, she had taken holiday from work, something she hadn't done for so long, something that had rendered Debbie speechless and Danny and the gang outraged. But no, not a holiday.

'Visiting family,' she qualified, cautiously.

He nodded and his eyebrows went this way and that, as if trying to entice a fuller conversation.

'You?' she asked

'I'm home to Barra,' he said.

Nell regarded him. She realized she had imagined that the islands' population stayed where they were, that only visitors came and went. 'You live in Barra?'

'Aye. Work in Glasgow four days a week. Then home.' He nodded at her. 'You been to Barra? When you've been visiting family?'

'This is my first trip. Harris.'

'Won't be your last,' he said sagely. 'And next time, make a holiday of it and fly in to Barra – you land on the beach.' He nodded and smiled. 'On the sands.' He sighed. 'You wouldnae believe it.'

It was obvious that he was ready to be home while Nell was pretty sure that this trip would be her last. Once she had answers, once she could finish sentences and lay mystery to rest, what point would there be of returning? No. This was not a holiday, this was duty. She had a duty to her mother and to her mum. Both lost, both deserving to be found.

'I just need to know.'

She hadn't meant to say that out loud, certainly not in a voice so hoarse and emotional.

Her fellow traveller's eyebrows rose then fell and he busied himself with his newspaper.

Know what? Dougie wondered. What does she just need to know?

He'd counted twenty-two people in departures. And that woman was the only one anxiously glancing at the board, picking at her nails and looking like she was embarking on an expedition she was both ill prepared for and dreading.

'Get you a drink, Da? A snack?'

Gordon was thirsty. Irrationally, though, he didn't want Dougie to wander off. He'd got him this far and felt compelled to keep him close. It was akin to the fear he'd felt when Dougie was just four, when they took him to visit family in Oban and the boy kept bee-lining into the roads. 'I'll get it,' he said, refusing his son's money with an expression of confusion and consternation.

Dougie watched Gordon at the vending machine, behind the girl who just needed to know. She'd dropped loose change all over the floor and his father was helping her gather it up. She went back to her seat with a packet of crisps she didn't open and a bottle of water whose cap she simply twisted off and on.

Gordon returned with snacks and handed them out to Dougie like they were mid-picnic but Dougie found he was no longer hungry. He wasn't so much ambivalent about this trip to his childhood home as he was apprehensive. What was it that awaited him – the island's open arms or the proof that he no longer believed his home to be there?

To Stornoway, to Tarbert

Nell had never been on a plane so small. It was unnerving, it was noisy, they were still on the ground and she was wishing that she'd chosen Florence's endless trudge of trains and buses and boats no matter how interminable. She felt fractious and emotional, scared of the plane, troubled by this distant land she was journeying to, burdened by the secrets it would either reveal or protect. But they lumbered into the sky and, across the aisle, Dougie chanced to see how the same girl who spoke to herself out loud and threw her money around the airport didn't dare look out the window, staring instead at the seat back in front of her.

But it didn't take long before the route headed for the Highlands and the plane felt stable and, at that point, Nell's attention was drawn to the barren beauty of the hills, sunlight and shadows moving in swathes, the climb and the fall and the swoop down deep into ancient lochs. There was still snow on the highest ground and the westward-facing rock faces showed the scars of timeworn battles against the elements. There seemed to be a pervading sense of melancholy alongside the grandeur. Isolated dwellings clung to the hills or tiptoed to the edge of the water and Nell wondered who lived there and why.

And then they were flying out and over the sea, millpond calm, and the drama appeared to be behind them. She could breathe now. She could eat the crisps she'd bought at the airport.

And so here are the Outer Hebrides. And Nell thought, what kind of land is this? Torn and pocked like moth-eaten fabric, water water water commandeering all the spaces in between. She looked down on the frayed edge of Lewis's coastline along which further small nuggets of land littered the sea, too small to be called islands. She watched how the land appeared to move when clouds cast mauve shadows while sunlight added clashes of gold and greens. The inland water shone still and violet but the sea coursed swathes of dull grey and bright silver, rich navy and, occasionally near the coast, turquoise too.

Descending, now, to Stornoway. Out of the window, down there, a small number of houses every now and then, lining up politely with their tended rectangles of a different green. And down. And down. An effortless landing. A smooth flight. And welcome. Steòrnabhaigh.

Gordon had his car and he and Dougie were making their way to it. He was careful not to make anything of how his son, on leaving the plane, had planted his feet for a long moment and just breathed, quietly but deeply. Dougie hadn't brought much, just a rucksack light enough to be slung over one shoulder. His walking boots stayed at the house anyway and, between them and his trainers, what more did he need? He'd brought his camera. And he'd brought a lot of film. Perhaps he'd take photos once he'd helped his dad, if he found himself with the time, the inclination. It would depend on the weather, on how he felt, it would depend on so much.

'Would you care to drive, Douglas?'

'I don't mind, Da.'

'I'm tired, so I am.'

'Let me drive then. How's she going, the old girl?'

'Temperamental. But I wouldn't part with her for the world.'

'Strange to be back.'

Gordon sensed that his son hadn't intended to say so out loud. He'd make no mention of it. Strange, aye – but good.

Nell wasn't sure how long she'd be staying so she had packed for all eventualities, which ultimately filled a sizeable suitcase. She'd wondered about the weather and decided to err on the side of caution and cliché and bring with her everything that she owned that was waterproof and everything she had that was sturdy in fabric or heel. She felt a bit stupid and self-conscious; it seemed everyone else on the flight had travelled light and here she was lugging her stuff in search of a car hire office that was so small she had missed it. She felt stressed and tired. She knew where she was heading and that she was unlikely to get lost, that there were only half a dozen public roads anyway. The drive was apparently straightforward with stupendous views, but Nell was overcome by an evaporating sense of why she needed to get there.

Through the relatively nondescript edge of town she drove until quite suddenly the bleak growl of sodden moors opened to either side, the road continued straight, unfurling for some way before it started to turn and bank and undulate, water to the left and the land ahead increasingly lumpy. Everyone must be at home, there were few cars on the road. Every now and then, simple plain houses nestled on a hillside or near the shore. But the hills of North Harris were coming and the views over Loch Seaforth were breathtaking. Two cyclists hunkered down over their handlebars as the vast hairpin bends hauled the road higher into the Harris hills, the upward drama of the land taunting while beckoning. Nell had never driven roads like this and she'd never seen a landscape like it either. She was mesmerized by it all, by how the heathery surface looked so soft, how the land soared and swooped, how some of the hills were finished with scone-like tops while the higher peaks exposed their slashed edges and monumental faces. And the water, always the water; navy silver black. She was but a tiny speck in a strange and ageless land; a place which seemed to be closer in time to the moment of its violent creation and yet felt more ancient than anywhere she'd ever been. She was traversing a land formed of Lewisian gneiss in melancholy grey streaked with darkness and light, folded, flawed and heaving, and three billion years old. It made Roman Colchester seem prosaically modern.

Back home could have been on the other side of the world and in another time zone. And Nell wondered, how were they all at the Chaffinch today? Did everything run smoothly? And will Frank be all right? Will there be walnuts for the birds, will Frank cook spaghetti and toast? It's dustbin day tomorrow. And under her breath, glancing to her left and her right, at all this unimagined beauty and solemn, solitary strangeness, she murmured everything will be all right, everyone will be OK.

Finally, Tarbert, the town on the cinched waist of land between North and South Harris, nestling at the foot of Beinn na Teanga. Nell pulled in and re-read the directions to the hotel even though she'd already seen a sign for it and knew it was just ahead. For the first time now, there was a short run of pavement and a few people. Every time she saw anyone of a certain age she wondered, did you know Florence? Might you know what happened? And she wondered, did you ever see *me*, as a baby? But she told herself to shut up. You sound ridiculous. Perhaps no one would remember anything. It was likely that Florence was forgotten.

It was normal for Gordon and Dougie to speak little in the car but it was an affable quiet rather than a loaded silence. Every now and then, Dougie would ask after some person or other and at irregular intervals Gordon would pass comment on a vista that was looking fine this afternoon, or a building that was for sale or that the car going the other way belonged to Old MacKenzie.

'Your man MacKenzie,' said Dougie. 'He's still *alive*?'

'Aye, son.'

'He's still *driving*?'

'Aye.'

They detoured to Mrs McKeon's to pick up Ben the dog who was beside himself to see Dougie and they stayed for tea and her incomparable cake before heading for the house. There'll be many who'll be wanting to have a look at you, Shauna warned Dougie lightly.

The Munro house looked as it always had, looked as it should. Unlike his old school which now seemed to belong in Toy Town, or Mrs Mackeson who was actually a benign soul and not the terrifying harridan of his childhood memory, to Dougie his house never changed. It was as he remembered, always the same. Positioned at an angle to offset the wind, the house looked askance at the coast, its end walls solid and windowless, each bisected by the thick artery of chimneybreast. He'd always seen his house as a face, kind eyes either side of the deep-set front door, the dormer rooms in the roof liked raised eyebrows. His grandfather had planted many trees but only the conifer and rowan to either side had taken and these Dougie saw as the bushy whiskers to the house's physiognomy. Sheep had made themselves at home in Gordon's absence but mumbled off as they drove up. Ben scrabbled from the back seat as soon as the door was opened and performed joyous laps. None of the dogs ever strayed – they had all instinctively known where the perimeter of the homestead reached even though there was no proper fence. Gordon led on to the house, tipping his head at the *cruach*, the peat stack, as he passed. Dutifully, Dougie lifted a *fàd*, a chunk as glossy and rich brown as chocolate, and brought it in.

The house. It smelt the same and nothing had changed. Everything about it was solid and steady and without whimsy. There was no place for trinkets and frivolity, only for decent furniture and functional rugs and throws; the pictures and maps on the walls alluded to places or people known and a gathering of framed photographs on the mantel, on the sideboard, further preserved memories. As Gordon lit the fire he could sense his son standing still on the flagstones just inside the front door, the worn topography familiar under his socked feet. If the boy's mother were still alive, she'd say he was *just having a moment*. Dougie could hear her too. I know, Ma. That's what I'm doing. *A' gabhail mionad*. I'm just having a moment.

His room upstairs. Clean and welcoming. It wasn't kept as a shrine. Over the years, the posters had been removed once the Blu Tack had ceased to hold the corners, rolled up and stored. And when the patchwork of photos above his bed had furled and faded they'd been taken down too and placed in a shoebox for safekeeping. All those trophies for running and swimming had been put inside the cupboard because otherwise they'd just attract the dust. The bed was stripped so that the mattress aired and the linen didn't stale. But it was still Dougie's room.

He unpacked his rucksack, returning his things to their designated drawers. Into the bathroom he took his wash bag, noting only the one bath towel. It struck him then how his father had not known whether his son would be returning with him. Momentarily, Dougie imagined Gordon arriving home today alone and his heart creaked. But I'm here. He took a fresh towel and placed it on the rail. On the landing, from the airing cupboard, he collected sheets for his bed and took them back to his room. I'm here.

Nell's room at the Harris Hotel was cosy and clean and quiet. The furniture was satisfyingly mismatched and the pictures were unique little oils and faded watercolours of hills and lochs and blackhouses. The view was to the giant rise of the hill whose peak she could not see. Delicious wafts of chips and fish and pies had accosted her on her way to the hotel reception and now, an hour later and still sitting on her bed, Nell realized that beneath the exhaustion she was starving. She left her room, taking her notebook and pen even though she doubted that her first evening would bring someone who knew everything. It wasn't a new notebook. There was a page with an old shopping list, another with a phone number with no name, film times for a movie she knew she hadn't seen. These sheets she tore out. She needed blank pages for the facts, which she'd document in this notebook. This would be where she would write the final full stop. Draw a line under it all. Close the book and go back to life as she'd always known it.

The restaurant was quiet so Nell chose the bar which, though not crowded, had a buzz. The man behind the bar – he seemed the right generation. And that couple sitting over there. And him. And him. And those two ladies. See. Everyone friendly, everyone acknowledging her. Most said hello but Nell, who usually found smiling and conversation to be contagious, felt herself clam up. She was struck not so much by shyness, as she was unnerved by the presence of people who really might know. She felt a sudden reluctance to get the ball rolling because once it rolled she didn't know how fast it would go, what route it would take and what it might pick up on the way. Ultimately, where would it come to a stop, where was the end? And was she really ready? No, just then she didn't think she was. She considered going back to her room and making do with a cup of tea and the two shortbread in the packet by the kettle.

But the smell of chips. And the warm lighting, the comforting and characteristic swirls of hotel carpet and the snug conviviality of the bar. Nell took a seat and concentrated on the menu, ordered, and while she waited, she filled the first page of her notebook with awkward, hasty doodles and not very good ones. Her food arrived and she ate her fish and chips, staggered by how much she could shovel in and how profoundly delicious it was. She had pudding too and a cup of tea and she asked for a jug of water to take upstairs with her. She closed her notebook and made eye contact with no one.

It was not quite 8.30 when she returned to her room and there she stayed for a full twelve hours. Her phone was switched off – there was no signal anyway. She hadn't told anyone she'd arrived. No one knew where she was staying. Just that she'd gone to Scotland. For a bit. She flicked aimlessly through TV channels. She did not know how to think about anything and was desperate to dream of nothing.

Gordon was happy enough with his fire and his pipe and his dog whose eyes flicked between his master and the stairs. Dougie would come down when he was good and ready. There'd be stew for dinner and Mrs McKeon had picked up bread and milk for them so plenty to eat. The day drew dark and Gordon tuned in to the utter silence of the house. Followed by the dog, he went upstairs where the last of the light bathed the outside mauve and the inside sepia. The sea could be heard but hardly seen and the sky hung low and heavy.

Dougie's door was ajar. Gordon had fixed the creaking hinge a few months ago and it opened soundlessly. There he was, his boy, sound asleep on top of his bed, facing away to the wall with an old tartan blanket pulled over him. Thirty-eight years old. What did that matter or mean? Meant Dougie was a man – but this man was also Gordon's boy and that was that. Gordon rested his hand on his son's head and then he backed away, leaving Ben curled on the rug beside the bed. He'd go downstairs, check the fire, put the stew on and listen to the radio. That's what he did this time of day anyway.

Wednesday, Thursday

Nell spent her first day walking slow and self-conscious mis-shapen circles of only slightly increasing diameter, doggedly avoiding all eye contact. She justified that this was the day to get her bearings, just get a feel for the place and not worry about conversing with local folk, never mind asking questions to facilitate her search. The town was much smaller than she'd thought, just Main Street and Pier Road forming a T from the harbour to the top of the village though protracted traffic flow made it seem busier. But she felt conspicuous mooching about: it was a working day and people walked with purpose. Akram's. John Morrison. A D Munro. Tarbert Stores. In her notebook she jotted down *bank, post office, medical centre, garage.* If she wanted sheep dip, she could buy it in Tarbert. If she needed a broom or a bucket, she'd find it here. The place felt sensible and moderate. Tarbert's main focus was the island-ers and, to that end, pandering to tourists was not a priority. Even a very old shop selling traditional hand-woven Harris Tweed was practical and not prettified. It was inside here that Nell wiled away a portion of the afternoon. Racks and stacks of jackets, coats, skirts, suits, hats, dog leads, table mats, slip-pers, shawls – there was a durable warmth to it all. The colours of the wool and the patterns woven reflected the spirit of the place; the hills, the heather, the peat, the machair, the salmon, the plumage of golden eagle and corncrake, the water. No one hassled her, they just let her be. Had Florence ever been in here? Had they responded to Florence the same way, with quiet equanimity, just letting her be? Or was there discredit and scorn for a pregnant teenager seeking shelter on their isle? Nell couldn't know without asking. But she wasn't ready to ask anything other than how much the cushion cover was. It was woven with mauves and pinks and shot through with a little mid-blue and just a touch of rust red. It would make her love seat look not so empty. Maybe she'd buy it tomorrow. Or before she left on Tuesday. She mumbled thank you as she headed for the door.

In the bar that evening, over fish and chips again, Nell busied herself with her notebook with its one page of doodles and one short list of businesses in Harris. She turned the page and wrote *THURSDAY*, embellishing the letters as she thought about tomorrow. Tomorrow, she told herself, she would start work. She'd ask questions and would dig for details. Definitely. Because, she said to herself, I don't even know if Florence actually lived in Tarbert. And if her home wasn't here in the town, however will I find her?

She woke early but stayed in her room late until she felt fuggy and irritable with herself. She went downstairs, determined to approach the man who was usually at reception, a cheery fellow whom she reckoned was manager on account of the camaraderie and attention bestowed on him by clients and the scurrying efficiency he elicited from the staff. He was there indeed but chatting to someone, so Nell went through and had breakfast. He was deep in conversation with another person when she'd finished so she decided she'd just pop back to her room for a bit. However, he'd gone by the time she came downstairs again. She'd have some fresh air, then. It was almost lunchtime before she dawdled back to the hotel, determined now to speak to the man.

He was on the phone, having a good blether.

She loitered as inconspicuously as she could before deciding better of it and she was heading to the stairs, to her room, when he called after her.

'And how are we today?'

Nell, though, faltered. 'Oh,' she called over her shoulder, 'very good. Thank you.'

'Anything I can help you with, missy? I was on the phone, there, to Morag Fraser. And can she talk!'

Nell turned to face him. There he was with his beaming face, ruddy and kind; his happy paunch and jaunty tie. 'Um.' She paused. 'Maybe.'

'And what would that be?' He was perhaps forty years old. Too young to have known Florence. But still – he seemed to know everyone.

She clung to the banister. 'I'm trying to locate someone,' she rushed quietly. 'A young woman – a girl really – who came to live here from England over thirty years ago.'

He tipped his head to one side and considered her expression, the way her eyes darted from her feet to criss-crossing his face. She looked pale, tired. He wondered what sort of a trip it was that this Englishwoman was making, midweek at this time of year. She wasn't a hillwalker or birdwatcher, she wasn't rugged enough. Perhaps some kind of artist, maybe a writer. Or perhaps she was an undercover detective, now that would be quite something. He walked over to her.

'Alasdair Scott-Goddard, general manager – but please, you can call me Al. Paul Simon said so. Thirty years ago, you say?'

'And I'm Nell. Well, 1969.'

'And her name?'

'Her name was Florence.'

'Florence—?'

He was waiting for a surname. Nell faltered. What would it have been? Her mind had emptied. Nell had Jimmy's surname – Hartley. That was what her mother still went by. Wendy Hartley. Or, to Sylvie and most of the staff, Mrs H. What was her mother's maiden name? What *was* it?

'Florence—' she repeated unsteadily, looking at Al blankly. 'Florence Something.' She scratched at her memory. 'I've gone completely blank.' She felt her cheeks scorch with self-ridicule. She could cry. Wendy and Florence What? For fuck's sake *think*! And then suddenly her embittered spinster aunt sprang to mind and though mostly Nell banished thoughts of Marjorie, just now her presence was welcome. Dr M. Lawson.

'Lawson,' Nell said, the choke in her throat painful.

'Florence Lawson,' the man said thoughtfully.

Nell wrote the name on the next clear page of her notebook, eased the paper away from the steel rings and handed it to him.

'I shall make enquiries,' he told her. 'There'll be someone who knows – of that I'm sure.' He looked at her enquiringly. 'Have you had your dinner, Nell? Will I make you something?'

No one had called her by her name for days.

He watched her falter, her eyes fill. 'A cheese toastie, perhaps? On the house,' he added.

But Nell shook her head; the offer alone was nourishing enough. She thanked him and retreated to her room for the afternoon. She'd made a start and it had worn her out.

Florence Lawson. Arrived here 1969.

And Wendy Hartley, in her room a million miles away closed off from the real world, unaware that she had a daughter hunting for her sister.

It never left Dougie – his innate knowledge of the vagaries of the land when he ran. The contrast to London was stark. There, tarmac and kerb and concrete paving caused his legs to stammer and his breath to falter. Here, he could run for hours, his proprioception and endurance intuitive. Here he instinctively tempered his cadence and breathing; he could fleet-foot his way over the squelch of saltmarsh, spring between ankle-twisting tussocks, counteract the scuff and skid of unsurfaced track and road, propel himself from boulder to boulder, skip over burns and calibrate his footfall between firm sand or the suck of the shoreline. The main difference between running here or in London was that here, Dougie never looked down. Look down and you're done.

It was his second morning and he was awake early, before his father. He made thick salty porridge and ate it standing up, looking out beyond the garden to the sea. He left no note – there was no need. Gordon would see that Dougie's trainers were gone and there'd be nothing to worry about.

And so he ran; mile after mile through glens shaped when glaciers had bulldozed their way through, up hills scarified by the strips and ridges where man had worked the land over thousands of years. He ran alongside the *gearraidh* – the skinned ground where the peat had been dug down to the boulder clay. He ran through the bickering between rock and land, where elephantine slabs dominated a riot of acid greens, pale blondes and rust browns, red deer grass and heather and the white stars of bog bean. The air was pure and cold at this time in the morning, but there was a watery sun climbing into the sky and the cloud cover was scrawny. It was going to be another fair day and, by the time he arrived back at the beach, the terns and gulls were in full squabble above the running waves. The tide was retreating, leaving a sinewy network of rivulets and lagoons across the vast Luskentyre sands, and here Dougie sprinted hard until, finally, his lungs burned and he had to stop, his legs trembling and his heart pounding in his mouth, in his ears. He clasped his hands behind his head and panted against the gusts from the sea, then he stripped naked and strode over the sand into the water. The slashing cold lanced through to his bones and halted his breath completely. Facing away from the beach, from the house, finally Dougie cried out with everything he had. It was the sound of pain and of exhilaration, of torment and triumph, of love, loss and frustration, but the difference between them was indistinguishable and the sea swept them away.

What was he doing back here?

How was he going to leave?

Mr Buchanan says I'm to call him Iain.

He said, enough now, Flora – will you not just call me Iain?

Every day he cycles to work south along the coast towards Leverburgh. He is something to do with seaweed – he says they make puddings from it, which quite turned my stomach, and he saw my face and laughed. Mr Buchanan, I said, where I come from no one eats seaweed for dessert. I said, haven't you heard of blancmange, Mr Buchanan? He laughed again and his face went as soft as George's and he said, enough now, Flora – will you not just call me Iain?

For a while until it came naturally, I called him Mr Buchan-Iain. But now he's simply Iain and we rub along fine. In the month that I've been here, I've kept myself busy. I've had to. I realized early on I have to occupy my time to stop everything grinding to a halt – which is when I think of Joan or Wendy or any of the others living their normal lives at precisely that moment. I've never been so completely on my own and I have had to fight hard not to feel just desperately lonely and blue. So I taught myself not to remember what my life once was, because it's too big to think about and brings with it a horrid churn of emotions. I've learned that I must not recall Eld Lane or Castle Park or our corner shop or the walk to school or our amazing zoo that opened five years ago. Now I stop myself from conjuring my old room, the smell of my bed and the feel of my pillow, my things on the shelves that I had to leave behind. I don't allow my mind to tour around the house. I cannot think of Joan because I miss her so desperately. Nor do I think of my mum because doing that rips my head and my heart into strips and twists them into one massive knot. I don't think of Wendy because it makes me long for her daftness and her lovely face and her crazy talk. It's hard not to think of George because Iain looks so similar – but he's not George.

I absolutely do not think about Peter. He's not a part of any of this. It's easy not to think about any of that.

But I do think about my dad. He is company that it is safe for me to keep because nothing has changed there.

So with all the time that not thinking frees up, I've taught myself this and that. On the shelves to the side of the fireplace are folded maps of the islands and books on birds and flowers. There's a dictionary, a really huge old Bible, a book in Gaelic called Gràs am Pailteas, a weighty tome on Scottish history and a slim leather-bound edition of poetry by Robbie Burns which I try to read out loud. The more ridiculous an accent I put on, the more understandable the poems become and I love them. But best of all is Mrs Buchanan's box of recipe cards, which Iain has translated for me. Her writing is so neat and chatty that I feel like she's here. She's taught me to how to bake fruity bannock cakes and I can make her lovely Cullen skink soup – with smoked haddock, onions and potatoes. I cook supper for us every evening and Iain leaves porridge for me on the stove as he goes out to work early. It's salty – but I've grown used to it. Iain says he'll teach me to skin a rabbit but I'm in no hurry for that. The first week I was here he presented me with 'poached salmon' but it was whole and raw, in fact it was quite fresh out of the water. Then I realized he meant he'd gone poaching for it. Most Saturdays he disappears at night – and on a Sunday, we have salmon. He taught me to gut the fish after which I fried it with a little butter and it tasted heavenly. I bake delicious pies and puddings and I don't use seaweed in any of them.

Every single day I go for a walk on the beach, weaving my way through the acres of marram grass. Sometimes the wind is so vicious it whips up the sand, which can give you quite a thrashing. Even when the rain comes down in heavy curtains, sweeping from the sea and across the land all day long, I'll still go out. Whatever the weather, I don't see a soul. Beyond the dunes are the start of the endless Luskentyre sands which run for miles. According to the weather and the tide, sometimes rivers and lakes will appear across the vast beach and there's no way through other than to swim. Iain told me that after winter storms, the dunes can change shape entirely. The sand here is white, it's actually shell sand and the islanders of old saw how it was spread by the wind over land near to the coast and the soil became really fertile, that if they dressed it with seaweed it made for sweet grazing pastures. They'd graze it in the winter then take their sheep up to their summer shielings, up in the hills all summer, and let the land by the sea rest and burst into bloom. That's how things grow here. Protected by the marram grass growing by the dunes and by the sea sedge, which acts as a soft green covering for other plants to take root. These sea meadows are called the machair. The flowers are here now and there are far more to come, Iain says. The rarest of birds visit, and the rarest of bees too. Sometimes all the mussells are open on the beach, they look like butterflies.

There's a mobile shop we call the Van which stops nearby every week but I still like to cycle into Tarbert or Leverburgh for bits and pieces like finnan haddie, which is smoked haddock that I could eat by the shoal. There are currently sixteen shops, two cafés, the post office, the meeting hall, a Masonic hall, the Harris Hotel, two churches and a school. In town, there are a few people who greet me now. They call me Miss Buchanan or Flora Buchanan. These days, Florence Lawson just seems like an old nickname. It's May; I'm gone five months pregnant and cannot be mistaken for chubby any more. There are some who look disapprovingly at me. There's a busybody lady who's always in the grocer's, never shopping just gossiping, and she looks me up and down in a snooty way but the shopkeeper doesn't; Morag is lovely to me.

I've noticed other girls around my age titter behind their hands if they see me while some look away quickly – as if they've been told I'm the lesson to be learned. Some do smile, though. There's a girl called Jessie and we've snatched a chat now and then, mainly about music. She loves the Beatles. She told me she lives off the Golden Road and she laughed when I said wow! I also see Jessie when I go to church with Iain. It's never really been my thing, church. I think religion causes wars. I think the world would be better off with a unilateral philosophy of peace, love and kindness. But I live here now and church is very much the way. In England I found church boring and cold and meaningless. These days, here, I find that church is somewhere to sit and have a think, I'm alone with my thoughts and yet I'm not alone. It's also somewhere simply to be with other people – the community – because I can go days without seeing a soul, only Iain each evening for a few hours.

I sent Wendy a letter. I wrote to Joan too. There isn't a telephone at Iain's. I've heard nothing from anyone. It's as if England has slid off the map of my world.

My world, though, is You.

It sounds stupid to say that I take you everywhere with me because of course I'm helpless not to. But I mean I'm never not aware and tuned in to you. Everything I see I describe to you; whatever I'm planning to do I tell you, too. I'll explain how to cook Mrs Buchanan's recipes, how to crumble up the butter against the flour for pastry, how to make oatcakes. I've described for you every step of our walks. In the house I ask you if you'd like a little Robbie Burns. Out on the road, I'll tell you 'nearly there, we're nearly there' when I have to get off the bicycle and walk the steep parts and then I promise you that we'll go to Mary Munro's Chip Shop when we get there.

You're a night owl, doing cartwheels all evening and nudging me awake when I want to go to sleep. It's like you're saying 'Be with me! be with me!' I tell you about the weather as soon as I'm awake even though I sense you're still asleep. We know each other off by heart.

All this newness is our *newness. I'll say look! a seal! We've learned the difference between the Atlantic grey seals with their roman noses and the harbour seals with their splotches and their gentler, dog-like heads. If Iain asks me about my day, I tell him about what we've done. We* think *we saw a Golden Eagle, I told him last week. He told us this: if you only 'think' you have, 'twas probably a buzzard. You'll know when it's an eagle, aye, he said.*

But today we did see our eagle. I was so awe-struck that I called out to it. Hey! Hey! You'd been asleep but suddenly you were awake, jiggling around inside me. We both waved at the bird, you and I. She was wheeling and soaring and with just a tilt of a wing feather she was slicing fast through the air, controlling the wind, flying for the thrill of flying, heading without a care to wherever she wanted to go.

And I said to you, I said to you this: see all that strength and that freedom? See the confidence she has in herself? See how she makes her way to where she needs to be? See how she can move so fast or stay so still? See how she makes all her own choices? See how she flies for the sheer joy of it?

I said:
That is what I want for you.
That is what I hope you'll find.
This is how I hope you'll be.

That's what I said to you, Little Wing.

Nell

Al had nothing for her other than a warm smile the next morning but Nell knew it would have been unrealistic to hope for more. Just knowing she had an assistant made her mission seem not quite so overwhelming now. She wondered whether she should phone England – someone, anyone – but the scant signal relieved her of the obligation. If they were not missing her, it would assuage any guilt of her not missing any of them. Of course she could use the landline in her room, but today she wanted to be out and about, following footsteps, picking up leads. She walked the short distance to Tarbert briskly, her head up, attempting eye contact with strangers and discovering that smiles and nods were readily given. The main grocer's seemed like a very good starting point but the sales assistant was around her own age.

'I'm sorry to trouble you – I just wondered if anyone else works here?'

The assistant looked confused. 'There's Mrs MacDonald who works part-time – and young David who works Saturdays.'

Nell took a moment. 'And Mrs MacDonald – she's——?'

'Part-time.'

'She's – older?'

'I'm sorry?'

'I need someone older than us. Than you. Anyone, really.'

'Is it a medical matter?' she asked Nell covertly. Not often that someone came in with a query like that. Usually they came in wanting to talk about a verruca, an opinion on nits, to know whether they should pop this blister or let it do its thing. Sometimes they came in red in the face, looking at their shoes, and mumbled intricate synonyms. But what was it, then, that afflicted this English girl much her own age, that only the older generation could help?

'No,' said Nell. 'Not really. Sort of.' She looked around hastily and picked up a lip balm and some herbal pastilles. 'Um – just these.'

'Shall I tell Mrs MacDonald you were looking for her?'

But the door had closed behind Nell's answer, if indeed she'd given one.

So, which café to choose? She fully intended to visit each before she headed home next Tuesday. Nell opted for the one nearest, ordered tea from a teenage waitress and gazed thoughtfully at the older woman, busy with her crumb-collecting, behind the counter. It was an excellent brew but after one sip Nell left her table.

'Everything OK with your tea?'

'Did you know a girl called Florence Lawson? About thirty years ago?' Nell's words came out in a tumble and the woman looked befuddled. 'The tea is amazing,' Nell said. 'But—?'

'Do I know who?'

Nell sighed. The sentences came out by rote. 'She was sixteen and she came here in 1969. Her name was Florence Lawson.'

'Florence Lawson you say?'

'Yes! Did you know her?'

'Where did she live, Florence Lawson?'

'In Harris!'

The woman's expression softened. 'Do you have an address? Not all of Harris live in Tarbert.'

Nell could see the problem. She shook her head. 'I only know that she must've arrived in 1969.'

''69.'

'Yes.'

'Florence Lawson.'

'Yes.'

'But you don't know where in Harris she lived.'

'No.'

These weren't questions; the woman was just stating the facts that Nell had dispensed. There was more, of course there was, but just then Nell felt reluctant to mention Florence's pregnancy, as if aspersions might be cast. To reveal that actually, she was Florence's daughter just made the whole thing sound unhinged.

'I wasn't here, back then. I'm from South Uist – I came here in 1974, when I married.'

'Oh.'

'I've been here ever since and I'd know anyone from 1974 onwards, but your Miss Lawson – before my time, dear.' She watched Nell's shoulders slump. 'Will I refresh your tea? It'll be cold now. Let me make you a hot cup. Looks like you need it.'

Nell sipped gratefully, looking out of the window at the comings and goings at the pier. Someone, somewhere, must know something. The name Florence Lawson had to ring a bell, even if muffled. Nell thought, if I was here for longer, I could put a notice up in the newsagent, in a local paper. But she had only four more days.

'You should try at Leverburgh too.'

Nell jotted it down in her notepad.

'Any news?' Al greeted her, halting his conversation with a whiskery old boy.

Nell shook her head. 'Any news at your end?'

'I'm sorry,' said Al. 'Nothing yet.'

It was ridiculous the amount Nell had brought with her, but she had packed for all eventualities. Just because there was no hint of Florence in Tarbert, there had to be signs elsewhere and that, Nell told herself, was why she'd lugged her walking boots and all this other waterproof stuff. That afternoon, she decided, she'd drive off in the little hire car and work her way along the few roads which traversed the island like veins on a hand. She spread the map out on the bed, drew her finger down the main road she'd taken from Stornoway to Tarbert. Should she head into South Harris and if so, branch off to the east of the island or stay on the road as it tracked to the west? Nell had seen pictures in the guidebooks of the stunning beaches along the Atlantic coast but Florence hadn't come here for a holiday and neither had she. She'd also read about the Bays on the east side, to where islanders had been expelled during the Clearances, having to survive on the thin soil of the rocky and torn coast of jagged inlets. Was that where Florence was sent, as some sort of penance? Nell tapped the map with her fingertip. It seemed to call to her. That's where she'd head.

'I'm going east to the Bays,' she announced to Al, as if embarking on an epic expedition. 'And I'm going to follow the Golden Road.'

Al chuckled. She made it sound so exotic. 'So called because of its expense,' he explained. 'It's not an easy drive – but it's rewarding, aye.' He helped himself to her map. 'The views of Skye from here.' He pointed, shaking his head. 'Unbelievable. Have you been to Skye?'

Nell didn't want to chat, it was almost midday and she wanted to get going. 'No,' she said. She tried to take her map back.

'Aye, you'll want to visit Skye at some point,' he said. He was putting his glasses on and her map was all his. 'You know they filmed *2001: A Space Odyssey* along here?' He tapped at the map. She didn't. He drew breath dramatically. 'You'll see why.' He handed it back to her thoughtfully. 'And you'll have heard of the whalebacks?' She hadn't. 'Aye. You'll see.'

He watched her go; her anorak looked like it had seen better days. It was dull in areas where the waterproofing had gone, creased and cracked across the back, its hood hanging thin and misshapen. It was old and cheap. They didn't make them like that any more; they used performance material now, concealed zips, ergonomically shaped and taped hems and cuffs, breathable fabric in crucial places and you paid, aye, you paid high for them now. Al thought she looked ill at ease in her walking boots, as if she'd bought them for one rugged holiday and they'd been back in their box ever since. He'd guess she lived in a city, that one. And he didn't think she was in the film business if she didn't know about *2001: A Space Odyssey* being filmed right here. He no longer thought that she was a detective of any sort – she seemed too soft. And she didn't know how to find this Florence Lawson. Nor, he feared, did he.

Never had Nell been frightened by a landscape but she was now and the emotion was rather thrilling. This was a coast created by some sort of extreme elemental violence; prehistoric rocks sheared off, spliced and thrashed at by Ice Age glaciers; bays and inlets sharp and tattered that had endured millennia being ravaged by the sea. The whalebacks, Nell came to see, were the vast boulder humps breaking through the ground. Everywhere, there was a pervading melancholy. A fair few houses stood empty and occasionally a rusted car or disintegrating boat slowly being absorbed into the landscape. It struck Nell that if it was hard to live along here in the twenty-first century for those who chose to do so, what had it been like for those with no alternative during the Clearances? Was this where Florence ended up? Negotiating perilous terrain, hands on her belly, protecting unborn Nell? Craving stability in a house that sat uneasily on its precarious plot? Had her mother navigated the ankle-twisting trudge along the tracks which clung, almost desperately, to the coastline? Had Florence stood, as Nell stood now, looking down on the swell of seaweed choke heaving in the inlets, gazing over the sea to Skye? Did her mother automatically sing 'Speed Bonny Boat' to herself, just as Nell was doing?

Was this where I was born? In a brave little cottage like that – in this stone-hard lunar landscape?

A few miles on, she came to a small gallery in a valiantly renovated cottage with a sign for refreshments. It was open and Nell stopped. She felt rattled. The cake, though, came in a large wedge and the tea was strong and served by the mug. The proprietors were happy for her to sit, lost in thought, cupping the mug, long after its contents were finished. Quietly, it was refilled.

'I love these paintings,' Nell said in a sudden rush. 'Did you do them? And I'm wondering if you can help me. I'm looking for someone. Her name was Florence Lawson. She came to Harris in 1969. A teenager.'

'Florence Lawson?'

Nell anticipated the answer before it was given.

'Sorry – no. I don't know that name.'

She walked, scrambled, tentatively for a couple of miles but the weather was glowering and so she returned to the car and sat there while fat drops of rain soon obscured the view from the windscreen. She had planned to go on to Leverburgh but, just then, she saw little point. Instead, she listened to the radio as if it was the most normal thing to do: to sit in a stationary car in the middle of nowhere looking for someone who appeared not to want to be found.

Back in Tarbert, the rain had stopped and a ferry had come in and the small town bustled. Boat fumes and clangs and chatter and traffic, visitors arriving and locals returning; hire cars, a coach and a few vans laden with the prosaic requirements of the islanders. It was a tonic to be amongst mundane human activity after the drama and isolation of the landscape she'd just left.

'Miss?'

If the tweed shop was open, maybe she would buy the cushion cover.

'Hey!'

And perhaps she'd have something other than fish and chips tonight.

A hand gently on her shoulder. 'Miss?'

It was the shop assistant from the morning, next to her, an older woman with rock-dark eyes and wire-grey hair twisted into a modest bun.

'I said it was you,' she said. 'I said it was you! Even under all that!' She gestured at Nell's anorak. 'This is the Mrs MacDonald who works part-time. She was in to town, to the shops, and I saw her. And then I spied you.'

Mrs MacDonald regarded Nell quizzically, her mouth giving a little twitch every now and then. She was not the type to covet attention and she appeared uneasy as to why she was wanted. The ferry honked and a car horn sounded and a group of lads laughed raucously as they passed. Measuredly, Nell gave out her hand and spoke.

'I'm Nell Hartley,' she said and she took a beat. 'My mother came here when she was sixteen.' Mrs MacDonald's eyes startled. 'She was unmarried. Her name was Florence Lawson. She was pregnant with me. 1969.'

The woman regarded Nell for some time, tipped her head and looked at her unblinkingly whilst leafing back through over thirty years of memories. In 1969 she was sixteen too, at school up in Stornoway.

'Lawson, you say?'

'Yes. Florence Lawson?'

She shook her head and shrugged. She vaguely remembered a Buchanan, but not a Lawson. 'I'm sorry – I don't remember anyone of that name.'

Mrs MacDonald and the shop assistant watched the anorak deflate as the shoulders holding it up gave way a little.

'I'm so sorry,' Mrs MacDonald said again. 'I can ask around for you?'

'Please do,' said Nell. 'I'm staying up at the hotel. Until Tuesday.'

'Have you asked at the medical centre – it's back up there? They'll have records. They're sure to know.'

The surgery was closing but Nell knocked and pressed her hands in prayer at the window. The receptionist let her in and listened intently. She was a similar age to Nell and apologized profusely for the fact that she wasn't going to be much use to her at all because the surgery was bound by Hippocratic oaths and patient confidentiality. But she put her finger to her lips and left Nell watching her as she nimbly flicked through files in a steel cabinet, then tripped her fingers over old brown folders in a long dark-wood box. She came back to the desk and whispered to Nell.

'No Lawson. No Florence.'

'Will you ask around, please? I'd be so grateful.'

'Oh aye, of course I will! I hope you find her before you go. Try Leverburgh too.'

Al, again, only had a smile for her the next morning.

'I asked five people yesterday,' she told him, 'between here and Rodel. I asked in shops and cafés and at the medical centre. But no one could shed any light.'

'Ah – but they'll each ask around.'

'I hope so,' said Nell. She faffed around in her knapsack for her map, which she then crinkled out in front of her.

'And where are you off to today?'

The anorak was tied by the arms around her waist and she'd tucked her jeans into her walking socks which frilled over the tops of her boots.

'Today I'm going to go west – to Hushinish.'

'That's no bad idea. The beach at the end – you might find people taking a walk. Or you might not. They might be happy to talk. Or maybe they won't. But you'll not regret the journey, either way.'

'And you'll keep asking – here?'

'Aye, Nell. *Florence Lawson*. I'm asking around.'

In weather that changed from season to season within moments, Nell drove into North Harris again but now took the smaller road west to the Hushinish peninsula. Under the watch of An Cliseam and the other high hills, she navigated cautiously through the twisting single-track road which rose and fell and switched back in unpredictable cambers. A sweeping glen kept peace between the competing peaks down which burns sped over rock and moor. The scenery in this part was rugged and expansive, soaring and monumental; there was a stern but gracious benevolence unfolding with the rhythm of the hills in contrast to yesterday's pervasive melancholy and bleakness. The route was not without its sudden surprises; the old whaling station with its unbefitting terracotta chimney and, a mile or so further on, a lone tennis court positioned so defiantly in its remoteness that Nell saw no incongruity and she batted questions at herself.

Who'd be mad enough to play there?

I would.

Where the hell am I?

In the middle of nowhere.

Is any of this a good idea?

Time will tell.

Will I find someone who knows something, anything, today?

You have to believe that you will.

Would my mum – would Wendy – want me making this journey?

Hard to tell.

Would she want me burrowing for information she's kept from me?

Will I even tell her where I've been?

Has she even noticed my absence?

And then.

Would Florence want me here?

And then.

Did Florence even want to be found?

Between Nell's thoughts and her better judgement, the volley of questions went unreturned.

And then there was a castle, quite literally, in the middle of the road. Standing so steadfast in such an extraordinary location, it super-elevated the landscape that Nell had thought couldn't be bettered. The narrow road passed by its front door while a busy stream tumbled its way gregariously over boulders as it cut its chattering path to the sea. It was all so unexpected, so peculiarly fairy-tale, that it brought her out of her thoughts abruptly and into the day. There was an archway under which the road continued and Nell parked up. She emerged into fast weather, which was coming in sighs of sunshine and growls of sudden cloud that spat short, sudden rain like insults.

Would the laird come charging out with deerhounds and a rifle if she walked too close? The windows were right there! But however tempted she was to nose, she was also compelled to keep a respectful distance. Had it not been for two other cars and the warning signs about walking the hills in stalking season, she could have believed that she was the first person ever to have come across it. But just look at it all! How Nell wished she had Danny and Rachel and AJ and Alex and Sanjay and Libby here right now, in their quirky crocodile formation topped by Debbie, tailed by Nell. What would they make of it? At once, she saw her surroundings with the wonder they would and for the first time since leaving home she smiled broadly. Even if she found no trace of Florence, Nell was here in this very moment. A seductive kiss from the sun and a bolshie shove from the wind proved it, as she stood her ground near the dancing water while a castle watched her back.

She found a door ajar to a small shop of sorts set within the castle's outbuildings. It was unmanned, just an honesty box and a surprising array of fine, locally sourced food. Nell thought of all the fish and chips she'd eaten. She took an apple, a bottle of water and some oatcakes, put coins in the box and went back to the stream, cajoled by a lengthy break in the clouds. There was no one around, no one to help with her mission but, just then, all of that was irrelevant. If nothing else, this would be what she could take home with her, this justified the trip, this poured value into every moment spent under a mountain, by a castle at the water's edge.

It was therefore with some reluctance that Nell finally left to continue her drive to Hushinish; her way hampered a few miles on by a small herd of highland cattle that were quite happy not moving. She turned her engine off and one by one the cattle came to inspect her; wearing their horns like crowns, a shy curiosity peeping through their flaxen shaggy fringes. And she thought, I'm on an island thrust out into the Atlantic surrounded by creatures from *Dr Dolittle*. And she thought, Mum – do you remember Whipsnade? Even though we have a zoo on our doorstep, you insisted on Whipsnade? Do you remember how you stopped the car though the signs told us not to, because you said you needed to talk to the monkeys? And I was terrified? One starting fiddling with the windscreen wiper and you tapped the window gently and wagged your finger, tut-tutting and calling it a cheeky little bugger.

'I remember,' Nell told a cow staring at her through the window. 'I remember being terrified that the monkeys would pull the car apart. They were everywhere, cackling and thumping. They looked wholly vicious. But my mum said, oh hush, Nell! We're chosen! Can't you see? She said, monkeys are a superior form of human being and don't let the church or the science teachers tell you differently.'

The cattle ambled off, their pace so passive it almost made a mockery of their wild horns and untamed coats. Perhaps she was the leader, that one over there; the chieftain of her clan. Perhaps she was giving Nell her seal of approval to travel on because she didn't take her herd away, just to one side so she could pass.

'I thought my mum had magic powers that day,' Nell said. 'She talked with the animals and kept me safe. One of the guards told her off. Are you *mad*, he kept saying. But I thought she was very sane that day.'

And as she drove, Nell thought about Wendy and she wondered why she was here, in this beautiful, strange land searching for a mother she'd never known when her own mum was incarcerated on her own confused island.

Eventually, the road ran out at Hushinish. Nell stilled the engine and said oh my God over and over again. A swooping and deep bay where the beach was of the whitest shell sand and the sea was in bands rippling from deep navy to indigo through to ultramarine and finally a dazzling cerulean close to the shore. Nell thought it could well be mistaken for the Caribbean were it not for the wind that rocked her car and wailed through invisible gaps in the windows.

The beach was empty, not a footprint to be seen, and with her anorak inflating and her hands cupped over her ears, Nell tracked a ragged line to the shore. All her senses were accosted. The feel of the sand beneath her feet, the wind rocking her this way and that, messing with her hair, eliciting tears from her eyes and snot from her nose, the taste of salt on her lips, the sounds of water and air, the views of Taransay and South Harris over the water. Please let Florence have been here. Please let her have stood here and felt what I'm feeling now.

The sands stretched inland and she followed them through the machair to the other side of the peninsula where she stood and looked out over a deluge of tumbled pink granite to the island of Scarp. To her right, a trail led on and a couple with a dog walked towards her. This was her chance, just as Al had predicted.

'Hi! I like your dog.'

'Hello!' they said. 'You walking to Crabhadail?'

'Er – should I be?'

'You'll want to get going if you are. Bit of weather coming in.'

'What's there? How long does it take?'

'Three hours. Views. And the best beach. That's what's there.'

'Actually, I'm looking for someone.'

'Oh? We haven't seen a soul, have we, Steven? Not a soul.'

'No – I mean, I've come here to see if I can find out what happened to someone.'

'A missing person, you say?'

'Well, yes. Florence Lawson – that was her name. She came here in 1969. From England. She was sixteen. She was pregnant – with me.'

'Oh! Oh, now there's a thing! Oh my!'

'You wouldn't have known her, would you? Might it ring a bell?'

'Oh, but we're from Aberdeen, darling. We're just here on our holidays. But out here back then! Out *here*? Six*teen* you say she was? And pregnant? Oh my.'

Nell waited for the couple to disappear from sight. She had no intention of walking for three hours, no matter how beautiful some bloody beach might be. A beach is a beach is a bloody beach, she thought to herself and the black wingtips of the gannets seemed to echo the darkening of her mood. Sand and more sand and all that sea. She laughed harshly at herself. It struck her that any clues would have been washed away years ago. In its place, just sand and sea. Had Florence wanted to be found, she could have ensured it. Instead, her mother had given her secrets to the tide to carry away and her story, like footsteps in the sand, she'd left to the waves.

Dougie

It took three nights for Dougie to know exactly where he was on waking and for thoughts of his life in London to settle dreamlike, only mistily flitting across the back of his mind's eye silently and without drama. On the third morning he woke up early yet rested and felt no need to leap up, grab his trainers and pound miles. Instead, he lay in bed staring at the ceiling and felt sweeping gratitude that, no matter how often it had been repainted, the same crack always reappeared. Lazily, he followed its passage, knowing the route by heart. Just then, Dougie decided he wouldn't see cracks as something to gloss over; instead he'd find comfort in their continuity and determination. This crack never reached anywhere. It just stopped, took a little fork off towards the centre of the ceiling and then stopped again. That was its journey.

Dougie looked at his clock and said fuck me! forty minutes philosophizing about a crack along the ceiling! He told himself to haul his arse out of bed and go for a run now. But ten minutes later he was still lying there as it slowly occurred to him how he hadn't so much forgotten the pace of life here as he had actively denigrated it over the last few years. Slowly, he sat up, swung his legs out of bed and looked down at his toes scrunching into the rug. He remained doing so for quite some time, contemplating how he'd trained his brain to think that life lacked meaning if it lacked pace. He knew he'd conditioned himself to believe that to be busy was to be productive. He'd spent the last few years chasing the same goal each day: to not have the time to think. But actually, just then, it felt good to be just a little more still. His feet on the sheepskin rug. One hand on the edge of the bed, the other loosely across his knee. He tuned in to the sound of his breathing, the sensation of air in his nostrils warm cold warm cold warm. He noticed the feeling of his leg hair being pulled just slightly by his hand. Fingernails. His heartbeat. The scorch to his eye on casting a glance straight to the daylight streaming in through the window. Birdsong beyond. A creak somewhere in the house. Above his head, his lifelong friend, the ceiling crack.

Amadan gòrach, he said to himself. *Daft bugger.* Get up.

Gordon liked a hearty whistle in the mornings; it seemed to him that whistling could spin a positive note to the start of any day. And Ben seemed to enjoy it as much as he did, the dog turning circles and skittering around on the flagstones. Gordon had whistled brightly on noting Dougie's trainers were gone from the front door the first two mornings his son was home. But today they were there and there was silence upstairs and he and Ben looked at each other and agreed that they'd keep the house soundless for a wee while longer.

Footsteps across the landing. The clunk of the door. The flush of the loo. The sound of the shower. Gordon wet his lips and puckered them and found his tune. Ben found his dance. And that's what Dougie heard as he came down the stairs.

'Morning.'

'Morning.'

'Porridge?'

'Aye – thanks, Da.'

'You not off running?'

Dougie looked deep into the porridge as a fortune teller might read tea leaves. He gave a stir. Stilled the spoon. How long had he conditioned himself to believe it was better to run than to walk? To start or end the day with his heart racing? He looked across the table to Gordon. His father was wearing his mother's pinny – he always did in the kitchen, even though he was the tidiest man Dougie knew.

'Fancy a walk, Da? Will we go up Beinn Dhubh?'

Gordon thought at first that he'd misheard. 'You'll never keep up with me, son.'

Dougie spooned porridge into his mouth. 'Want to bet on that?'

Gordon smiled, gathered up the breakfast things and whistled his way over to the sink.

Watching his father stride so confidently, negotiating the boggy terrain to the vast slabs of the ascent, it struck Dougie how much bigger his father looked here. This was the man he remembered, not the small man shrouded in a coat against the cold in a slump on his doorstep last week. Here he looked right; in the city he'd looked all wrong. In London, Dougie had felt his father to be embarrassing. On the hill, today, he felt in awe and proud to be his son. Gordon was robust for his age, confident in his surroundings, at ease. Strong and invincible. Dougie thought that those two adjectives were what every father should aspire to and what every son should see. They walked almost shoulder to shoulder, Dougie mindful for Gordon to lead.

Gordon had noticed that Dougie had brought his camera. Nothing unusual about that. What was unfamiliar was walking a good two hours without a single photo being taken. He glanced at his son, all that hair flopping around the place, flicking at his eyes, catching in his mouth. The lad tended to tie it back when he was in the still house yet let it fly wild in the open. *Amadan gòrach.*

'Loch a Siar not good enough for you?' Gordon chuckled darkly.

'Huh?'

'Views not what they were?'

'Da?'

'Sea a bit nothingy, is it? Sunlight wanting?'

'What are you going on about?'

'Your camera, Douglas.'

Dougie laughed. 'I forgot I had it with me.'

'Like your mother—'

'—with her handbag!'

'Took it everywhere. Took it upstairs and back downstairs too.'

'Took it to the beach.'

'Took it to the end of the garden. She took that thing everywhere. Said *you'll bury me with this bag.*'

Ahead, a slab of stone roared up from the heather and Gordon sat while Dougie stood, hands on hips, his face to the sun, breathing in sweet air, his eyes closed. When he opened them his father was munching on oatcakes. He sat down beside him and, as he ate, he wondered what it was in the air that changed the flavour from its perfunctory norm on a plate at the kitchen table to some kind of delicious and energizing manna. The stone beneath him was that ageless contradiction of hardness and warmth. And Dougie thought if I could be only one place in the world with only one food ever to eat, it would be right here with these oatcakes. He took another to keep the concept alive a little longer.

'Did it strip it?' Gordon wanted to know. 'College? Your job? Is that what happened to the pleasure, the passion?'

Though he knew exactly what his father meant, Dougie gave it space before he answered with a shrug.

'I don't know,' he said quietly and he thought about it some more. 'When I'm looking, when I'm seeing, it's a sensation. I feel my eyes focus in on the subject, assess the light, find the form and understand the spaces, sense the sides you can't see. The camera takes it one step further. It stills it all. If it captures anything, it captures a dimension that's hidden.'

Dougie could feel Gordon looking at him. His answer was erudite but it wasn't what his father was looking for, he knew that.

'It has to start with the eye,' Dougie persevered. 'Not gadgetry.'

And he wondered, do I sound like a bit of a prick?

'And you get all this, do you?' Gordon asked. 'When you photograph the hidden forces of a wheelbarrow? For a *catalogue*? You experience all those complex things about light and form when you photograph models in bad clothes for mail order? You sense the sides you cannot see – you attain that stillness?'

Dougie started to laugh partly because he knew his dad was being quite serious and it was unsettling. 'It's a *job*, Da,' he shrugged. 'The money is good.'

'That's an excuse,' Gordon said, 'and in the long run, it'll cost you more than it pays you.'

Dougie didn't like where the conversation was going precisely because he had no idea of its path. Usually, he and his father conversed so benignly, avoiding contention. It wasn't their style to chatter either, that had been his mother's speciality and oh, how she could draw it out of him and Gordon. Today it was uneven, uncharted ground. Dougie didn't like it. More so because it appeared his father knew where he was headed.

'Don't scupper your gifts, laddie. Pursuing an easy life will tire you out far more quickly.'

They sat in silence, Gordon's words settling on the heather before the wind picked them up and swirled around the two of them. Today there was an edge to his father's voice that Dougie seldom heard. He wasn't sure how to acknowledge it.

'Or is it because of what happened?' Gordon said very carefully. 'Back then? That business?'

Dougie answered this by not moving an inch.

'Because that's a long time done, Douglas,' Gordon said. 'You have this gift, God-given, of capturing and magnifying what so few of us have the ability to see. Use it.' He took a beat. 'You are built of stronger stuff than to be captive to old memories.'

Dougie looked away.

'Well,' said Gordon. 'All this sitting around is no good for old bones.' He clapped his hands against his legs, stood and set off at his hearty pace, climbing on.

As a kid, Dougie had rarely needed cautioning or disciplining. He'd always been a good lad, never easily swayed, naturally kind, ever motivated. A boy who'd take himself off for a run in the wilds then be home and laying the table without being asked, who'd respond to his name being called just the once, who'd notice if help was needed, who rarely provoked a raised voice. But, just then, Dougie felt the sting of reprimand, of his father's frustration, and he sat alone on the rock waiting for his head to make sense of the discomfort.

How could his father be right about this one? Dougie had long felt a gentle and private superiority after leaving home, leaving the island for a different country altogether. He was the one who'd got a degree, who'd travelled extensively, who was paid well in his job and could afford rent that would make his father reel in disbelief. Were not these the accoutrements of savvy living in the modern age?

'I'm the one living in the real world,' Dougie said out loud, looking down at his boots and the quivering heather.

But.

How had his father worked it all out before Dougie had?

Dougie knew it was true. He got paid for what he did. But he got nothing from it. He'd sought out a career which did not require him to look or see or focus. The gadgetry could do all of that. What he did, he felt nothing for. The photographs he took these days brought him no stillness. Just an easy numbness. He knew it and yet he hadn't truly seen it until his father had pointed it out by pointing at heather, at the water, at the sky. Dougie looked at his camera. It had not captured feeling or depth for years and years.

And yet.

Was he not a paid photographer?

Had he not made a life for himself?

Were not all the decisions his own?

'Have I not earned the right to choose what I look at and what I don't? What I decide to feel, what I choose to forget?'

Still the heather shivered in the wind and Dougie stood and stomped it down underfoot. But it sprang back. It always did. His father was now just a blue Gore-Tex smidge, marching his way through all the barren beauty that his son had turned a blind eye to for so many years.

Dougie was tempted to go the other way. He was also tempted to sprint a vindictive route and get to the trig point and the cairn before Gordon. But thoughts careened through his mind without purchase and the more they tumbled away from him, the less steady he felt. He tracked his father cautiously, unsure of what he'd say when he reached him. Perhaps he could explain in detail, but that wasn't their way. He could lay out his secrets in front of his dad; like a road map of his life, jab his finger at the crossroads and dead ends of the past fifteen years. But he wouldn't. Maybe he'd just say he was going to leave the next day.

The view, anyway. The view after the final push to the top. Taransay. Beinn Losgaintir. The Harris hills. The sands. The Atlantic. Father and son standing quietly alongside each other, attempting to absorb the vast beauty that flooded their eyes.

'You can't put that in a photograph,' Dougie said quietly. And he knew the truth of it was that when he had stopped looking, he'd squandered almost everything.

Jessie is now certainly my friend.

We meet up midway on the Bealach Creag an Eoin – or am Bealach, the Coffin Trail. It's the old road that links the Bays where Jessie lives on the east, with where I live on the west. I like Jessie's Gàidhlig *name for it because it sounds moody and romantic, but the truth is darker: when the islanders were banished to the east coast from their fertile land on the west during the Clearances it was too rocky and the soil was too thin there to bury their dead so they'd walk the coffin back to the west coast along this route.*

I've been there – to Jessie's. Hers is a happy home, scampering with siblings and dogs. But it makes me pleased to be on the west. Her landscape glowers and wails with the rocks and the drops and the serrated bays. She likes it well enough though she says she'll leave when she can.

'Everyone leaves,' Jessie told me. 'All the young. There's no jobs here. There's just—' And she waved her hand around at the island like she was swatting midges. 'There's just – this. All this island and nothing on it.'

'What'll you do, though? Where'll you go?'

'I don't know. Have you heard of Sussex University? It's meant to be very groovy there.'

I told her I had. I told her that I quite wanted to go there myself, at one time, when I thought I might be a writer not an artist.

'I don't know if I'm clever enough,' she said.

'Oh, you're bright all right,' I told her.

'Or Liverpool University – because of the You Know Whos.'

She makes me laugh, my friend. She calls the Beatles the You Know Whos like she's taking the Lord's name in vain if she doesn't.

'If I don't get a place, maybe the Merchant Navy – like so many from here. But I don't have sea legs though. Maybe I'll jump ship at Liverpool and find a job at the Cavern Club. Did Jimi Hendrix play there ever?'

'1966,' I tell her.

'You're an encyclopaedia of modern music, so you are, Flora Buchanan.'

Not really.

We meet twice a week, usually. We don't have telephones so I can't phone her like I could Joan. When we see each other we just say, same time Thursday or same time Monday. The route is only four miles end to end but it's a slog because I'm bigger now. It also feels longer because the changes in the landscape are so stark, like walking through one land into another. When I set out, I think of Jessie setting out too, and then the walk isn't as intimidating, as lonely as it might feel otherwise. We have our favourite boulder that is pretty much halfway and we usually share carrots or a slice of cake or some bread and butter. And there we sit, my friend and I, chatting or singing our music. Jessie loves a boy called Lachlan McCrae. I said to her, your parents will worry I'm a bad influence on you. And Jessie said ach, not a bit of it.

I worry that her mum and dad won't want her being friends with someone like me but she said they don't disapprove of me. Quite the opposite, she said. She told me they feel for me and the wee bairn.

Today was proof. We met on our rock – I brought two slices of Mrs Buchanan's jam sponge that I made yesterday and Jessie had a bag with her.

'These are for you.'

But it wasn't carrots.

Inside was a woven shawl in patterns of gentle cream and pale grey and golden honey. Very soft. And inside that, little miniature clothes. Baby clothes.

I didn't know what to say. I was flabbergasted by their tininess.

'They are for you – for when the baby comes. This one – I wore this.'

It was a cotton nightie, with a yellow duck embroidered and a little frill around the wrists.

'This one – this was my wee brother Glen's.'

It, too, was white cotton, with three embroidered fish: blue, green and turquoise.

'My granny did the needlework.'

There was also a bonnet and a cardigan, hand-knitted, the colour of butter. There were muslin squares and terry nappies and a dozen safety pins with white safety caps, all clipped onto one very long one. They reminded me of birds sitting on a wire.

I didn't know what to say. I hadn't thought about any of this, about clothes for You. That you will be so tiny as to fit them, so real as to fill them.

Sometimes I gladly forget that you can't stay ripening inside me for ever. Sometimes it's a bit too much to consider that you will appear, in just over three months' time.

I didn't know what to say because I was scared as well as too choked at the kindness of it.

'Och, don't go crying, Flora Buchanan – you'll start me off.'

I put Jessie's hand on my belly so she could feel you wriggle.

We sat like that for a while. Not a cloud and the breeze was gentle, warm, it lifted Jessie's hair revealing all the freckles on her forehead which I'm sure I saw multiply before my eyes.

'What's it like?' she asked.

'Oh,' I said, 'it's like butterflies. Or imagine a bunny getting comfy in a burrow.'

'No,' she said quietly. 'The – intercourse, I mean. The sex.'

I had to think about it carefully because I constantly shy away from memories of my old life, that night in particular. So I sat in the sunshine on our rock and I thought about the party and the delicious punch and the tiptoeing upstairs, hand in hand with the handsome boy who said relax, baby, relax.

I put my hand over Jessie's over you.

'I wish I hadn't done it,' I whispered. 'And I wish it hadn't been with him.'

My tear dropped onto my hand and we looked at it as we might a crystal ball.

'Don't go upsetting yourself,' Jessie said and she put her arm around my shoulder.

I looked at Jessie. 'Sometimes,' I told her, 'sometimes I'm so scared I can't breathe. Sometimes I'm so upset I can't cry. Other times, though, I'm so at peace, so excited that I float above the world.'

'I wonder if it's a boy or a girl,' Jessie said.

'I don't know how it's going to get out,' I said because just then the thought dawned on me for the first time.

'Same way as it got in,' she said.

'I know that – but. I just don't know how an entire baby is going to get out.'

I started to cry again. 'Is it going to hurt? Will everything be OK?'

I didn't expect Jessie to have the answers but these were questions I couldn't exactly ask Iain.

'Well,' she said. 'We were all born at home and certainly it sounds like it hurts. I've heard my mother cry and holler and bellow like a cow and pant like a dog – but there's the joy and peace that follow so quickly and that carries louder and for longer.' She looked at me quizzically. 'Can't be that bad,' she said. 'After me she went on and had another four. Have you not seen the nurse yet?'

'The nurse? No?'

'Aye – you'll want to see the nurse.'

'How will I find her?'

Jessie laughed. 'Oh, she'll find you.'

And she did.

Eventually.

It took a couple more meetings on our boulder along am Bealach with Jessie asking if I'd seen the nurse and me shaking my head.

'You need to tell Mr Buchanan,' she said.

And it struck me then that Iain and I have not spoken once about the day I'll give birth. We just rub along in the here and now. My actual baby is as unreal to him as, currently, it is to me.

'I don't know how to,' I said and we looked at each other, worried.

But then, Iain told me that he'd spoken to Jessie's mother. He told me she'd come to the house and given him a ticking-off for not seeing to it sooner.

'I'm sorry, leannan,' Iain said to me last night. 'This is new ground for me as well as you.'

He said tomorrow you have a visitor; tomorrow you'll meet Fire.

Fire?

Mid-morning there was a knock at the door and I'd forgotten about this conversation. I thought maybe it was the postman. I opened the door and there she was. Around forty years old with her hair cut short and the most beautiful curls the colour of liquid chocolate. She wore a little hat on the back of her head and a uniform with a white collar, white cuffs, a wide belt, one of those upside-down watches and a special badge too. There was a small black car at the end of the path and I didn't know how I hadn't heard it. I had been drawing at the kitchen table, a million miles away.

'I'm Nurse Keaton,' she said. 'Some people call me Nurse Fire. As in Sophia – which is my given name. All the kiddies like to say they are playing with Fire. How should you like to call me?'

I was so flabbergasted by all of it that I just stood there, in the doorway, gawping at her.

'Well, you can decide once you know me a little better. May I come in? It's lovely to meet you – and I'd like to get to know Baby too.'

'I don't have the baby yet,' I apologized. 'I'm not due for another three months, I think.'

And she smiled. 'Oh,' she said, 'I can get to know Baby very well before then – and when it's your time we'll be quite the little team, us three.'

I was still standing in the doorway.

'May I come in?'

And just for a moment I thought if I let her in, this becomes very, very real. If I let her in then the baby will most certainly come out.

I think she's a mind reader.

'You'll be a little scared, Flora – I understand. But I have all the answers to all those questions that you'll not have asked a soul. I am your nurse. I am all yours. May I come in?'

So, took her into the kitchen and made tea.

'Did you deliver Jessie's brother wee Glen?'

'No, pet, that was Catherine – Nurse Morrison.'

'Am I to have the baby here?'

'What – here in the kitchen? And where will poor Buchanan take his evening meal!'

'I meant – or in hospital?' I was so nervous her humour had quite slipped off me.

'I know, Flora, I know – but no, you'll have your baby here at home. Just not right here in the kitchen, Iain'll never get over that.'

I took to her so quickly. She's another incomer – as we are known here. She's from Yorkshire and brimming with kindness and so upbeat. She saw my drawing on the table and she was wowed by it. I said that Jimi Hendrix's music inspires me. She loves Jimi too. She asked me what film stars I love and what I'm reading.

And would you like to see the dress I made from my friend's mum's tablecloth?

Oh yes, she said, I'd love to.

It doesn't fit me at the moment, I told her.

And she said – well perhaps it will fit me!

She did some gentle feeling, some measuring, asked me to pee, took my pulse, listened to my heart, read my blood pressure. Best of all, though, was her look of joy and excitement when she listened to you.

She says you are one bonny baby without a doubt.

She's to come every fortnight for a while, and then once a week.

I am very happy about all of it. I believe she'll know what to do because it's struck me I haven't a clue.

Jessie.

And her mother.

And Nurse Sophia Keaton.

We're being looked after, baby – you and I. We are cared for.

Every now and then little surges of excitement trample over the thudding worry.

Sunday

'Will you come to church, son?'

It was the last thing that Dougie wanted to do.

'Even if it's not your thing any more,' Gordon said, 'would you consider it today – here?'

Father and son had been cautious in each other's company since the day on the hill, not wanting to continue the conversation, but not wanting an atmosphere either. Dougie had been out running. Gordon, walking or pottering. When they were together, they walked quietly around each other and into routine conversation. Dougie cooked and Gordon cleared the dishes. Gordon cooked, Dougie washed up. They watched *Taggart*. They read peaceably in the sitting room, the tock of the clock, a wee dram, Ben's eyebrows rising from one man to the other, as though the dog was umpiring a silent game of tennis. All the while, photos of Dougie's mother on the shelves and the mantle, casting an eye.

Dougie was due home Wednesday. It hadn't been mentioned. 'Sure,' he said. 'I'll come to church.'

Nell was not used to this type of Sunday. Sunday, for Nell, was a day for doing: washing, supermarket, bookshop, menu planning. The hotel was quiet when she went for breakfast and there was no sign of Al, only the young Australian waitress.

'Gone to church, all of them,' she told Nell. 'I'm a Buddhist.'

In Tarbert, everything was shut. Nell had planned to buy the Harris Tweed cushion cover today, to pick up some souvenirs for the Chaffinch crew, whisky for Frank, some shortbread for Debbie, stock up on tablet for herself. All the while, she was going to ask about Florence, she was determined to ask anyone. Because someone somewhere must know something. But nowhere was open. The town was quiet; the sky was a still, uniform grey and the water hardly moved. Somehow it felt neither dead nor empty, just peaceful. Tomorrow was her last full day. She couldn't afford for today to yield nothing and she cursed herself for her inactivity earlier on in her trip.

Maybe she'd find people enjoying a Sunday walk. Maybe they wouldn't be from Aberdeen this time. They'd be local and, as luck would have it, maybe they'd know all about Florence. Danny's voice piped up. *Think positive*. It was one of his sayings. Think positive, he'd say if something was dropped, if they ran out of tomatoes, if there were too many customers or too few. Think positive, he'd chant to himself going to clear tables, hoping for tips. Nell passed by the medical centre, closed Sundays. Dear Danny – how she missed him just then. How were they all, her motley and colourful little bunch, a world away on another island altogether?

The hire car, a nondescript hatchback, was now as familiar to Nell as her own car at home and she saw in its headlights and radiator grille a friendly face. Come on, it said. Hop in. Let's go. She sat in the driver's seat in the car park and just traced her finger over the badge on the steering wheel. Perhaps she'd go back to the Hushinish peninsula, sit by the busying burn next to the castle, maybe the shop would be open with its honesty box. If she left now, she'd have the time to hike to Crabhadail beach. Perhaps Sunday afternoons were when the locals did their long leisure walks and she'd meet them and they'd tell her all about Florence. She looked at the map. Leverburgh. She needed to go there and ask. She could take the road from Tarbert to the west. The infinitely scenic west with the views and the most famous stretches of white shell sand. Maybe everyone goes to those beaches on the west after church on Sundays.

This was the same route that had taken her to the Golden Road but today she didn't turn off to the east, she drove on instead into a huge sky as the road burrowed along a route blasted through the colossal rock. And then into view came the unimagined beauty of the sands at Luskentyre and, beyond, the sound of Taransay. Following the sign, Nell took the single-track lane trailing the northern shore in rises and dips, bends and right angles, past the township, past a cemetery set peacefully on soft, rolling land and onwards to a car park. There were no cars. Think positive. There might be walkers.

Nell walked her way through the dunes and suddenly, stretching before her was a long and breathtaking beach. Over the water, Taransay. To the north, the Harris hills and the Hushinish peninsula. South, the sands ran on. However, apart from a convention of oystercatchers with their bright red bills and their tuxedos breaking the Sabbath busily working the shoreline, she found she was alone.

White white sand. The surface pinched by thousands of miniature pyramids sculpted by the wind. She'd walked far. And

Nell wondered, why was there no one else around? She felt utterly fed up with all the wild beauty. Why was it that everywhere she'd been had been so empty? She'd travelled for miles; she'd travelled so far. She'd got bloody nowhere. Above, the sky was starting to bruise purple and a wind was whipping from the water; the marram grass on the dunes danced into and away from it while sand was blown along the surface of the beach like a fine rolling mist. The water was turning the colour of ink and the sea now slapped rather than lapped at the shore. It was orchestral. Nell looked around; she was in the midst of deepening drama and brooding.

And then the rain. Initially the drops fell so far apart that Nell could kid herself she was imagining it. Fat splashes put paid to that before the sky opened in slices and threw down walls of water, hard and fast.

Dougie didn't mind the rain. In fact, he preferred running in the rain to harsh sunlight. And today, the wet would help wash away church. Church itself had been fine, comforting in some ways for its nostalgic scents and sounds. He'd smiled at faces known so well and not seen for so long; his favourite teacher these days stooped and grey, one of his classmates now gloriously rotund, those who had always seemed old suddenly positively ancient, those who'd been kids now grown and with families of their own. Hymns he thought he'd forgotten he found he sang word-perfect, his voice closed and reluctant at first, then shy, soon tuneful and strong. A smile from his father, watery-eyed. And on the way out, his mother's best friend Peggy.

'Is that you, Douglas?'

'Aye, Peggy.'

'Oh my! Gordon! Would you look at that! Oh my!'

And she stood on tiptoes to kiss Dougie; put her hand to his cheek and simply marvelled at the sight of him. He'd loved Peggy when he was young, with her vivaciousness that counterbalanced his mother's calm. Always stories to tell and sweets in her pocket and her wee boy who looked up to Dougie as a superhero.

'Are you here long? When did you come? Oh my! Douglas! Dougie! Angus is in Edinburgh these days – two little girls he has now!'

'Send him my best.' It was odd thinking of Angus as a father of two. And in Edinburgh too.

Peggy linked her arm through Dougie's, squeezed him close against her, on her tiptoes again, *sotto voce*.

'You here alone?'

'Aye.'

'No girl?'

'No.'

Her grasp tightened.

'Aw, Dougie!'

He knew what was coming.

'Your mother, dear soul that she was, she wanted to see you settled more than anything in the world.'

He smiled at Peggy kindly while adding a levelling in his eyes he hoped warned her to go no further.

But Peggy didn't have her glasses on.

'That terrible business,' Peggy said, shaking her head, her eyes downcast. She looked up at him and he found he could not look away. 'But that was a long time ago, Douglas. A long,

long time ago.' She gave him a little shove. 'You must move on, Douglas. Aye – you must.'

So after church, Dougie ran through the garden, over the road, though the machair and along the marram ridge. On he ran, up the dunes, down to the beach, straight through a tidal rivulet and across the further dunes, headlong into the rain, welcoming it to wash away Peggy's words. Would he ever not be known as the boy with all that terrible business? Fuck's sake. And my dad wonders why I don't come back more often! Dougie decided he'd sprint the frustration out of his system, that's what he'd do.

But Dougie didn't sprint. In the dunes above Tràigh Rosamol, the furthest stretch of sands, he stopped. It appeared he didn't have the beach to himself. There was someone else down there. A woman, on her own, pacing left a bit, right a bit. Stamping and stomping, obviously vexed. She was raising her arms and slapping them down in exasperation, grabbing her hair either side of her head and giving herself a good shake. He thought he could hear her shouting at the sea. And Dougie thought to himself, she looks how I feel. And Dougie wondered, what sort of terrible business has she encountered, then?

It wasn't because Nell was drenched that made her look so bedraggled to Al when she returned to the hotel late afternoon after a fruitless trip to deserted Leverburgh, it was her demeanour too. It was as if the stoating rain had washed the spirit quite out of her, soaking the very stuffing holding her upright and sunk it down heavy into her boots. It was still raining out there but lightly so and the sun was now spinning through the smirr. Nell, it seemed, had absorbed most of the black cloud.

'Afternoon, Nell,' Al called over. Look at you, all drookit!'

It raised a half-smile but she continued her squelch to the stairs.

'Nell – will you wait up?'

If she'd looked at Al she'd have noted the dance in his eyes, the flush to his cheeks and his broadening smile. Her head, however, was hung low.

'Say, Nell – there's someone here. Someone to meet you. I found someone who can help.'

Slowly, she turned.

'Come,' said Al. 'Please – come through to the bar.' He knew that she was soaking wet, that perhaps it would be decorous to suggest she go up to her room, dry off and change. But – all these days had passed and she was away home soon and finally, just today, finally *something*. Nell looked at him almost fearfully; she hadn't the capacity just then to wonder who or how, her mind was full of the statement that right here, in the hotel, there was someone who could help.

'Follow,' said Al. 'Come.'

She walked behind him. The bar was empty but for one man sitting with a cup of tea at the far end. He had white hair in puffs, which seamlessly blended with his beard, and round spectacles that appeared to be welded to his face. Nell thought, Father McChristmas.

'Hello.' He stood. He was huge, but soft. 'I'm Reverend Sinclair.'

'Hello,' said Nell. He motioned for her to sit and his eyes, intent on Nell, glinted with delight.

'Now,' he said, stroking his beard. 'I didn't know your mother,' he said, 'but I have for you someone who knew her very well indeed.'

Nell knew she couldn't speak, she could only hope that, in spite of her deafening heartbeat, she'd be able to hear.

'Aye,' he said, drawing himself tall and then pouring another cup of tea. He sipped thoughtfully as if calibrating the portent of the information.

'Miss Keaton,' he announced. '*Nurse* Keaton as she was then. She looked after Flora and she delivered *you*.'

Nell's shoulders dropped so heavily that her forehead bounced down to the surface of the table. She found she could not lift her head. 'But my mother's name was Florence.' Her voice hoarse, flat, hampered by the tired choke of tears. '*Florence Lawson.*'

A hand on her shoulder. A gentle squeeze. 'That's as may be,' Reverend Sinclair said, 'but *here* she was only ever known as Flora.'

Nell lifted her head, which was so heavy with information and so besieged with emotion she could do so only slowly.

'She was known here as Flora Buchanan,' he continued. 'On account of Iain Buchanan – God rest him – who took her in.'

The name Buchanan rang a distant bell, but it was too muffled for Nell to hear clearly.

'Anyway, young lady – it's Sophia Keaton you'll be wanting to meet. And I've phoned her already and she's wanting to speak to you too.'

'The nurse?'

'Aye – your mother's nurse.' Father McChristmas with his sing-song voice and his happy eyes and his kindly face. '*Your* nurse.'

Nell's voice gave up; she took her hand to her neck and tried to ease the pain of the welling emotion constricting her throat. An oily tear crowded her eye until it slid hot and fast down her cheek.

'Aw, m'darling,' said Al, who'd been sitting there all the while, agog.

'Tomorrow,' said Reverend Sinclair. 'You're to meet each other tomorrow.'

'Where?' Nell asked.

'She lives in Scalpay,' Al told her. 'It's another island.'

'Another island? But I have to leave the day after tomorrow.'

'Well,' said Al, 'it's a good job we built a bridge linking Harris and Scalpay eight years ago, then. We must've known you'd come one day.'

Will you keep me waiting?

Six weeks until we say hello, a month and a half until I see your real face. Mid-September when everything – everything – will change. Terror and excitement are my bedfellows at night while panic and calm take my hand by day. It's exhausting, all these feelings. It's exhausting carrying you – Nurse Keaton says you're bonny. I think that's a tactful way of saying big.

If I think of England Essex Colchester, I don't think of it as 'back home' any longer. I've written to Wendy and Joan and told them that they must come to visit – and I realize that it's not because I miss them so actively any more, but that I'd like to show them around, to show them where I live, to see the wonder on their faces, to introduce them to the people here who are my friends. Jessie and Nurse Keaton. And Morag from the shop. And of course Iain. I dream of George coming to stay – how I'd love to sit quietly while he and Iain are in the same room. But George won't come; my mother will make it impossible. I doubt, really, that Wendy will, either. She'll be all married now and skipping around a new home with Jimmy. I can imagine her so clearly in all her bonkers glory and Jimmy coming home to chaos and cocktails and his wife, my sister, wafting about throwing kisses like confetti and serving banquets for two of goodness only knows what.

Joan won't come for a while yet. Her mother wouldn't have it and she has no money anyway. She replies to my letters with whole novels. They must take so long to write which is why I hardly ever receive them.

Joan and Jessie. They'd like each other. They'd like each other on account of me being the common denominator because actually they aren't alike at all.

I love Jessie.

All through July we've spent so much time together, whole days on picnic blankets in the machair, while the meadow pipits, stonechats and skylarks sing. We try to count how many types of flower, making up names for those we don't know.

Wee pinkypoo.

Shyface.

Blue blink.

White ghosty girl.

Peaches and cream.

We mimic the birdsong, very badly. We paddle in the water and nod at the seals and wave at the dolphins. We go through list after list of names for You.

Anna. Rebecca. Lucy. Emma. Marion. Jeannette. Rennie.

David. Daniel. Alfred. Harold. Nathan. Jack. Michael. Antony.

JohnPaulGeorgeRingo.

Jimi.

Mainly, though, we loll, Jessie and I. We just take to our blankets and loll all day. There's eighteen hours of daylight at the moment. Jessie's mother says God doesn't give us days like these to ignore. Jessie's arms are so freckled, her face so rosy and her nails and her neat little teeth gleam. My skin has turned nut brown and we both have gold in our hair. We've pulled out strands to compare. Identical. We share secrets and dreams, Jessie and I. She's not in love with Lachlan now; her affections have returned to Murdo whom she's known since she was a girl, who's back from the Merchant Navy for a little while. He's been to Australia and Canada and New Zealand. He told Jessie she wouldn't believe what's out there. I've tried to tell her it's not that big a deal – that back in Essex I had no idea what was out here.

We talk about the news. Apollo 11 landed and Neil Armstrong walked on the moon. Brian Jones from the Rolling Stones died. John

Lennon and Yoko Ono were holidaying in Scotland but had to go to hospital after they crashed their car. There's terrible rioting going on in Northern Ireland. Jessie likes to hear, over and again, how I marched for peace and freedom for all. What is London like? she wonders. And all those people on a protest, she marvels, how many people does 200 feel like? And when I tell her make that 20,000 her jaw drops in awe and disbelief. But I know that London would swallow her up. She'd hate it.

Jessie and I practise what we'd say if we met the You Know Whos. I asked her to choose between Murdo and George Harrison and she said, Flora Buchanan, what are you like! I have come to realize that, actually, I'm far more at ease being Flora Buchanan then ever I was being Florence Lawson.

And You. We talk mostly about You. We watch my belly undulate, pucker and poke when you let it be known that you're awake and playful. We talk to you and we sing to you and we tell you how we just cannot wait until we meet you.

Iain has been spending quite a lot of time on the mainland at the moment. I'm still not sure how the stinky slither that is seaweed can be so desirable or profitable but our alginate industry is the second largest in the world.

See — I said 'our'.

Thank goodness for Nurse Keaton. From a glance she can tell how I'm feeling and knows what to say. She's very impressed with You. She says I'll know what to do.

I don't. I don't know what to do. I'm going to get this all wrong.

I told her this yesterday, crying my eyes out. She tipped her head to one side and watched me as I paced about. I won't know what to do, I told her. I don't want it to come out. I don't know about being a mother.

I'm. Too. Young.

I'm. Too. Stupid.

I'm. Too. Scared.

Nonsense, she said and she can say 'nonsense' in a way that is both kind and an order. She said I may be young but I am not stupid and that I've nothing to be scared of. She says I'm in the safest hands and in the best place in the world. She said I WILL know what to do. She said that she'll be here, every step of the way, when my time comes.

Nurse Keaton says I'm dead brave. She says I'm the bravest young woman she's ever met.

Less than one month to go now.

I sleep sitting up because you're such a bonny baby that it feels like you're in every nook and cranny, there's not much room for anything else and the acid has been pushed right up into my chest. Jessie's mum says it's a sign that you'll have a full head of hair. Nurse Keaton laughed like a drain and said it's only gastric reflux and that Vidal Sassoon needn't book his ticket to Harris just yet.

There was a ceilidh in Tarbert last night after the Agricultural Fair. Oh, I loved the fair! The sheep that are usually all scraggy were puffed up and snowy white, their little black faces proud as punch. And the cows – or coos as I'm to call them these days – all the colours of caramel and toffee and liquorice, their fringes fluffy and their horns gleaming. There was a tug of war and food galore and ponies and tractors and best of all, the pipers. That sound pulses through the blood and I felt quite teary but as I looked around I saw I was not alone.

I'm dog-tired in the evenings. I didn't want to go to the dance. I don't like being stared at. These days, more people now smile and greet me than gawk or look sharply away, but there are still those who pass me with pursed lips or an eyebrow raised. However, Morag, from the grocer's, will have none of it. Morag has come to my defence more than once. 'Now that'll be a shilling for your shopping, Mrs McKenna – and two more for all those nasty glances you've shot at Miss Buchanan in my shop.' And I'll be for ever grateful for her telling Old Woman Gillies to take her holier-than-thou-ness and stuff it in her pipe. Old Woman Gillies does smoke a pipe – and she can sour the milk and freeze the blood in your veins. But even though she growled at me and spat curses at my baby, she was no match

*for Morag. That's why, when Morag told me that I will come to the ceilidh,
I wasn't going to argue with her.*

*In mid-August it seems the sun is just too happy to set. The hall in
Tarbert was packed, some of the older women were sitting in little groups
sewing and telling stories; the young children were in a writhing scamper,
just like the salmon that flurry and leap at this time of year. Men were
deep in discussion and deals – there was a lot of smoking and nodding and
backslapping and handshaking. And the music! And the dancing! And
Jessie danced and danced with her Murdo and I watched their eyes lock and
their fingertips linger ever so slightly when the dance was done. I hope he
comes back to the island to live when he's done with the Navy, though he
claims he never will. I want Jessie to have more and more reasons to stay.*

*I was too slow and full of baby to dance much, let alone nimbly, but still
I was dragged in to join the reels. Everyone laughed at my clumsy footwork
but I was quite content to be part of the entertainment.*

And You, you little rascal, you out-danced everyone.

'Flora – here, will you?'
Iain is calling me now.
I am in the garden, pegging washing.
I go inside.
He takes me to the front door and opens it.
'Look!' he says.
Outside is a pram.
Outside is a small crate with some toys in it.
Outside is a bag with a bundle of baby clothes tied with a ribbon.
*From the MacLeods. From the MacKinnons. From the Martins and
the Frasers.*
From all of them, for you and me.

Little One.

   You came.

   Ten days late and you took your time and had me screaming blue murder and bellowing like a cow and swearing like a navvy and crying that surely I was going to die. Poor Iain, downstairs at a godforsaken hour, heating the water while my caterwauling shifted the mortar from the stones. And all the while I squeezed the blood out of Nurse Keaton's hands while she told me that I was doing brilliantly, that I was a natural. She reminded me all about breathing when I clean forgot how to.

   But none of that matters any more.
   Because you're here now.

   My beautiful, beautiful baby girl.
   My daughter.
   Born 21ˢᵗ September 1969, in Harris, at home.

   Mo leannan bhòidheach – *my darling sweetheart.*

Monday

The bridge was only 5 miles from Tarbert, and its single lane with one passing place spanned the 300-metre Sound of Scalpay in a simple, elegant and unobtrusive way. For an island measuring little over three miles by two, Nell was struck at how distinct Scalpay felt with its tighter rolling landscape of mounds and lumps in a very different shade of green. The road here twisted and turned, the rises and falls were more pronounced and the houses were grouped more closely together; denser, jostling for position on little knolls or in small dips. It seemed more populous than anywhere she'd been over the last few days.

Sheltered by a series of small islands scattered like a handful of rune stones along Loch Tarbert, Scalpay's two natural harbours nestled, protected. Sophia Keaton lived in the North Harbour which, on a Monday morning, was bustling. Nell found the bungalow easily. For a while however, she just sat in the car, focusing her gaze instead on the North Harris hills over the water, the morning light glancing off all that steady grey rock. It was an easier option than trying to remember all the questions she wanted to ask. More difficult still would be trying to keep a check on the surges of emotion that had done away with her sleep and deadened her appetite. But an appointment had been made for her and Nell was now a few minutes late. She left the car, walked to the front door, steeled herself and knocked.

When Sophia opened the door, she and Nell just stood still, lost in a soft silence that transcended time and cancelled out all the sounds around them that spoke of an everyday Monday. Sophia had been anticipating this day for well over three decades, not knowing when it might be. And it was now.

This is Flora's girl. Here she is. Unmistakable. Unforgotten.

'You took your time,' she said at length. 'But I always knew you'd come.'

'You're not Scottish!'

Nell was immediately mortified that this was her opening observation but Sophia just laughed.

'You're dead right – I'm not. I'm a Yorkshire lass, from Leeds originally. Come in, Nell. Come in. I'm Sophia. Folk still call me Fire. Your mother always, always called me Nurse Keaton.'

Sophia's sitting room overlooked the water and two arm-chairs were placed either side of an occasional table on which was a plate of biscuits and two mugs as if conversation was already under way. Nell said yes to tea. She said yes, the open window was fine. She said yes, her journey here was easy, lovely. She was offered a seat, to which she replied thank you – yet she followed Sophia into her little kitchen. And there they stood together, watching the kettle come slowly to the boil.

'My mother,' Nell murmured. 'I mean – my birth mother.'

Sophia, deep in thought, poured the water into the teapot. 'Come on through, Little Wing, come and sit down.'

'Little Wing?'

'It was your mother's pet name for you. On account of her being Jimi Hendrix's greatest fan.'

They sat and looked at each other over the rims of the mugs, the drama softened by the steam from the fragrant tea, the gentle breeze from the open window.

'I didn't know about this – about me – about Flora – until pretty recently,' Nell said.

'Must've been a terrible shock,' Sophia said. 'Baffling too.'

Nell took her time to think about just how shocking it all had been.

'I didn't even know that my mum – my mum Wendy – had a younger sister.'

Sophia nodded thoughtfully. 'Is she still alive? Has she said why she never told you? Does she know that you're here now?'

'Yes. No. No,' Nell said. 'My mum – Wendy – she's. She's always been – well, it's worsened over the last two or three years.' Suddenly Nell felt like she was betraying Wendy and it made her want to cry. She fidgeted with her fingers and her words. 'She's unwell – she's never been well. She has mental illnesses and the symptoms have been worsening. She's deteriorated quite a lot.'

They sat quietly.

'I'm sorry, pet.'

There was something about the timbre of Nurse Keaton's voice, the way she considered Nell's words. Nell knew for sure that she'd cared for Flora with those same kind eyes, with this soothing tone.

'She – Mum – Wendy – had been calling me Florence for a while. That was Flora's actual name. Or in England, at least.'

'She was only ever Flora to all of us.' Sophia cleared her throat. 'And she spoke only fondly of her sister, I promise you. Didn't much like the oldest one, I might add. I met her, you know – your Wendy mum.'

Nell was shocked.

'In Glasgow. When you were twenty-one months old. When I handed you over. After Flora had died. When you had to leave us here for your family down there.'

'She came to collect me?' Nell had never really pondered the logistics. 'My mum?'

'With your granddad.'

And now the bell rang clearly. '*Buchanan* – of course – that was my granddad George. He died a long time ago.'

'Iain Buchanan's brother. I met him that day. The spit, they were, the spit of each other.'

'Is he alive? Iain?'

Sophia shook her head. 'A good twenty, twenty-five years, I reckon.'

Nell's questions were backing up in a logjam; she sipped quickly at the tea, chiding her mind for being in such a muddle.

'You do look like her, you know,' Sophia said.

Nell felt her eyes smart. 'Even though I'm pretty much twice the age she was when she died?'

The blunt fact sounded horrible, tragic.

'Yes, Nell – you do look like her.'

'I can't remember all these things I wanted to ask you. There's so much. I don't know where to begin.'

Sophia put her cup down. 'Well, I've plenty to tell you. For starters I want you to know how much you were adored. Adored. You might not have been planned – but you were very much wanted, right from the start. That's how she found her way here.'

'Did she run away?'

'She was sent.'

'She was banished?' Nell remembered the pain of being that age, even for a normal sixteen-year-old in a liberal household. She layered upon that the abject fear, the rejection and shame that Florence must have shouldered. Flora. She'd only ever call her that from now on because her mother had found her strength and her bravery and her happiness being Flora.

'If Flora hadn't died—'

Sophia sighed fondly. 'She'd have stayed up here. I'm quite convinced.'

'Really?'

'Absolutely. She loved it. She had plans, you know – she wanted to be an artist.'

'An artist?'

'Here.' Sophia picked up a piece of paper resting on top of the books on the shelf beside her. She handed it to Nell. Tessellating swirls and arabesques and spirals and paisleys in many shades of mauve and gold and deep greens and rich browns. 'She was dead good.'

'It's the Harris hills, isn't it? I've been places that feel like this over the last few days.' Nell turned the page.

For Nurse Keaton, we love you! Flora and Nell xxx

And it struck Nell that there had been a time when it really had been just Flora and Nell and she wished, how she wished, she could conjure up some tiny memory. Lightly, she traced her finger over the shapes.

'I wonder whether I'd've stayed too.'

Sophia sighed. 'Probably not. Employment – prospects – opportunity. So many of the youngsters leave the islands. It's a problem. It's always been a problem. Some do return but mostly they go to the mainland or seek their fortunes elsewhere. It was lovely that Flora was intent on making a life here.'

'But she died,' Nell said softly. 'Flora died. Before she could be an artist – before she could fulfil any of her dreams.' She sensed Nurse Keaton flinch and Nell realized that she too wanted to overlook this fact for the time being, to keep Flora alive, now that she'd found her at last. 'Did she like being a mother? At only seventeen? I mean – was she good at it? How did she cope? Was I a good baby? Did we have – a bond?'

Sophia gazed at Nell. 'Her eyebrow did that – what yours just did. That little tremor and twitch when she'd fret.' She watched Nell touch her eyebrow. 'Let me tell you – Flora was a natural. You made the world make sense to her. The pair of you – it was really something.'

'Where was I born?'

'At home – at the Buchanan house.'

'Where did she die?'

'At the other house.'

'The other house?'

'She'd moved by then. She was renting a tiny cottage.'

'She didn't stay with Granddad George's brother?'

'Oh, she didn't move far – but she was feeling so settled, if you like. Earning a little – but enough. Of course, everyone helped everyone in those days. I remember her saying it was time for her to put down roots for the both of you.'

'So – she was happy? Coping? Excited?'

'There wasn't electricity in her cottage, there were parts of Harris still off-grid back then. So she just had her peat and Tilley lamps. But that little cottage breathed warmth and light. She felt blessed, Little Wing. She felt her life could not be bettered.'

'Are they still there? The house I was born in – and the cottage where she died? Can we go?'

Sophia nodded. It would be a good thing to do. It would infuse the places with Flora's spirit again, keep it strong by tying Nell's to it. But she wasn't going to tell Nell that she hadn't been back to either place for many, many years. She hadn't yet told Nell that it was she who'd discovered Flora. How was she going to tell her what she found that afternoon? All these years gone. Flora dead, Nell at her side, trying to revive her mamma with her toy tea set?

'Now?' Nell asked. 'Can we go now?'

'I've an appointment in Stornoway this afternoon.' Sophia said. 'I'm having a hip replacement soon. So it'll be tomorrow – we'll go tomorrow.'

But I'm going home tomorrow, Nell thought.

And then she thought, no, I'm not.

* * *

Dougie was aiming to run am Bealach, the Coffin Trail, fast, knowing well what his personal best was for the eight taxing miles. The fact that he'd achieved it at eighteen, over half his life ago, made the challenge all the more compelling. It was his last chance, really, for a good run. He was leaving on Wednesday and tomorrow he'd spend with his dad. They planned to take the ferry from Leverburgh over to Berneray, walk the length of West Beach and drive on to Lochmaddy for a meal. Dougie had never been over the causeway that now linked Berneray with North Uist but Gordon had spent the last six years since it was built eulogizing to his son that it was the closest he'd get to walking on water. So, today he'd run. What he was not expecting was to trip up just two miles in and see Duncan MacAskill's face peering down at him.

He knew it couldn't be Duncan – he'd been dead many years, but Dougie sat a while longer on the rough and stony ground, his arms loosely across his knees, gazing at the slab of rock in whose furrows and dinks and streaks old MacAskill's face had momentarily appeared. Dougie could no longer see it. He called himself a silly twat, picked himself up off the path, brushed the dirt off his calf and inspected the graze. You'll live, he told himself. He ran on for a few metres more and though the soreness was surface only, his pace was off. He slowed to a walk, then to a stop, put his hands on his hips and slowly turned a full circle. This God-given place. How did he feel about leaving? Was he even ready?

'Duncan MacAskill,' he murmured quietly. 'Bless you.' Dougie turned for home, his personal best irrelevant. He sauntered, keeping time with his thoughts. He passed the rock again. It looked nothing like Mr MacAskill from any angle or with any level of squinting. But still Dougie put his hand to the stone. It was cool to the touch and yet he sensed energy deep beyond the surface. His mother had always told him that some would say that rock was just stone hard cold, the deadest and greyest of things – but that the lucky ones could feel through to find a force billions of years old. Same as what's up on the moon, she'd told him, same rock, same powers.

He thought of his mum just then, how she had stories and sayings that could narrate almost anyone's life. He chuckled; how many had she simply made up? He thought of his father; did he not find the house intolerably silent now? Did he not find his life these days unbearably lonely? He thought of the house; it had always been a peaceful space, whether bouncing with sound or stilled by silence. And Dougie knew that Gordon was pretty much like the rocks amongst which he lived, solid enough to withstand a bit of harsh weather. Seventeen years his mother had been dead. Thank goodness she hadn't borne witness to anything that came after. She'd been spared what Peggy had referred to as 'that terrible business'. No, thought Dougie. But then he thought of how his father had had to shoulder it all on his own. No, he said to the memories. No.

Dougie walked on, glancing behind him. Just a slab of rock. Duncan MacAskill wasn't there.

But I know where I can find him, Dougie said to himself. He picked up the pace and headed straight home.

'That was fast!' Gordon said.

'I fell. Stupidly.'

'You all right, son?'

'Oh aye – just a graze.'

'But you didn't run on? For your personal best?'

'No, Da – I remembered something I have to do.'

Up in his room, Dougie searched through the cupboard, not allowing himself to be waylaid by unfurling posters and alluring glimpses of Kim Wilde and Clare Grogan. Nor was he distracted by the see-through box in which a mass of ribbons and their clank of medals documented his sporting prowess. He shoved everything onto his bed, knowing that the box would be right at the back. It was one of four, sizeable and stout, made of acid-free cardboard. They'd been expensive and he'd had to send away for them. The top two he dumped on his bed. It was the third that he wanted. The fourth, however, needed to stay where it was, right at the back, at the bottom, in the dark. He barely glanced at it.

Dougie sat on the rug by the bed with the box next to him. He lifted the lid and immediately the scent accosted him. Photographic paper and leaves of treated tissue. If he closed his eyes, the darkroom came through, a heady mix of vinegary fluids, the three trays, the lines and the pegs and even the dimness itself. It occurred to him that everything in one's past has a scent even if it went unacknowledged at the time. All these years later, it was this that came to the fore; this was the key to travelling backwards – regardless of whether the more obvious details were remembered.

In the box was his project for his final year at art college. A collection of photographs perpetuating his chosen theme, *On the Edge*. He read his mission statement.

I grew up on the Isle of Harris in the Outer Hebrides.
Like many my age, I have left for the mainland.
Who is left to watch for the weather and to judge the tides, to buain the
peats and gather the crotal, to walk up the high hill and run over the
white sand?
Here are the faces that know.
They know that while I may perceive opportunity to lie further and further
away, my heart and soul will always be that of a Hearach.

Dougie remembered sharply how the five sentences had taken him almost as much time to develop as the photographs themselves. He looked away from the box and over to the window. How long he stayed there, lost in thought, he did not know but when his focus returned his father was standing there, puzzled, in the doorway.

'Spring cleaning, Douglas?'

'I wanted to find my photograph of Duncan MacAskill. I thought about him this morning.'

'Now there's a name I've not thought about for many a year.' Gordon chuckled. 'MacAskill, eh! Will we bring that box downstairs, then?'

And Dougie thought, why not. The projects by all the final-year students had been exhibited, after all, for anyone to see. His parents had come to his graduation, walked quietly around the show, wearing the same polite expressions for all the works. Nudes, graffiti, decaying food, abstracted trees, the Notting Hill Carnival, people living in boxes under a bridge in London. And Dougie's Harris. It was the time they spent that gave away what they liked and what they didn't. They nodded and smiled at all Dougie's fellow exhibitors. Very good, they said, very good.

'Yes,' said Dougie, content that his father should want to carry the box. 'Let's.'

The portrait of Duncan MacAskill was third from the top.

'There he is!' Gordon chuckled, then sighed. 'You know he was Tarbert's oldest shopkeeper when he died? Never left the island again once he came home from Gallipoli.'

Dougie knew. He'd spent quite some time with the man, a number of days; judging the light outside and watching for the light behind his subject's eyes until he knew the portrait was ready to capture. They looked at the photo. Duncan MacAskill in his shop, his wares in a higgle in the background. Wearing his shirt and tie under a thick hand-knit jumper, over it all his Harris Tweed jacket that may even have belonged to his father. Peaked cloth cap and the kindly, craggy face beneath, eyes darkened by the war he wouldn't speak about.

'Remember how he'd jump over the counter?'

'Aye. Remember how there was no chair – he'd pull out a drawer from the counter, pop a cushion over it and sit there.'

'I'd give him 10 pence,' said Dougie, 'and he'd give me a line and fish hooks and I'd catch eels on the shore.'

'God rest him,' Gordon murmured. 'Did all right, so he did. You'd go in the shop for one thing and come out with seventeen others.' But Dougie didn't comment; he was absorbed with all the prints. He could still remember the precise conditions when he pressed the shutter for each.

Black-face sheep.

Isobel in the bakery, aproned, hands on hips.

The cruachs – the herringbone stacks of peats.

Slabs of striated, folded, compressed Lewisian gneiss.

Lobster creels.

The carvings at Rodel Church.

Bolts of tweed.

A nurse vaccinating alarmed children at school.

Sanderlings in a frolic on the beach.

Mrs McGregor dyeing her wool.

Eilidh Campbell weaving on her Hattersley loom.

Fish guts on a boat deck.

Old hands fixing nets.

A red deer.

A self-portrait against the folds and jags of the eroded rock at the summit of An Cliseam. Twenty years old he was then, and home for the summer.

Two men, hauling kelp.

The minister, preaching.

Lachina, one hundred and two years old, with no teeth and the widest smile.

A traditional blackhouse with its thatched roof and deep-set windows not dissimilar to the face of a highland coo.

His father, dozing.

His mother doing battle with the wind to peg her washing.

At the time, Dougie knew that technically and aesthetically these photographs were outstanding. He saw now what he'd truly achieved; every image defined and encapsulated Harris and even the seemingly inanimate personified the *genius loci*, the spirit of the place. But more than all of that, these photographs were his homage and his love song to the island of his birth, the island on the edge of the long sea.

He sat quietly with Gordon as they took it in turns to lift the sheets of tissue paper off the prints.

'And now,' Dougie said. 'Now I photograph agricultural gubbins and racks of polycotton clothing for a living.'

Gordon noted the hoarseness to Dougie's voice, observed his son carefully restacking the prints. He knew, just then, that he needn't say a thing. He put his hand on his boy's back and left it there for the crucial fraction longer than a moment.

Back up in the bedroom, Dougie restored order to the cupboard; this time briefly unrolling the posters to gaze at his teenage crushes before he put them away for God knows how many more years. Back went the shoebox full of tickets and stubs and coasters and leaflets from his inter-railing trips. Back went his medals. The ridiculous straw hat he'd worn every day on that one long hot summer in Greece. A rugby ball. The box of random letters and birthday cards. The tin of button badges and pins of the musicians and quotations that had brought deep meaning to his teenage years. Everything stacked to the left. To the right, the four acid-free boxes. Three on his bed, one for each year of his degree course. The fourth untouched, right at the back, always at the bottom of the stack. All the other boxes and mementos he could deal with; they brought a gentle nostalgia, they were a commemoration of sorts. That other box? Lifting the lid would serve only to slice through a scar and open a wound that had taken so long to finally heal.

Your name is Nell.

Well, it's Neilina Joan but you're known as Nell even though I call you Little Wing mostly. Neilina means 'cloud champion' in Scots. I love you I love you I love you. You are perfect and noisy and gorgeous and exhausting and terrifying. I don't think I've ever sung so much in all my life – I just sing to you all the time, mainly because you don't understand many words. I sing to help you sleep. I sing because it makes you smile. All of Jimi's hits can be adapted into soft, lilting sing-song lullabies. Even 'Purple Haze' and 'All Along the Watchtower'. Of course, I sing 'Little Wing' to you most of all. It's your song. You – among the butterflies and zebras and moonbeams. You of the thousand smiles. You who have made life into one strange and beautiful fairy tale. I read that Jimi was inspired by Native American legends where spirits inhabit nature and animals and birds. I like that.

I also sing to stop myself panicking when I'm not sure what I'm meant to do, the times when I haven't a clue and feel completely out of control and utterly useless. When I'm so tired my head won't balance on my neck. Nurse Keaton tells me, 'You'll muddle through – you'll find your own way.' She says there are no rules.

That's not what Mrs MacSween said when she came visiting. She's a kind soul, all bosom and smile and busy busy efficiency. But by the time she left I felt I'd been doing it all wrong, I felt I couldn't trust my own judgement. She says I'm to feed you at 6.00, 10.00, 2.00, 6.00, 10.00, 2.00. But I don't have a watch and I can't be checking the only clock in the house and anyway, the one day I tried it you weren't hungry at 2.00 but at 3.05. Then not at 6.00 but at about 7.23. Mrs MacSween also said I have to let you cry because it's good for your lungs. She says I'm to wrap you in a tight bundle, pop your pram outside and let you holler till you're done. If you ask me, Mrs MacSween knows everything about baking the best cake on the island but NOTHING WHEN IT COMES TO BABIES – even though she's had five of her own. That's when Nurse Keaton found me sobbing because you were screaming but it was only 9.35, not 10.00, and my chest was swelling and oozing and I had no voice to sing. That's when she gave me a hug and told me I'd muddle through. So I feed you when you're hungry and sing to you whenever you like. And when I don't know what anything is about, or if there's a better way of doing something, or if I've no idea what's going on or what the right or wrong way is, or how I'm going to make it through to lunch or tea or bedtime, I sing a little ditty I've composed:

> *I'll muddle through,*
> *you'll muddle through,*
> *you and me Little Wing a Ding Ding,*
> *we'll muddle through.*

I've even heard Iain humming it quite a few times.

*   I remember nothing of the early days – they just passed in a fog. The early weeks seemed to move very slowly, like we were inching our way along a tunnel. Some days I didn't manage to get myself dressed I was so busy with you. Some days I didn't have the energy to even be bothered. Thank goodness for Nurse Keaton. But in the last month or so, since Christmas really, our days have found their own rhythm and we're muddling along just fine. You're star of the show, you're the dish of the day for miles around. Oh! the fuss that was made of you the first time I took you to Tarbert! All the little children crowding round to marvel at your tiny fingernails, to dimple your cheeks with their thumbs. People crossed the street to meet you, they rushed out of shops to admire you and even Old Woman Gillies came*

over and took her pipe out her mouth and peered into the pram. *Leanabas!* *Leanabas! She cooed at you softly in* Gàidhlig *and then started laughing like a drain. She pinched my cheek and her eyes were all watery and, dare I say it, gentle. The kindness of everyone – the little parcels left at the door, the extra bun or the creamiest milk from Morag. The tiniest little shoes from Duncan MacAskill's shop and ice cream wrapped in newspaper from Bean Angie's.*

And Nurse Keaton. And Jessie. Always there for you and me.

Jessie is often with us. She'll take you in your pram for fresh air so that I can have a little time. Earlier on, I used that time to slump into a crazy deep sleep. Now I use it to tidy or cook or wash my hair. I sent Joan a photograph and a long, over-emotional letter. She sent me a tiny pair of mittens and the dearest teddy bear. She's desperate to meet you, desperate. We neither of us have a clue how or when we'll get to see each other.

I wrote to Wendy too but her letter back was odd. She must have had a million things to ask, a zillion things to tell me and out they all tumbled and she obviously forgot to read her letter through when she sent it. Not a single full stop. Iain went to the hotel when you'd been born, to telephone George. I like to think that George might have kept the news to himself for a little while, before letting my mother know. I imagine my mum told Marjorie at some point. It has probably never been spoken of since.

But poor Iain. For one so small your presence is everywhere and you have taken over his house. Every chair-back has a muslin square or baby clothes draped over to dry. There are buckets of nappies soaking, bowls of bottles. You have more wardrobe changes in a day than royalty, young lady! It's midwinter now and there are seldom days dry enough to peg the washing outside. I say sorry to Iain all the time but he just says 'Ach!' and blows raspberries on your tum while you grab on tight to his whiskers.

Before I came here, to Harris, all I wanted to know was how long I'd have to be here, when I could go. But I haven't been here even a year and I know for sure I will never leave. Not because George told me that I must stay, but because I don't want to be anywhere else. Where else would we go anyway? Where else would have us? Here, in Harris, I want for nothing more than to be here with you.

Winter. Days upon end when the icy blasts of gale-force winds are vicious. It seems to be a very very long season. And dark – there's not much light now. Day after day of rain and more rain – often with wind I'm convinced could move the entire house and an angry sea that can savage the beach night after night. The rain washed part of the road right away last week. The gale brought sand right to the front door. The hills raged with churning, charging water and the storm last week mashed the seaweed into thick foam. I'd never before heard what truly wild weather sounds like. But weather doesn't last for ever and there are some days when it's dry, even bright. There are flocks of snow bunting wintering in the machair. There are rockpools to explore. There are days when it's calm and afternoons when the rain stops and the sun breaks through and there's a watergaw – a floating portion of sudden rainbow pouring out between the clouds. There are nights when it's clear, when it's cold and still and the Northern Lights – the Fir Chlis – *sing out across the blackness.*

Nurse Keaton – she often says call me Sophia, but I like calling her Nurse Keaton – brought me a special sling and taught me how to tie it. I love it because it's a trippy batik design in soft strong cotton and she showed me how to wrap you up and fix you against me. And that's how we walk for miles each day, Little Wing! If it looks like rain I wear Iain's enormous waterproof coat, with a couple of buttons undone so you can see where we're going. Me with you like a human kangaroo.

We found something this morning, you and me. Since then, I've done my usual singing and cooking and boiled the nappies and a hundred other things, but half my mind has been fixed on what we saw.

It's a small cottage – just over the way there – at Luskentyre and it's for rent. We went up to the windows and tried to see in and then I laughed at myself for forgetting that this is Harris and we don't need to lock ourselves in or anyone out. So we opened the door and stepped inside. There's a small, light sitting room, a tiny kitchen and next to that a room with a tin bath and a sink and a rack from the ceiling for drying. The loo is in a lean-to fixed against the house. We tiptoed around whispering, even though the place was empty. We went upstairs where there were two little rooms in the roof. Everything is small but plenty big enough.

What do you think, Nell? I said.

And you kicked your little legs about so much that I took your answer to be a resounding Yes!

Of the £20 George gave me, I still have over £17 left.

I'll ask Iain if he knows anything and if he doesn't Nurse Keaton surely will.

I can't wait to show Jessie.

Flora & Nell Buchanan
Am Bothan Geal
Luskentyre
Harris

Our address!!!

Am Bothan Geal means the White Cottage. I have given £3 to Mr MacDonald who owns it but he said I'll be doing him a favour just keeping the weather out.

My very own place. Honestly – how lucky am I? How many people my age have what I have? I can't believe it!

Iain said I didn't have to go. He also said we can always come back. I said Iain, I can practically see your back door from my front door! I said Iain, when the tide is right out we can walk across the sands to you. And it's only two miles by the road. I told him that, before we know it, Nell will be going to the little school in Seilebost. I said Iain, I want to put roots down for Nell and me – right here, in Harris, a stone's throw from you.

Despite my excitement, it was so hard leaving Iain's house, the house where my daughter was born, the home that was open to me when I had nowhere else to go. It was desperately hard leaving Iain. I have grown to love him like another father. He and Nell adore one another. There were tears. He tried to hide his from me but mine gushed out uncontrollably. For some reason, it gave Nell fits of giggles so, amongst the sadness of the day, happiness reigned.

Our home has a table and two chairs. We have an armchair and a wooden stool, a short bookcase and a fireplace and a rug. We have a bed big enough for both of us for the time being until Jessie's father brings over their cot. I'm in no rush, I love sleeping alongside my baby.

We have food in the kitchen cupboard, a stack of peat outside and gas for the Tilleys. And the Van comes twice a week if we don't feel like a trip to Tarbert. We have nothing to complain about and everything to be thankful for. There is a little land at the back and I'll plant potatoes and carrots. Peas in the summer. We even have neighbours about a quarter of a mile away and they have a toddler. We have Iain a couple of miles around the bay. We have visitors all the time.

Often, I stand at the windows with my baby, just gazing out at the views for ages. Or we cuddle up in bed in the mornings, in the armchair in the evenings, just marvelling at the steady walls around us.

Best of all, though, best of all is what's outside.

On the other side of the path, towards the sea, there is a small stone building I didn't even know about.

As I stood in there looking out beyond the dunes, I sensed the power of the sea and the energy from the sky propelling an even, fresh light straight into the building. And then the revelation came. I don't know what the place had been used for, but it's going to be a studio. Its roof is sound and the stone floor is level but it is missing a wall where it faces the sea. Iain said not to worry about that, he says it's an easy enough job to fix.

So I AM going to be an artist.

I shall paint my pictures and sell them and then one day, perhaps I can buy the White Cottage from Mr MacDonald.

Flora Buchanan. Mother. Artist. This is who I am.

Tuesday

'Where to?'

'Back over the bridge to Tarbert, then the road west.'

Nell looked at Sophia sitting beside her, and Sophia looked at her. 'Nurse Keaton – I have to tell you I'm so nervous. I came only for facts – I never expected to *feel*.'

'You know I'm retired? You can just call me Sophia.'

'I know,' said Nell, slowly. 'But I'd rather not.'

And Sophia nodded. It was a way for Nell to feel closer to Flora. And Sophia liked it. It also reminded her of a career she'd loved, a position within the community she'd cherished – as respected as the policeman, the minister, the doctor. She still couldn't quite believe this was Nell. All grown up. And here.

'I didn't sleep,' Nell told her. 'I've barely slept since Sunday.'

'We don't have to do this today – you can rest. We can meet tomorrow?' Sophia said. 'When do you leave?'

But Nell put the key in the ignition and fastened her seat belt. 'I haven't booked a ticket home,' she said. 'It didn't feel right to do so.'

Sophia nodded approvingly and then laughed. 'Your boss must be understanding, then?'

'I rarely take any leave.' Nell thought of the Chaffinch. It was just after nine o'clock. They'd be in full swing. The builders would be first in for their takeaway teas and their Danny chats. Debbie would be overseeing the salads. AJ would be wiping the coffee machine. Libby would be folding the paper napkins very carefully, very slowly. Alex and Sanjay would be bickering amiably while constructing sandwiches. And Rachel would be carrying the trays of brownies and millionaire's shortbreads with her shaky hands that made everyone hold their breath. 'I've never really felt the need,' Nell qualified. 'I'm part of the furniture now.'

'What is it that you do?' Sophia asked, as if she'd be telling Flora oh, you must be so proud of your daughter. 'Tell me everything.'

'You'll tell me which direction to take?'

'Oh my goodness,' Sophia said. 'Stitching wounds, delivering babies, inoculating children, plastering broken bones, treating the elderly, the infirm, the insane – all that I can do. But I can't give careers advice.'

'I meant,' said Nell, starting the engine and pulling away from Nurse Keaton's house, 'the directions to the house where I was born.'

Though she didn't know the precise location of Iain Buchanan's old house, Nell liked it that she did have a feel for the roads now, the etiquette of passing places and giving a smooth wide berth to sheep and cattle. She drove at a speed that was confident and yet allowed ample time to appreciate the views and details both distant and close. Sophia commented that she drove like a local. Nell told her that she didn't actually think she'd ever driven north of Peterborough.

'Flora had a bicycle,' Sophia said. 'She was still cycling into Tarbert eight months pregnant – and later, she'd often cycle in with you in a basket seat behind her. When you were really wee, you'd be in a pouch and she'd walk you for miles. She developed this thing for fresh air. When she was doing her painting, if the weather was nice, you'd be happy as a lark in a playpen outside that she made out of old sheep hurdles.'

Nell breathed deeply. Flora was coming to life and she wasn't like Wendy and she wasn't like Marjorie. And though Nell wanted to ask but how did she die, why did she die, when did she die – she swerved away from asking, not wanting the stories to end.

'Did she – did Flora – ever mention who my father was?'

And Sophia thought that Nell was going to hear so many fundamental truths that to be spare with details would be prudent. 'Yes,' she told her. 'But I don't know his name. I do remember her saying he was dead handsome. It was one night. It was her first time. I do know that he emigrated.'

'Where to?'

'Off the face of the earth,' Sophia said.

Nell absorbed this. 'A lost mother and a missing father,' she said quietly.

Sophia looked at her. 'Seems to me that Flora and Wendy were excellent mother-fathers,' she said. 'Look at you, Nell – *look at you.*'

They drove on.

'Luskentyre,' said Nell, nodding at the sign. 'I went there. The weather was shit and I was despairing a bit by then.'

'That's our second stop,' said Sophia. 'Keep going to Seilebost. Another mile or so. We're so nearly there, Nell.'

Nell's heart was starting to pound, she needed to keep calm. 'Nurse Keaton – how did you end up here, from Leeds?'

'I wanted to join the best nurses in the world,' Sophia told her. 'Almost forty years before the creation of the NHS, the Highlands and Islands Medical Service provided district nurses for the islands of the Outer Hebrides. These nurses were so rigorously trained, so resourceful and adaptable, they were respected the world over. And I was dead sick of redbrick and grime and my dad was a drunk and my mam had died and I won a place at the Queen's Institute of District Nursing in Edinburgh.'

'And you've been here ever since?'

'Started off in North Uist in 1950 when often I had to row a boat to patients. I was twenty-two years old. Came to Harris when I was twenty-seven and they gave me a cottage and a motorbike. Eventually, a car. But Nell,' Sophia said, 'that's another story. Slow right down now and indicate – because that stony track coming up on the right, that's where your story begins.'

And Nell gazed at the billowing expanse of sea meadow and dunes, the broad swathe of white sand beyond. And the sea. And Nell thought, here I am.

The car rattled along, and then around a bend the Buchanan house stood before them, achingly familiar to Sophia but new and unexpected for Nell.

'This is where you were born, pet, in this house here. Upstairs in the little bedroom at the back that looked out and over the dunes to the sea and over to the isle of Taransay which was still inhabited back then.'

Nell couldn't find her voice. Just then, she had no thoughts of Flora or of Wendy – only for herself. This is where she came into the world, right here on 21st September 1969. She'd always assumed it was hospital and Colchester because she'd been given no reason to think otherwise.

She walked tentatively towards the house; Nurse Keaton at her side letting her set the pace. There was no car, no dog; the house seemed still and quiet. They stood by the front door and, with an encouraging nod from Nurse Keaton, Nell knocked. There was no answer. They peered through the windows and Sophia thought how different everything looked, all trendy grey walls and tasteful artwork and a sumptuous-looking L-shaped sofa.

'Come around the back,' Sophia said.

She hardly recognized the garden. It had been fenced all around and a bank topped with well-tended turf now rose level along one side of the short stretch of stone wall while the other side had been beautified into a rockery with alpines already spilling forth between the old stones. The clothes on the washing line were like a family portrait. Here is Daddy and Mummy and Big Sister and Baby Brother. Sophia noted that an extension had been built, modern yet unobtrusive, with a spectacular wall of glass doors. What would old Buchanan have made of this?

'There's no one home,' Nell said with her face up close against the window. 'Nice kitchen.'

Sophia took a look. So sleek! It made the room look far bigger. 'She wasn't a bad cook at all, your mother,' Sophia said. 'Taught herself from the late Mrs Buchanan's cookery cards.'

'There's no one home,' Nell said again. 'Should we leave a note?'

'We can do.'

'Which was my bedroom?'

'That one there, that one on the left. That's where you were born. You had the tiniest cry – like a kitten – for the first two days. Then you found your lungs. Bloody hell, that was a right pair you had on you.'

Nell stood and stared at the house. The presence of the current family was so strong that it dominated and she felt her own story had receded; faint, silenced and covered up, like faded wallpaper hidden behind three decades of redecoration.

'I don't know why but I expected it all to be preserved – like a museum to Flora and me.' Her voice was thin. 'Shall I still leave a note, though?'

Sophia nodded. 'Do that. I don't know this family.' She looked at the washing all ordered and clean, wafting gently in the breeze, as though the family were dancing together. 'But I get the feeling that they're nice.' She watched Nell write a note, tear it carefully from her spiral-bound pad. 'A long time has passed. The next place might have changed a lot too. Best prepare yourself, pet.' She was aware that she was speaking to herself as much as to Nell.

* * *

'That'll be Roddy,' Gordon said to Dougie on hearing the doorbell. '*Diabhlaidh càr* – bloody car.'

Dougie glanced at his watch. It was gone 10.30. If the car could be fixed quickly, they could make the next ferry from Leverburgh. However, if Roddy was still the inimitable Roddy, then the man liked a good long stroke of his chin and a lot of pensive humming before he even looked under the bonnet. His father and Roddy were old friends and Gordon wouldn't hear of anyone else coming to see the car. Fixing it was something of an institution; it was a ritualized dance of sorts, with mugs of tea, loaded silences considering worst-case scenarios and every tool in the box, unrushed reminiscences, rags and a tub of Swarfega. Dougie accepted that he might not be walking on water between North Uist and Berneray this trip either. As his father went through to greet Roddy, Dougie put the kettle on and dropped teabags into three mugs.

Only it wasn't Roddy.

Gordon opened his front door to two women standing on his doorstep. He was so flummoxed at not seeing all six foot two of Roddy with his oily hands and his ancient, stained boiler suit, he could only stand and stare.

'Gordon?' Sophia was charmed that, apart from the colour of his hair, he really hadn't changed all that much.

'*Fire?*' Gordon rubbed at his eyebrows and blinked, as if that might produce Roddy. 'Fire! Well now! You're not Roddy, not Roddy at all – but what a fine surprise!'

'Gordon – this is Nell. Nell, this is Gordon Munro.' Sophia faltered. She didn't quite know where to start. It would be far easier giving a potted history to the new people at Buchanan's old house. But Gordon would remember, and memories revisit pain as much as benign nostalgia. 'Might we come in?'

Gordon gave his head a little shake as if to still the futile attempt to change the nurse into the mechanic. 'Aye – of course. Come in. Please – do. Dougie, another mug, please.'

And Dougie thought that if Roddy had an assistant these days, perhaps they would make the ferry.

'Hello, Dougie.'

Dougie hadn't seen Nurse Keaton in years. But hers was a face he'd never forget and a voice that sounded just the same. In just those two words, memories were triggered of wanting to be brave when there was an injection to be had, trusting her to pop his dislocated shoulder back into place, finding comfort in her commiseration that a broken ankle meant no running for a good six months. He'd bled on her, been sick on her, cried like a baby and, once or twice, fallen asleep on her lap.

'*Fire?*'

Dougie was so focused he didn't take much notice of the young woman standing next to her. He just wanted to allow his mind to tumble back through the years, to all those occasions when this remarkable woman had patched him up, stitched him back together, bandaged him better, jabbed him with needles, stabilized broken collar bones and come to school to talk about contraception.

Sophia gave a little shrug. 'It's me.'

'Are you come to give me a jab?'

'No, Dougie,' she laughed. 'I'm assuming you're all up to date.'

'Dougie,' said Gordon, 'the tea, lad, the tea.'

'Fire!' Dougie shook his head in happy disbelief. 'It's just so amazing to see you! You're in Scalpay still? Are you well? You look well.'

'I am, pet.'

'*Pet!*' Dougie laughed.

'And you're still in that London, are you? Keeping out of mischief or making a whole bunch of it?' Handsome boy, Sophia thought. He never did like his hair cut short. 'Still running your socks off?'

'Aye.'

'We've some cake,' said Gordon.

'Milk and sugar?' said Dougie.

'Just milk,' said Sophia.

'Where is my man Roddy?' said Gordon.

'Sorry,' said Dougie, 'did you say sugar?'

'No, pet, just milk.'

'My name is Nell Hartley,' Nell said suddenly.

They all turned and stared at her, as if she'd appeared from nowhere. 'My name is Nell Hartley,' she said again. 'I'm Flora Buchanan's daughter.'

'Flora Buchanan?' Gordon's voice was paper-thin. Then silence. '*You're* Flora's wee girl?'

'Yes,' said Nell.

'She is,' said Sophia.

And Dougie thought, I don't know who Flora Buchanan is but I do know that this is the girl with the huge suitcase who threw her money around the airport and shook like a leaf on the plane to Stornoway.

Gordon's eyes darted from Nell to the past and back again. This he couldn't quite believe. 'You're wee Flora's wee girl?'

'Yes,' said Sophia quietly. 'She is. She's come back.'

He pulled out a chair for Nell. 'Please,' he said, with not much voice. 'Will you sit down awhile?'

Nell sat, Sophia next to her. Dougie brought tea over. 'Will you have tea?' he asked Nell. She looked up at him and nodded, needing to hold the mug as a warm anchor. 'Sugar?' he asked. She shook her head. He brought her a mug and sat down next to his dad.

For a while, no one said anything. Nell cradled her cup while the others sipped and stared at her.

'Did you know my mother? Did you know Flora?' Nell asked Gordon.

'I did, m'dear. We all did. We knew you too. Me – my late wife Màiri – even my boy here.'

Nell looked at Dougie. 'I knew *you*?'

Dougie was confronted by her eyes; they were glossy, deep, earnest. But he couldn't remember knowing her at all. He looked at his father.

'You'd'a been only about three years old, Douglas,' he said quietly. He turned to Nell. 'Your mother – Flora – well, she'd bring you here and the bairns'd play while she and my wife would do whatever it is that women do.'

'I used to come here?' Nell said. 'To play? With *him*?'

It sounded comically rude and the other three laughed a little. She looked to Nurse Keaton who nodded.

'Aye,' said Gordon. 'When you lived at Am Bothan Geal – at the White Cottage. And my wife would bring young Dougie to play at yours too.'

Nell and Dougie greeted the fact blankly, regarded each other quizzically, smiled shyly.

'Of course, Dougie was a bit older. But he loved the little baby – always gave you a present. A train. A stick. A piece of bread. Once – I remember this – a pair of his underpants because he said yours were too big and baggy. I don't think he quite understood nappies.'

'I remember that,' Sophia laughed. 'I was there that day.'

'Did I – have hair?' Nell wasn't sure why the question was so important to her.

'Not for months on end,' Sophia said.

'Then curls,' said Gordon. 'Like curls of butter.'

'Did you *know* my mother? Flora? I mean – really *know* her?'

Gordon considered the question. 'I was at work, you know. But aye – I knew her as our neighbour. I knew her as your mother. I knew her as my wife's friend.'

'Was she—?' Nell faltered.

'She was very good,' said Gordon levelly, 'in all those roles. I'd say she was wise and calm beyond her tender years.'

Nell took her hand to her neck. Her throat was aching with tears under tight control.

'Do *you* remember me?' Nell turned to Dougie. 'Do you remember my mother? Do you remember giving me your train and the stick and the bread and the pants?'

They all looked at Dougie who cast his eyes down, deep in thought. 'I'm sorry,' he said. 'I'm not sure that I do.'

Gordon put his hand on his son's wrist and he spoke low and quietly. 'But you'll not have forgotten the story, Douglas. About the girl. In Am Bothan Geal. All those years ago.'

Dougie looked at his dad. Then he looked at Sophia. Then he looked at Nell. 'The one who died?'

His father nodded.

Dougie kept his focus on Nell, his eyes and his voice soft. 'That was your mother?'

Nell nodded. 'I only just found out she was my mother at all.'

'I'm so sorry,' Dougie said. 'My God – I'm so sorry.'

And it was the first time, Nell realized, that anyone had said how sorry they were that her mother had died. She nodded and suddenly she craved sweet, sweet tea. The other three watched as she spooned in sugar and they let her sip undisturbed until the mug was finished.

'Gordon,' Sophia said at length. 'Would you know who the White Cottage belongs to these days? We've been to old Buchanan's house but there was no one in. I think Nell here would like to see her home.'

Sophia and Nell saw Gordon and Dougie exchange a look and watched as a smile broke from father to son.

'It belongs to us,' Dougie said.

'Well, officially Douglas here bought it maybe ten years ago,' Gordon qualified. 'We rent it out – as a holiday home.'

'Is there anyone there at the moment?' Nell all but whispered.

Dougie looked at Gordon who shook his head. 'It's empty for the minute.'

'Could we possibly borrow the keys?' Sophia asked.

But Gordon had already left the table to fetch them.

'I'm to wait in for that Roddy man to fix the car,' Gordon said, rolling his eyes as he handed the keys to Sophia.

'And I'm waiting on a new hip,' said Sophia. 'I'm not sure I could walk that far.'

'Douglas?'

'Dougie?'

And Dougie glanced from his father to Sophia and then he looked at Nell.

'Sure,' he said. 'I'll take you there.'

The wind had picked up. It was blowing thin, sharp and low. Douglas led the way; through the Munro garden and onto the machair where a scatter of sheep regarded them with momentary alarm before returning to their cuds. Along the marram-fringed dunes, they looked down on the beach where small, fractious waves hissed along the swelling sea surface and shadows of the clouds ran fast across the sands. The grasses around them shivered and shook while Nell and Dougie walked in amiable silence.

'There.' Douglas pointed. 'That's your house.'

The cottage was some way off, nestled into its plot much like the sheep around them. Nell stopped, her eyes fixed on the distant cottage, her hands cupped over her ears.

'Wind giving you earache?' Dougie asked.

Nell nodded. 'It was like this at Hushinish,' she said.

'Ah – you've been to Hushinish?'

Nell nodded. 'I've been everywhere,' she said, 'looking for Flora.'

It dawned on him just then that it was of course Nell who'd been at Luskentyre on Sunday, marching about in despair, shouting at the sea. At the time, he'd resented her presence, felt she was an intruder, believed he had priority. However, now that he knew she was Flora Buchanan's wee girl, he felt himself to have been the trespasser. She had needed that beach to herself more than he had that day, and that was OK by him. He looked at her and she looked at him. A small smile passed between them and on they walked, the sun and the wind in a bicker at their faces. Dougie observed Nell again, saw how she was squinting, her nose wrinkling, her hands still over her ears. It was as though she didn't want to see and she didn't want to hear.

'Here,' he said, pulling a beanie out of his jacket. 'Put this on.'

'You sure?' said Nell, not waiting for an answer. 'Thank you.' The knitted hat was warm and soft and carried the gentle scent of another person. 'What's it actually like, living here?'

Dougie stopped. 'Oh,' he said and he looked out over the bank and flow of the feather-soft dunes to the sea. It was spectacularly beautiful. 'I don't live here any more. Not for some time.' He watched the spume bibble in frenetic squibs over the surface of the rolling water. 'London now,' he said quietly.

Nell thought about this. 'Nurse Keaton says that many of the young folk leave the island,' she said. 'My mother, Flora, was here to stay.' Her ears were warm now and because the hat was a little too big for her, it afforded her eyes some shade too. 'I'd like to think I'd've stayed.'

'Where do you live?'

'Colchester.'

'That's some contrast! What do you do?'

'I work in a café,' she said. 'You?'

'Catalogues. Production side.'

She wanted to stand and gaze out to sea for a while longer before the final advance to the cottage. 'Actually,' said Nell, 'it's more than a café. It's the beating heart of a community project – all my staff have various disabilities or challenges. We're the definitive motley crew. Yet – somehow, it works. It's a well-loved institution. I wouldn't work anywhere else.'

'Well, that's all kinds of amazing, Nell,' said Dougie. 'I bet there's never a dull moment. What's the food like?'

'Delicious. Comfort food with a healthy twist, I suppose.'

And Dougie stopped briefly. Thought for a moment.

'Actually – to be honest, I'm just a failed photographer.'

Nell watched as Dougie nodded gravely at himself, the wind lashing cords of his hair against his face as if in punishment while he sent his shame and disappointment out to sea. 'It was everything to me – and I was good. Once.' He turned to face her. 'So it's nice to hear of your success, your love for what you do.'

They walked on. Nell frowned. 'How did you fail?'

Dougie thought about this. 'I stopped looking. No true photographer ever stops looking.'

'Did you fall out of love with it?' Nell asked. 'Has what was once your craft just become a chore?'

He thought about it. 'Maybe,' he said. He thought about it some more. 'Not so much,' he said warily and left it at that. Nell saw that he was done talking.

'Bollocks,' she said. 'I left my own camera in the car.'

'And this is the one time I forgot to bring mine,' said Dougie. 'Told you – failed photographer.'

'Maybe I'll come back,' she said.

'When do you leave?'

'It was meant to be today. But then I found Nurse Keaton. I haven't rebooked my ticket yet. What about you?'

'Tomorrow.' He turned his focus back to the sea as if soaking up the sight of it, then he gave her a little nudge and nodded ahead toward the cottage.

'Ready?' Dougie asked.

They had reached the cottage after strolling for twenty minutes, during which time their questionnaires had eased into relaxed conversation. And now they were here. Whistling, Dougie opened the gate and busied himself with the keys, until he was aware that Nell was standing stock-still and pale a few steps behind him. He looked from her to the house and back again.

'Do you remember it? Are things coming back?'

When she brought her eyes to his they were shot through with tears. 'It's just the *knowing*,' she told him. 'Just knowing that this is where I lived. Me – here. Baby Nell and young Flora.'

Dougie considered this. 'I'm sorry I can't remember stuff for you,' he said.

'That's OK – you were only a toddler yourself.'

'Are you ready to go in?' He touched her elbow. 'We can wait a bit – just hang out here in the garden?'

'It's OK,' Nell said. 'I'm ready.'

'You should open up,' he said, standing to one side.

So Nell unlocked the back door and pushed it open, Dougie just behind her. Inside, everything was very still, very quiet, very polite. It was simple, plain, tasteful. It was very much of today.

'When you first bought it – what was it like?'

He wished, just then, that he could provide details beyond the mundane, that he had information or anecdotes that would have significance for her, but he had none.

'I think your ma rented it for the time she was here – and it's been rented or sold on again a few times over the last, well, thirty years.'

'All the treasures are gone?'

Dougie shrugged. 'It's a treasure in its own right, is it not?'

A cosy yet airy sitting room, a small but sweet kitchen, a compact but bright bathroom downstairs. Walls painted in a contemplative soft white, enlivened by curtains and cushions and a throw over the armchair in tweed the colours of heather. They went upstairs and looked into the two tiny bedrooms in the roof: simple, spruce, neutral. They gazed out of the window. The sea was calmer now and there were lengthier gaps of sky between the clouds.

'That's the garden,' said Nell.

'You don't say,' said Dougie and it could have been rude but it wasn't. She was glad for the tone to be lightened. The air in the house hung heavy and forlorn with inaccessible memories and sealed history.

'That's where you and I played,' she said, looking down to the grass.

'With my pants and a piece of bread,' he said.

Dougie left Nell to walk back into each bedroom and head downstairs when she was ready. They stood quietly in the sitting room, spent some time looking out of the kitchen window.

'Did you do much to it, when you bought it?'

Dougie took a moment. 'To be honest, my dad called me and told me it was for sale – he dealt with everything else, including organizing Christopher MacKay to come and fix whatever needed fixing and paint everything white. Then there's a company in Stornoway that came and fitted it out for the holiday market. The furniture, the kitchen stuff – even the framed prints.' Dougie paused. 'I'm sort of ashamed to say this is probably only the third or fourth time I've been in.'

Nell nodded. 'It's purely an investment, then?'

'Yep.'

'You're a property magnate?'

Dougie looked at her, caught her half-grin and laughed. 'A rented one-bed in Camden and a tiny house on the edge of a distant isle. Aye, I'm a property tycoon.'

'I rent the most boring flat in the world,' she told him. 'By choice. You actually *own* a house in this extraordinary place.'

Dougie rooted around in a cupboard. All those years he'd thought of the island as anything but extraordinary. 'Tea?' He looked in the fridge though he knew it would be empty. 'Sorry, no milk.'

'Happy to have it black,' said Nell. 'What's that?'

He filled the kettle and flicked it on, then came to stand beside her and followed her gaze to the stone building beyond the garden.

'Storage now, I'd imagine,' he said. 'It's probably older than the house itself. Might even have been another dwelling. It was most likely a loom shed at some point – for weaving tweed.' He made two mugs of black tea and led on into the garden. The wind had dropped, the sun was out and they sat on the bench. They sipped quietly, enjoying the open moments preceding Nell knowing what she wanted to do next.

'I just want to sit here for a bit.'

'That's fine.'

'It's all been so much to take in.'

'Understandably.'

'I should have brought my camera. Idiot.'

'You're welcome to visit again.'

They looked at each other. She turned her attention back to the house. 'I lived in *there*. I played in this garden. I *wish* I could remember. I wish I could recall *something*. Anything.'

Dougie was suddenly aware that neither of them had mentioned her mother dying here. He glanced at her. She was still wearing his beanie and her hair peeped out in little flicks. It was rather cute really. She should keep the hat.

'Who brought you up, Nell? In Colchester?'

'My mum – well, my mother's sister.'

'Your aunt, then.'

Nell thought about it. 'My *mum*.' She qualified. 'Flora was my mother – Wendy *is* my mum.'

'She's still alive?'

An image of Wendy came to her mind's eye and she smiled tenderly. 'Yes.'

'But all this – this truth – is new to you?'

Nell nodded and shrugged. 'I had no idea.'

It seemed pretty fucked up to Dougie.

'I'm so sorry,' he said. It sounded lame. 'And I apologize for being nosy. Anyway, I think it's amazing and brave that you're up here. Looking. Finding.'

Nell focused on her hands around the mug. Brave was the last thing that she felt. She sipped thoughtfully. 'As yet I don't know if any of this has been a good or bad idea.' Dougie watched her about to elaborate but then check herself and stop. 'Anyway, I guess we should mooch back,' she said. 'I don't want to keep Nurse Keaton too long.'

'It's funny you call her Nurse Keaton,' Dougie said.

'But apparently that's what Flora – my mother – always called her.' Nell finished the tea. 'Shall we just have a quick look in there?' She motioned to the shed.

'Sure,' said Dougie. 'You go on ahead. I'll just take this stuff back in.'

He watched her from the kitchen window. He thought she was lovely.

The small building was more substantial than a hut and felt more refined than a shed or stable. It was stone on three sides and the fourth, facing the sea, had a pair of glass doors flanked by two glazed panels. The glass itself was very dusty and the frames were peeling, the paint lifting from the wood like old lichen from stone. It wasn't locked. And there wasn't much in there – just some old garden loungers, a hose reel and various gardening tools, some cardboard boxes that had buckled and bowed from the damp. Nell swept her foot in an arc over the floor – stone slabs that were well worn, somehow warm and not cold. The light coming off the sea fed the interior completely. The view over the machair, to the sands, to the sea, was almost paralysingly beautiful.

Dougie had joined her.

'So much more than a shed,' she said. 'It's pretty cool in here.'

But Dougie didn't reply. Nell turned towards him and found him standing quite still, his lips parted, his eyes widened, gazing way beyond what was around him.

'I remember,' he whispered. He reached for her wrist. 'I remember *here*.'

It is warmer now.

*The days are finally longer and you are seven months old and robust –
a chunky bundle of squidgeable gorgeousness – so it feels the right time to
bring the studio to life.*

*Those winter months have been both the happiest and the hardest I have
known. It was so cold, unbelievably windy, and almost constantly wet. No
one in their right mind ventures out in it – and there were days on end when
we didn't see a soul. Day after day when we had to make do with standing
outside and taking some kind of company from seeing the distant lights on
in Iain's house and those of our nearest neighbours. Or, if we're lucky, the
Northern Lights. The garden was one unholy squelch. There were three
whole weeks when it was just impossible, dangerous even, for Jessie and I
to meet up. Nurse Keaton, however, came once a fortnight and never let us
down. She'd bring groceries with her, tinned goods too, even hand-me-down
clothes for Nell from other families.*

But sometimes I wasn't able to get a single fàd *of peat to light, not even
the smallest* caoran. *It just smoked without smoulder, without warmth.
Twice I ran out of gas for the lamps and matches for candles. You didn't
seem to mind. You had me. But I cried into the dark, cold house. Filling a
bath is a chore, which is why you and I splash around together only once or
twice a week. And the toilet is a hateful place last thing at night and first
thing in the morning with its corners creeping dark with damp. But this is
our home. This is home.*

*There have been days that ran into nights when I didn't sleep at all
because you wouldn't settle. 'Caidil m'ulaidh', I'd sing to you – sleep, my
treasure. Teething is torture for babies – I think it's a very bad design fault.*

Sometimes, we've gone to bed at four in the afternoon, wearing layers of clothes over our pyjamas. You have a cot now – and your tiny room is pretty – but at night you're still in with me because that suits us both. Often when you're awake I'm tired. Sometimes, though, when you've been asleep I've been hair-tearingly bored. And, occasionally, howlingly lonely. Probably just the winter blues. They say: tha an duldachd seo trom air duine – *that such dullness is heavy on a person.*

Winter out here is all about waiting and you and I have done plenty of that. We've waited for the softer weather, we've waited for your teeth to break through, we've waited for visitors, we've waited for the peat to take and our clothes to dry and the kettle to boil and the potatoes to cook. We've waited for light to lift the long hours of dark. We've waited for the right time to work on the studio. Now's the time. This is our reward.

My neighbours are the Munros – but they're still a good walk away. There's Gordon, the man. Màiri, the woman. And Wee Douglas, the boy. He's three years old. I've only spoken to Gordon a few times – but I often see him striding by on some epic walk or other and he always waves. I am terrifically fond of Màiri. She is twenty-five and Jessie and I could listen to her for hours. She's not like a big sister – she's more like the cool girl in the upper sixth. She says such outrageous things about Gordon in the bedroom department, she has Jessie and me in fits. All that laughter is so good for the children – I love that the soundtrack to Nell's early months has been mostly laughter and song. Màiri knows everything about being a mother and between her and Nurse Keaton, I've been kept sane and Nell has been kept healthy. Wee Douglas loves Nell; he sits very still and pleads to have her on his lap. He inspects her fingers and asks for a tissue to clean her nose. He likes to feed her, spooning in the porridge while singing crazy made-up songs that make Nell chortle and coo so much that she and Wee Douglas end up wearing most of the food. You can tell that he is a very kind little boy.

284

It was Màiri and Jessie who helped make the studio shipshape. Iain, Gordon and Mr MacDonald fixed the open wall before the weather set in and, for a building that is so old and hasn't been used for years, it's dry and stable. I swept and swept and swept the floor. Jessie, Màiri and I then saw to it the old-fashioned way, like their grannies used to do apparently. It was such a slog, but seemed fitting, somehow. We gathered mealtrach *– the very fine roots of the marram grass – and buckets of shell sand. We scrubbed the floor with carbolic soap then used the grass as a scourer before covering it with the sand. Two days later, when it was dry, we brushed the sand away and the floor was clean enough to eat off. We sat on upturned buckets, drank tea and ate scones. That afternoon, while Màiri jiggled Nell, and Wee Douglas had a nap on the sheepskin, I did a drawing and Jessie wrote a poem. It became our studio that day.*

Jessie is torn between staying here, sharing the studio and being a poet – and applying to university on the mainland. These days she likes the sound of Edinburgh. She tells me that wherever she goes, she'll still write her poetry and that every holiday she'll be back. She really believes that. She says that we can start a business – selling art and poetry. We talk about it for hours. But there's a little voice in me that says once she leaves she may not return. I bet she will be swept up by all that the city has to offer. I bet she'll see things, feel things and experience things that life on a far-flung island can never, ever provide. I bet she'll meet new people and they will band together like a tribe and be carried on the tides of opportunity and excitement that come their way.

I don't want her to go. I'm closer to her than to anyone I've ever known, even Joan. Jessie is my sister-friend. When she dithers about what to do I want to cry please stay, Jessie, please don't leave. I hate myself for not encouraging her, for hoping that she'll make the wrong decision – which would be to stay. Murdo is back with the Merchant Navy heading for Canada for goodness knows how long. But these days Jessie has decided that she doesn't want to be tied down by love, she says she wants to stretch her wings and fly free. Màiri said that one day, she hopes for us both to find men as good as Gordon.

Jessie rolled her eyes. 'This is the 1970s now!' she exclaimed.

'And you, Flora,' Màiri said. 'Aye – may someone make it their life to cherish and look after you and Nell.'

Jessie started laughing her head off. 'Flora doesn't need a man – look at the fine job she is doing! Our Flora is the epitome of feminism. Aren't you, Flora – aren't you!' Màiri had to shrug and nod and agree. 'This is the 1970s!' Jessie sang out again.

And I thought yes, it is. I thought this is the 1970s now. And I wondered just then, where the decade would take my daughter and me? And then I thought, who on earth would be able to find us all the way out here anyway? And then I realized that we are not lost. And that we are looked after and cherished by the island itself.

The Studio

Still holding Nell's wrist, Dougie led her over to the back wall. With boxes and junk to clamber over, it was as if they were mountaineering. He brushed away the veils of dusty cobwebs that hung like shredded curtains until the whitewashed stone was revealed. Without letting go of her, he peered silently at the wall.

'But it used to be here,' he said at length. 'It's been painted over.' He dug his nail into a chip in the surface to see if the layer of paint might lift. 'It was *here*.'

'What was?' said Nell.

'A mural,' said Dougie quietly. 'I'm telling you, this entire wall was covered with eddies and swirls of colours. The surface seemed to move – like a giant kaleidoscope. I remember a zebra. I can see its face, Nell – I know that face. It was over here – right here. And I remember butterflies too. Butterflies everywhere. The entire wall was all the blues and all the purples and silver and white. It was a night-time scene. It was magical.'

In their slim corridor between the junk and the clutter, Nell and Dougie stared at the wall, willing the white to recede.

'It's just white,' said Nell.

'But it was *here* – you have to believe me.'

'I do,' said Nell quietly, 'I do.' She was strangely touched by his frustration. 'But it's OK,' she told him. 'I'm resigned, now, to collecting other people's memories in lieu of having any of my own.' She shrugged and smiled sadly. 'Anyhow, it's way more than I had on Sunday.'

Dougie was staring at her intently, as if using her eyes like some sort of portal to the past. 'A tea set,' he said, brushing his hair away from his face. 'I remember a tea set.' He let go of her wrist and rubbed his eyes. 'I remember making tea with a toy tea set.' He touched her cheek, softly, quickly. 'I remember making a little baby cups of toy tea. It was you. It was *you*.'

Nell didn't know that a tear was going to rise and spill, but she let it and her voice, when it came, was a whisper. 'Please – what else do you remember?'

The sunloungers were old-fashioned with metal frames supporting a sling of green canvas with eyelets all along the edges, through which thin plastic rope was spiralled to secure it. There were matching folding chairs as well, but they had been collapsed and propped against the side wall and hemmed in by a rusting barbeque. The loungers, however, locked open with age and beyond folding, had been left as they were and Nell took one and Dougie took the other and there they lay, curled on their sides, facing each other.

'Bright red flowers,' Dougie said. 'A bright red flower pattern on a dress – and a matching hat.'

'Me?'

'The baby,' said Dougie. '*You*. And songs and giggling – always. In *here*. Women – my mum.'

'And Flora? Maybe?'

He shrugged. 'I don't know. The only face I truly remember other than my mum's is the zebra's.'

'Written in your memory in black-and-white,' Nell smiled.

Dougie laughed a little. 'Except this zebra was navy and magenta and silver.'

Nell closed her eyes to try to imagine it. She conjured Dr Seuss and Walt Disney and a little of *Where the Wild Things Are*.

'There was a day with a bucket – an old-fashioned steel bucket.' Dougie seemed amazed at the sudden recall. 'It was turned upside down as a seat for me. I'm kicking against it with my heels because the sound is so satisfying but I'm told off for waking the baby. The baby asleep on a sheepskin rug.'

'Is this the same day?'

Dougie shook his head. 'The bucket day was so warm in here – must've been high summer. The dress with the red flowers was a birthday party – yours, it must have been. But I so remember the tea set – it came in a little tin case painted to resemble wicker.'

Nell and Dougie looked at each other searchingly.

'Seems that you've always been making me cups of tea, Dougie.'

Outside, the wind had lessened but the marram grass still waved; the sun was dissipating all but the most feathery high clouds. The machair was showing signs of what was to come: sea pink, daisy, harebell, knapweed, gentian, eyebright, centaury and orchid. At the shoreline, two otters gambolled in a slither amongst the seaweed. But inside, Nell and Dougie lay curled towards each other in the dusty quiet of the small storeroom that once had been a little studio. Their gazes were direct and intent, going way beyond the undoubted attraction of each other's surface details and deep into the past; into thought, into emotion. Every now and then, their eyes met in the moment and the world at last seemed steady.

'It was you,' Dougie said quietly. 'It was you.'

*   *   *

'There was a zebra, wasn't there? Fire – do you remember it?'

More than four hours had passed before Dougie and Nell returned. Roddy had been and fixed the car and idled over coffee with Sophia and Gordon. Gordon knew that the planned day trip would not happen now but he was fine with that as it left something unfinished for Dougie to commit to. He'd offered to drive Sophia to the White Cottage but she'd been reluctant, telling him they could well enough leave the kids to it. The truth was she didn't much want to go back there. Gordon sensed it too, though he said nothing. So he made cheese sandwiches and they caught up on all their news. They talked fondly about his late wife and Gordon confided that no, Dougie didn't come home much at all and that yes, it was upsetting but what could he do? The boy was a man who had chosen a life hundreds of miles away.

But now that man was a boy again, standing in his childhood home, asking about zebras.

'Is it not there?' Sophia asked. 'Has it gone? All of it?'

'It's been painted over,' said Dougie. 'It's not a studio any more.'

'You loved that zebra,' said Sophia. She turned to Nell. 'Flora painted that back wall the most magical dreamscape.'

'Blues and purples and silver,' said Dougie.

'The zebra,' said Sophia. 'And butterflies – and moonbeams. Fairy tales. From the lyrics to Jimi Hendrix's "Little Wing".'

Everyone saw the smile lift Nell's face. 'That was Flora's nickname for me,' she told Gordon and Dougie, proudly.

'Will you have a piece?' Gordon offered the remaining sandwiches to Nell and Dougie.

'Thank you,' she said to Gordon; she was famished. 'And thank you for the key. It unlocked more than the cottage.'

'You're very welcome,' he said. 'Would you like another tea? Dougie, put the kettle on.'

Gordon and Sophia saw a smile pass between Dougie and Nell.

'I also remembered a wee tea set,' Dougie said. 'In a tin case painted to look like wicker.'

Sophia nodded and fixed her mouth into a smile but her eyes belied it. And she thought, when's the best time to tell the girl what happened? And she wondered whether now would be good, here, in this familiar kitchen with a family who knew. But then she thought about how Nell had yet to ask. And she thought what if Nell had decided she doesn't want to know anything else? What if seeing where she'd been born, visiting where she'd lived, meeting the boy who'd been her friend, the nurse who'd brought her into the world, all the while learning about the land and the light and the water of her early years – what if all of these were enough for Nell?

'Did I have a dress and a hat with huge red flowers?' Nell broke into Sophia's thoughts.

'Yes, pet, you did. You wore them on your first birthday.' Suddenly Sophia actively wanted to avoid the subject of Flora's death. It was the worst thing that had ever happened to her. District nursing was hard in itself out on these islands, especially in the years she'd been active when the roads were rough and resources were unreliable and communication was patchy. But in all that time, though there had been deaths – some of them terrible, some tragic – at least she'd been there, at least she'd been able to try. With Flora, she hadn't been there. She'd found her when it was too late.

Sophia tapped her hands lightly on the kitchen table and smiled at Gordon and Dougie and Nell. Then she took a slightly theatrical glance at her watch and smiled around at them all again.

'Probably best we head off now,' she said. 'I've my sister arriving all the way from Leeds tomorrow – to lend a hand when I have my hip done.'

'Yes, of course,' said Nell, 'look at the time!'

At the front door, she turned to Gordon and thanked him. Then she held out her hand to Dougie. He didn't take it; instead he slipped his hand along hers and encircled her wrist again. 'Thank you,' she said.

He nodded. 'And thank you. If I have any more memories of buckets and zebras and tea sets – I'll be sure to let you know.'

In a gaze that lasted seconds but stretched back years, Nell and Dougie said goodbye.

Pulling up to Sophia's house, Nell stilled the engine.

'Big day,' she said. 'My brain is aching.'

Sophia nodded. 'It'll take a while to sink in.'

'Dougie's lovely and I love the thought of the mural.' Really it was two sentences.

'He's dead nice, our Dougie – always has been. And the mural – yes. Flora was talented but what we all loved about her was that she was so idealistic. Not so much a daydreamer as someone who was dreaming big. She didn't *want* to be an artist – she was going to *be* an artist.'

Sophia watched Nell's gaze cast downwards to her hands in her lap. And she knew, then, that it was coming.

'How did she die?'

The question was finally here and yet Sophia didn't shirk from it. It wouldn't have been right in the Munro house. It would have been too painful at the White Cottage and just not fitting at the Buchanan house. Nor had the time been right yesterday, when she first met Nell. Was that only yesterday? But here, in the neutral bubble of a hire car outside her home, it felt OK. Where to begin?

'Was it suicide, Nurse Keaton?' Nell whispered, unnerved by her silence.

Sophia turned to her sharply. 'Heavens, no! No, Nell – nothing like that.'

Nell's voice creaked. 'It's just all my points of reference have become skewed,' she said. 'I ask because I've grown up secretly fearing that my mum's mental health issues are hereditary. Now I've been wondering whether both sisters suffered – whether it's genetic – whether I'm susceptible.'

'Nell, love, Flora was perhaps the strongest and most emotionally stable person I have ever met. She had a quick, bright mind, that one.'

Nell slumped and exhaled deeply. The relief, though, was swiftly tinged with a biting sense of betrayal. How could she be relieved that Wendy was not her mother? The woman who'd always done her eccentric best by her, the woman who'd always made her feel loved, the woman currently sitting in gaga land confused as to who was Florence and who was Nell and who she was herself at any given moment.

Sophia had tuned in to Nell. 'Flora talked about her sister – about your mum Wendy – in the fondest of terms. Zany, mad-cap, daft – those were the words she used and she obviously adored her.'

'So was it cancer then?'

'No duck, not cancer.'

'Then how did she die? Will you tell me?'

'It was an accident.' Sophia took a moment. 'It was because of the pneumonia, pet.'

'Pneumonia?' Nell thought about this. 'Isn't that treatable?'

'Yes.'

'But?'

'She didn't know. Knowing Flora she'd've passed it off as a tiresome bout of flu and told herself to get on with it.' Sophia's face was striated with pain and regret.

'I should've looked in on her. To this day – to my dying day – I'll regret that. I failed her – and you. You see, I'd sometimes pass the Luskentyre road, sometimes I'd be along it, with a patient to see, even passing right by the White Cottage, on my rounds and I'd always say to myself oh, I'll pop in and see Flora soon. But you were by then twenty months old and the pair of you were doing so well – there was no urgency, really, no need.'

Nell nodded. 'That's good though – that Flora and I were getting on with life just fine.'

'I found her,' Sophia said and she started to dab franti-cally at her eyes. 'I found her. I was passing – on my way back from the Macleans, actually, as Mr Maclean had a boil to lance. They'd get them, the fishermen – from their thick waterproofs rubbing against their necks. All that oily salt, all that wet and wind.'

And oh! Sophia could have talked about the Macleans for hours – each one of them – and theirs was a family of seven. And then she could go on and tell Nell all about the various health conditions pertaining to the different trades of the islanders. She could even tell her about the poachers who'd steal to her house in the godforsaken hours because they had a cleek speared into their backside. But Nell was holding her breath, her eyes wide and waiting. Sophia knew she had started a story that she would have to finish, for Flora's sake as much as Nell's.

'Well, after the Macleans I thought I'd just pop in on Flora and the little'un. I remember being pleased that I had time that day. There was nobody at the cottage – back door was open and all the signs of life were there – washing-up, toys on the floor, a bowl of potatoes on the table, the cat. I don't know why I expected you both to be in the house because Flora spent most of the day in the studio or walking. So I called out Flora! I called out Flora! Little Wing! Guess who's come to tea!

I thought you must be napping.

I thought Flora must be deep into her painting.

It was dead quiet.

It was dead quiet.

She was on the floor of her studio, pet. She was on the floor like she was having forty winks. And you were there with your toy tea set, offering her a little tin cup of tea. You had the jug there, the sugar bowl, plates – all neatly around her. And you were sitting by her, by your mammy, saying *wake up, Mamma, cuppa tea.'*

Nell reached for Nurse Keaton's hand and held it tightly as they stared at fat raindrops suddenly blotching against the windscreen.

'I'm sorry, pet. I'm sorry, Nell.'

'It's not your fault!'

'I wish I'd known. I could have done something. I wish there was something I could have done.'

'It's not your fault, Nurse Keaton. It's awful.'

'She'd hit her head – we reckon she'd been standing on a bucket balanced on a chair trying to paint the ceiling. She'd sketched out a design in pencil up there. All her trademark swirls and curls. She shouldn't have been up there – but how was she to know? Weakened by what she thought was the flu, being in that position trying to paint the ceiling, lungs tight with pneumonia. It's thought she passed out and fell. A possible blood clot. I'm sorry, pet, I'm sorry.'

Sophia started to cry, low deep sobs. Nell held her hand in both of hers.

'And there you were, making her a cup of tea,' Sophia wept. 'With your little runny nose and tear-stained face. *Wake up, Mamma, cuppa tea.'*

'How long had she been there?'

'She was cold. But not—' Sophia looked at Nell. 'She looked asleep, pet.'

Nell shuddered. 'Bless her,' she said and she was thinking of her little self as much as Flora. 'Where is she buried?'

Sophia blew her nose. 'At Luskentyre,' she said.

Nell thought back to the cemetery, peaceful in pasture, that she and Dougie had walked by. Nell had passed Flora without knowing, passed right by.

But Sophia was taking Nell's chin between finger and thumb.

'Three and a half weeks,' she was smiling. 'For three and a half weeks after that you were Harris's baby. You stayed with Iain Buchanan and we came to see you every day. All of us. Everyone who'd known Flora. Every day. You were our baby. But then, from the mainland, came the news. The instruction. The legals. It was all set. Iain and I took you to Glasgow. We weren't to know your surname would change and they weren't to know that you were known as wee Flora Buchanan's wee Nell. It was all rushed and emotional and the station was busy and noisy and dirty. I placed you in Wendy's arms and there we said goodbye. And your mother's sister became your mum. We hadn't an address. We lost our island baby to England.'

There was no more talking to be done. There was no more listening possible. Nell took Nurse Keaton into her home and hugged her long and close. She drove slowly back to the hotel, relieved that reception was empty and she could return to her room unnoticed. She slept, deep and dreamless.

Wednesday

'Next time, Da – next time we'll go to Berneray.'

Dougie had checked his room, stripped the bed, checked the bathroom, taken his towels down to wash. He never found it difficult to leave the house because he never doubted that the house would always be here, quiet and steady. There would be peat stacked outside to keep it warm, water in the taps, food in the fridge, a dog by the hearth called Ben. And his room would always be his, with its cupboards guarding his history and keeping his secrets until the next time.

'Next time.' Gordon raised an eyebrow at his son.

'Maybe the summer,' said Dougie, glancing away. 'Unless you fancy a trip back down to London.' They both laughed at that but the truth was that neither of them knew when they'd see each other next.

'Aye,' said Gordon. 'Now, you'll have your breakfast before we leave.'

Dougie wasn't really hungry, it was a good hour before he normally rose, but he sat at the table with his father. They ate in convivial silence and then loaded the car.

'Bonny day to fly,' said Gordon, passing his son the car keys.

The sea was millpond calm. They didn't see another car all the way into Tarbert, where the road to Lewis, to Stornoway, then took them past the hotel. Nell's hire car was bright red and one of only three vehicles in the car park. They both noted it.

'Amazing,' said Gordon. 'That the wee girl came back at all – never mind that we were here, for her to find.' He glanced at Dougie. 'Amazing, too, what you could remember.'

Dougie nodded. 'I don't think you ever forget memories,' he said. 'Seems to me you tuck them away until they are needed.' He crunched the gears badly.

'Easy, son – I'm not wanting to see Roddy for quite some time!' Gordon laughed.

'What happened, Da? What happened to Flora – to Nell's mother? I only know that a young woman died there.'

As the road climbed and fell and swung around hairpins, Gordon told Flora's story.

'The baby was *there*?' Dougie asked. 'Nell?'

'Aye. Wee mite.'

'And Fire found them both?'

'Aye, so she did.'

'Jesus Christ.'

Gordon shot his son a stern look. He wouldn't have that language in the house, nor in the car.

'Sorry, Da.'

Gordon nodded.

Dougie crunched the gears again. 'Sorry.'

And then, on the stone track to someone's farm Dougie swung the car in, turned it around and headed back the way they'd come.

'Sorry, Da.'

They drove back along the road in silence, Gordon aware that his son didn't quite have a hold on the explanation just then.

'I can't go yet,' Dougie said at length. 'I'll get a later plane.'

'Are you made of money, son?'

'No – but I know how best to spend what I have.'

Dougie drove into the car park of the hotel and stopped the car. He gave Gordon the keys. 'Don't wait,' he told him. 'I'll phone.'

Dougie wondered at himself as he took a table in the restaurant and had his second breakfast. This was not like him. His week in Harris had been about duty and his dad. His return to England, to his life, had been about himself. He ate the sausages, the black-and-white pudding, and gulped at the bitter coffee; he asked for more toast. He'd have to run up An Cliseam twice to work this lot off. What had this morning been about? Why was he still here? And then it struck him that he wasn't here for himself. He was here for Flora, for all those days he'd played in her studio and romped around her garden. And actually, he was here for Nell too. For the baby she'd been, for the woman she was now. Today, his life felt like it had significance and that was something that his dogged self-sufficiency had precluded for a long, long time.

Nell didn't see him. She had a little routine now, which played out each morning on autopilot. She did this while she waited, not so much for her breakfast, but for her thoughts to settle and for the aim of the day to transpire. The same table, the same order, the same absent-minded repositioning of the cutlery, nestling the salt and pepper pots right up against each other, leafing through the sachets of condiments, doing brickwork with the individually wrapped butter pats, constructing small towers with the miniature tubs of jam. Her notebook, open at her side, pen lid off, a clean page for a new day. *WEDNESDAY.*

The waitress brought her a rack of toast and a pot of tea.

'Oh – but I ordered coffee.' She'd only ever ordered coffee and she was always served by this Australian girl. She felt a bit affronted.

'I know,' said her waitress. 'But that guy over there asked me to bring you tea. Bit of a low-rent version of sending you a glass of champagne but, you know, whatever.'

Nell looked over to that guy over there, and there was Dougie. Tea; it made her smile.

'You're *always* making me tea,' she called over and the only other guests taking breakfast, a pair of elderly sisters, thought this very interesting. They watched the young man leave his table and take his plate over to the young woman's table. She'd been on her own this last week or so. They'd spent a lot of time wondering about her. But whatever was going on now? They nibbled their toast and sipped at their tea and relished chewing over fanciful thoughts all day long.

'Aren't you going to miss your plane?'

'I'm taking the later flight.'

'Do you have more memories for me?'

'I'm sorry – no.'

'I gave you my number, though, didn't I – in case you remember anything else?'

'You did – I have it.'

Dougie and Nell ate thoughtfully, felt the eyes of the sisters upon them.

It was nice to see him.

It was lovely to see her.

They'd shared a lot yesterday.

Dougie tapped his fingers against his cup, took a breath and regarded Nell.

'It's just I think I know where you'll be going to today,' he said. 'And I don't want you to go alone.'

The drive back to Luskentyre was beautiful but the journey itself was full of portent for both Nell and Dougie. Nell dealt with it by concentrating on the road, Dougie by asking questions of Nell that he himself could answer as well. What was her favourite part of Harris so far? Did she go out much at home? No, nor did he. Did she do sport? Well, he was a runner – but it's different running in London. Was there a husband waiting for her back home? No – he was also single. Did she have pets? He also lived in a flat and yes, someday he'd like a dog as well. Siblings? Another only child. Tell me about Frank. Tell me about Danny. Tell me about Debbie. Tell me about AJ and the coffee machine. What do you do in your spare time? Yeah, that's funny – he tried not to have any spare time either.

'Look how calm the sea is,' said Nell.

'There's a saying in *Gàidhlig*: a wave will rise on quiet water.'

'How bleak is it here, in winter?'

'Well, it's wild and it's wet. Dangerous, sometimes. We had a terrible hurricane this year which was devastating – five from the same family died in South Uist. You have to remember that the Outer Hebrides are like this one-hundred-and-thirty-mile stone windbreak taking the brunt of all that the Atlantic is hurling. There's less snow these days than when I was a kid – though we can have snow in April and May during lambing, we call it *sneachd nan uan*, the lamb's snow. Mostly, though, winter is just dark and sodden – we've a saying for that too, that the raindrops are like bull's bollocks.' Dougie thought about winter in Harris. 'It has a wild, terrifying beauty – aye. Sometimes it feels relentless. But it always passes. Turn right here, Nell.'

'I know – I was going to.'

'I forgot – you'll know this road well enough yourself, by now.'

'I do – I like that I do. I used to live here, you know.'

'I saw you on the beach, on Sunday. You were – shouting at the sea. You were stomping on the sand.'

'I was running out of time and there was no sign of Flora.'

'You were in distress.'

'I was. Shall I park here?'

'Aye. Do that.'

'Nell?'

'I'm nervous.'

'You want to take a minute? Is it too much?'

'I'm OK. I'm OK. I'm just – *nervous*.'

'And why wouldn't you be? When you're ready – only when you're ready. We can just sit here awhile.'

The burial grounds at Luskentyre are both ancient and modern. Absent is the whimsy of the higgledy headstones of a crowded English country graveyard. Absent is the gut-wrench of the endless row upon neat row of a municipal cemetery. At the Luskentyre burial grounds – one old, one modern – the dead are laid to rest at a quiet but genial space from each other, on sweeping meadows protected by the dunes with a vantage point out over the sea. Many of the headstones face the sea, some don't; those young laddies finally coming home from the Great War who drowned when the *Iolaire* went down on New Year's Day 1919, they look to the land.

The old burial ground, after a tight bend in the road and over a small bridge with a burn running, sits behind a stone wall. At the furthest point on the road is the new cemetery. Plots are spaced at respectful distances and headstones are in black, in grey, in white, each packed tight into the earth; steady, solid, enduring and from a distance not unlike sheep hunkering down close to the ground when the gales blow.

'I don't know where to find her,' said Nell.

'We'll find her,' said Dougie.

And he gave her his beanie again.

'Well,' he said after a while, 'here's my mum.'

Nell stood back as Dougie touched the headstone.

Ah – Mam. Miss you still. Aye, Dad's all right, Dad's the same. Aye, his health is good – still wearing down the paths with his walking. Me? My life is ridiculous but I'm going to make changes. I promise you. I'll look out for Da. I will. You rest easy. All will be well.

'Seventeen years,' Nell said. 'You must miss her still.'

Dougie nodded.

'Were you close?'

'Aye. She was an amazing woman. Took no nonsense and gave out love. She knew what to do. Always knew what to do.'

'Was it hard for your dad?'

Dougie smiled sadly. 'I heard him talking to her just the other day.'

'We don't have to leave – if you want more time?'

Gently, Dougie put his hand against the small of Nell's back and guided her forward. In his head he could hear his mam saying, get going, laddie – you haven't all day.

In the old burial grounds, eventually they found her. They found Flora. Some of the headstones were blurred with orange and grey lichen. There were family plots and war graves and the oldest, now just nubs of rock amidst a thicket of roses, belonged to those brought along the Coffin Trail during the Clearances. But they found her, they found Flora.

Nell pulled back and her breath caught because before she even reached the plot she somehow knew that it was her mother's. Her world polarized just then. And though he stayed by her side, Dougie blended into the background. So did Colchester. And Wendy. The Chaffinch. Flying into Stornoway. The hotel room. The wall of photos in her kitchen. Nurse Keaton's front room. Debbie's front room. The Coronation teacup. Frank and his blackbirds. They were all part of someone else's life because, just then, it was only Nell and Flora – exactly as it had been once, for twenty precious months.

Flora Buchanan
2nd June 1952–29th May 1971
Mother to Neilina
Loved by all

Nell leant by the grave, put her hand tenderly to the head-stone and traced each letter, each number.

Thank you.

Thank you.

Heartfelt and silent, Nell spun her gratitude back in time and hoped, how she hoped, that Flora would receive it.

She stayed as she was, deep in her connection, until Dougie touched her shoulder. As she stood and came back into the day, sunlight spun through the cloud and blessed her face and the wind amplified the grasses whispering that it was OK, it was OK, Flora was OK and it was OK, now, to let go and finally to cry.

Dougie wasn't sure what to do so he wrapped her in his arms and tucked her head under his chin while she wept against his chest. He had his own tears to understand. Some were for his mother. Some were for Flora. Some were for Nell. Some were for Gordon. Some, still, after all these years, were for Daisy. But some were also for himself because his tears could only mean that he could feel again and this was finally something to celebrate as much as it was something to also fear.

'We're a long time dead,' Nell said, her nose snotty and her face blotched. 'But look – look where we are. There is no better place for Flora to be.'

Dougie faltered.

'You need to make peace with the beach, Nell.'

She looked from the car key she was holding to Dougie's outstretched hand and turned her face to the sun. She was flooded with warmth; from the weather, from finally finding Flora, from this man who'd offered her his hat and his hand.

'Here,' she said, giving him back his beanie and squeezing his hand quickly.

'Keep it,' he said and he walked on. 'It suits you,' he added, over his shoulder.

They walked away from the graves and toward the dunes, walking through narrow twists between sandy knolls fringed with marram which led down steeply to the beach.

There was calm. At the shoreline the waves, which had started 3,000 miles away, had run out of steam today and were lapping benignly. The lagoons and rivulets, which plotted and pierced the sands of the wide tidal plain between Luskentyre and Seilebost, were still. Nell, though exhausted, felt at ease and Dougie found he was happy to mooch and meander over the beach that up until now he'd only ever sprinted across.

'What'll you do next, Nell?'

'I'm going to buy this cushion cover I saw on my first day – as a keepsake,' she said. Then she laughed at herself. 'To brighten up my flat, to add a little warmth.' He looked at her quizzically. 'When you've grown up in a house tumbling with chaos and crammed with stuff – you set yourself up in a sort of monastic environment.'

'Tell me?'

Nell stopped, stooped at the water's edge, dipped her hand and then took her fingertips to her mouth.

'Salty,' she said.

'You don't say,' he said. It made her laugh.

She went quiet for a while. She didn't usually talk about this. She shrugged at Dougie.

'My childhood home was at best colourful and eccentric – at worse frantic and chaotic. On some days there was a crazy vibrancy to it all. When my Mum was "up" it was a place full of colour and song and the mass of knick-knacks and paintings were like cast members in a play. The furniture and the wafts of shawls and scarves and throws and random pieces of fabric draped over the doors became the stage set on which she danced through the day.'

Dougie liked the way Nell talked, he liked the way her eyes narrowed but glinted on her route back through memories.

Nell opened and closed her hand; the seawater had dried and the salty tightness felt nice.

'But when my mum was "down",' she said, 'then the air at home was drenched in a claustrophobic silence.' Nell looked at him. 'I'd go looking for her but all that stuff would be in the way. Everything seemed threatening. Horrible carved wooden tortoises and leering china figurines and cackling Venetian masks and scarily decorated rain-sticks and dark, oily paintings of people we didn't even know – they were all menacing. And the scarves and the throws and the drapey things – strangulating. Anyway. Anyway.' Nell stopped. 'You don't want to hear all this. Why am I telling you all this? Sorry.'

'Actually, I want to know,' said Dougie.

'Well, in a very roundabout way, what I intended to say is that in my own space I choose simple. I choose open and bare. So I can see everything. So there is calm.'

'But you liked the cushion in the tweed shop?'

'Yes.'

'It's a cushion – it's functional?'

'Yes,' Nell faltered. 'But it's also a solid piece of Harris for me to take home.'

'My grandparents were cottage weavers,' said Dougie. 'My mother too. For it to be *Clò Mòr*, or the Big Cloth as we call Harris Tweed, it must be woven in the home of an islander. I wouldn't be surprised if Flora's studio had a loom in it at some point.' He flopped down onto the sand, his arms loosely over his knees. Nell sat beside him. 'And I have my granny's crotal spoon.'

'Her *what?*'

'It's an old spoon – with one side cut diagonally. She'd scrape the crotal off the rocks – it's a lichen, a dye – for the wool. It turns it a deep red-brown.' Dougie looked at Nell; he appeared confused and amazed. These memories weren't just pleasurable, the recounting seemed to him suddenly significant. 'They taught me. I know the ways. I'd never mistake goat's beard for crotal. I could show you. I could show you, Nell.'

'Show me what?'

'I could show you the ribwort that gives a blue colour, heather tips for pastel green and hogwort for dark, willow leaves or bracken roots for soft yellow, peat soot for warm cinnamon, *sealasdair* – iris – for black and the sorrel used for colour-fastness. *Dathan nàdarra*, Nell – true earth colours. I know where these things grow and I could show you.'

'Except you're flying back to London today!' Nell laughed. 'It must've been amazing growing up here – but the kind of amazing you only truly understand much much later.'

'I couldn't wait to get away.'

'And you so rarely come back?'

Dougie shrugged.

'I couldn't wait to leave home,' said Nell. 'I went back, for a little while, when my mum really wasn't in a good place – but I had to go. For my own well-being.' She looked desperately sad. 'She can't live alone now.'

'Your mum,' Dougie said cautiously. 'Wendy.' He paused and looked straight out over the water, his voice suddenly raised. 'I *hate* the way when we say "mental" it immediately has derogatory implications. Like poor mental health is somehow unsavoury, inferior, even shameful compared to poor physical health. What I'm trying to ask is – your mum Wendy—'

'—has mental illnesses,' Nell finished for him. 'Yes. Severe.'

Dougie nodded.

'Yes,' said Nell softly. 'Bless her.'

'When she was bringing you up?'

'Yes. Undiagnosed for years and years. She'd just be called bonkers. Crackers. Bit of a nutter. As if it was self-indulgent. Not real. As if she should know better.'

'And she brought you up on her own?'

'Yes.'

'When you left here?'

'She was still married for a couple of years after.'

'You see your da?'

'No.'

Dougie thought about this.

'My childhood wasn't unhappy,' Nell rushed. 'It was just – well.' She looked at the sand, focusing hard on a square inch, wanting to shrink down and get inside that world for a while. 'You know, I always feel like I'm betraying my mum when I speak about any of this.'

Dougie brought his attention right to her. She could feel it. Warm. Intent.

'I worried a lot when I was young,' she said. 'I had the most amazing, loving, unforgettable mum who just wasn't able to be amazing and loving all the time. And those are also the times that, unfortunately, are unforgettable.'

'Where is she now?'

'She lives close by – in a care home. She's safe *there* because she's not often *here* these days.' She looked at Dougie and shrugged sadly. 'So, really, I have two lost mothers. One lost in a different time, one lost in a different place.'

Dougie thought about this. 'No, Nell, no,' he said. '*You* have lost two mothers.'

She listened to his words. She'd never thought about it this way.

'And I really feel for you,' he said.

I'm not going to cry I'm not going to cry I'm not going to cry.

They sat quietly. There was just a gentle breeze and the sound of the water lazily slapping the shore was soothing. And Dougie thought, I never knew the beach could be like this. He thought, I'm always using it as a running track, I'm only ever running away from it. And then Dougie thought, perhaps for the first time, how to sit still, to just *be*, might give him more power and strength than running at full pelt. And he thought about what was then, what had happened all those years ago. How he'd left the island for college without a backward glance yet six years later it had received him home without question at a time when he couldn't stand up and he couldn't talk and he couldn't distinguish between day and night. And hadn't he turned his back on all that it had given him, all that was here, ever since, really?

Dougie glanced at Nell; she was gazing out over the sea to the velvety form of Taransay. His home hadn't had ornaments and trinkets and shawls and people who danced on furniture. His home, his family, was plain and strong and always there.

And yet.

'I went to art college in Manchester and I met a girl and fell head over heels and I didn't properly notice her depression because

I didn't want to see it and she committed suicide when she was twenty-two and then I got heavily into the rave scene and I fucked myself up on drugs and had a nervous breakdown.'

Nell stared at Dougie aghast. He'd said it in one breath and now she held hers. His eyes were closed and he was swallowing hard. Who was this man she'd met only yesterday whom, it seemed, she had known all her life?

So this was his story?

She put her hand between his shoulder blades and let it rest there.

'That's why I don't shoot portraits any more,' Dougie said. 'Because of the time when I couldn't see what I should have seen.' He glanced at Nell. 'The camera should be an extension to the eye – not a substitute. If I saw emotion, fear, love, secrets, pain, dreams in a person I could capture it with my camera – a hidden moment that not even the subject was aware of.' He looked away from Nell, away from the sea, down the beach to the looming growl of the North Harris hills, a bank of bruised clouds hunkering on the peaks. 'I don't trust myself with a camera these days. For work, yes. For the inanimate, yes. For vast landscape and crammed cityscapes – yes. That's it. Photography is my wage, not my calling. Because it lied. It lied the same time as my eyes failed me – when I took all those portraits of her, when I couldn't see what was staring back at me in black-and-white and vivid colour.'

'What was her name?'

'Daisy.'

Nell moved her hand and swept her arm around his shoulders.

He turned to her and gave her a little nudge. 'So I take your bonkers mum,' he said, 'and I raise you one suicide girlfriend.'

Dougie's words hung emphatic in the air. And yet, as callous as they could have been, they weren't. Somehow, they worked. They worked because he'd said them to someone who he'd sensed wouldn't judge, who'd empathize, who *knew*.

Nell was the first to go. With a snort, laughter wracked her body so hard that she was soon lying on the sand in a twisting side-stitch of giggles. Dougie joined shortly after and there they stayed with their glee and their grief, with the tears and the laughter and the understanding and the connection and the sand in their hair and the unseen eagle high overhead and the sea, always the sea, rolling in to take a little of their sorrow deep into the water and away.

'My bum's wet,' said Nell.

'So's mine,' said Dougie.

He got to his feet, held his hand out for Nell to pull her up. This time, she let her hand be held and on they walked.

'It was 1990,' Dougie said. 'It feels like a lifetime ago. Like someone else's life. MDMA. Acid. Whatever, really. Getting off your face – that's the way you grieve when you're twenty-three.' Dougie nodded. 'My poor da.' The memories were still too stark to focus on for more than a moment, like the spiked dazzle of looking straight into sunlight. 'He brought me back here, me and my rucksack of Prozac. And all I remember of that time was that day became night became day became night. Again and again and again. God, I was a mess. I probably still am.'

'I like your dad.'

'My Mum had died not two years before. He'd had all that. And then he had to have me and all my shit. I've never really thanked him and I've never really said sorry.'

Nell listened quietly. 'But you know, I doubt he thinks you've anything to apologize for.'

'I should say sorry for being such an arse more recently,' Dougie said. 'Ignoring his calls, feeling irritated by his concern. Being insensitive – bigging up the merits of life in a place as far from my upbringing as it's possible to be.'

Nell gave Dougie a poke in the ribs. 'But look at you now,' she said. 'I mean, yes, your hair is all over the place and a bit of a tousled cliché – but it seems to me that you're pretty bloody fine. You're strong,' she said. 'You're kind. You care.'

Dougie raised his eyebrows.

'It's a compliment,' she mumbled. 'I'd take it, if I were you.'

And Dougie looked at where he was. Luskentyre. On primeval land that had more grace and solidity and substance and longevity and meaning than the shiniest modern metropolis. And he knew he had a choice. He could take Nell's compliment and pop it in a box and keep it in his cupboard in his childhood home to revisit when he was next here, whenever that might be. Or, he could take it with him when he flew away from the island in a few hours' time. He could take it with him back to Camden, to his day-to-day, and allow it to change the way he saw himself and the way he'd chosen to live his life. Much as Nell was taking home with her a cushion cover in Harris Tweed because she'd grown away from the bare neutrality she'd thought was so necessary.

'And the island,' Dougie said quietly. 'I turned away from it and I don't even know why. I've resisted coming back. I've stopped calling it home. And yet it's the place where I'm most *me*. But listen to me blethering on – I have a plane to catch.' And he changed direction and walked back along the beach, Nell having to jog a little to catch up to him.

An hour after she'd dropped Dougie at his home, with a fond smile and a shy kiss on the cheek and a reminder that he was to call her with any new memories, Nell was still sitting in her car outside Flora's old cottage. What had she looked like, Flora? Nell attempted to clothe her imagined mother in mini-dresses and Mary Quant, and then Woodstock and flowing hair and robes. She tried to picture herself with butter-gold curls and dimpled elbows and knees, a sagging nappy and a grubby face. Maybe her mother had painted on the walls of her bedroom – perhaps doe-eyed animals and flowers with smiling faces and a rainbow that stretched from one side of the wall to the other. Maybe her mother had sung daft, made-up tunes to entice baby Nell to eat. But how could she know? She couldn't. The only thing she could do was feel. And her overriding feeling was that she had been loved.

She left the car and walked through to the back of the house and looked up at the bedroom window. Yesterday she and Dougie had looked down from there onto the garden. *That's the garden*, she'd said. *You don't say*, he'd said. She laughed today as she had yesterday. She peered in through the kitchen window, from where she'd first caught sight of the stone building at the back of the garden. Yesterday. Only yesterday. Now, a day later, she had enough facts to fill in the blanks and pack the pages of a virtual photograph album that she hadn't known existed. What a charmed and happy life she'd had for 21 months.

Nell walked across the garden and opened the glazed doors to the studio. There was no mural but there had been once. Right there, all over the back wall. And there was meant to be one up there, on the ceiling, but that wasn't to be. And here on the floor, this was where she'd kicked her chunky baby legs on a sheepskin rug while three-year-old Dougie bashed his heels against a steel bucket. And here in this studio she'd toddled around. This is where she'd had her first birthday party in a dress with great big red flowers. And here, on this floor, she'd made cup after cup of tea while her mother lay there still as still can be. Nell knelt down and ran her hands over the floor, and felt warmth not cold from the old, old stones.

*   *   *

Al was at reception when Nell returned later to the hotel.

'You eating with us tonight? Fish and chips?'

'I may surprise you and choose the daily special.'

'Which today is – scallops. But you could have that as a starter and the haddock for your main.'

'Thank you, Alasdair.'

'Och, it's only fish and chips.'

'I mean, thank you – for everything. But I'm going to check out tomorrow morning.'

'You are? You've found all the missing pieces to your puzzle?'

'I think so.'

'Well, I hope we'll see you again. You'll always be welcome.'

'I hope so too. But I need to go home,' said Nell. 'I want to see my mum.'

It's May 1971.

Jessie is coming home for the summer soon. The machair is exceptional this year, as if to welcome her back. And I want the painting to be well under way by then.

The Munros will be back by then too – Màiri has taken wee Douglas up to Stornoway to stay with her mother for a while as she had a fall. Jessie left not soon after Nell's first birthday party last September. Oh, I loved that day – and Nell looked like a little dolly all dressed up in the frock and hat with the bright red flowers that the Munros gave her. She was like royalty that day, visitor after visitor. If I'm that proud of her turning one, whatever will I be like when she turns six, or double figures, or becomes a teenager, or passes a zillion O levels or graduates from Oxbridge University or on her wedding day or when she has her first child! One day I'll be a granny – imagine that! If this wretched bloody cold-flu thing doesn't kill me first.

So Jessie left for university last September, to study Politics and Something Else at Edinburgh. Joan was busy training to be a teacher, but her father was offered a job in New York and the whole family moved there just before Christmas. We don't know when we'll see each other again and our letters take ages to arrive. She cannot believe she hasn't met Nell. And neither can I. Joan says that the Outer Hebrides still feels further away than New York.

Joan and Jessie – I love them I hate them I'm proud of them I envy them I miss them I want to hear about everything and I don't want them to forget me. Jessie is a far better pen pal than Joan but that's alright – whenever I receive their letters it's a treat. I read them out loud to

Nell – but I've taken to whispering the racy bits to myself because even though she's a baby, it doesn't seem right. She can't exactly talk yet but she can say words. 'Garden' was her first word. Anyway, I don't tell her all about Jessie and Joan and the boys they're in love with. I don't tell her that sometimes I have a little envious wonder about what their lives must be like. I haven't seen Jessie since she was last home at Christmas, almost five months ago. I haven't seen Joan in over two years but I love her just the same – even if she is the worst correspondent in the world. Well, she's slightly better than Wendy who sends me huge ramblings every once in a blue moon. But that's just my sister. When her letters arrive the envelopes are practically bursting because she folds the various sheets of paper over and again. She says Jimmy is 'a one'. I don't know what that means. 'Oh, Jimmy is a one.' I can't hear her tone of voice. I'm not sure if she's saying this is a good thing or a bad thing.

I haven't been well. Stupid flu thing. Every time I cough it feels like a plank of jagged splintered wood is trying to break through the back of my ribs, it feels like my lungs are being crushed between rocks. I'm easily out of breath too – but maybe that's because Nell is now a wee chunky lump of loveliness. She can walk – but obviously not too far and the little dips and tussocks of the land are like mountaineering to her. How can I resist her when she puts her arms up for a carry? I can't, that's the answer! But at the moment, with this rotten cold, even climbing the stairs is hard work. If I don't feel any better soon, I'll call for Nurse Keaton – I'll walk to the Munros and ask if I might use their telephone. It's frustrating feeling so poorly. It's exhausting.

My new mural peps me up, though. It is for the studio ceiling – hardly the Sistine Chapel but I thought that, as the back wall is a night scene inspired by 'Little Wing', I'd paint a daytime scene on the ceiling. I borrowed a book about Van Gogh from the mobile library which comes by every fortnight. I'm inspired! However, instead of his great big sticky blowsy sunflowers, I'm going to paint all the machair flowers – but ten times the size – against a background of swirls and swooshes to signify both the hurling wind and the whispering breeze, to describe the swell of the sea and the waves of the storm, the slick of dolphins, the swoop and rise of eagles.

Iain once told me that in a square yard of machair you can find forty-five different species of wild grasses and flowers and that some of the rarest birds and bees make it their home for a few months each summer. I want the mural to look so vibrant, so pretty that people will imagine they can actually smell that lovely honey fragrance, that they can hear the skylark and the corncrake though they can see neither. Jessie and I plan to picnic with Nell and spend day after day in the sea meadows, in the machair, and I will sketch all that I find. Harebell and eyebright, red clover and white, tufted vetch and gentian and primrose, bird's-foot trefoil, the buttercups and the daisies and the orchids. I will paint the bees too – the moss carder and the great yellow bumble bee that's extinct in mainland Britain. I know my meadow will be upside down on the ceiling but I don't mind. My whole world is a topsy-turvy world. And I love it.

Who knew!

Who knew that this would be me at my happiest?

I am living a good life now on my island of hills and heather, of sand and flowers, of sheep and eagles, of bleak bare rock, of horizontal rain and sawing wind and dazzling sun and cerulean water. Here, I've been taken into the embrace of the kindest, gentlest and wisest of folk. I'm living on an island that is as refreshingly mundane as it is inspiringly mystical, where the sea is black and angry, where the sea is turquoise and benevolent. I'm living on this island on the edge – right on the very edge. Me and my beautiful baby girl.

Mainland

It was a normal Friday morning at the Chaffinch Café – in that it was as normal as ever. There were the usual struggles to wriggle incompliant hands into the blue latex hygiene gloves, the customary bickering over who was going to arrange the pastries and who was going to give the tables a wipe-over, as well as the standard inadvertent clumsiness that precluded anything being done speedily. A glass had been broken already. The coffee machine had been polished and thumped but was finally up and running. A sudden discovery that there were no bananas had led to only momentary panic. A lazy wasp threatened to keep everyone hostage. In its own peculiar way, however, an unconventional efficiency played out and the café opened punctually at nine o'clock.

Timing her arrival with the slim breather between workers grabbing breakfast to go and school-run mums commandeering every table, Nell slipped in to cheers and tears, bear hugs and kisses.

'Everything all right?' she asked.

'Broke a glass,' said Libby.

'Killer wasp,' whispered Rachel.

'Coffee machine keeps almost dying,' said AJ.

'Bananarama drama,' said Danny.

'Did you miss me?' Nell laughed.

Sanjay positioned his finger and thumb an inch apart. Alex said so-so but kept his arms wrapped around Nell's waist. Danny said is the Pope a Catholic. And Debbie said yes. Yes, said Debbie coming through from the kitchen and giving Nell a bowl of salad. Yes, we missed you. Welcome home.

'I found her,' Nell whispered to Debbie. 'I found her.'

Later, after closing, once everywhere was wiped, swept and scrubbed, Nell and Debbie sat at one of the tables with coffee and a plate loaded with broken cookies and the nub ends of cake.

'And this little cottage – it's a holiday rental?'

'Yes,' said Nell.

Debbie went to the back to fetch her bag and brought out her laptop, scurrying her fingers over the keyboard. 'Show me,' she said, swivelling the screen towards Nell. 'Which one is it?'

'I didn't think of doing this,' Nell marvelled, scanning through properties. 'I was kicking myself for not taking my camera that day.'

'Now you can visit from the comfort of your living room,' said Debbie. 'No need to bugger off to the Outer WhereTheFucks for days on end.'

Nell searched and found the little white cottage. It was called Am Bothan Geal – the White Cottage.

'Here.'

They clicked through the pictures, lingering and enlarging, Nell annotating each room in turn, elaborating on what the view was truly like and all the while recounting what she'd seen, what she'd learned, who she'd met, how she'd felt. Debbie clicked backwards and forwards, marvelling.

'There.' Nell pointed. 'You can just see the studio at the very edge of this one.'

'I've always thought this place could do with a mural,' Debbie said and Nell looked at the long side wall of the café with its Morse code of scuffs and dints. 'Don't you think so, Little Wing?'

Nell laughed. 'My name is actually Neilina. I think it means "cloud champion".'

Debbie raised her eyebrow at Nell. 'So we'll be ordering a new apron, then?'

Nell shook her head and traced the embroidered name on hers. 'I *am* Nell,' she said. 'To everyone. And I always have been.'

'And tell me more about this Dougal bloke?'

'*Douglas*,' Nell said. 'Dougie, really.'

Debbie knew his name was Douglas but she just wanted to double-check on the faint rise of colour to Nell's cheeks, the ping of light in her eyes.

Yes. It was there.

How many times had Nell sat in her car in this car park, looking at the building that held her mother, steeling herself for the unpredictability of her visit? She'd lost count. She'd never been able to simply skip out of her car, wave blithely to whomever was on reception and take the stairs two at a time to be welcomed by her mum with open arms and intelligible conversation. There were times when they gamely chatted – but over two disparate conversations. There were times when they embraced – but neither felt sure who was in the other's arms. Today, though, as Nell gazed beyond her windscreen at the trees softening the angles of the redbrick block, at the rose bushes planted sympathetically to raise a smile and an ooh for anyone walking in or out, she sensed something new weaving through her usual trepidation. It was a gentle emotion, a softly spoken one, but she wasn't quite sure which. It made leaving the car and heading for the doors less onerous. Once inside, the staircase didn't seem so steep, the corridor not so cold. It was an odd sensation but a welcome one.

Nell knocked gently on the door and went in.

Wendy was watching television.

Of course she was.

But that's OK, thought Nell. She thought, that's what my mum likes to do.

She sat herself down on the side of the bed and studied her mother's profile and she thought if Flora had been half as beautiful as Wendy, she'd have been blessed.

When Nell was young, television wasn't merely something for her to watch with her mum, it had been a springboard for things to do. These were the times when Nell and Wendy occupied the same world and spoke the same language. *Dallas* and *Dynasty* meant that they had to play with big hair and talk in broad Texan for hours afterwards, sometimes days in Wendy's case. *Great Expectations* saw Wendy dress as Miss Havisham and Nell as Pip for a trip to the shops. And repeats of *I, Claudius* had them perfecting, even bettering, Derek Jacobi's stammer – which made a taxi ride to the station slightly mortifying. And best of all *The Young Ones* had them playing Rick and Vyvyan, jumping up and down on the sofa, hurling cushions and newspapers about and stomping around on the kitchen table shouting unintelligibly. But today, Wendy was watching *Friends*.

'Who's your favourite Friend?' Nell asked.

'Joey,' Wendy said, her eyes not leaving the television set.

'Mine's Phoebe.'

'Smelly cat.'

'How are you?' Nell touched her arm. 'You're a bit cold.'

'I am a little chilly.'

Nell went to the cupboard and found a soft cardi. 'Here.'

'Which friend are you?' Wendy was looking at her, puzzled.

'Monica?' Nell tried tentatively.

'No – not off the telly. In real life?'

Nell smiled sadly and put her palm softly against her mum's cheek. 'It's me, Mum. It's Nell.'

Wendy looked startled. 'You're Nell? Look at the size of you!'

'I'm thirty-five.'

'Never!' Wendy clapped her hand to her forehead before peeping through her fingers spryly. 'That makes me *ancient*.'

'Don't be daft, Mum.'

Wendy reached for Nell's hand. 'I haven't seen you for *years*.'

'Well,' said Nell, 'about a fortnight.'

'A lot can happen in a fortnight. Believe you me.'

'A lot did happen these past two weeks.'

'But look at you! Where have you been?'

'I've been to Scotland, Mum.'

'You don't say!'

'I do. I went to Harris, Mum.'

'To Harris?'

'To Harry's.'

'To Harry's?'

'I went there for you.'

'For me?'

'Yes, Mum. But for me too.'

'For you?'

'And for Flora.'

'Flora? Who's Flora?'

'Not Flora – *Florence*. I went there for Florence.'

Wendy's eyes darted all over Nell's face as though they were caught in a pinball machine. However, the confusion that Nell had so frequently seen criss-cross her mother's face was absent. Nor did her eyes have that alarming blankness. Today was very different; today Wendy's expression was fearful.

'Did you find her?'

'Yes, Mum – I did.'

'My little Florence?'

'Yes.'

Nell took a beat, not knowing what best to say next. Should she suggest that Florence was still alive? Should she pretend she was Flora? Should she make out that it was still 1969?

'My darling little naughty *naughty* Florence?'

And then Nell realized that perhaps Wendy just needed straight facts.

'Florence had *such* a good life out there, in Harris,' she said. 'She had a little house and she was an artist. And a mummy. And she was very much loved. Everyone thought the world of Florence. And she was safe. She was cared for.' She paused; Wendy was looking at her unflinchingly. 'Everything is OK now, Mum. Florence was very happy before she died. Her life was good. She is at peace now. Florence is at peace. Everything is OK now.'

'Oh,' said Wendy, her voice tattered with relief and sorrow. 'Oh.'

'I visited Florence's house. I met her friends.'

'You did?'

'I did. I saw where she is buried. It's beautiful.'

'And the baby? The little cheruby-blonde pudding baby?'

Nell inhaled deeply and brought her face close to her mother's. 'Oh, Florence was an excellent mother. And she is so grateful to you, Wendy, for all that you've done. Florence is so happy that you were there for her, that you stepped up to be such a good mummy to the little puddingy cherub-blonde baby.'

'Yes?'

'Oh yes.'

'Because look at you!'

'Look at me, Mum.'

'Yes – because I mean *look at you*! Look at you!'

'I'm all grown up.'

And Wendy put her hand on Nell's head and kept it there.

'What a beauty!' said Wendy.

'Thank you,' said Nell.

'I mean it!' said Wendy, stroking Nell's hair, tucking a lock behind her ear. 'Look at you!'

'I meant – *thank you*,' said Nell with her eyes closed, able to rest her face against her mother's steady hand for the first time in however long. 'For being my mum. Thank you from Florence. Thank you from me.'

There they stayed, recognizing the moment long enough to make peace with the past.

'I didn't really know what to do with a baby,' Wendy said, forlorn. 'But I loved trying. I really loved it. And I really tried. I know that I did.'

There they stayed until the Rembrandts struck up 'I'll Be There For You' as another episode of *Friends* aired.

'Who's your favourite Friend?' Nell, eyes still closed, asked Wendy.

'Rachel,' said Wendy. 'No – Chandler.' She tutted at herself. 'No,' she said. '*You* are. You're my favourite.'

When Nell opened her eyes she saw that Wendy wasn't engrossed in the television screen, she was gazing intently at her and a tear was slipping its way down her cheek.

'Oh, Mum,' Nell said, and she took the tissue peeping out from the corner of Wendy's cardigan sleeve and gently dabbed her mother's eyes.

Nell had always thought of the building as *holding* her mother, as if it was holding her in, keeping her captive, holding her against her will. But as she left that evening, she realized that it wasn't like that at all. It *held* her mother, held her compassionately and safely in its own embrace. And when Nell returned to her car and began to drive home, she gazed back at the building keeping her mum safe, its dull red bricks now suffused with warm toffee tones by the evening light. Finally, she could identify the infiltrating emotion.

It was gratitude.

*   *   *

Two weeks. Two weeks Dougie had been back from Harris and though a steady stream of work kept him occupied, the general dullness of the jobs gave his mind time to wander. It chanced upon no old memories and that meant there was no reason, therefore, to contact Nell. For Dougie, however, Nell was herself the subject of new memories and these flowed across his mind's eye unbidden. Each time one surfaced, he stayed with it for a while before telling himself *for God's sake!* and turned away from it. He told himself to pop Harris back in its distant bubble. He reminded himself of the blueprint he'd painstakingly designed for his life, one that avoided complication, challenge or complexity. He was the architect of his own steel structure, clad with one-way glass; he had not configured room for changes and he was reluctant to tinker with the efficacy of the design.

However, his week back in Harris, where so much was familiar and so much was new, had created a distinction between what had been before and what could be now. It had served like an umpire in the ring, keeping two boxers apart. Nevertheless, there had been a gentle shift in Dougie since his return. He was debating with himself more. And so, when the phone rang and clicked through to the answering machine and his father cleared his voice to begin an awkward ramble, Dougie picked up.

'Hey, Dad.'

'You're there? That's you? Douglas – hello?'

'Aye, Da – it's me. How are you? How was your day?'

What Gordon hated most about phone calls was that the bloody handset seemed to suck away anything to say. But on that night, it was as if Màiri was at his side with her pad of paper. She used to do that when they spoke to their boy after he'd first moved away aged seventeen. She'd scribble little suggestions for questions Gordon could ask, anecdotes he could recount.

Ask him how work is.

'Work? Oh – it's busy. A catering industry catalogue this week and then medical gadgetry all next week, near Chelmsford.'

'Chelmsford, eh?'

'Yes.'

Ask him if he's been in touch with Nell.

'You've been on your runs, Dougie?'

'Only in the gym, on the treadmill.'

Gordon laughed. 'Why on earth would someone want to run for all they were worth but get nowhere?'

Ask him if he's been in touch with Nell.

'And you've been out walking, Dad?'

'Oh aye – every day.'

'The weather?'

'You know how it is here.'

'Aye – I do.'

'And all is well with your flat, is it?'

'Yes,' said Dougie, 'everything's fine here. How's the house?'

'Ah, just the same.'

'And Ben's well?'

'Aye – Ben's well.'

Ask him, you old numpty – ask him about Nell.

'So!' said Gordon.

'So,' said Dougie.

'And have you been in touch with Flora's wee girl?'

Gordon liked the momentary silence that followed. Whatever the answer, his boy was having a think.

'I haven't had a reason to,' said Dougie. 'I've not been able to recall anything else about that time.'

And Gordon wondered, what would Màiri say about that? But the old house was strangely silent.

'As if you need a reason,' Gordon chided lightly.

And Dougie thought, Jeez, Dad, you sound just like Mam.

So Dougie photographed medical gadgetry the next week. Every day, he drove to Chelmsford and every day he negotiated road signs for Chelmsford that also had Colchester underneath. And then there was that sign that put Colchester above Chelmsford. And then, soon after, the fork where Chelmsford was one way and Colchester the other. Colchester, Dougie reasoned, was neither on his route to work nor on his way home. But it was on his radar. And when thoughts of Nell came barging into his mind while he was at work, he tried his best to blink them away, to look through his lens and focus on all the shiny lifesaving equipment instead.

You can't just turn up on someone's doorstep without phoning first.

You can't phone unless you have something specific to talk about.

Yes, you can.

* * *

'What are you doing later?' Debbie asked Nell.

'Visiting Frank,' said Nell.

'I mean *later* later.'

'Oh – you know,' Nell shrugged.

'Gazing at the rental cottages in the Outer Humdingers?'

Nell laughed. It wasn't far off the truth.

'You don't want to try my ceramics class?'

Debbie was expecting Nell to react as if she'd suggested she join the Moonies.

'Actually, I might,' said Nell, giving Danny a wink who gave her a massive blink in reply.

The Chaffinch was busy. They'd run out of soup and, predictably, Debbie's jambalaya but there was no time to rub the items off the chalkboard.

'Two cappuccinos, please,' the next customer ordered. 'And a cheese-and-ham toastie. No! Cheese-and-tomato. Actually, can I have cheese-ham-*and*-tomato?'

'Yes,' said Nell.

'And could one of the cappuccinos be decaf soya?'

'No problem – AJ, you've got that? One cappo, one cappo decaf soya?'

'I've got that,' said AJ.

'I'll have soup, please,' ordered a woman who looked like she was having a very bad day. 'And a tuna baguette. And a giant chocolate-chip cookie – but can I have the second one down, the one that's poking out a bit?'

'You may,' said Nell. 'But you can't have soup. Soup's finished.'

'Oh. Oh. I'll have the tuna baguette and the giant chocolate-chip cookie – second one down, that one there – and a smoothie. What smoothies do you have?'

'Green, red, orange, yellow,' said Nell. 'You can kind of guess the ingredients from the colours.'

'Which smoothie is most like the soup?'

'Sorry?'

'Which smoothie is most like the soup?'

And Dougie, standing quietly in line, wondered how Nell would answer that.

'Green,' said Nell. 'It was watercress soup – so I'd say the green smoothie.'

'OK. The green smoothie. And the—'

'—tuna baguette and the second choc-chip cookie,' Nell said. 'Eat in or take away?'

'In, please. I'm literally dead on my feet.'

Nell put the order through the till. At the same time she reached down without looking to hand a wodge of paper towels to a mother whose child was wearing his meal, while also admiring Danny's handful of tips, saving the jug of straws from going flying and calling out *next please!*

'Just a cup of tea,' said Dougie. 'Please.'

'Dougie?'

'Just thought I'd see how your tea-making skills compare to mine.'

Rachel, who rarely spoke, noted Nell's sudden silence; that the queue stretched to the door and that Debbie wasn't in sight.

'Eat in or take away?' Rachel's scratchy little voice asked Dougie.

'In – if that's OK?'

'Want a cookie or cake?'

'Lemon drizzle, please,' he said.

'Pay her,' Rachel told Dougie and pointed to Nell. But Nell suddenly had no idea what anything cost or how the till worked.

'It's on the house,' she said.

'Join me?' he said.

'We're crazy busy,' said Nell.

'Join him,' Debbie said, suddenly there. 'We're fine. We're always fine.'

Danny brought Dougie's tea over, much of which was in the saucer. He went back for the cake and brought another slice for Nell too.

'Debbie says Don't. Rush. Your. Food,' Danny told them.

'Are you the famous Danny?' Dougie asked him.

'Yes, I am,' said Danny. 'You can leave a tip if you like.'

'Danny!' said Nell.

'I'm worth it,' said Danny.

'That I don't doubt,' said Dougie.

'OK, well I'm very busy,' said Danny, walking off with a dismissive wave.

'He's just as you described,' Dougie said. He looked around the café. 'Everything is just as you described. I've been into every single bloody café to find you. I couldn't remember what it was called. I knew it had something to do with birds.'

Just then, Nell loved him for defining the café by its name, not its workforce. Dougie sipped his tea and tried the cake, swooning as he did so.

'But Dougie,' said Nell. 'What are you doing here?'

Dougie thought how best to explain. 'I was working in Chelmsford. I finished early. I wanted a slice of cake.' He looked at the cake. 'I wanted to see if I recognized you not in your crappy old anorak and walking boots.'

Nell tipped her head to one side and gave him a long look. 'Meanwhile your hair does its Heathcliff thing out of the Harris wind too.'

Dougie laughed.

'I like your café.'

'I like it too,' said Nell.

Dougie nodded, as if in private conversation. He looked at Nell. 'I would have phoned – but I haven't been able to remember anything else for you.'

In her peripheral vision Nell could see Debbie staring straight at her, hands on hips, her head cocked, as if urging her on and blocking any escape routes.

'I was hoping you'd phone anyway,' shrugged Nell with a mumble and a blush that Dougie found strangely bolstering.

'Aye.' Dougie sighed. 'I'm a dick. And there it is.'

Thoughts were colliding so fast that they pushed through all his barriers and he had no time to censor what came next. 'But that's not to say that I haven't thought about you. Because I have. And yes, I didn't want to phone – but I wanted to see you. So here I am.'

'But I have to go,' she said. 'I have to go now, Dougie – to see Frank.'

'Frank of the Walnut Whips?'

'Yes.'

Dougie stared into his cup, hoping to read signs in the tea leaves about what to do next. But it was a teabag and he'd already squeezed it and put in the saucer.

'Well, Nell,' he said. 'Maybe another time? If you fancy?'

And Nell looked over to Debbie who'd managed to keep one eye on her, one eye on a customer, and the eyes in the back of her head on the staff, and Nell knew that Debbie would say that the ceramics class could wait.

'Or maybe later?' Nell said. And then she told herself to say something else, quickly. 'I won't be too long.' And she told herself to say more. 'Or maybe come with? Frank doesn't have many visitors.'

In Frank's flat, Dougie had been given the seat of honour, the olive-green velvet armchair with the tasselled fringing and the antimacassar, and there he sat in the still of the afternoon watching Nell and Frank and the ritual of the birds. Frank was just as Nell had described too and Dougie told himself that he could learn from her powers of observation. The ability to see things just as they are, thought Dougie, rather than faffing with filters, rather than wondering if it could somehow be bettered or manipulated.

The birds had their walnuts and Nell and Frank came away from the window, their heads haloed by the golden graze of the afternoon sun. How Dougie wanted to say stop! be still! to reach for his camera. His camera was just there, in his satchel by the side of the chair, but Nell and Frank had now moved and their ethereal counterparts had disappeared.

'You have me to thank,' Frank said, Zimmering his way up close to Dougie. 'I was the one who told this young lady to speed-bonny-boat her way to Harris.'

'I took a plane, Frank.'

'You're spoiling the romance,' he chuckled. 'Now, young man, young Douglas, you're a photographer, are you?'

'That's one way of putting what I do for a living,' said Dougie immediately regretting how sardonic that sounded.

'Come,' said Frank. 'Come.' Dougie stood up and followed Frank's slow passage over to the corner cabinet. 'The only thing I can bend these days is the truth,' Frank said, wheezing at his wit. 'So if you could please bring me that black photo album down there on the bottom shelf, I'd be grateful.'

Nell helped Frank back into his chair and she and Dougie sat together on the sofa, the album between them. The pages took them into another world, one in which a time and a place long gone were saved for posterity in mesmerizing sepia.

'My sister Josephine, 1933,' Frank annotated. 'There was no vanity in having one's photograph taken in those days. It was dear – but that's what we saved up for. We didn't want snapshots of mundane moments to glance at, we wanted style. We wanted substance. That's what having one's picture taken was all about. It was about us, at our best. It gave us an everlasting mirror to look back at who we were. Look at this one!'

'Frank – that's *you*!'

'Yes – that's me. Twenty-two years old and off to war.'

'Look at you!'

'Handsome devil,' Frank laughed. 'Had 'em lining up, I did. That uniform had magic powers, I'm telling you.'

Page after page of faces to be named, lives to be remembered, anecdotes to resurface; Frank's recollections spun bright colour into the shades of cream and mocha of the old photographs. Dougie was utterly absorbed. Who had photographed these people? Where had they learned their art? What equipment had they had back then? How did they elicit such natural smiles yet such poise, such character, such life in the eyes from such formal poses? The dance between light and shadow, between surface and depth.

'These are quite something,' he told Frank. 'They're very moving. I find them quite humbling. Who's this chap?'

'That's my big brother, Alfred. Died in Burma. Bless him. Bit of a bugger – but always looked out for me. We were orphans, don't you know,' said Frank. 'And I'd trade in all these photographs for just one of my parents.'

'I'm just going to get Frank's meal ready,' Nell said, walking quietly away.

In the kitchen she set about her usual routine of switching the oven on, emptying the bin, refreshing the water in the kettle, checking what was in the fridge, re-washing the plates and the cutlery as required. She could hear birdsong but wasn't sure whether it was in her head. She touched her cheek; her hand was cool but her skin was warm. She tuned in to her heartbeat; it was strong, it seemed elevated.

It was good to see Dougie again. More than good. She stood in Frank's kitchen a while longer with her warm cheek and her strong heart. She thought, listen to your heart, Nell. Listen.

'Frank,' said Dougie.

'Yes, boy.'

'Could I take your picture?'

'You want to take it away? The one of me in my uniform? The one of me at the dance? Oh no, I don't think so.'

'No – I mean your portrait – to photograph you. Here. Now. I have my camera. May I photograph you?'

Frank looked at Dougie as if he was mad. 'This old bag of bones, this wrinkled old sack?'

'I wouldn't describe you that way.'

'I'll probably crack the lens. I'm no longer the handsome lad you see in that book. I don't know where he's gone. It seems to me I blinked my eyes and suddenly I'm not twenty-two, I'm eighty-eight.'

And Dougie wanted to say yes, you were handsome then but you are far more beautiful now. 'Your face is the map of your life – and the light just now is stunning.'

'Barmy,' said Frank. 'But – all right. How do you want me?'

'Just as you are.'

'Right here?'

'Right here.'

'Having my picture taken – fancy that.'

Dougie took his camera and placed it on his lap. 'I haven't taken portraits for a long while.'

'That's a shame,' said Frank. 'I'd say they are very important.' He thought about it. 'If you have the know-how, I'd say it is your duty. They document our stories, they keep us living.'

Unseen, Nell observed Dougie at work. Or was it work? He seemed so in tune with his camera, with his subject, and he appeared confident and relaxed. As he photographed Frank, Dougie chatted away, every now and then touching him gently to alter an angle, to remove a bit of fluff from his pullover (today, peacock blue). Nell remembered all that he'd told her in Harris, about why he no longer photographed faces; now she was witnessing him vanquishing that. Against the satisfying rhythm of shutter clicks she approached quietly, carrying the tray with Frank's starter, today pâté with crackers. She placed the tray on the table and as she straightened Dougie said her name.

'Nell,' he said and, in the moment that she turned to him, the edges of her features caught the light and her eyes were all his. His camera clicked. She looked at him and he looked at her and he released the shutter again. 'Sorry,' he said. 'I should have asked. I should have checked if you're OK with this.' He gazed at his hands, at his camera, knowing what was in it, what he'd achieved. 'Are you OK with this?'

Nell nodded.

'Might you sit beside Frank?'

She sat beside Frank.

And Dougie waited, watching all the while. He observed their soundless interaction, the trust that was conveyed through a wink and a smile, the pat of a hand, the happiness and gratitude sown deep in Frank's heavily furrowed face, Nell's fondness for him glowing in the softness of her skin and the gentle glint to her eyes. He understood now why they meant so much to each other. As he watched and as he looked he could sense the depth of mutual affection. Could he infuse a single photograph with all of that? It wasn't purely about releasing the shutter at precisely the right confluence of light, shade, expression, form and ephemera and then controlling the developing process of the print. Dougie's skill had always been to go deeper and to enable his sitters to forget he was there. He was able, therefore, to catch the moment Nell and Frank thought they heard one of the blackbirds and turned at the same time to look. And the moment afterwards where they brought their faces close to each other to commiserate. And the moment when Frank looked like he was nodding off but Nell kept surreptitious watch. And the moment when Frank began to reach for his glass of water but Nell intercepted and handed it to him. And Nell tucking in

Frank's napkin. And the two of them laughing about something incomprehensibly funny about pâté. And Nell subtly checking that Frank was managing fine. And Nell looking straight to camera and her expression appearing to say to Dougie I'm so pleased you're here.

And then Dougie was out of film. Frank's dinner was out of the oven. The light was flattening. It was time to leave.

'I'd better get back,' said Dougie, looking from his car to hers. Nell's was red, just like the hire car.

'Thank you for coming.'

'Are you kidding me? He's amazing!'

'Not just for Frank. Thank you for coming – for me.'

'Och.' Dougie scratched arcs with his foot in tarmac planings of the car park. 'You're welcome.' He looked at Nell and shrugged. 'But I should've phoned. I'm a bit of a twat, really.'

Nell knew what Debbie would tell her to do. 'Well – I mean – if you want we could get a snack? Or something?'

All Dougie had eaten since late morning was the lemon drizzle cake at the Chaffinch.

'It's not the centre of the culinary universe, Colchester,' said Nell. 'But I know a couple of really nice places we could go.'

Dougie thought about this. How easy it would be.

'I'd better go, really,' he said to Nell. 'I've got stuff to sort out.'

Nell nodded as if her suggestion had been idiotic. Dougie thought to himself, never a truer word spoken.

'OK.'

'So.'

Clumsily they hugged.

And Frank, who'd left his pudding untouched to dodder his way to his window in the hope of seeing lovebirds instead of blackbirds, sighed.

'That's not the way it's done,' he muttered from the third floor down to Dougie. 'Give her a kiss, you silly arse.'

Dougie called himself a lot worse during the drive home. Not least when he stopped at a garage, bought a disgusting meal deal and gulped it down while he drove. He could have been eating something lovely somewhere nice with Nell, as she'd suggested. It did his hunger no favours. And what Dougie realized as he drove was this: it would have been far simpler in Harris. In Harris the light is in its continual bounce between sky and sea and makes everything seem clear. In Harris it was just Dougie and Nell against a complicit backdrop of otherworldly scenery and shared history. In Harris, they were a world away from their everyday.

He didn't go directly home. He drove to Soho, to Joe's Basement, and had them develop his film and run off a contact sheet. When he arrived back at his flat, he beat himself up a little more then turned on his computer and uploaded his day's work, scanning through frame after frame of medical gadgetry. Then he took a shower. Watched the ten o'clock news. Then he went to bed. Got up after ten minutes. Paced around his bedroom. But then, for two hours he studied the contact sheet of the photos taken at Frank's. It was, he knew, a beautiful collection. Three or four of them were good, really good; they were exhibition good. And there was one of Nell that was so – so Nell.

Diabhlaidh amadan fuilteach. Bloody idiot.

When Nell's phone rang so late she assumed it would be Philippa in New York. Last night they'd sat in their respective homes, in their discordant time zones, and looked on their laptops at the White Cottage on the rental website. Philippa had sobbed. 'Oh, Nell,' she'd cried, 'little baby Nell.'

'Yo, girl!' Nell answered. But it wasn't Philippa this time.

'It's Dougie.'

'Oh – I thought—'

'Listen,' he said. 'Listen.'

So Nell listened thoughtfully to the ensuing silence.

'I don't know,' Dougie said. 'But. Nell – it's Dougie.'

Jesus Christ! he chided himself. I sound just like my father.

'Nell.' Come on, man! 'It was so good to see you. Danny, Frank and the cake. Colchester.'

Nell just listened. What else could she do? She'd simply have to wait for something to make sense.

'I've been kicking myself ever since,' Dougie said and then he muttered something unintelligible in Gaelic at himself before continuing. 'I would have loved dinner. But – I don't know. I've spent years. Years! Defiantly on my own. You know? I've been single too long. I've forgotten the tune. The dance.'

'I never realized there was a tune,' Nell said quietly. 'And I've got two left feet when it comes to dancing.'

'Look,' said Dougie, tugging his hair like an old-fashioned doorbell, as if hoping something would miraculously open before him. 'Look. Can I – please – could I see you this weekend? Do it all a bit better.' His mother would tell him to spit it out. 'I've thought of you so much,' he said. 'I think of you all the time.' And then he waited. He calibrated the weight of silence at the other end of the phone and however she responded would be

OK because he'd stood up tall and he'd been truthful out loud. In his own clumsy, fearful way, he'd been honest.

'I'd like that,' said Nell.

Dougie's sigh of relief was so audible it made her laugh.

'For what it's worth,' she said. 'I've thought about you too.'

And she didn't know, just then, how much this was indeed worth to Dougie.

He looked over the room to the box he'd brought back from the depths of the cupboard in his childhood bedroom.

'Good,' he said to Nell. 'All good, then.'

'Goodnight – *oidhche mhath*,' she said clumsily.

'Aye, Nell,' said Dougie. '*Mo chridhe.*'

Nell assumed it meant sweet dreams or something.

'My heart,' Dougie said quietly into the stillness of his room.

And in Colchester, in her bare little flat, Nell sat on her underused love seat in pleasant surprise and hugged the Harris Tweed cushion she'd bought in Tarbert. It was pinks and purples and reds and browns and the yarn was not without the characteristic tickle. But that only made her hold it all the tighter.

Slàinte

While Nell paced around her bedroom, assessing the various outfits she'd draped across her bed, Dougie lay in his and allowed thoughts to meander through his mind like a stream in high summer. The flat above was playing reggae and the beat and the bass were akin to his heartbeat. He felt calm; calm about the day ahead and steady about Nell. She was connected to Harris and yet independent from it too; she'd appeared out of nowhere in a place that was everything to him and she'd arrived bearing this lifelong attachment, this intrinsic bond. And in Colchester, being with her again, he knew he wasn't imagining it, he knew it wasn't one-sided, he knew they both felt it. And he knew, after so long, it was time. There was an inevitability and, intriguingly, it was this that brought a sense of calm.

If he was honest with himself he also fancied the pants off her, pretty much since she'd first pulled his beanie on. At the time, though, he'd snubbed the sensation – focusing instead on being her guide, leading her through the tussocky grass and along the edge of the dunes to the White Cottage, accompanying her back in time to the place where she'd spent those first happy months of her life.

But his last night in Harris, in the secrecy of his bedroom, he'd thought about her – ordered up for his mind's eye a vivid recall of her lips, her eyes, the swell of her breasts, her neat bottom as she walked across the garden to the studio while he'd watched from the kitchen. He'd imagined her naked, of course he had. He'd imagined kissing her. The feel of her. It hadn't felt wrong or ridiculous, that night, but it had felt refreshingly illicit. It wasn't as if he was going to call downstairs to Gordon, hey! Dad! I'm fantasizing about Nell – much as he wouldn't have called downstairs when he was fifteen, hey! Mum! Dad! I've got a porn mag under my mattress. It was private, it was tantalizing, it was his. And that's what Nell had been to him ever since, some strange talisman suddenly in his possession to feel overwhelmed by sometimes, and enthralled by at other times. For a while, it had felt dangerous and unsettling, something to brush off and turn away from. But his trip to Colchester had changed that. And in three hours' time, she would be his for the day.

The heartbeat.

The reggae.

The thoughts.

From Harris via Colchester to here.

No expectations but a whole lot of hope.

Daft bastard. Get up.

In Nell's flat, the potential outfits she'd pulled together from the decent clothes she owned lay lifeless on her bed – as if there'd been bodies within which had vaporized. She thought about it. Dougie had seen her in crap jeans and a shit anorak and appalling walking boots. He'd seen her with flour in her hair and an apron emblazoned with her name. So – no, not jeans again. She was bored of jeans. And no, not the cargo pants – supremely comfortable yes, but not flattering. And certainly not the outfit she'd worn on the disastrous date with that bloke that Debbie knew. She couldn't remember his name just then. Public schooly. Rufus or Jasper or Simeon or something. It seemed such a long time ago. For Nell there was before Harris and there was now. And of course there was Harris itself.

Since her return, in her mind's eye and whenever she could, she had spent a lot of time back there. She pored over her maps and re-tracked her routes with her finger. Even by gazing at a heavy bank of mauve-grey clouds which hung beyond the river rising up from the horizon and blurring her eyes a little, she could re-imagine the Colchester scene as those heather-heavy hills far away. She'd dedicated evenings well into the small hours online, searching and scrolling through photographs of the Outer Hebrides, videos on YouTube and, of course, lengthy periods spent on the holiday rentals website advertising the White Cottage. And Dougie's beanie was on the hook on her bedroom door. He had said keep it, hadn't he. And yes, she'd frequently held it to her nose and closed her eyes and inhaled. It wasn't just Dougie's scent, its fibres seemed to exude the fragrance of that day – salt and sand and grass and sheep and clean clean breezy air, white paint in a holiday home and the old walls and the dust and the warm stone floor of a forgotten studio.

But if she didn't hurry up and make a decision about what to wear, Nell was either going to miss her train, or have to run for it in her underwear. She told herself to stop faffing and opted for a layered top that was clingy but soft, a gauzy skirt just grazing her knee and her favourite brown boots. Boho. They called it Boho for Kate Moss. Nell thought her attempt was probably more So-so. But she didn't care. She felt happy, she felt excited and intrigued, charmed – and her reflection positively shone back at her when she checked the mirror before hurrying out.

Philippa had sent a text message telling her to kiss the face off him. Debbie had left a voicemail just saying good luck and to remember to enjoy it. Debbie also passed on messages from Danny and Libby and Sanjay, who wished to tell Nell that she was to behave, not to get married and not to be late to work on Monday because of silly love. Danny had also told Debbie to tell Nell not to have sex. But Debbie had no intention of relaying that.

For Dougie and Nell, suddenly nerves were in an utter tangle in the minutes leading up to them meeting, but they dissipated immediately when they saw each other. The hug was longer, more tender, and the kiss, which was initially directed to each other's cheeks, brushed lightly over lips and tasted good.

'Come,' said Dougie and it felt natural as anything to take Nell's hand. And though they were headed for the National Gallery, they found themselves doing laps around Trafalgar Square while they chatted nineteen to the dozen. And when they entered the gallery, though they had tickets for the Caravaggio exhibition, they were continually waylaid by conversation so they walked a random and circuitous path towards the exhibition through room after room, only half-looking at the art. And they marvelled that there was so much to talk about. And they relished all those gaps to fill in for the years that had passed since Nell had left the island at the age of twenty-one months. Occasionally, a painting silenced them and they'd stand where they were, filling their eyes while they continued to fizz inside. Stubbs's *Whistlejacket* had done it for Dougie. For Nell, it was *The Enchanted Castle*, by Claude.

'Look! It's like Amwin Swede,' she said.

Dougie peered at the canvas carefully. 'Like where?'

Nell frowned. 'A Moon Suede?'

'Huh?'

'The castle,' said Nell, giving Dougie a little shove. 'On the road to Hushinish. Surely you must know it? It's a bloody great castle right there on the road! Don't tell me you've never been there?'

He was mindful to stifle laughter because her earnestness was touching. 'You'll be pronouncing that Amhuinnsuidhe, Nell.'

He repeated it and they said it together. 'Avn Soo Yeh.' She looked so crestfallen that he laughed and hugged her. 'Call yourself a Hearach!'

'A what?'

He laughed and spontaneously kissed her forehead. He liked her face when it was all flustered.

'What did you just call me?'

'Hearach,' said Dougie. 'One who is from Harris.'

And Nell stood stock-still. That was who she was. And she thought that perhaps the reason she was so obsessed with looking at the map and the photographs and the websites wasn't just about the trip she'd just made, or even about finding Flora. She'd found something of herself she didn't know had been lost. She thought about the misplaced little girl she had so frequently felt herself to be during childhood when Wendy was up or Wendy was down or Wendy had disappeared into her room or somewhere well beyond the house for hours on end.

There was a bench in the gallery and Nell sat down heavily. She looked at the painting of the castle. Actually, it wasn't anything like Amhuinnsuidhe. It was simply a springboard. She realized how she'd been continually looking for connections to Harris since her return, no matter how vague, how tangential or fanciful.

'It's a funny thing, identity,' said Nell, as Dougie sat beside her.

Dougie nodded and sighed. 'Sometimes, I think we redefine who we are according to the shit that happens. But actually, I've come to learn that it's enmeshed and we can never shirk off what's always been there. Because it's always been there.'

Nell thought about this. 'There's so much I never knew.'

'But it's always been there, Nell. Don't you see? Waiting. Waiting.'

She shrugged. She looked downcast. She thought of Marjorie – why had her aunt set out to deny her only niece the truth? And in those periods that Wendy had been in her right mind, why had she said nothing either? Why had no one, anywhere, contacted her?

Dougie watched her. OK, he thought. OK.

'You know,' he said, 'what happened to me in Manchester back then – I set myself up in a different guise after that,' he said. 'I became Camden, I became deludedly self-sufficient, I became resolutely unreachable.' He paused. 'I turned the temperature right down – on what I felt, and on what I'd give out. I actively sought out the beige in life – in my career, my social life, women.' He slid his hand over hers. 'But that's not me.'

Nell nodded. 'When I was a child, I often didn't feel like a child on account of being a carer, I suppose. So I think I've always set my own dials on low because of my mum. I couldn't forge ahead – I couldn't – I had to remain close by for her.' Her fingers curled around his like a new fern and they contemplated their woven hands quietly.

'I was so protective of my mum – yet I've spent most of my life focused on being the opposite of her,' Nell said quietly. 'When I was little, I'd kneel by my bed clasping my hands piously – like I'd seen in paintings – and *pray* not to be like her.' She looked down beyond their hands to Dougie's boots with the brogue pattern at the toe, the brown leather burnished with wear and polish. 'Such guilt, Dougie, that accompanied that. And my terror and dread of her illness being genetic.' She shook her head at herself. 'Dougie – the *relief* that Flora died only of pneumonia. The joy – yes, *joy* – that Flora had no mental illness.' She paused. 'What sort of person does that make me?'

Dougie took a beat. How he wanted to wrap his arms around her. 'One who wants to embrace life?' he said. 'One who is happy to live in the real world. One who wants to be well. I'd say that makes you an extremely healthy person.' It was a statement and he said it levelly.

Nell had never thought of it like that. 'For years I've told myself that it meant I didn't love my mum enough.'

Dougie looked at her in disbelief. 'Nell,' he said, 'that love can never, ever be doubted.'

'But Dougie – this terrible, cruel relief that Wendy isn't my birth mother. What sort of daughter does that make me?'

'Seems to me you've absolutely nothing to doubt on that front.'

'And yet – since finding Flora, since learning about who I am, how I came to be, how I came to Wendy – now I know how she had to step up to being a mum against all the odds, in the face of all her challenges. How hard – almost impossible – it was for her.'

'And look at the great job she's done with you,' said Dougie.

Nell brushed away a hot tear. 'It's occurred to me that it doesn't matter, really, if Wendy does think I'm Flora every so often. Doesn't mean she doesn't love me. Because what's very clear to me now is how much she loved her little sister. Her little sister who had the blonde-cheruby pudding baby. And Wendy loved that little baby with all that she is.'

Neither of them was expecting the Caravaggio exhibition to be so uncompromisingly dark, so dramatic, so morbid, so sexual, so sinister. Spotlit, and hung on walls of dark red and blue-grey, were sixteen canvases. That the paintings mostly alluded to biblical scenes appeared to be a foil. Pierced and swiped by dramatic chiaroscuro lighting, bodies writhed and drapery gaped and faces were twisted in torture and ecstasy. The gallery was crowded but nobody talked, not even a whisper. They felt like voyeurs witnessing all manner of death, violence, sex and corruption.

Trafalgar Square in all its dirty grey glory was incongruously bright when they emerged.

'I need a drink after that,' Nell laughed.

'I need to show you something,' said Dougie quietly.

Nell stood in Dougie's flat. It was west-facing and warmed by the late-afternoon sun. It smelt good, it smelt clean and of fresh washing. He hadn't prepared for her arrival; it hadn't been his intention to ask her back and his clothes were drying on a rack in the living room. Nell noted that he hung things out the way she did; precisely, neatly, minimizing creases and any need to iron. She was transfixed by his great-grandfather's beautiful hand-drawn map of Harris, all the place names in *Gàidhlig*, and Dougie stood behind her, telling her about his family history. She browsed the books on his shelves; he had the same old Penguin copy of *The Catcher in the Rye* with the silver jacket design as she did. And she liked the way he'd put the remote controls back by the TV, not strewn around the sofa. Most of all she was captivated by the framed photographs of Harris.

'Are these yours?'

'Yes. They're old.'

'They seem pretty timeless to me.'

'Thank you. I keep meaning to change them – I have stacks.'

'I have four,' said Nell. 'Stunning photographs of Yosemite by Ansel Adams. Well, from a calendar. The framing cost a hundred times more than it did.'

Dougie tipped his head. 'You know, sometimes photography isn't a caught moment. The photograph – the emotion behind it – is fluid for the photographer. There's no such thing as a straight print. Ansel Adams would often print the same negative perhaps ten years apart, altering the exposure according to how he felt, to how he perceived his subject on any given day, in any given year. Melancholy one year, lightness the next.'

'I had no idea,' said Nell.

'Some say photography is an art – some say it's a science. I think it's both – but there's alchemy too.'

'And now you take photos of tools and buckets?' She looked at him quite levelly.

He shrugged. 'Product photography is lucrative,' he said.

'But Dougie—' she said, and she pointed at his framed land-scapes, raised her arms and dropped them.

He stared at her right back. 'Did you still feel like you needed that drink?' And she sensed he was telling her not to go there. Not yet.

'It's not even six,' she smiled. 'But why not – let's live a little.'

'Red?' he called from the kitchen. 'Or an awful white? Or beer, but it's warm.'

'Whatever you're having,' Nell called back. 'By the way, what washing powder do you use?'

Dougie stood in the kitchen and smiled. He liked this. He liked the way that Nell and he could bounce around from one topic to another, dip their toes into the profound, give the mundane resonance. He came back through with two glasses of red wine and a pouch of Fairy capsules.

'Here,' he said, 'happy birthday.'

'It's not till September.'

'I know – I was at your first ever party. It's just in case I forget. It's just in case we're not – we don't . . .'

But Nell stilled his sentence. She kissed him on the lips. 'But we will be,' she whispered. His eyes sank into hers and he pulled her close, his hands in her hair as he kissed her back. He smiled at her reddened face and touched her lips with his finger.

'*Slàinte*,' he said, raising his glass.

Nell and Dougie sat and drank and sometimes they chatted and other times they were still.

'What's in the box?' Nell asked. It looked oddly out of place, just randomly plonked in front of the bookshelf.

'Are you hungry, Nell?'

'I am a bit.'

'What do you fancy?'

'I could absolutely murder a burger – a monumentally big juicy one that drips down your chin, with posh French fries that come in a little tin mug.'

'Well, as luck would have it there happens to be such a place right around the corner – shall we go?'

'Let's. What's in that box, Dougie? More photos?'

'Wait!' said Dougie. 'I almost forgot.' He went to his desk in the corner of the room and brought back a large white card envelope. He placed it on Nell's lap.

'Go ahead,' he said.

She opened it, pulled out the contents and gasped.

'It's Frank!'

'Aye.'

'And me!' She stared at the photograph. There she was, glancing at Dougie as she placed Frank's tray down. 'I don't remember you taking this! But it's so – *still*. Like I'd been standing there, lost in thought, for hours. The light, Dougie!'

'Like a modern-day Vermeer, Nell,' Dougie grinned. 'Aye, the light was just perfect. Actually, I like this one.' It was Nell and Frank turned to the window in the hope of catching their blackbirds. 'And this.'

Nell took the print from him and studied it. Frank with his rheumy-eyed smile and a depth to his gaze that spun through the decades of his history for all to see, as colourful as the clothing he now wore to brighten up his eighties and his inevitable passage to the ultimate dark.

'I love my Frank,' she said quietly.

'I can tell,' Dougie said.

'May I keep this?'

'Of course.'

She looked through the other prints. 'Your photographs are beautiful, Dougie,' she said. 'It's like your eyes see things differently.'

'Shall we go and eat?'

'And that box, though – is that more photographs?'

Dougie regarded the box that he'd brought back from Harris. Energy seemed to vibrate between it and him. His head was full and his appetite had gone. Here's my can of worms, Nell, he thought. Here's Pandora's box. Open it at your peril – and mine.

But Nell was looking at him intently, affection criss-crossed with a little confusion at his sudden silence. And Dougie thought then that it might just be safe now, to lift the lid on what had been.

'The box is what I was talking about earlier,' he said quietly. 'This is what I need to show you. What I want you to see.'

He brought it back to the sofa, placing it on his knee, his hands gentle and protective but holding the lid down firmly. And just then, Dougie thought that it wasn't a very big box to contain such monumental contents, undisturbed for so many years.

'At college, my tutor used to bang on about Caravaggio. She believed the artist invented cinematic light. She taught me to look, to really look, to elicit the inner light of a subject. I always remember her telling me to *find the hidden darkness and illuminate it.*' Dougie glanced at the box and looked at Nell. 'I was good, Nell. I was bloody good, aye, so I was. I won all the prizes at college and when I left, that's what I wanted to do. I wanted to photograph significance meaningfully and beautifully.'

Nell's eyes were wide. She sensed this was a prelude.

'Really, a camera is just a gadget,' Dougie said. 'It's inanimate, it's designed to work, not feel. In essence, the camera is just a fancy, clever conduit between the photographer's eye and the subject. Click – and there you have it. The truth be told for all to behold year after year after year. Like Frank's beautiful photographs, Nell, in his old black album – as relevant and vital today as the day they were taken. That's what the camera should do.'

Dougie breathed deeply.

'But the eye – the eye is different. The eye should detect, draw to the surface the very essence for the camera to blink-capture in its mechanical moment.' He looked at Nell and then he looked at the box. 'It's just that Daisy is in here – and I haven't looked at these photographs for over ten years.' He paused. 'But three weeks ago, when I was leaving, finally, for the airport, I told myself it's time. So I brought this box back with me. Because I saw the way you dealt with pain and it had an impact on me.' Dougie took his hands off the lid and cupped them around Nell's face. 'And I've thought of you so much, so much,' he said quietly. 'So I know it's time.'

Nell took Dougie's hands away, kissed them and held them in hers. Then she took the box and placed it on her lap and slowly, tenderly, lifted the lid.

Daisy.
Nell smiled at her.
Hello, Daisy.

Daisy was just a normal pretty girl with late-1980s hair and clothes almost identical to those Nell had worn back then. She was smiling for the camera, smiling for her boyfriend who was probably calling out *Cheese!* There were no snapshots, just beautiful portraits printed eight inches by six. There were eleven of them. Five in colour, six in black-and-white. Four were indoors, the rest were outdoors mostly in calm weather, two in the wind with Daisy's hair whipping around her face. Nell didn't recognize the indoor location but she knew where the rest were, she knew that light, she knew that wind, she knew the fuzz and suck of the moors slapped hard every now and then by the blunt bulk of primordial rock.

Nell looked at the photographs carefully, compassionately, smiling at the girl who smiled emptily back at her.

'But can you see it?' Dougie asked, his voice hollow and wretched and suddenly Nell was aware he was focusing directly ahead, that he hadn't looked at the photographs at all.

'See what?'

'In her eyes?'

Nell looked at the photograph of Frank that was to her side. His eyes drew her down deep into the soul of the man. But Daisy – her eyes were shallow, they had a flatness, like a footfall on concrete rather than on sand.

'Dougie,' Nell said gently, 'there is little to see in her eyes.'

'The distress,' Dougie said, 'the helplessness, the terrible knowledge she had of what she was going to do.'

'No, Dougie,' Nell said. 'It's not there.' What Nell saw was a girl not hugely bothered about having her photograph taken or by the man taking it. Smile! Say cheese! Come on, Daisy. Fuck's sake, Dougie.

'But I should have seen it,' Dougie said. 'That was meant to be my skill, my gift. That's what I won prizes for. What I trained to do. When I looked through the lens at her, I should have seen it.'

Nell looked at him closely. Carefully, she turned Dougie's face towards her, insisting that he look at her. 'It's not there, Dougie. You could not see what really wasn't there. And never mind the naked eye, even a camera with the most powerful lens in the world could not capture what was not there.'

'Why did I not know? My stupid fucking eyes!' he whispered. 'Ten days later, Nell. Ten days later she was dead.'

'And you've spent every day since wondering – torturing yourself – why you didn't know and what you could have done?'

'Not every day,' said Dougie. 'There were six months when I was so off my face I didn't have a single viable thought – and another six months when I was a monosyllabic lump being cared for by my father.'

'Dougie,' said Nell. 'You could not have known. It is not your fault that Daisy did what she did. There are no clues in these photographs. Please, Dougie – you need to look.'

And so, finally, Dougie looked.

Daisy.
There you are.

Nell was right. The photographs were just of a girl smiling for the camera on a weekend at her boyfriend's when the weather changed every five minutes.

'I didn't know,' said Dougie. 'I just thought she was – zany.'

'It wasn't your fault that you did not know.'

'She was pretty bloody maddening,' Dougie said. 'I thought Harris would be good for her, that she could take a breather. But the truth is, she didn't seem that bothered. I remember at the time how that disappointed me. And I kind of knew that our relationship was coming to a natural end anyway. But ten days later, Nell. Ten days.'

'Sometimes, darkness doesn't encroach, it just swoops,' Nell said. 'The times when my mum went down – and I'm talking chasms-deep – I never saw it coming. Because she'd been up and laughing and dancing and taking me to drag clubs and to see the floodlit castle and cooking crazy banquets for just the two of us. It felt like I'd turned my back for a second and bang! down she'd gone, so deep into a fug she couldn't move or be moved, she couldn't talk or be spoken to. She was this heavy shell of herself. Terrifying. And I always blamed myself – I used to get furious with myself – why hadn't I seen it coming? Why could I not see the hole so big it swallowed her in a single gulp? I tried, sometimes, to pinch and poke her. And some-times, I'd pinch and poke myself to stay awake, stretching my eyelids open with my fingers, so that I could keep watch. Stop her falling.'

'Nell.' Dougie stroked her hair, tucking it behind her ear.

Nell shook her head and smiled. 'It wasn't my fault,' she told him. 'This much I know. There was no way of knowing and nothing I could have done anyway.'

'Daisy was twenty-two.'

'Dougie, you cannot incarcerate her in this box – because doing so imprisons part of you in there too. And you don't deserve that. You did nothing wrong. There must be no more punishment.'

Nell looked at the eleven photographs again, each in turn. The images were exquisite.

'These should be seen,' she said gently. 'What were you telling me about Ansel Adams? About how a negative isn't fixed? Why don't you print them again, alter the exposure, develop other aspects – see her in the light of today, Dougie?'

Cautiously, Dougie looked through the prints.

'Which is your favourite? Which do you think is the best photograph?' Nell asked. 'Show me.'

He chose an interior shot.

'So the other ten photographs,' Nell said, 'they need a home. They need to be on walls and shelves and looked at and chatted to each day.'

'Her parents lived in Guildford,' Dougie said.

Nell laid the photograph of Frank on the arm of the sofa and, next to him, the print of Daisy that Dougie had chosen. She put the lid on the box and turned to Dougie. 'You were there with me – when I walked into the studio. I will be there for you when you take these to Daisy's family. These are theirs, really. They are no longer yours to keep. Daisy was their beautiful lost girl.'

* * *

The fries came in a tin pot and the burger juices ran down their chins and Dougie asked Nell if she had a spare hair-tie, which she did. He made a ponytail and she took the piss mercilessly which he loved the sound of.

'Stops the sauce getting in my hair,' said Dougie.

'Whatever you say, Heathcliff,' said Nell.

'You're eating my chips.'

'Oh, sorry – I thought they were mine.'

'No, you didn't.'

'Do you begrudge me your chips, Dougie?'

'No, Nell – go ahead, knock yourself out.'

'Dougie—?'

'—Nell.'

'Would you photograph my beautiful chaffinches?'

'It's funny you should ask,' said Dougie, 'because when I sat in your café and Danny asked for tips and that wee quiet girl offered me cake and the tall gangly laddie was shining the coffee machine for all he was worth – I was struck by this desire to photograph them. I would love to. I would love to.'

'I would love all their portraits framed and on that long side wall of the café.'

'I've a quiet week coming. I'll bring a couple of cameras – they might like to have a go themselves.'

'Oh, they'd love that. And Dougie—?'

'—Nell?'

'Maybe not next week but one day – will you also come and meet my mum? Though she might think you're someone you're not. Oh, and she hated my ex.' Nell laughed. 'It was before I'd moved her from our old house into where she is now. I brought him over – twice. Both times she chased him around the place with a broom yelling, out! out! out!'

'Listen,' said Dougie, reaching across the table for Nell's hand, his cuff dipping into the ketchup. 'If Flora liked me at three years old, Wendy is going to love me. Just you wait, Nell. You'll see.'

And Nell looked at Dougie, looked at her hand held by his. 'We can't understand a person unless we know the content of their memories,' she said. 'I'm glad to have shared mine with you. Thank you for trusting me with yours.'

It was just a Saturday night as May was slipping into June. There was an enticing half a bottle of red remaining at Dougie's. The trains to Colchester ran into the early hours. Nell didn't have a shift at the Chaffinch the next day. Wendy hadn't a clue what day it was and she didn't know what year either but that was OK because she'd had a delicious supper and now Sylvie was watching *Inspector Morse* with her. Marjorie was studying journals and planning lectures and telling herself she wasn't lonely, she wasn't lonely at all. Frank was never lonely, he had his blackbirds and his Walnut Whips and his friend Nell, and his dressing gown tonight was a green-and-orange check so bright that surely it could be seen from space. He would wave at the astronauts before he Zimmered his way to bed, that's what he'd do. It was pizza and DVD night at the Chaffinch residential home for those who weren't with their parents this weekend. Danny wasn't there; he was at home watching *Back to the Future* for the zillionth time cuddled up with his mum and a tin of Quality Street while his dad dozed off in the chair next to them. Debbie was cooking her grandmother's Jamaican spiced corn soup, following the recipe diligently with a view to having it as a special on the menu for the café the following week. In New York, Philippa was looking into flights back to the UK for August, to escape the insane humidity in the city. In Colchester, the floodlights came on to illuminate the castle. In the Outer Hebrides, the days were now long; the sun was only vaguely thinking about setting and in a most leisurely manner at that. In the machair – safe beneath the buttercups and corncockle, the sea spurrey and wild orchids, the milkwort, the sorrel, the campion and the centaury – the elusive corncrakes rested, some on their backs with their legs in the air to hold the sky up. Amongst the myriad flowers, petals curled inwards to hold on to their honey-sweet fragrance until the morning light. In the rocky inlets the otters were still playing, but the dolphins further out were gone until tomorrow, and on slabs of ancient rock in the shallows the harbour seals reclined on their sides like portly ancient Romans after a gargantuan feast. In their nests, the eagles were settled. And over 3,000 miles away waves were forming, ready to make their way across the Atlantic to lick clean the white shell sand of the Hebridean beaches. It was going to be mild tomorrow, it was going to be a glorious day. In Scalpay, Nurse Keaton was loving her new hip and telling her sister to bugger off back to Leeds before she killed her. In Harris, Gordon was in the garden with Ben the dog, thinking what a beautiful evening it was. Thinking maybe he'd give his boy a phone call. See if he'd been in touch with Flora Buchanan's wee girl yet. That's what Màiri was telling him to do.

And in Camden, Flora Buchanan's wee girl Nell, and Gordon and Màiri Munro's son Douglas, were kissing like teenagers at the corner of his street.

'Will you stay? Will you stay with me, Nell?'

'Yes, Dougie. I will stay with you.'

Epilogue

Harris, 21st September 2005

The day before Nell left for two weeks in Harris, she had a visitor. It was a quiet afternoon at the Chaffinch and she and Rachel were trying to make the paper napkins resemble swans, without much success. Debbie and Sanjay were decorating cupcakes and Danny was lost in a daydream when the door opened and Marjorie walked in.

'Cappuccino, latte, Americano, flat white,' AJ called out to her. 'Mocha. Black.'

'I'd like Nell, please – my niece,' she told him. 'Is she here?'

AJ thought the lady looked spiky; he wasn't sure whether he was going to like her so he hollered for Nell.

'*Aunt Em?*' Nell was flabbergasted.

'Hello, dear,' said Marjorie. 'I'm popping in on Wendy in a while, so I thought I'd drop by.' She said it as if it was a most common occurrence.

'To see where I work?'

Marjorie thought about that. 'Well – to see *you*.' She held out a small cardboard box. 'And I came to give you this.'

Nell couldn't remember Marjorie giving her anything but that wasn't relevant just then. The Chaffinch gang loved anyone unwrapping packages, often gathering around a table if there was a customer with birthday presents. Now, they were in a jostle to be closest to Nell.

Inside the box, under a pad of bubble wrap and behind leaves of tissue, was a set of the Clarice Cliff Coronation china. The teacup and saucer, the plate. The frilled edging, the turquoise, the gold and the Queen.

'It's yours,' said Marjorie with a softness to her voice Nell wished she'd heard more often. 'It belonged to your mother. It was Florence's.' But Marjorie wasn't one for emotion and Nell's suddenly welling eyes were disarming to her. 'Well – I think I will have a coffee.' She turned to AJ. 'Young man – would you mind telling me again what's on offer?'

Marjorie stayed for half an hour. She had black coffee and a chocolate chip cookie which she ate daintily in front of an audience. Rachel gave her a scrunched napkin and said it was a swan, which Marjorie did not contest. Danny wanted to know who was the lady on the cup and the plate. Libby told him it was the woman off *Coronation Street*, silly. Marjorie laughed at that, a deep, honking sound that set everyone off. It struck Nell just then that of the three sisters, one was dead, one was contorted by early-onset dementia but the eldest was living really quite a small and lonely life with rarely more than dry lecture notes for company. So Nell sat with her aunt and told her a little of her trip to Harris. Just a few details today; there would be another time to tell her more, a time to ask as well.

Back in her flat, Nell placed Flora's Coronation trio on one of the shelves that she'd put up the other week, which Dougie had kindly straightened for her. There it sat, pride of place, flanked by a community of framed photographs, various guide books to the Western Isles and a Toby jug she'd been unable to resist from the little shop on Trinity Street.

And then she went to pack, leaving her new anorak on top of her suitcase because you just never knew what the weather would do out there on the island.

The midges had all but gone but Gordon said the *meanbh chuileag*, wee buggers, had been pesky that year, which Dougie translated as meaning insanely terrible. He'd been home for a fortnight already and Nell was joining him tomorrow. He'd come home to reprise his graduation project, to track down and photograph again those islanders who'd sat for him, the locations that had always spoken to him. Some were changed. Some had changed little. Some were gone. But Dougie's sense of home, of being a Hearach, was in sharp, sharp focus. And actually, he'd come home – two full weeks before Nell arrived – so that he could spend time, proper time, with Gordon.

'Da,' said Dougie, the night before Nell arrived, as he washed and Gordon dried and Ben mooched around the kitchen hunting out crumbs. 'I'm sorry.'

Gordon did not understand. But Dougie had stopped what he was doing, turned to face Gordon full on. His eyes were soft and settled on his father, his voice tender yet serious, strong.

'For what I put you through. Back then. And to thank you – for helping me back on my feet.'

'Ach,' said Gordon, brushing the air. He and his boy didn't talk like this together, they'd always left anything of magnitude to Màiri. But Gordon was touched, intrigued even. It had been such a good fortnight.

'And I'm sorry – truly sorry – for being an arse,' Dougie said. 'And not coming home often enough. And I thank you for the patience you've shown.'

Gordon chuckled and stroked Ben's head.

'No, Da,' said Dougie. 'Please – my apology and my gratitude – please accept them.'

Gordon regarded his son levelly. Dougie was his boy but he was also a grown man still growing and that seemed right to Gordon. He nodded. He opened a cupboard and took down the Glencairn crystal and the Balvenie and he poured a good dram for himself and his son.

'*Chan eil thu tuilleach's sean airson ionnsachadh fhathast,*' he said.

'Aye,' said Dougie. And he said to himself, we are to learn as long as we live.

'You know,' said Gordon, 'peace isn't just where there is no noise, no trouble, no hard work. Peace is when you can be in the midst of all those things and still be calm.'

'Thank you,' said Dougie, pressing his glass against his father's. 'It's taken a while.'

Gordon smiled at him. '*Slàinte.*'

'*Slàinte,*' said Dougie. Sharing a Scotch, a nod and a smile between father and son and all was well with their world.

The White Cottage had been booked all summer and was rented out now to an American couple until the end of October. Nell wondered whether she would have wanted to have stayed there anyway. Maybe on another visit. She and Dougie were with Gordon who'd put an ancient Z-bed into Dougie's bedroom as if they were kids having a sleepover. But Nell didn't mind. She pushed the beds close together. And Dougie fulfilled every teenage fantasy he'd ever had by having the most beautiful girl in the world slip under the covers of his single bed in the wee small hours and make silent urgent love with him. Kim Wilde and Clare Grogan remained rolled up in his bedroom cupboard with the medals and the trophies and the old letters and concert programmes and birthday cards and now just the three acid-free boxes of photographs.

On the morning of 21st September, Dougie woke first.

'Happy birthday, Nell,' he said, and he reached out his hand still heavy with sleep down to the Z-bed to loll on her head. 'What do you want to do today?'

What Nell wanted to do on her birthday was everything so Dougie gladly set about making that happen. Before breakfast, they clambered over the dunes and raced each other to the water's edge, Dougie letting her win because it was her birthday. They drove to Amhuinnsuidhe Castle and put their money in the honesty box, filling a bag with smoked salmon and pâté and cheese and bread and oatcakes and also venison to go in Gordon's freezer. They went on to Hushinish and walked the ragged trail over clifftop and moor to Tràigh Mheilein where they flopped on the sand, Nell closing her eyes to listen to Dougie recount the tale of Herr Zucker who, in 1934, launched letters from Scarp in a rocket to Harris, an experiment that failed spectacularly.

'Anyway,' Dougie told Nell, 'there's the Clach na h-Eigheach, the shouting rock, right over there – a point where the voice carries right over the water to Scarp.'

And Nell thought what *is* this magical place, this birthplace of mine? And she thought how blessed she was to be a Hearach.

They had lunch at the hotel, treated like royalty by Al who said Nell was to have the fish and chips whether she wanted it or not because he didn't like change and they'd missed her since she'd been away and they were all very pleased to welcome her home. And in the afternoon, they drove to Scalpay, where they walked to the Eilean Glas lighthouse and gazed over the Minch to the shadowy velvet mass of the towering cliffs of Skye before visiting Nurse Keaton at teatime. Sophia suggested a walk to the harbour so she could show off her new hip and how nimble she was without her cane. Everyone said hello to her. Mrs Ross said she'd be over for a chat later. Mrs Muir reminded her that it was cards on Thursday night, not to forget. Nell linked arms with her and gave her a squeeze. As Dougie ambled a little way ahead, Sophia squeezed Nell back, nodded in Dougie's direction and gave Nell the broadest smile which proclaimed that everything made sense, everything was as it should be.

'Don't think I don't know what day it is,' Sophia said, when they sat together having tea and biscuits later, looking out of her window to the higgledy drop to the harbour beyond. 'Happy birthday, pet,' she said, gazing fondly at Nell. How was she thirty-six years old? And was she too old, now, to be called Little Wing? And then Sophia thought had Flora been alive, she'd bet she'd still call her daughter that. So much had happened and yet no time had passed. And now that Nell was back, it made a nonsense of all those years that she'd been away.

'Look,' said Nell and she showed Nurse Keaton the photographs that Dougie had taken of the Chaffinch flock. 'And look,' said Nell and she showed Nurse Keaton another set of portraits that Dougie had taken. 'This is my mum Wendy,' she said.

Sophia looked through the photos thoughtfully. 'Well, it's been well over thirty years,' she said, 'but I recognize that smile. I do, pet, I do. And I have something for you, Nell,' she said. She left the room and returned a few minutes later. 'After you'd gone in the spring, while my sister was still here, we turned the whole house upside down because I knew they were here somewhere. I knew I hadn't lost them or thrown them away. I *knew* it. I just couldn't remember where they were. Well, we found them.'

She passed Nell a small white envelope.

Inside there was a business card and also a piece of paper torn from a lined notepad. They both had names and addresses on them.

Nell studied them. 'Thank you,' she said. 'But what are these?'

Sophia felt a twist of emotion at her throat. Oh, how she'd hoped for this over the years, prayed for it, prayed for everyone concerned and now the day had come. At last, it could be done.

'Mrs J. Kingsland.' Nell read the business card. 'Leavitt Lane, Saxton's River, Vermont.'

'Mrs *Joan* Kingsland,' Sophia said. 'I don't know what her maiden name was, I'm sorry. But this is Joan – Flora's best friend on the mainland, since childhood. She sounds all American – she came here, must be at least fifteen or twenty years ago, and she tracked me down and sat a while and gave me this card.'

Nell ran her fingertip over the embossed type. 'Do you think she still lives there?'

'I hope so,' said Sophia. 'She said she was a teacher, at the school there.'

'We'll find her, easy,' said Dougie.

'Maybe she'll know something about my father,' Nell said quietly as she studied the card intently. 'And this?' Nell looked at the torn piece of paper with a name and an address handwritten in confident loops. 'Mrs J. Gillespie?' The address was Edinburgh and there was a telephone number too.

'That's Jessie,' said Sophia proudly. 'Our very own Jessie Gillespie. She and Flora were the closest of friends. Oh, she adored you! Jessie was going to be a poet and sell her poems alongside Flora's art in the studio. That was the grand plan.'

'And she came to find you too?'

'Yes, pet, say eight years ago. Maybe ten. I'm old. I forget.'

'Did she say if she was a poet these days?'

'Jessie Gillespie?' Dougie interrupted. 'As in *the*—?'

Nurse Keaton nodded at him, then turned to Nell. 'Just after your first birthday, Jessie left the island to go to university. Politics and Something or Other.'

'Nell – Jessie Gillespie is *amazing*,' Dougie said. 'She's a Member of the Scottish Parliament. More than that, though, she's the special advisor who was instrumental in campaigning for *Gàidhlig* to be recognized, that every child has a right to learn *Gàidhlig*. The first piece of legislation to give formal recognition to the Scottish Gaelic language was passed just a month ago, thanks to her. Call yourself a Hearach!'

Nell looked from the card to the piece of paper. Somewhere in the background Nurse Keaton was telling her how Joan and Jessie had tried very hard to find Nell in and out of the years. All Nell could think, however, was that all questions could have answers now. But then she thought that perhaps some questions would never be asked. However, there were two women out there hoping that their friend and Nell's lost mother would be found. Two women, Joan and Jessie, who could add a little more colour to the black-and-white of how Nell came to be.

It was only when they arrived back at Luskentyre that Dougie gave Nell his birthday present to her. He took her hand and they walked through the machair though only devil's-bit scabious, lady's bedstraw and a few tenacious harebells remained of all the wildflowers. On the beach, oystercatchers went about their business along the shore while giggles of sanderlings skittered and jollied together just above the surface of the sand, like impish schoolchildren at play. Over the tussocky grass Dougie and Nell walked, along the edge of the dunes to the house where she'd once lived. The little cottage that Flora had loved so much. Only it wasn't called Am Bothan Geal, the White Cottage, any more. A new sign stood, the lettering bold and emphatic:

Tigh Floraidh.
Flora's House.

Harris, 21st September 1970

This time last year I was writhing around in agony, feeling like my insides were on the outside, as I gave birth. Oh, I screamed blue murder at poor Nurse Keaton. I squeezed the blood cold out of her hand and called her a liar when she told me that of course I wasn't going to die, all I had to do was breathe and push. Today, I think back and though I know that it was terrifying at the time, I remember it now with only a brimming heart and a ridiculous grin. And my baby girl is one today! She is the best baby in the world and I'm giving her a birthday party!

I have baked a cake and made pink icing. It makes my teeth hurt it's so sweet but it looks very gay. There is one candle right in the middle and I have tried my best to write HAPPY 1ST BIRTHDAY NELL in white icing around it. I have made sandwiches and sausage rolls. I have a bottle of blackcurrant drink and some chocolate. We're having the party in the studio and I have painted a colourful banner: One Today 'Hip Hip Hooray!' The words are strung between a parade of cats and dogs and rabbits that I've painted all the colours of the rainbow. Jessie is coming, with her mum and her smallest brother. Nurse Keaton will be there. Iain too. Also Màiri and wee Dougie. I have made a pass-the-parcel for all of us to play and also little party hats out of coloured card for everyone to wear. The daft thing is that the birthday girl herself isn't remotely aware that today is so special and she is unlikely to remember any of it. Who remembers anything from when they were one? Or two? Three, even? I don't think I can. But I'll never forget this day. I'm fit to burst with pride and happiness.

My daughter is growing into a bubbly little soul and so beautiful that sometimes when I catch sight of her I just want to cry. I gaze at her for hours and hours when she's asleep. She is perfect. She is so very precious. She is the making of me. How can one so very very tiny make such perfect sense? What if I hadn't had her? What then? Jessie is off to university next week, Joan has a job helping at a school – maybe I would have gone to art college. Or perhaps I wouldn't have got into college anyway and I'd be skulking around Colchester feeling sorry for myself. But I like to think that I am proof that one doesn't need to go to art college to be an artist. My mural at the back of the studio takes people's breath away when they first see it. And Morag and a couple of the other shops now stock my bright little landscapes which are proving popular with tourists and locals alike. More and more people have visited the islands this summer, the youth hostel at Stockinish is still full and the Harris Hotel has been doing a roaring trade. Iain took me and Jessie for lunch there, on my eighteenth birthday in June. The manager said that when Nell goes to school he'd be glad to have me work there. I think that would be most sensible, fun too. Just in case I can't make a living from my paintings alone.

Yes, this is the place to be. I cannot think of anywhere else I would rather live.

And so today is Nell's birthday. Jimi Hendrix died three days ago and I have wept a lot about that. He was only twenty-seven. His legacy is his music and it will always provide the soundtrack to my days and the songs I sing as I walk, as I paint, as I do almost anything. The mural at the back of the studio is my homage to this great artist – and how I hope in years to come people will see it as a memorial and he will never be forgotten. There is a beautiful saying in Gàidhlig:

> Thig crìoch air an t-saoghal,
> ach màiridh gaol is ceòl.

Life will come to an end but music and love will endure

Ah, my Little Wing, toddling over the garden in your special party dress with the great big red flowers! A daisy and some grass in one hand and a stone in the other. For me? Thank you, baby girl, thank you! Happy Birthday, little one. Happy Birthday, Nell. Daughter mine. Thank you.

Will you ever know how much you give me and how much love I feel? I don't think I'll ever be able to find the words or even the paint to truly express it. But I hope that you'll always feel it, always know that it's there even when you're all grown up. You've taught me all I'll ever need to know about love.

If it wasn't for you, we wouldn't be here. Because of you, I live in a place that makes perfect sense to me, somewhere that I belong. Harris is our island and how can it be anything other than safe and steady – it is formed from the oldest rock there is. Three billion years of rock steadiness.

Home is truly here, amongst the hills and heathers and wild weather. You and me together in our little white house next to sand the colour of angel wings, on the edge of the island, on the very edge of the ever-stretching sea.

Acknowledgements

Though this fifteenth novel of mine was in embryo back in 2016 (when it went by the working title of *The Lost Mother*), *Little Wing* really took flight during the first lockdown in the Spring of 2020 when, each day, I'd gladly escape to my world within the world. Though I was safely holed up on my little farm in Hertfordshire, I spent my days back in Harris, albeit in my mind's eye. Writing this novel kept me sane, stimulated and happy. It holds a very special place for me – of a place so special to me.

It was highly emotional for me to return to Harris in September 2020 when the book was complete and lockdown was lifted. I owe a debt of gratitude to Isobel Mackay (the perfect host) and Rebecca Hutton (weaver extraordinaire). Thank you for answering a thousand and one questions, for checking my *Gàidhlig* and sharing your anecdotes, reminiscences and local knowledge. This book would be the poorer were it not for both of you.

Also in Harris, Sarah Scott and Andrew Morrison at The Harris Hotel – always so lovely to see you. Sally Lessi at the much missed Anchorage Restaurant, thank you for great food and introductions. Waving over the Sound of Harris to Berneray and the super-talented Eilidh Carr – go visit her Coral Box Gift Shop and follow her on Twitter. Eilidh Mackay in Lewis – thank you for the delicious homemade shortbread, the chat and the views. Once again, my posts on social media sparked enthusiastic and useful assistance with my research – so big thanks to Ruth Dawkins, Jane Fulton, Cathy Ann MacPhee, Julie Davies, Jenny and Murdo Morrison, Mhairi Parker, Isobel Rogers and Mairi Crockett.

In Colchester – my thanks to my friend Zoe Davidson.

In Glasgow – thank you to my lovely Shirley Doig for Columbo and Tunnocks and Jura and the Beatles blanket and so much more.

I'm also very grateful to my excellent photographer friends Phil O'Connor and Dan Weldon.

Keaton, Sophia (see what I did there?!) and Luke – we first went to the Outer Hebrides in 2017 on an unforgettable research trip that took us from Barra to South and North Uist and onwards to Harris and Lewis. We were on the trail of the real district nurses of the Outer Hebrides. In 1913, over three decades before the foundation of the NHS, a programme of state-funded healthcare was bestowed on the Outer Hebrides via the Highlands and Islands Medical Service in the form of the district nurse, many of whom had trained at one of the prestigious Queen's Nursing Institutes of Scotland. This lasted until 1971. As Sophia tells Flora and Nell, they were a unique and special class of district nurse – astonishingly resourceful, resilient, indefatigable and respected women who provided top class healthcare to the islanders (and often their animals too). We had the honour of meeting many of these nurses. We remain passionate about our project – a TV drama series – and I've written the pilot.

I am indebted to a remarkable woman Catherine Morrison, a retired district nurse whose memoire, *Hebridean Heroines*, based on her PhD, became our bible. She helped us so much, was always generous with her time and knowledge and introduced us to many wonderful nurses. Catherine died before *Little Wing* was published – I will never forget her and am so grateful for her kindness and support. It's still our dream that this TV series will be made: a medical drama based on true stories, quirky characters and the incomparable setting of the Outer Hebrides . . . Our audience is surely out there – let's do this!

To my publisher Welbeck – thank you for welcoming me so warmly into your fold. Your love for Flora, Nell and Dougie means so much to me. Jon Elek, Annabel Robinson, James Horobin, Rob Cox, Rosa Schierenberg, Maddie Dunne-Kirby, Nico Poilblanc, Angie Willocks, Alex Allden, Carrie-Ann Pitt, Sophie Leeds, Louise Howard – cheers, chaps!

Thank you to the world's finest copy-editor, Mary Chamberlain – all these years and all these books later, finally I'm getting the hang of track it and changelings or whatever it's called.

At Curtis Brown Ltd – my thanks to Olivia Edwards, Sophia Macaskill, Lucy Morris – and of course to my beloved agent Jonathan Lloyd who has represented me throughout my career and to whom this book is dedicated.

Finally, on the home front, during the period of lockdowns which meant I couldn't see, let alone hug, friends and family, your support and love from afar was crucial. As ever, the inner sanctum remained steady and positive and full of laughter: Fee & Gee, Antony, Ma & Pa, Luce, Mel, Emma, Simon & Mo, the gentle folk of Cucumbria, the girls on The Yard and my beloved GCC – thank you. I love you all.

Links you will love:
Weaver of tweed and stories and all round extraordinary human being: Rebecca Hutton: www.taobhtuathtweeds.com
I stayed here – with thanks to Isobel Mackay: www. luskentyre-beach-holidays.co.uk
These websites were invaluable:
www.north-harris.org
www.westharristrust.org
www.visitouterhebrides.co.uk
www.hebridespeople.com
www.isle20.com
www.facebook.com/groups/isleofharris/

Reading List:
Hebridean Heroines – Catherine M Morrison
Harris & Lewis – Francis Thompson
The Outer Hebrides – Alan McKirdy
Hebridean Memories – Seton Gordon
The Fragile Islands – Bettina Selby
The Heather Isles – Bruce Sandison
Outer Hebrides – Mark Rowe
A Harris Way of Life – Gisela Vogler
Crowdie and Cream – Finlay J Macdonald
Crotal and White – Finlay J Macdonald

The Corncrake and the Lysander – Finlay J Macdonald
Place-names of Scarp – Calum J Mackay
Hebridean Light – Alan Warner, Gus Wylie

Oh – and this is us:
www.shoutingrock.co.uk

in loving memory
Liz Berney 1968-2005
Hannah Berry 1983-2013
Jonny Zucker 1966-2016

A Letter From Freya

I first went to Harris in the Outer Hebrides in 2017, researching an idea for a screenplay. The landscape, the weather, the wildlife, the people, the ever-stretching sea all had a profound and enduring impact on me. That trip to the island will always hold great significance for me – it was 2 months after my back surgery and I took my first run along the white sands at Luskentyre.

There is a robust spirituality to Harris quite unlike anywhere else I have visited – a close-to-the-earth, majestic but gritty poetry to the place and it feels so very far away. Here is an island where weather truly dictates and shapes the lives and the land, and a dynamic, elemental energy exists that can overwhelm as much as uplift. In Harris, you can simultaneously feel closer to the ground and yet nearer to the sky. It is brooding, beautiful, wild and sometimes unforgiving. So I wondered what if . . . ? I wondered what if I sent a character here – how would they fare? I thought what if that character hadn't chosen to go, but had been banished to Harris, in disgrace at 16 years old, in the late 1960s? And then I thought what if, in the early 2000s, there's someone finally looking for her? This, for me, was the springboard into *Little Wing*.

Written at home in Hertfordshire during the first lockdown, this novel kept me sane during that time – transporting me each day to Outer Hebrides, back to the wild weather, the hills, the moors, the flowers of the machair, the burns, the peat, sand the colour of angel wings, and land itself which rises out of the Atlantic on rock that is 3 billion years old. I knew from the start that Harris could never be just a backdrop, a mere setting for the story; it was always going to be a leading character in this 15th novel of mine.

I was able to return to Harris for the first time since lockdown in September 2020. It was an emotional trip. The book was finished but I needed to follow in the footsteps of my characters. I like to believe that all stories pre-exist – that they are like dust motes floating around. I feel privileged to be the author to tell Flora, Nell and Dougie's story. This book was a joy to research and write. I hope you like it and I hope it inspires you to visit one of the most beautiful places on earth.

Freya North

WELBECK

PUBLISHING GROUP

Love books? Join the club.

Sign up and choose your preferred genres to receive tailored news, deals, extracts, author interviews and more about your next favourite read.

From heart-racing thrillers to award-winning historical fiction, through to must-read music tomes, beautiful picture books and delightful gift ideas, Welbeck is proud to publish titles that suit every taste.

bit.ly/welbeckpublishing